CLOCKWORK PHANTOM

AETHER PSYCHICS BOOK TWO

CECILIA DOMINIC

ABOUT CLOCKWORK PHANTOM

Everyone wears a mask. But the deadliest secrets hide in plain sight.

Marie St. Jean's supreme acting talent comes with a price: Every spellbinding performance extracts a piece of her soul. When she reluctantly steps into a role abandoned by another leading lady, she encounters the ghostly spirit that caused the other woman to flee in terror. And who promises to fix Marie's affliction – for a price.

Marie's other problem – her attraction to alluring violinist, Johann Bledsoe, a temptation she dares not explore. However, with the Prussians surrounding Paris, she is well and truly trapped.

Johann left disgrace and his gambling debt behind in England, but a murder outside the Théâtre Bohème makes him fear he's been exposed. He'd love nothing more than to claim Marie as his own, but after the siege is over, his past will catch up to him again.

Under the baleful eye of steam-powered ravens, more murders drive Marie and Johann closer to the truth of what really lurks below the stage, and what dangers hang over their heads. Their only hope could lie in exposing their darkest secrets—and surrendering to the Eros Element in a way that could push them irretrievably close to the edge of madness.

Clockwork Phantom is the second book in the Aether Psychics, a thrilling steampunk series with puzzling mysteries and hints of magic. If you like historical mysteries with a scientific – or is it supernatural? – twist, then you'll love Cecilia Dominic's Aether Psychics series.

Note: Clockwork Phantom can be read on its own or as part of the Aether Psychics series. It was originally titled Light Fantastique.

PRAISE FOR CLOCKWORK PHANTOM:

"This deftly woven adventure is cast with well-developed characters that round out an entertaining mystery...a complex tale of murder, mayhem, and romance." - Romantic Times

"Light Fantastique gets a 'highly recommended' from me! It is complex and magical, mysterious and romantic. If you like steampunk that is powered by romance and mystery, you too will appreciate Light Fantastique." – Smart Girls Love Sci Fi Romance

"I highly recommend this book to anyone who likes romance, mystery, and steampunk - you won't be disappointed!" - 5-star Amazon review

ACKNOWLEDGMENTS

Classical music has always been part of my life. My Belgian grandfather was an organist at the famous Antwerp Cathedral, and he passed his love of music down to his children and grandchildren. While my opera tolerance stops with Andrew Lloyd Weber's *Phantom*, I do have fond memories of my mother listening to Bizet's *Carmen* and Strauss's *Die Fledermaus* during the holidays.

This book is dedicated to those share their joy in music with others. I'd particularly like to thank Patsy Arnold, my very patient piano teacher from third through twelfth grade and Jim Parker, my band leader in high school. Also Ronald and Barbara Shinn and Dennis Herrick, college professors at Huntingdon College in Montgomery, Alabama. This book is also in loving memory of Professors James Glass and Harald Rohlig. Here's hoping those angels are not singing with too much vibrato. Huge thanks goes once again to Dawn P., my archaeologist on call. Any historical errors or exaggerations in this book are mine alone. I did have to change around a few things, but having an alternate version of history is part of the fun of writing in this genre.

My gratitude as always goes to my husband and family for their unswerving support.

Finally, most importantly, thank you to my readers. I couldn't do this without you!

LOOK FOR THESE TITLES BY CECILIA DOMINIC

Steampunk Series

The Aether Psychics
Noble Secrets
Eros Element
Clockwork Phantom
Aether Spirit
Aether Rising

Inspector Davidson Mysteries
The Art of Piracy
Mission: Nutcracker

Urban Fantasy Series

The Lycanthropy Files
The Mountain's Shadow
Long Shadows
Blood's Shadow
A Million Shadows

Dream Weavers & Truth Seekers
Truth Seeker
Tangled Dreams
Web of Truth

Copyright© 2017 Cecilia Dominic

ISBN: 978-1-945074-47-9

Edited by Holly Atkinson

Cover by Karri

First ebook edition: December 2015

Second ebook edition: June 2017

This is a second edition of the novel titled Light Fantastique that was released by Samhain Publishing in December 2015.

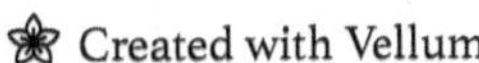 Created with Vellum

1

Théâtre Bohème, Paris, 1 December 1870

Screams were not uncommon at the Théâtre Bohème, mostly because on stage, one was expected to express emotions in an exaggerated way for the benefit of the audience. But the scream that sliced through the usual midday din of the theatre held a note of pure terror, and Marie nearly dropped the costume she held up for the examination of modiste Madame Beaufort.

"_Sacre bleu,_" Madame said. "What could that have been?"

"I don't know, but I'll check it out," Marie answered. "I'll let you know if the Prussians are upon us." She handed the dress to Madame and lifted her own skirts to make her way through narrow hallways from the costume room to the theatre itself.

Now shouting echoed through the wooden and brick hallways.

"I will not go forward with this!"

Marie recognized the slightly nasal but resonant female voice as Corinne, her mother's go-to lead after Marie had left. She had become quite the _premiere femme_ while Marie was away, but rather than sounding snobbish, her tone held an edge of panic.

"You must. The first performance is next week, and I don't have time for this nonsense."

And that was Marie's mother, Madame Lucille St. Jean. Marie took a shortcut through a secret passage, which allowed the sound to carry. She emerged in the theatre to see the two women almost nose-to-nose.

"What's wrong?" Marie asked before she could stop the words from tumbling out of her mouth. "You two do realize others are trying to work here."

"Oh, Mademoiselle." Corinne's face melted into a mask of tragedy. "I saw a ghost backstage. It raised its finger at me to tell me I am doomed. I must get away from here!"

Lucille looked at Marie. "What are you doing here? I have told you that if you refuse to take the stage, you do not belong in the theatre. Go back to helping Madame Beaufort with her pins and pinches."

Marie ignored Lucille. *This is the most interesting thing that's happened since I returned.* "What did the ghost look like?"

"He was tall and thin, and his hand looked like a skeleton's. He wore a long robe, and I could not see his face. He was Death come for me!" She placed the back of her hand on her forehead and swooned.

"Actresses." Marie sighed. Two stage hands came and picked Corinne up from the floor—she'd pulled the fainting trick before, but this time she didn't jump up with protestations at the "filthy peasants'" hands being on her.

"Well?" Lucille asked, apparently forgetting she'd banished Marie. "What are we to do now? I have a play with no lead actress and apparently a ghost has taken up residence in the theatre."

"Not my problem." Marie turned to go, but her mother grabbed her arm with surprising strength.

Lucille switched to English and lowered her voice, both signs she didn't want the workers and other actors to hear and understand what she was going to say to her daughter. Since the American "Civil" War had become a proxy war between England and France, not knowing English had become a point of pride among the common folk, particularly as the hard consonants and flat vowels sounded a lot like Prussian, spoken by the invaders who massed outside the city.

"And 'ave you forgotten that I am housing you and your friends for free?" she snarled in Marie's ear.

"And have you forgotten we're trying to help replace the faulty gas lighting system?" Marie snapped back. "You can't have a performance without light."

"The professor isn't proceeding as I'd hoped." Lucille's eyes glittered as the gas lights subsided and then flamed back to light. "I doubt he will have anything installed in time for dress rehearsals, and I am not sure I want to try the holiday play with an untested system."

Marie couldn't argue. "Science takes time," she said, echoing Professor Edward Bailey's oft-repeated sentiments. But she'd watched him in the laboratory they set up in a room at the top of the apartment building. The space itself received a lot of illumination, but the scientist within didn't seem to. Seemingly mesmerized by the isolated drop of aether within the glass globe, he would only sit and stare at his equipment. Inventor Patrick O'Connell proceeded better with developing the actual aether lighting equipment, but without the substance itself in usable form, the system would be useless.

"I cannot support you if we do not have a performance. We cannot have a performance without a leading actress. You are her understudy. Therefore, you must take the stage again." Lucille punctuated that last statement with a finger held up in triumph.

"The only reason I accepted the understudy role was

because I knew there was no way Corinne would back out. She may still do it." Marie looked to where the actress had been set, but—uncharacteristic for her—Corinne had left quietly and without any kind of announcement. "*Merde*, she really was frightened."

"Congratulations, Henriette," Lucille said. "You have tonight to memorize your lines. Rehearsals start for you tomorrow. Now Gerard, let's get back to the scene in the graveyard. I'll stand in for Marie as Henriette today."

Violinist, artist, and now disgraced gentleman Johann Bledsoe snuck in the back door of the theatre. Or at least he tried to, but he ended up holding the door open for the blonde actress he'd bedded two nights previously. Or had that been three? Either way, he tipped his hat and smiled, bracing himself for an onslaught of emotion and reproach.

"*Merci*, Monsieur," she said with uncharacteristic meekness, at least from what he could remember. She'd been a tiger in bed, or at least an alley cat. This change in character intrigued him.

"Where are you going?" he asked.

"Away. Death has come for me, and although I know it is futile, I shall run to the ends of the earth to escape her."

"All right, then. It figures death would be female." He watched Corinne hurry away, but before she reached the end of the alley, she turned.

"Beware, Monsieur! *La Mort* has come to the theatre, and she will not leave until she has claimed enough souls to satisfy her insatiable hunger."

"If it's insatiable, then she won't be sated," Johann pointed out, but she only shook her head and picked up her pace, her satin slippers splashing in the puddles from last night's rain.

Johann tried to enter again, but this time Marie St. Jean dashed out and nearly bowled him over.

"Where is she?" she asked. Her chest heaved, and Johann dragged his eyes away from her generous décolletage, which didn't need that much help from a corset. Not that he would know. She'd kept a careful distance from him since the incident in Rome when it was revealed how much of an ass he was. Had been. All right, was.

"Who?" His befuddled mind wondered if Marie ran after death.

"Corinne, the lead actress in *Light Fantastique*," she said and gave him a look that would have shrunk the balls of a lesser man back into his torso. Johann's balls barely took notice except to shoot an impulse to his brain to kiss her. They said such things frequently about Marie, so he told them to shut up.

"She ran that way," he said and gestured to the end of the alley.

"*Merde,*" she muttered and picked up her skirts to run after the escaped actress, but a gust of wind made her gasp.

Johann followed her through the alley. Now he really had to try not to look at the front of her dress to see if the wind had done him a favor and peaked her nipples. "You really shouldn't be running about without a coat. You'll catch your death of cold."

Another cool gust ruffled both their hair, and he shivered both internally and externally at his unintentional mention of whatever had scared the actress.

"I should be so lucky," Marie said through gritted teeth. They reached the street and looked in both directions, but the only thing to be seen was the disappearing back of a cab. "Damn, now we'll never catch her." She dropped her skirts and rubbed her hands over her bare forearms.

"What was that all about?" Johann took off his overcoat and draped it around her shoulders.

"I don't need your help," Marie told him, but she tugged the wool closer around her.

Lucky coat. "I wasn't offering it, merely curious, that's all."

They turned back and walked toward the theatre's back door. The alley concentrated small gusts of wind into blasts, and Johann tried not to flinch whenever one hit them.

"But perhaps your way with women could be useful," Marie told him with a sideways glance that brought surprising warmth to his middle.

"How so?"

"Something spooked her. She said it was a ghost that looked like Death."

"And it wasn't the costume they're using in the play?"

"Of course! Someone was playing a trick on her. She's certainly been nasty to enough people to warrant it. Thank you!" Marie stood on her toes and kissed his cheek. "I'm going to her lodgings to explain. Then she'll come back."

Once inside, Marie handed his coat back to him and with a grin dashed off, presumably to get her own cloak and go to Corinne's apartment.

"Shall I accompany you?" he asked.

"Normally I would say no, but..." She sighed, and she hunched her shoulders when Lucille's voice floated down to them from the backstage area.

"Marie, come quick. The new phantom costume has arrived. You must see this."

"Your mother isn't good for your posture," Johann observed.

Marie straightened. "Or my sanity."

Reluctant to let this moment of detente pass, he followed her up the narrow wooden stairs.

Lucille held the mask for Marie to admire. "It is made from a material that will appear to glow, or at least I hope it will, in the Professor's new aether light."

"What happened to the old costume?" Marie asked, afraid of the answer. "And when did this one arrive?"

Lucille waved a hand. "I sold the previous one to one of our noble patrons for his parlor games. He has a mistress who likes strange bedroom role-plays. Death should be tattered, but that old costume had so many holes you could see the person underneath. Another reason it was perfect for the Count."

Marie had long since grown out of the tendency to blush at the mention of sex, but the image of her and Maestro Bledsoe playing out a scandalous scene with the costume flashed through her brain. He stood beside her, and she couldn't help but be aware of his broad shoulders and chest that tapered toward a narrow but still manly waist.

"Well, this leaves us with a problem," he said.

"Several," Marie murmured and widened the distance between them as she reminded herself that he was a selfish sort, as the English would say. "But yes, we're back to needing to know what frightened Corinne."

Lucille put a hand on Marie's cheek. "*Mon Dieu*, your skin is cold. What did you do, go chasing after her, you silly *fille*? You need to preserve your voice, not risk it by running into the cold without a cloak."

"I had a coat," Marie said with a sideways glance up at the musician. He grinned but didn't say anything, for which she was grateful.

"As for what frightened Corinne, bah!" Lucille banged her cane on the floor. "She was always a silly, superstitious girl, particularly once she became the *premiere femme*. As for you, go to the *Chambre d'Etoile*. You need to practice your lines, and I will send Madame Beaufort to start fitting the costumes to you. They will all need to be let out." She pinched Marie on the waist.

Marie moved away from her mother's critical, prying words and fingers. "Yes, that would be wise, so I don't burst through the seams on opening night." The look on Johann's face made heat bloom in her chest. "I mean, it's not going to be that kind of show." *Still not helping. I need to get rid of him.* She curtsied and said, "Maestro, thank you for your assistance. I'm sure you preserved my ability to perform in this detestable play."

"Any time," he replied with a cough. His cupid's bow lips were pulled back into a grin that said he tried not to laugh at Lucille's ridiculous antics. "And I think the costumes will look better on you, anyway. You have a more classical figure."

"Thank you. If you'll excuse me."

Marie fled from the genuine admiration in his eyes and the answering expansion of gratification in her middle. *Silly girl, you can't get stupid over a man who does something nice for you.* But her mind turned to the feel of the soft wool coat being placed on her shoulders by his large, strong hands.

Maybe having to take the lead in this play is a good thing. If I'm going to lose part of myself, I'd prefer it go to a role than to a man.

Now anxiety replaced any warm feeling she'd gotten from the maestro's complimentary look, and she had to catch herself and lean against the nearest wall while waiting for her heart to stop its pounding in her throat. She would have to take the stage again and face the loss of part of her soul.

2

———

héâtre Bohème, 1 December 1870

"Now as for you..." Madame St. Jean turned to Johann, and he had to take his eyes from the retreating figure of her daughter. He made it a policy not to ogle young women when their mothers were present—he'd almost gotten trapped into marriage that way once—but he couldn't help himself. Since Rome, he'd found himself slipping in his policies around Marie, and he'd need to find a new distraction soon. One that would stick or at least do a better job of getting her out of his head.

"What about me?" he asked with the lopsided grin he used to charm women of all ages.

"I have been looking for a first violin who can lead the stage orchestra in the Overture and Entr'acte pieces with the kind of emotion Berlioz's music deserves. So far I have not found anyone, but I have heard you play."

"You've heard me practice," Johann corrected her. "Not play. I'm taking a break from performing in large venues at the moment."

"I am aware of your reputation, Maestro. All of it." She fixed him with her glittering black stare. "And need I remind you that you and your friends have been staying under my roof with no recompense to this point?"

"Professor Bailey and Mister O'Connell are working on a new lighting system for you, and I believe Doctor Radcliffe set one of your stage hand's broken wrist a few weeks ago," Johann pointed out.

"Working on is not the same as installing or fixing, and all of you owe me more than a set wrist."

Johann took a deep breath and did what he usually did when faced with a difficult woman, ask what she truly wanted. Not just from him, but from life. The answer came to him—Madame wanted to have control down to the smallest detail. She acted with the aggressiveness of someone who had let it slip once and had lost a great deal. He wondered if it had something to do with her hatred of Parnaby Cobb and the past connection with him that Marie refused to talk about.

Then he asked himself how he could use the situation to his advantage. Not getting kicked out and having to return to England and face the men who wanted to kill him seemed beneficial enough for the moment. Not that he was going anywhere during the siege. No one was, at least not unless they could bribe their way on to an airship.

"I'll look at the score," he said, unwilling to give all the way.

"*Bien.*" She walked to the orchestra pit—without the aid of her cane, he noticed—reached down to a shelf, and gave him a first violin score. "This should not be difficult for you."

"I'm sure it won't be." *Especially since I've played the* Symphonie Fantastique *before.* But again, he wasn't going to say it. He'd learned the hard way not to reveal all his advantages in antagonistic situations like this. But he also knew there was more to the situation than Madame St. Jean let on.

❧

IRIS ASCENDED the steps to the multi-story townhouse Madame St. Jean owned next to the theatre. A year ago, Iris had been living in a modest but nice house in a little town in England with her father. She had few friends since other young middle-class women didn't share her interests in archeology and science. Now she attended the new French *Ecole d'Archaeologie* and shared a room with—*how scandalous!*—an actress, who also served as a maid when Iris needed some extra help, although she was proud she could mostly take care of herself. And she had friends, a strange group, to be sure, but friends nonetheless.

The first person she saw when she crossed the threshold was the member of the group she liked least but perhaps understood the best, for they'd both had to deal with the aftermath of dangerous secrets coming to light. She tried to be pleasant to him for that reason and because he was the best friend of her almost fiancé, Professor Edward Bailey. And today she was happy to find him alone because a question had grown in her mind over the past few months since she'd returned to Paris after her father's funeral.

"Good afternoon, Maestro Bledsoe."

"Good afternoon, Mademoiselle McTavish." He sat in the parlor with his violin on its stand beside him and a score spread on the table in front of him. "How were your exams?"

"Fine. We should have our results by the end of next week." She tried not to say too much about her studies because she didn't want to bore the others. She'd alienated friends in the past by going on too much about sarcophagi and coins. Now she tried to figure out the best way to broach the subject on her mind. Heart, really. "What are you doing?"

He looked up from the music in front of him and ran a hand through his hair. It had gotten long in Paris, and he'd grown a beard. He looked like a bohemian musician, particularly when agitated gesturing made his curls loosen and stand in a blond nimbus around his head.

Like he's the scruffy angel of the Théâtre Bohème.

Her cheeks heated with the thought.

"I'm being put to work with the orchestra," he said. "Madame St. Jean is impatient. We've not made enough progress with the lighting system to please her."

"Oh." Iris glanced up the stairs, where she knew Professor Edward Bailey, the author of her greatest joy and anxiety, toiled in his laboratory in the converted attic workshop. Or at least she thought he was. She tried not to disturb him, but the few times she'd been up there to tell him it was a mealtime or bring him a delivery, she'd found him gazing at the biscuit-sized swirling aether in its glass globe. He never seemed to move much beyond that. As for Patrick O'Connell, the tinkerer/engineer who was working on converting the theatre's lighting system so it could be used once Edward made enough aether gas—whenever he figured out how—Iris suspected he protected Edward out of sympathy for his mental state. She'd come to find the Irishman liked to exaggerate for dramatic effect, but also to shield those to whom he was fiercely loyal.

"Yes," Bledsoe said with a sigh, "have you heard the *Symphonie Fantastique* by the late Hector Berlioz?"

"Only the snippets they've been rehearsing for the production." Iris imitated the disapproving look on her former headmistress's face and intoned, "Young ladies do not listen to scandalous music from the continent."

The musician's beard made his smile seem all the wider and emphasized the evenness of his teeth. "So you're getting an education in many things these days."

And many things I'm not. With that thought, Iris placed her books on the hall table but didn't enter the parlor so she at least wouldn't be unchaperoned in the same room as a bachelor with a rake's reputation. Her current living situation had caused her to become good at finding loopholes to Victorian convention, particularly since the French had a tendency to flaunt silly societal rules. So she continued to talk to him from just beyond the doorframe and fidgeted, wanting to ask him but not wanting to seem foolish.

Finally, she blurted it out.

"Why hasn't Edward kissed me since Italy?"

All right, it was a clumsy way of asking, but she'd got it out.

"Doesn't he still love me?" she clarified. She wouldn't meet Bledsoe's eyes, and the music she focused on blurred so the notes slid across their scored terraces.

"I believe he does still care a great deal for you. You know his limitations," he said, but his tone was gentle, not chiding.

"Everything seemed fine when I went back to England for father's funeral. And Jeremy Scott's," she added. "But when I came back, Edward was different, distant. Was it because I went to Jeremy's funeral? I didn't want to tell him, but I promised I'd never lie to him ever again, and..." She had to stop and breathe. She could understand Edward's reticence on some level. No matter how hard she tried, she couldn't shake the feeling that if she had handled the situation differently, the odious Lord Jeremy Scott would still be alive and with a better understanding of her. Intellectually she knew his death at Edward's hands was the best possible outcome—aside from Edward having a part in it, of course—and that he would have never ceased pursuing her, but she couldn't shake the memory of his heartbroken family.

"Yes, you had to tell him you attended Lord Scott's services," the musician said in a gentle tone. "Edward broke the strictest of his rules in the underground temple, and it's taking him a while to recover. Radcliffe said that sometimes when someone has experienced a great upheaval, they snap back to their previous way of being in spite of progress made."

"But how long is it going to take before he returns to how he was?" Iris chewed her lip and reminded herself not to. It was a bad habit she'd picked up since coming to Paris.

"Has another young man caught your fancy?" Bledsoe asked.

"N-no," Iris stammered. Although she thought his beard quite dashing, she didn't feel that way about Bledsoe. And the young French men in the archeology institute generally ignored her in favor of the few French women there. She didn't mind—she was accustomed to being an outsider—but she was glad for the holiday break.

"You're sure."

Iris blinked, but not fast enough to keep the tears inside her eyes. She wiped them from her cheeks, which stung from the salt sliding across the sensitive skin—the air had teeth lately. "Yes! How could you be cruel like this? I care for Edward. I had just hoped…"

He stood and crossed the room so he stood in front of her. He tilted her chin up with one finger so she had to meet his eyes. "You hoped that something in you would transform something in him, like the meeting of two elements to make a new substance," he finished for her.

She pulled away and looked down at the pattern on the rug. "It sounds so ridiculous when you say it like that."

"Your hope isn't ridiculous. But like the aether experiments, it will take time before the effect you have on Edward becomes something of significance."

"Why are you being so kind?" she asked and moved away from him. "It will ruin your reputation as an insensitive cad."

He glanced back toward the theatre, and his grin returned. "Perhaps I like to keep you guessing."

Iris shook her head and grabbed her books from the table. *Men are incomprehensible.*

EDWARD HEARD Iris's voice below talking to Johann. He couldn't make out the words, but she sounded upset. He put his head in his hands. She never showed that side of herself to him, not since returning from her father's funeral in England. Now he only saw the false bright smile she put on every time she saw him.

As much as he tried not to be jealous of his friend and the ease with which she spoke to the musician, he was. But he didn't want to frighten her with his dark thoughts, and they had become dark indeed since his first attempt at integrating the aether into a mock theatre lighting system a few days before. Patrick O'Connell, his partner in engineering, hadn't said anything, but he'd been remarkably absent since.

Edward tried to do something himself earlier that day, injecting a little of the aether gas into the part of the system they had set up in the corner, but he could only get so far with just two hands and his improving but still basic understanding of engineering.

The footsteps that ascended the stairs was too heavy to be Iris but too light to be the Irishman. As Edward anticipated, Johann poked his head around the laboratory door, his lips drawn back in a grin too wide to be innocent, but not big enough to hint at diabolical scheming. Wary, Edward drew back.

"I thought you couldn't do the experiments without sunlight," Johann said and moved toward the window, which was covered by heavy curtains.

"Don't touch that. The aether light is fine." Edward gestured to the writhing opalescent mass of light and color in the center of the glass globe in front of him. "I'm seeing how long it takes for it to decay without light. I'm still unsure what its fuel is."

Johann sat on the stool beside Edward's. "That makes sense. Wouldn't want it to disappear in the middle of a performance. How long has this one been going?"

"One week." *Yes, keep talking about the experiment. Don't make me discuss other things.*

Now Johann raised an eyebrow. "You must be anticipating some long plays."

"I'm being thorough." There, that would keep the questions coming. There were always questions. He used to like being the one to ask them, but now...

"Or you're avoiding something." Johann stood and walked to the window, where he yanked back the curtains. Watery late autumn sunlight poured through, and Edward squinted.

"Now you've ruined my experiment!"

"It's been a week, Edward. We don't have time to waste."

Edward decided not to argue about how he spent his days because then he would have to talk about things he wanted to ponder further. Thus, a change of subject was in order. "Your hair and beard are getting longer," he said. "You look like a wastrel."

"You have no room to talk—you look like a vagabond. How long have you been up here without a break?"

Edward looked at the aether mass. "I don't know. The servants bring me food and take the trays away. They also manage water for quick washes and the chamber pot at the appropriate times. O'Connell reminds me when I need to rest. What more do I need?" He stuck his shaking hands between his legs and squeezed so his friend wouldn't notice his tremors.

"What more, indeed? You've reverted back to how you were before we left England last summer. Worse, actually. At least then you'd talk to people." Johann resumed his seat and leaned in close to the aether chamber. "I could watch this stuff all day."

"Don't get so close!" Edward shoved him away.

"Fine, I'll wear goggles."

"You'll need more than goggles if it destabilizes," Edward gasped. His lungs felt too big for his chest, and he could barely expand them to breathe in the tight space they inhabited. His heart thumped in time to the aether's undulations, and he again squeezed his hands between his legs to stop their shaking and tingling.

"Edward, what...?" Johann stood and searched for something. The room spun, and Edward barely stayed on his stool. Something covered his nose and mouth, and he breathed into the paper bag his friend held to his face until his lungs shrank back to a reasonable size and he could take more than mere sips of air.

"Do I need to call Radcliffe?" Johann asked.

"No," Edward said. "I'm all right now. Just don't get close to it. How many times do I have to remind you it's dangerous?"

"And how many times do I have to tell you that it's not going to act like it did in Rome?"

"How do you know? You're not an aetherist. A stray frequency, a rumbling outside... It's not safe to move forward with it."

Instead of arguing as he usually did, Johann paused and gave Edward a measuring look. "Is that why you're stuck? You're afraid it's going to do something unpredictable?"

"Everything is predictable." *Like my inevitable descent into madness and Iris's disappointment in me.*

"So what is it, then? Madame is getting impatient."

"Science takes time." Edward couldn't help a little grin, remembering an argument from another lifetime.

"And money doesn't grow on trees," Johann replied with an answering smile. "But it has to come from somewhere. We're reaching the ends of our expedition fees from Cobb. I have to join the orchestra for the upcoming performance so Madame doesn't kick us out."

"Don't worry, no one will recognize you. We haven't seen any clockworks since returning to Paris. The Prussians have scared them away."

"They're more persistent than you give them credit for." Now Johann's expression mirrored Edward's doubt.

A flapping noise outside startled them both. A raven sat on the roof between the townhouse attic and theatre and gazed at them with glowing red eyes.

3

____

Rue de Gris, Paris, 1 December 1870

That evening, Marie paused outside Corinne's apartment building. Situated in an older part of Paris, it didn't match the bright, sparkling nature of the actress who lived there.

But how many of us match on the outside what we keep within?

Marie found Corinne in a flurry of packing. She raised her eyebrows at some of the dresses the woman had laid out—silk and satin, which she'd either had since before the siege began or had made from materials flown in by airship during the cover of night—but didn't say anything. She was here to cajole, not antagonize. In any case, they were much more expensive than an actress, even the *premiere femme* of the Théâtre Bohème, should have been able to afford.

Ah, right, she has been seen with the marquis...

"I am not coming back," Corinne said and flung ribbons, gloves, and stockings into a trunk. "I don't care if the Prussians shoot us down. I am leaving Paris."

"Is something else going on?" Marie asked. "I've never known you to turn down a part, especially not a lead role."

Corinne sat on the chaise, and her face crumpled. It wasn't a pretty crying face, so Marie suspected the woman's tears were real this time.

"Today was not the first time I've seen the angel of death."

"Oh? When else did it appear to you?"

Corinne shook her head so vigorously hairpins clattered to the floor around her. "He has never appeared to me before today. But I have seen him. Yesterday in my dressing room, he was in the mirror beside me, but when I turned, no one was there. And I didn't hear the door open."

"In your dressing room." Marie knew that room well. The door squeaked horribly no matter how many times they oiled it, and it opened on to a busy corridor. Even if someone had managed to go in or out quietly, they would have been seen, and a person in a death costume, even if there was one in the current production, would have been remarked upon. Plus there was the irritating issue of the fact the costume had been sold and not replaced for weeks.

"*Si*, and last week, he appeared in the hall where the musicians come and go from the stage." She lowered her voice. "He came out of one wall and walked straight into another one."

"Have you been drinking the marquis's brandy again?"

"*Non*." Corinne stood and put her hands on her hips. "If you have just come to mock me, I will not speak to you. How do I know this wasn't a trick for you to get to play Henriette, and now you are here to gloat?"

"Because I am not interested in taking the stage again."

"Why not?" Corinne leaned forward, her eyes wide and nostrils flared, a predator on the hunt for gossip. "You keep saying that, but I don't know whether to believe you. You were once Fantastique, the greatest actress in the city."

Marie didn't care to explain, especially not to someone who wouldn't understand. "I'm just trying to figure out what happened so I can convince you to come back. You'd make a much better Henriette than I. I'm too tall. Poor Gerard will have to wear lifts in his shoes."

Corinne wrinkled her nose. "Yes, all the tall ones have gone to war. You would think Death would be busy enough at the front without having to bother a poor actress like me."

Or even a good one. Marie didn't voice the thought. "So about you returning…"

Corinne stood, all trace of warmth gone from her face. Marie wondered if she'd been taking lessons on expression severity from Lucille.

"You can ask all you want," Corinne said and placed a slender hand on her not-so-slender throat. "I will never return to the Théâtre Bohème lest Death claim me once and for all."

"But how do you know it's truly Death?" Marie asked. "It could be someone playing a prank on you."

"That is a good prank, Mademoiselle St. Jean, if a man can walk through walls."

Marie bit her lip. She and Lucille knew of the myriad secret passages that riddled the theatre, but they'd agreed to keep them secret. Who else could know? "There are many tricks that can be done with mirrors," she said.

Corinne's look would have skewered a lesser man or woman. "Mirrors. You are not serious."

"Yes, I am. Perhaps you only saw the reflection of someone in the hallway."

"And yet I did not see my own reflection? I do not understand how this could be done. No, it was the specter of Death come to haunt the theatre. Mark my words, Mademoiselle. You will all be doomed, even the delightful Maestro Bledsoe."

"What does he have to do with—?" Marie stopped when she saw Corinne's lips spread into a smug smirk. "Oh. I didn't know you had a relationship."

"Some connections do not require the empty promises and

doomed commitments of a relationship." Corinne tossed her yellow curls. "We have an understanding. That is all."

"What sort of understanding?" Marie hoped jealousy didn't bleed through in her tone.

"One based on mutual interest. Now, this interview is over." Corinne stood. "Begone with you. The marquis said he would help me leave on tonight's airship, and I have to choose what is most important to pack."

"WHAT IN THE BLAZES IS THAT?" Johann asked. He peeked around the curtain at the raven, which turned its head, its beak slightly open.

"I told you to keep the curtains closed," Edward grumbled. He'd taunted Johann about his appearance, but the scientist's hollowed cheeks and sunken eyes told Johann he was slipping into a worrisome state. Johann had never seen him this far gone, not even when he was finishing his degree or during the incident that drove him to a life of predictability at the cost of grave limitations.

Johann slid the curtain along the rod, and the demonic bird seemed to fix on the sound. It opened its beak wider, and smoke emerged.

"It breathes fire?" Johann asked.

"No, it is obviously some sort of steam-driven automaton," Edward said with a look that expressed his low opinion of those who might believe in fire-breathing birds.

"Obviously. Why are we hiding from it?"

Another exasperated glance. "Because you don't know what its makers have instructed it to do in response to certain stimuli."

The furnace of anxiety that always had active coals flared to life in Johann's gut. "Is it the Clockwork Guild?"

Is this it? My death at the hands, er, beak of a red-eyed fake raven?

"Doubtful. They don't use steam in their works, at least not from what I've been able to ascertain."

"Then who?"

"If I knew that, I'd know what to do beyond hide from it."

The bird opened its mouth wider, and Edward squinted at it. Then he pushed his side of the curtain to the center.

"Close yours as well! How could we be so stupid?"

"What do you mean?" Johann complied.

"The light reflected off a lens in the back of the bird's throat. I think it had some sort of camera in it, and it was trying to get a picture of what I've been working on. I hope we shut the curtains before it got a good image."

"Of your devices or of us," Johann muttered. "If the Guild gets a good look at my photograph, someone will recognize me."

Now the only light in the room came from the aether device. With its illumination, Edward's features were softened, and his physical flaws smoothed, and Johann couldn't help but imagine how it would affect theatre productions.

"If you can get the theatre lighting working with this, you will be doing all the actors and especially the actresses a favor." He recalled seeing Corinne in the light of day come morning. Without her cosmetics, she was not the beauty she appeared on stage, and he wondered just how much she had to put on her face before treading the boards.

"Perhaps, but one never knows."

"What do you mean?"

Edward shook his head. "Nothing. Go now. I need to continue working on other things. When O'Connell gets back, would you send him up?"

"Right." Johann found himself in the hallway. He scratched at his beard—damn itchy thing—and tried not to feel piqued.

He'd never shown much interest in his friend's experiments before, but he was honestly curious beyond the pressure for the aether lighting system to be working soon. Edward's behavior had been stranger than usual too.

What is going on with everyone, and who is behind the raven? Surely it didn't have enough time for a clear picture of me.

He shook his head, but his anxiety lodged in his brain. Now he would have to pick up his violin or find some other distraction before he'd be able to sleep that night.

The violin it is, then. I've had enough of neurotic people—male and female—for one day.

But part of him hoped Marie would poke her head in on his practicing.

THE NEXT DAY, Marie sat on her bed in her old room at the townhouse and gazed out the window rather than at the script on her lap. Rain fell from the sky, glazed the windows, and slicked the surfaces of the trees and street below. A strange large shadow swooped overhead, but when she craned her neck to see it, it had already gone.

"You're supposed to memorize all that by when?" Iris asked. She sat at the only desk, which she had taken over once starting school. With the addition of a cot for Iris to the room, there wasn't space for another. Marie didn't mind—she learned best when sitting in nontraditional positions, or at least whichever ones her skirts would allow. She much preferred the clothing she'd worn when she trained to be a female guard, but she didn't like the circumstances of her employment, so she supposed this was a fair trade-off.

"The show starts in a week, so I need to have all of it memorized by the end of the weekend."

"Music and everything?"

"It's no different from you learning all the different sizes and shapes of Greek vases because of what you want to be. I can't imagine learning all that, but your brain soaks it up. Mine does that with lines. Maybe I just want to be someone else."

Or someone else wants to be me.

She'd never been able to explain it, only that when she was preparing for a role and on stage, she felt possessed by whatever character she played. And when the production ended, she felt like she left part of herself behind.

Iris rubbed her eyes. "I'm exhausted from studying, but I don't know what else to do. Exams are over, but I feel I need to do *something*." She glanced up, and Marie guessed she thought about Edward, whom they all worried about. He hadn't been down for a meal in days.

"Me too." The edgy feeling had started earlier that morning, but Marie didn't know how to explain it or where it came from, only that it had been off and on the past few weeks. "I'm going to find a corner in the theatre to look over these."

Or not look over them without witnesses to scold me for avoiding my work.

Iris stood. "I can leave if you need me to."

"No, stay here, I'll go. Perhaps you should organize your notes so they'll be ready for you to pick up next term."

Iris grinned like Marie had just proposed the most brilliant of ideas. "Yes! That's exactly what I'll do. You're a genius."

Marie left Iris to her organizing, which already looked like an explosion of papers over every surface of the bedroom. She crept down the stairs so no one would accost her. Or maybe she moved slowly so someone would interrupt her on her fool's errand, for she didn't want the part of Henriette.

She emerged into view of the front door just in time to see it close behind Bledsoe, and her errant mind wondered if he was going to see Corinne. Not that he'd find her if she'd managed to make it on to the airship the night before. Marie shook her head. The privateers would have their hands full with that one.

When Marie emerged into the halfhearted light of the cloudy morning, she reflexively stilled to listen for the bass sound of cannon or engines. Of course the airship had long since sailed, but she and other Parisians always paused to see and hear if there was smoke on the horizon or other signs the Prussians had engaged the French troops, if they would invade or finally be turned back to slink heads-down to their homeland. Everyone knew something would have to happen one way or the other soon with winter coming on and supplies in the city running low. Meanwhile, they pretended life went on as usual, just with fewer imported luxuries to be had.

In fact, the city had an air of forced gaiety—look, the people seemed to say, we're not letting your silly invasion dampen our spirit. It made for irrational behavior, but it also helped fill theatre seats, even if tickets were half the prices they used to be with the economy of the city half shut-down. Still, with most of the theatres having been converted to hospitals, the Bohème drew good crowds since they were one of the few still running.

A fine mist clung to Marie's hair and clothing, and a chill breeze made her quicken her steps. She went in a side door just beyond the portico leading to where noble theatre goers left their drivers and carriages. Or if they were nice, just their carriages. Marie tried not to think about how she sneaked out that door and was bundled into a carriage by her former patron. Those memories carried too much regret, both for her and her mother.

See, Maman? *This is why I cannot take the stage again.*

She knew no one would be in Corinne's former dressing room and turned in that direction, but then she stopped. That was the star's dressing room, the one her mother wanted her to take. Was she doing it again, responding without intention to a role that had been thrust upon her? She closed her eyes, and the litany she had come up with long ago materialized in her brain and whirled around like a little aether cloud. She clung to its light, which pierced the haze of her anxious thoughts.

I am Marie St. Jean. I am twenty years old. I have brown hair and hazel eyes. I like pain au chocolat *and* cappuccino. *I am myself, not my role. I am Marie St. Jean...*

She opened her eyes to see she now stood in the hallway in front of the dressing room she wanted to avoid. Had she walked here without recognizing she did? Panic shot in an arrow's line from her stomach to her throat, to which she raised a hand. Wait, that wasn't one of her regular gestures, was it? The script fell to her feet, and when she knelt to retrieve it, she saw the stage direction on the page in front of her—*"Henriette: raises hand to throat."*

"Are you having difficulty, Mademoiselle?" a soft male voice asked with an American accent. Marie wasn't one to faint, but the hallway swam in front of her eyes, and the last thing she saw before she blacked out was a metal death's head leering over her.

4

Théâtre Bohème Townhouse, 2 December 1870

"Where is she?" Lucille swept into the room. Papers swirled in the eddy caused by her flinging the door open, and Iris dove to pluck her *Greek Pottery I—Prehistoric through Archaic Periods* notes from the floor so they wouldn't end up under the Frenchwoman's boots.

"I take it you mean Marie, Madame?" Iris asked in as polite a tone as she could muster while she straightened the stack in her hands. She reflexively looked around for her gloves, as she typically did when Lucille was near.

"Yes, Marie. She is needed to read through the play this morning." Lucille's black gaze swept through the room as if she could make Marie materialize from the books and notebooks that covered every surface.

"I think she was headed to the theatre to review the script."

Lucille's brows drew down in a black V. "The Théâtre Bohème is a large building, and she could be anywhere."

The defeated expression that flickered over Lucille's face made Iris blurt out before she could stop herself, "I'll help you look for her."

"*Bien.*"

Now Lucille beamed at her, and Iris wondered again just how much of what Lucille did and said was real and how much an act to manipulate others. She was coming to a ratio of about seventy to thirty percent unreal to real. Iris found Lucille to have a dizzying array of expressions like her own mother, but unlike Adelaide, Lucille didn't always seem to feel the emotion she projected.

Or did she?

"I need a break from this, anyway," Iris mumbled.

"Pretty girls do not mumble," Lucille said, and her voice and accent were juxtaposed in Iris's mind over Adelaide's.

"I said I need to take a break from this organizational effort," Iris said and enunciated clearly, perhaps exaggeratedly. Not that her schoolwork looked very organized.

Lucille either didn't notice or chose not to respond. She swept out of the room, and Iris followed her after making sure no notes flew too far. She glanced up the staircase toward the atelier, as Marie called it, where Edward worked on his aether-based lighting system. He hadn't come down to dinner again last night, or to breakfast that morning. She'd been so focused on her exams she didn't remember the last time she saw him, and now guilt sagged between her chest and stomach.

"Lucille, are the servants feeding Professor Bailey?" she asked.

"I believe so, yes," Lucille said over her shoulder. "He says he is getting close. But he has been approaching *close* for months now and never reaching it."

"I know. I'm worried about him."

"As well you should be. He seems possessed by a certain madness."

Lucille's words made Iris's stomach clench, and she almost stumbled on the stairs. "What kind of madness do you mean?"

"He is one who will always lose himself in his work. It is not a bad thing, Mademoiselle, but men like that require extra care. And patience."

They reached the front hall, and Lucille turned to Iris so suddenly Iris almost bumped into the older woman.

"Sometimes no matter how hard we try, we are not enough."

"What do you mean?" Iris asked. She found her gloves on the side table where she'd set her books the day before.

"You cannot hope to change him if you want to truly love him. Many women have ended up in unhappy relationships because they think they can transform a man into what they want him to be. In some cases, you merely have to accept."

Iris nodded as though she believed the woman's words, but she didn't allow the disappointment they engendered to take root. She didn't want to think that this would be her life with Edward, not seeing him for months at a time, always wondering if he loved her more than, or at least as much as, his science. She loved archeology and him equally—at least she thought she did.

Some impulse made her ask, "Is that what happened with Marie's father?"

Lucille barked a laugh and opened the front door. "Ha! No, mademoiselle. We had an arrangement. I wanted a daughter. He wanted a no-strings-attached dalliance. It was not a traditional arrangement, but it worked for us."

"What if you'd had a son?" Iris followed Lucille along the sidewalk. "You can't determine the gender of a baby."

"There are things one can do, but you are too young and innocent to know of them."

Iris fought to keep her shoulders from slumping, as they wanted to do when she ran up against the wall of women's wisdom she was "too young and innocent" to be worthy of learning. It was one of Marie's favorite conversation-avoiding tactics.

I guess I know where she learned it from.

The gloom of the theatre enveloped Iris along with the smells of old wood and the paint the scenery-smiths were busy using for the new production pieces.

Lucille paused in front of the ticket window and flared her nostrils. "There is something... You take the main auditorium and backstage areas."

"Where will you search?" Iris asked. She reached through the connection she had with Marie but couldn't feel anything.

I should be able to feel her if she's nearby unless she's asleep.

"The dressing rooms and passages."

"Secret passages?" Iris took her hand. "Oh, let me search with you! I knew there must be some in a building like this."

"No, Mademoiselle, it will be too dangerous." Lucille's eyes flashed like faceted jet beads in the flickering gaslight. "You stay where you can run if you need to and tell Marie to get back to the townhouse as soon as you find her, if you find her and we are not too late. I fear he is back!"

"Who?" Iris grabbed for Lucille, but the theatre owner had already dashed into the hall beside the ticket booth.

Who is he? What is going on here? Iris moved toward the auditorium through the nearest door, but a chill settled on her shoulders like the gaze of a malevolent spirit.

Don't be silly, you're letting your imagination run away with you.

But evil spirits belong in the myths of the past, not in the scientific present, don't they? Whatever was happening, she felt a flicker of Marie's panic and hastened into the auditorium.

MARIE WOKE inside Corinne's dressing room. Her mind wouldn't let her think of it as her dressing room. For one thing, the other actress had been much too fond of lace and gauzy fabrics. Marie didn't know how much stuff Corinne had stashed in this room, but she guessed it would be enough to keep some very lucky ragpicker fed for a month. If Lucille didn't sell it first, but would she want to attach herself monetarily to a doomed woman's possessions?

That's not a useful thought, and many women will be happy for such luxuries, especially right now.

Marie propped herself on her elbows and saw she lay on the chaise lounge to the right of the door. She kicked a pair of stockings to the floor. The script lay on the dressing table, but it was thinner than she remembered.

What...?

A movement in her peripheral vision made her straighten to full alertness, but the only person she saw when she turned her head was her own reflection in the full-length mirror that made the wall at the back of the room. That was why Corinne had liked this dressing room—she could admire herself from every angle and observe which men never took their eyes off her. Yes, Corinne knew how to find out who worshiped her and who merely saw her as a prize. It was one of the few things Marie admired about her.

Marie put a hand over her heart, which tap danced below her corset. How did she get here? The last thing she remembered was—

Now the mirror shimmered, and Marie dashed to the door, but the handle wouldn't budge.

I'm locked in!

She allowed herself one terrified glance over her shoulder, and her heart nearly froze its frenzied tarantella.

The same death's head from the hallway stared back at her.

No, not a death's head, a metal man's head. An automaton?

She decided someone played a cruel trick on her, but she didn't know of a passage behind the mirror. Lucille denied the existence of one, and Marie had never been able to find an entrance to it.

"Whoever you are, sir, I do not appreciate your prank," she said with as haughty a lift to her chin as she could manage. "Remove your mask at once. This theatre belongs to Madame Lucille St. Jean, and we do not abide trespassers."

The death's head approached from behind the mirror, which seemed to stretch and bend around it. Marie knew mirror effects and could concede it moved, but whoever this was manipulated it like they'd...

"...built it?" Marie murmured. She'd heard of a workman who'd been killed during the theatre construction, long before her mother had bought it with the help of one of her patrons, a stately duke who was long passed at this point.

No, no, let's not think about another dead man.

She tried to ram the door with her shoulder, but it wouldn't budge. Of course. The theatre had been constructed just before the Revolution, and they'd made the doors extra strong in case either side wanted to pay to keep prisoners there.

The air warmed like the inside of a toaster oven, and a droplet of sweat trickled from beneath Marie's hair line and down her cheek. Now she couldn't look away from the mirror, where the ghost stood and watched her, a rapier at his side.

"Are you going to kill me, sir?" she asked. *Maybe if I can draw him out, I can disarm him and then get hold of his mask.*

"Why would I kill you? You're banging yourself up beautifully without my help."

Indeed, Marie knew her shoulder and arm would be bruised. "Then why not show yourself all the way?"

The air clouded, and Marie darted to and fro looking for the source of it, the flame that could grow and consume the theatre in a matter of minutes. She'd entered to find burning candles—what if one of them had tipped over? But her movements slowed, and she felt as though she pushed through a tub of the greasy substance actors used to remove the stage cosmetics. The smell—earthy sweet and familiar—tipped her off that no wood burned, and she found the fainting couch just before she collapsed.

"You know that smell?"

The voice was back, and Marie used every one of her upper face muscles to pry her eyelids open a sliver. The sneering automaton face hovered in front of her.

Sick familiarity forced a memory to mind, and she struggled not to swim into it, but something weighted her body while her spirit floated above. "Go away," she murmured.

"What do you see?" the strange being asked.

"I'm in a club, a gentleman's club. It's the night, the first night I met him..." The words tumbled from her mouth in spite of her trying to keep her lips sealed in her lolling head. The smell of Parnaby Cobb's own personal tobacco brand, which he managed to get from his North Carolina plantation in spite of the ongoing war, threaded her past to her present.

"Sleep now, my beauty," the ghost crooned. "And may your conscience light your dreams."

CLUB L'OR, Paris, 16 May 1868

Marie entered the club, and although she kept her cloak around her and hood drawn, a murmur followed her like the foam at the crest of a wave—"Fantastique! It's the actress from the Bohème. But what is she doing here?" She knew her cheeks must glow as brightly as the lamps in their beaded red silk shades, which cast everything in a lurid, ruddy glow, but she pressed on. She didn't know what she felt, only that the emotion originated somewhere in the center of her pelvis, clawed its way through her stomach, and clogged her throat, from where it scratched at the corners of her eyes. But she held her head up as her mother had always taught her.

"You are a fatherless female from a culture no one understands. You have nothing and everything to lose, so must never let them take anything away, least of all your pride."

She had lost everything. She had given it to him as a stupid accident, and now she would swallow her pride to retrieve it.

Finally she found him. She should have known he would be at a table in the farthest corner, from where he could survey everything like a king. And of course a woman sat on either side of him. She'd heard he collected them. Their looks, like alley cats dressed up to be noble tigers from the far side of the British Empire, almost broke her composure because she saw her own future in their empty eyes and painted-on smiles. At least it would be if she continued her current course. Her mother would try to protect her, but she knew what kind of reputation actresses had, and it would only take one slip, one bad decision to fall into that role as easily as she had all the others that had been presented to her.

"Give it back," she said, the speech she'd rehearsed vanished in a puff of cigar smoke and whiff of expensive perfume.

He tapped his ash into a—what else?—gold-rimmed square ashtray. Everything about him said controlled extravagance— just enough to show his wealth, but not to a gaudy extent. "Give what back?"

"I'm not going to say in front of these creatures."

He dismissed the women with a wave of his hand. "Go find drinks for yourselves, Mademoiselles. Fantastique and I have business to discuss."

They scooted away with languid attitudes, but Marie caught their angry glances.

You're welcome to him, girls.

For girls they were, younger than she. She removed her

hood and sat at the edge of the banquette cushion, but he gestured for her to move closer.

"Come now, I don't bite," he said. He shook his empty glass at a waiter and held up two fingers to indicate another should be brought for Marie.

"No, thank you," she said, both to the invitation in his eyes and the drink, but she did move close enough to him to speak to him privately. She grasped for the role of outraged actress, but all she felt was young and foolish.

"Now what can I do for you?" he asked.

"The autograph I gave you earlier, I need it back."

His gray eyebrows signaled surprise before they drew together. "Now why could an autograph be so important?"

He drew it from his waistcoat pocket, and Marie clasped her hands in her lap so she wouldn't grab for it and cause a scene. She was too known here. Too known everywhere in Paris, actually. Facing others' expectations, feeling them crawling into her skin and under her pores until she couldn't help but be who they wanted her to be, had grown tiring. But she wouldn't reveal that to him.

"It isn't the autograph itself, sir. See? I've brought you another." She removed a folded piece of paper from her cloak pocket and handed it to him. He compared it with the one he'd removed from his own.

"You still haven't told me why this one is so valuable."

"I apologize, but when you visited me in my dressing room earlier, I picked up the wrong piece of paper." She tried to shrug in a nonchalant manner—*See? Silly me.* "So I would appreciate if you would return the other to me, for I need the letter on which it's written."

"I hadn't noticed." He unfolded the paper on which her first scrawl was written and scanned it. "You're planning to leave Paris and visit a relative in the United States?"

Another silly girl shrug. "Only for a short time. I'm ready for a change of scene, as it were."

His mustache didn't move when he smiled, she noticed, only the corners of his lips. "I can do much better than this," he said. "A talent like yours needs to be seen in New York or Boston."

Marie kept her own smile stuck where it was in spite of her jaw muscles tightening so hard they stung. "Where I want to go is none of your affair, although I appreciate your consideration." She held out her hand. "My papers, please?"

He tucked it back in his waistcoat and handed her substitute back to her. "We'll discuss it after tomorrow night's performance at a late dinner. Do you know where the Hotel Auberge is?"

"I'm afraid my mother will not look kindly upon me dining alone with a strange man."

The look he gave her made her wish she'd kept her mouth shut, for she now knew she was the prey.

"Your mother doesn't know about this letter. She has no idea of your intent to leave Paris." They weren't questions, so she didn't answer them, but she had to look away. "Then your proposed adventure is much more risky than dinner with me, Mademoiselle." He lifted her hand to his lips, and the brush of his whiskers put her in mind of a scraggly lion. But this one was far from toothless.

"Tomorrow, then." She stood and walked out. She tried to ignore the whispers after her, but she knew the gossip would be all over Paris by the following morning, by when she had intended to be gone. Now instead of "Actress Disappears," the paper would read, "Actress Entertained by American Entrepreneur at Gentleman's Club."

"*Merde,*" she whispered.

5

____

héâtre Bohème, 2 December 1870

Johann sat in the pit and tuned his violin. Sometimes when he played, it felt like part of him, and other times it seemed a creature with its own mind that required cajoling and gentle handling. And rarely it seemed to hold a tempest, and he had to grasp the bow with even more care lest it slip away from him in the middle of a passage.

Today feels like a tempest day, or perhaps that's how I feel.

Sometimes he was happy for Edward's preoccupation. Johann felt his friend was the only one who had truly forgiven him for his role in the airship crash in spite of being the one most hurt by it.

He made the tuning note a long and plaintive one. The tone hung in the air, but when he lifted his bow, a new sound floated to his ears.

"Marie?" The name was asked in almost a whisper.

Johann stood and saw Iris at the back of the theatre. When she saw him, she stepped backward, then squinted.

"Maestro? I hope that is you and not some strange spirit haunting the theatre."

Her words made the skin between his shoulders tighten. It wasn't like her to kid about the supernatural. "Mademoiselle, if there is a ghost in the room, it is not me."

She gave him what he'd come to think of as her analytical look and walked down the side aisle. "I hope you're jesting. Have you seen Marie?"

"Not since breakfast." And she had seemed distracted with barely a glance in his direction. Not that he expected anything from her, but he'd found himself oddly disappointed. "Why?"

Now Iris stood close to him. "I'm not sure what to make of it," she said in a quiet tone. "Madame St. Jean seems convinced there is something evil here, and she is concerned for Marie. I told Madame I would help her search."

"And you're sure Mademoiselle St. Jean is here?"

"She said she was coming over to study her lines for the production." Iris glanced around the theatre. "I'm to search in here and backstage."

"And if you find her?" Now Johann's nerves thrummed like someone stroked them with a bow. Iris seemed worried, and she wasn't easily disturbed, not after all she'd been through. Something felt off about the place today, but he didn't know whether to attribute the sensation to something truly there, or merely because he felt conscripted to be there and would prefer to remain hidden in the background, not front and center in the orchestra.

"If I find her, I'm to tell her to go to the townhouse, and to run if we have to." She glanced up at him. "This sounds ridiculous, doesn't it? Nothing in here could hurt us. It's the middle of a Friday morning." But she rubbed her hands together, and the strips of pale skin between her gloves and the bottoms of her sleeves showed goose bumps.

"I'll help you search for her," he said. "If only to prove that this is all nonsense. Madame seems a sensible woman, but the old have been known to start seeing things that aren't there."

"I doubt Madame is going senile, but yes, the sooner we can find Marie the better."

Johann placed his violin in its case and secured it. He'd return to practicing later. Mademoiselle St. Jean hadn't been far from his thoughts all morning, so it made a strange sort of sense he would search for her now. And when he found her? She'd probably be irritated at the interruption rather than rush into his arms.

"Maestro, look," Iris said. She'd climbed the stairs at the side of the stage and found something, a piece of the script, toward the front. "It's hers, I think. The notes are in her handwriting."

He joined her, and together they followed a trail of pages through the backstage area and green room and then down the back stairs into the hall where the dressing rooms were. They stopped in front of one of the doors, which had the name *Mlle. Corinne* scrawled on the nameplate.

"This is the star's dressing room," Iris whispered.

"I'm sure Madame will change the nameplate soon," Johann replied, also *sotto voce*. "And why are we whispering?"

"I don't know. But it's oddly quiet down here."

Indeed, noise from the street could be heard in the theatre itself but not in the lower levels. Now the only sound came from shadows, which was to say, none at all. Even the gas lamps flickered silently. Johann fought the urge to hunch his shoulders against an invisible threat. No matter which way he turned, he felt something stood behind him and watched.

Iris raised her hand to knock on the door, and her taps echoed in the corridor. "Marie?" she called, but still in a muted call. "Are you in there?"

A noise came from behind the door, and something rattled the handle.

"Iris? Is that you? I'm locked in!"

WHEN MARIE woke, she found herself back on the chaise lounge, and she scrabbled against the feeling of fingers brushing over her. No light illuminated the room, which was a normal temperature again, and the groping feelings subsided as she anchored herself by pinching the fabric against her skin.

A knock at the door made her run to it, but she found it was again locked.

"Marie? Are you in there?"

"Iris? Is that you? I'm locked in!"

"Stand back," a male voice said.

"Maestro?" Marie asked. Shame at being caught in that predicament warred with a strange relief he was there. "Whatever you do, don't damage your hands."

"Do you want me to get you out or not?"

Just hearing his voice calmed her and shredded the cobweb-like wisps of the dream that clung to her brain. "Of course, but let me think for a moment." The darkness behind her pressed in on her, and she resisted turning around lest she see the metal face leering at her. She couldn't allow Bledsoe to risk a broken hand or dislocated shoulder by breaking down the door—Lucille would surely blame her. Plus Marie hadn't turned to a man for help in a long time, so she knew she could figure this one out. She ran her hands over the door, and her right thumb brushed against something metal sticking out from it—the key.

In the lock.

She leaned with her forehead against the door. The key hadn't been there a moment ago, had it? Her brain must still be addled by whatever had been in the smoke that dragged her to the past. She wasn't even sure if she had described her vision out loud or if she had only dreamed it. And she had been fighting the role of a woman who went mad from opium—had she dreamed everything, even the man?

They're going to think I'm insane. "Never mind, I found the key." She turned it, opened the door, and squinted against the light in the hallway. Although dim, it was brighter than the darkness in the dressing room.

"You were locked in... With the key?" Iris asked. Her facial expression only showed concern. "We found these." She handed Marie the missing parts of the script. "They led right to you."

Marie rarely found herself speechless, but she had no explanation that would make any kind of logical sense. "I wish I could tell you what happened, but I'm not sure myself."

"What do you mean?" Iris asked simultaneously with the maestro asking, "Are you all right?"

"I'm fine." *Aside from my little involuntary trip into the past.* "What's wrong?"

"Other than you being locked inside with a key and parts of your script leading us to you in a trail?"

Marie could tell Iris's mind sifted through the possible explanations like her fingers would eventually search for shards of pottery or other clues to the past in the desert sands. The crease between her brows and sharpness in her dark blue eyes said Iris could not come up with any good, sane explanations for Marie's predicament. That was fine because Marie hadn't, either. Who would believe a story about an automaton that had trapped her and forced her to reveal a past she wanted to keep hidden?

"Yes, that. I may have had some help, but I don't want to speak of it here." She looked back into the dressing room, but it looked ordinary again, the mirror just a mirror.

"Your mother said we need to go back to the townhouse." Iris glanced over her shoulder. "She seems to be concerned that someone is in the theatre who shouldn't be, and that we're in danger."

"She's right." Marie couldn't suppress the shudder that overtook her. What did her mother know of the strange man in the mirror? And her mind batted the question around—was he even real or an invention of the role that tried to overtake her?

Marie led them out of the side door and into the cool, gray morning. The clouds hung low overhead, and she paused as she always did, but again no mortars or overhead engines overlaid the usual city noises. They encountered Frederic LeClerc, another violinist, on his way into the theatre, likely for some pre-rehearsal practice. When he saw Marie, his face transformed from a mask of artistic concentration to a fire burst of a smile.

Marie groaned inwardly—she'd been avoiding him since returning to Paris. Not that there was anything wrong with him, but he had a dogged devotion and had proposed to her at least once a month before she left Paris two years earlier and insisted she call him by his first name, although she never reciprocated the invitation.

"Mademoiselle St. Jean," he said and bowed over her hand. He continued in rapid French with tone and volume that hinted he spoke words of love to her. "What a pleasant surprise! I hear you are to take the role of Henriette in *Light Fantastique*. It is a part that was meant for you, I think, a sign that Fantastique should take the stage once again."

A chill shimmied up Marie's spine. Henriette—Hector Berlioz's idealized woman—was the type of role she most needed to avoid lest it influence her to become the ideal woman for someone like Frederic. As it were, when she was in character, she would likely only increase his perception of her as the perfect woman for him.

Merde, how am I to get out of this one?

"We were just leaving," Bledsoe said, and although his hand

hovered above and not on Marie's waist, Frederic stepped back, a look of dismay on his face.

"And so you are the new concertmaster? I have heard of you." Frederic's English was heavily accented. "But it is strange that you would be leaving. Are we not to start rehearsals today?"

"I will return shortly. I recommend you wait out here until I do."

Frederic looked at the sky, where the clouds sagged darker than before. "But it looks like it shall rain."

"Madame St. Jean is doing something in the theatre," Iris said. "She said for no one to come in until she finished. You're welcome to join us at the townhouse for lunch."

Marie sent Iris a sharp look. "Or perhaps you should wait here until the others arrive, warn them as well not to disturb *Maman*." She steeled herself against his crestfallen expression.

"Ah yes, Madame needs to work her magic," he said. "It is part of her genius, so I will wait here. I disturbed her once and shall not allow anyone in *my* orchestra to make the same mistake."

Maestro Bledsoe stiffened beside Marie, and she guessed he felt Frederic's barb, that as concertmaster he should take the lead. "I will stay here as well," he said. "Mademoiselles, please go to the townhouse. I shall join you as soon as I can."

Marie and Iris linked arms and turned on to the sidewalk. Marie couldn't resist one last glance behind her, and as she expected, the maestro and Frederic stood a few feet apart and appeared to evaluate each other.

"Will there be a fight?" Iris asked. She, too, stared at the men, and Marie directed her gaze forward lest they bump into a lamp-pole or tree.

"Don't be dramatic. That's my job. Plus, they won't risk their hands."

"It's romantic, don't you think?" Iris grinned up at her. "Two artists vying for your attention."

"Not those two. I don't want the one, and I don't trust the other." But she caught the disappointment on Iris's face. *Right, she's craving romance she's not getting. Taking this role is going to cause me nothing but trouble.*

6

T héâtre Bohème, 2 December 1870

Johann and the other violinist eyed each other. Johann still held his violin and glanced at the sky to see if it would, indeed, rain.

"What is your relationship to Mademoiselle St. Jean?" the other man asked.

Johann allowed his astonishment to show. "Perhaps we should start with our names and move on to more personal questions after. Proper etiquette and all."

"I am Frederic LeClerc." He didn't hold a hand out to shake. "And I am going to marry Mademoiselle. And I know who you are, English swine."

Johann gestured for LeClerc to follow him so they stood under the canopy of the portico by the side entrance to the theatre. "No sense in getting our instruments wet as we sort this out. How do you know of me?" *I've made it a point not to be known here.*

LeClerc shrugged as only the French do. Johann reminded himself to stay patient. "Word gets around, Maestro. Especially when someone with money is curious."

Now the iciness in Johann's lungs had nothing to do with the chill breeze that heralded the start of a deluge. The sound of sleet mixed with rain made him glad he was under cover, but a sense of being exposed caused him to step behind one of the pillars and out of view of the street.

LeClerc studied him with a shrewd look. "Oh yes, *Monsieur Bledsoe*, someone has been very interested in knowing where to find you."

"And who would that be?"

Another man ran from the rain and joined them, and Johann prepared to defend himself if necessary.

"Luc," LeClerc greeted the newcomer with a handshake and spoke in French, which Johann knew well enough to follow. "Where is Martin?"

The new man pulled a clarinet case from under his oilskin cloak. His hair and mustache dripped in spite of his attempt to dress for the weather. "He's on his way. Why are we standing out here?"

"Madame."

"Ah." He seemed to accept that as sufficient explanation. "And who is this?"

"Maestro Johann Bledsoe, our new concertmaster."

Johann cringed against his given name. He'd been using the pseudonym of Harry Sable.

Martin held a hand out, and Johann took it, bracing himself for Martin to say he'd heard of him or reveal some other sign he continued to be in danger of discovery from the Clockwork Guild. But Martin only introduced himself, as did the two men who joined them. When a knot of six or seven of them crowded under the portico, Madame St. Jean emerged and looked them over.

"*Bien,*" she said. "The theatre is clean. Practice can start."

Johann held back as the others filed in ahead of him. "Did you find what you were looking for?" he asked.

"*Non*, but I'm sure I will soon. Just be careful. And watch out for Frederic." With that cryptic warning, she disappeared back inside the theatre.

"Oh, I most certainly shall," Johann murmured. "We have a conversation to finish."

~

IRIS AND MARIE walked through the front door of the townhouse just before the rain started. Marie frowned as she shut the door. "I think I see sleet mixed with the rain."

"Perhaps winter is finally here." Iris stripped her gloves from her hands.

"You're not leaving those on?"

Iris glanced up at her with an inquisitive look. "Why should I? I've been here long enough that the objects around us don't ask to be touched or read, and I've gotten much better at controlling my...well, whatever it is."

Lucky girl. "It's chilly in here."

"The dining room will be warm enough, and I do believe it's lunchtime. By the way, you should talk to your mother. She might be able to help you."

Marie followed Iris through the hall and up the stairs to the first level, where the dining room and kitchen were located. "What do you mean? I don't need her help."

And her help will come with a price, like my staying here and taking the stage for the rest of my life.

"You were talking in your sleep, something about a mask that will consume you from within. It was very poetic, but you sounded frightened."

"I have nightmares." *Some of them more real than others.* "It was probably nothing."

They reached the dining room, and Iris exclaimed, "Edward, you've emerged!"

When Marie entered, she saw Iris embrace Edward, who held her stiffly before melting into her. She looked away and was glad to see she wouldn't be alone with the hopefully reconciling lovebirds. Doctor Chadwick Radcliffe and his friend Patrick O'Connell stood by the sideboard and helped themselves to a light lunch of salted meats, cheeses, bread and pickled vegetables—standard fare since commerce from farms outside the city had slowed to a trickle, and the growing season was long over. Although Marie thought her mother's cellar held plenty of food, she knew many pantries around the city bordered on bare, and soon there would be riots.

"Gentlemen," Marie said with a nod. Que sera sera—*enjoy the moment while you have it.*

The doctor and his friend greeted her, and she moved to join them. A certain energy trembled in the air, of expectation and hope. Marie glanced between the two of them but also took in the details of the room—the damask wallpaper, the sideboard with its chipped corner from where it had been moved clumsily after serving as a piece of a set. And the cocktail server, which had been converted to a tea server due to their English guests, trundled around the room on its little track inlaid in the wooden floor. Marie paused to allow it to pass before standing beside Radcliffe and O'Connell.

"What's new?" O'Connell asked. He held a bottle of some sort of alcohol.

"Looks like something got through on last night's airship." She gestured to his beverage. "Where's it from? And how did you get it?"

"Stu swore it's from Ireland, but the brew isn't black enough," O'Connell said. "As for how I got it, don't worry about it."

Radcliffe snorted. He rarely imbibed but held a snifter with some sort of honey-colored liquid.

"Perhaps I should ask what's new with you." Marie gestured

to Edward, who spoke with Iris in hushed but excited words and then to the two men with their beverages. "This feels like a celebration."

"We made a breakthrough," O'Connell told her. "Well, the professor did. We got the mock lighting system to work with the aether. It was disappearing when we tried to inject it in the hydrogen, but he made an adjustment and it worked. Lit up the atelier like a bonfire all morning."

"Oh, that's incredible!" Marie clapped her hands. Now she stopped the tea server, which had come around again, and opened a side door, where her mother always kept a small bottle of rum. She poured some in a teacup, which she then raised. "Here's to you, then, and the new era for the Théâtre Bohème."

They raised their glasses to hers, and Edward and Iris joined them. The professor appeared tired and worn, but there was a light in his eyes that had been dulled since the death of Jeremy Scott in Rome. From the look on Iris's face, she noticed it too, and a relieved happiness emanated from her through the special connection she and Marie shared.

Marie's shoulders relaxed a hair, but jealousy braided her lower guts. Not for Edward—goodness, she had no room in her life for neurotic scientists—but that Iris was one step closer to the chance for a normal life with a husband and family.

Marie gazed at the brown liquid in her glass, hating her friendship-betraying thoughts and the circumstances they originated from. She should be happy for Iris and not begrudge her the moment, for she knew there were still challenges ahead.

"Where's Johann?" Edward asked and startled Marie from the dark spiral of her emotions. "He should be here to celebrate with us."

"Why?" Marie asked. "He's busy. Working. He can celebrate with us later." She pushed away the sense of relief she'd had that morning when she heard him outside the dressing room, like he could pull her from her strange dreams into this world and anchor her in reality.

"Something he said yesterday was responsible for the breakthrough. His words bounced around in my head and made me see things in a new way." Edward smiled at Iris. "And then I knew what had to be done, what adjustments to make."

"He's a good friend," Iris said.

"Even if he has his faults," Marie added.

Like being irresponsible and a gambler and putting us all at risk from the Clockwork Guild. Her mind tripped through her reasons for not liking Bledsoe as smoothly as the tea server moved along its track.

"Right," Radcliffe said. "So let's toast to Edward and Patrick."

"And to Marie and Maestro Bledsoe, who will be taking part in the upcoming production," Iris added.

Marie reluctantly clinked her teacup to the others'.

"So Fantastique is taking the stage again?" Radcliffe asked.

"Not enthusiastically." Marie tried to ignore the impulse to step into the expected role of *premiere femme*, but her shoulders straightened, and her chin tried to move into a haughty angle.

Her appetite fled. *No, no, no!* She took a gulp of rum and ended up coughing.

"Are you all right?" O'Connell thumped her on the back.

"Uncanny," Radcliffe said. "You seemed to transform for a moment."

"And you've been working too hard. Perhaps you should take a break from your makeshift clinic, Doctor." Marie set her teacup on the table. "Excuse me, gentlemen. I have lines to memorize."

"Wait," Edward said. "I wanted to show you the system so you can tell me if you think the quality of the light will work for the stage."

"Very well." Marie allowed the others to file out ahead of

her and grabbed a couple of cornichons and a piece of rolled-up ham with a thin block of cheese in the center. She ate them on the way up to the atelier and repeated her litany.

My name is Marie St. Jean. I am twenty years old, and I am not going to allow my mother to make me feel badly about my size.

Maestro Bledsoe certainly hadn't seemed to find fault with her shape, not the way his eyes roved over her like—

I am Marie St. Jean, I am not going to allow the way a man looks at me to define me.

Thankfully she reached the top of the stairs before she got in a serious argument with herself. That was the problem with her little sayings—sometimes they conflicted. She didn't want anyone defining her but her, but it was hard to fight through all the messages and expectations, particularly with the strange talent she didn't want to acknowledge.

Marie hadn't been in the atelier since her mother's former renter, an artist who painted portraits of the gargoyles on top of the theatre but with his former lovers' faces, moved out. She saw it had been transformed into a laboratory of sorts, and a replica of part of the theatre's gas lighting system stood in one corner. It looked like a tangle of metal and glass tubes, and Edward started the little steam engine that powered it all.

"Typically a theatre uses hydrogen gas injected with some other gas to control the brightness of the lighting," he explained.

Marie nodded. Of course she knew that, but she also recognized he spoke for the others' benefit.

"Instead of oxygen, for example, we're injecting aether into the part of the system that illuminates the stage. At this frequency, which I only thought to apply this morning, it spreads quickly and seems to pull more aether out of the existing gas in the tubes."

Indeed, Marie could barely stand to look at the device, it

shone so brightly. "Is there some way to control the brightness?" she asked.

"Yes. This method is much more reliable than the tuning forks I used in—"

The word hung in the air—Rome. A spike of fear and concern stabbed through Marie from Iris, who stood near Edward. Her hand hovered by his shoulder, and confusion showed on her face.

"Than I used before," he said. The dark stubble on his cheeks gave them an extra haggard appearance, and Marie glanced at Iris, who clasped her hands together.

"Don't worry about me," Edward said and pried Iris's hands apart before taking them in his.

"But I do." The tears in her eyes fragmented the reflection of the aether light into sparks.

O'Connell cleared his throat. "The demonstration?"

"Right. If you will assist me, Engineer O'Connell?"

The Irishman increased the amount of coal in the engine, and when he nodded, Edward flipped some switches. The engine sounded like it ran faster, and the hue of the aether changed to a peach-rose color. Now everyone in the room looked younger and less tired, even Radcliffe with his dark skin and Edward with his sun-starved sallowness.

A flapping noise outside the window drew Marie's gaze away from the mesmerizing model, and Edward ran to the windows and pulled the curtains.

"What...?" Iris started to ask, but her question was cut off by a scream from outside.

7

———

héâtre Bohème, 2 December 1870

Johann found himself in the role of concert-master, conductor and cat herder during the rehearsal. Every time he suggested something, Frederic would argue with him about it, and by the end of the first hour, he was sure he'd lost clumps of hair due to pulling on it in frustration. Even worse, Frederic was his stand-mate, which put the Frenchman in an even better position to sabotage him.

"Let's try that passage again," he said and willed his jaw to unclench. He wouldn't show the little snot how much he'd allowed him to bother him.

He lifted his arm, but an ear-splitting scream punctuated the air before he could draw his bow across the strings.

"What the hell was that?"

"It's a theatre, you idiot." Frederic's accent didn't make his insult any more charming. "It is expected during rehearsals, *non*? Someone is merely practicing their lines."

"I'm certain all the women here know how to scream without having to practice." Johann put his instrument down, and his irritation allowed his tongue to get away with him with, "I've made certain of that myself."

"I am too much of a gentleman to boast of my conquests," Frederic replied with a sniff.

"Or you haven't had any," someone else in the orchestra put in, and the rest of them snickered.

Are sounds of terror so common that no one cares?

Johann left them to their chatting and made his way out of the auditorium to the front hall, where Madame St. Jean stood and peered out of one of the windows. Seeing her relieved him somewhat, for if Marie had been the one to scream, wouldn't she have rushed out there?

"That wasn't part of the show, was it?"

"*Non*, but it sounded like Corinne when she saw the ghost yesterday. There is a certain note to a woman's shriek when she encounters her worst fear in an unexpected place."

"Is that who you searched for earlier, the ghost?" He joined her at the window. A knot of people gathered around a body on the sidewalk, and a dark figure darted through the crowd. "That's Radcliffe. Someone's hurt."

"Go see who it is. I dare not show myself."

Johann frowned, but he didn't argue.

The rain had brought in colder air, and although nothing fell from the sky at that moment, he wished he'd thought to grab his cloak. He rubbed his hands together and approached the gathering crowd on the sidewalk.

"What happened?" he asked in French. The woman next to him gave him a haughty look and moved away, but a small man in dark clothing stepped toward him and spoke eagerly.

"Such a tragedy! Madame and Monsieur were walking along when the man in front of them turned, just there by the gate, and stuck a knife in Monsieur."

"Is he badly injured?" Johann tried to move forward to see, but the crowd pushed him back, and a few glanced at him with curiosity. Of course he would draw attention with his lack of cloak, hat and gloves.

"He is dead, Monsieur." The man spoke in a gleeful tone.

"And the murderer?"

"Ran off. Some men gave chase, but he slipped away."

The dark blue and red uniforms of the gendarmerie appeared amidst the blacks and grays of winter outerwear, and the crowd thinned as though the appearance of the authorities turned the spectacle into a serious occurrence. Johann turned to report back to Madame, but a heavy hand on his shoulder stopped him.

"Maestro?" The young man looked familiar in that his features appeared more English than French, and his accent spoke more of school than street. "What are you doing out here in the cold? Surely a man as clever as you could remember to put on his hat and gloves before coming out to see a poor murdered wretch."

"I'm sorry, do I know you?" Johann breathed into his cupped hands. Now that he thought about it, it was dastardly cold, and the sky spit snow rather than rain.

"I'm Inspector Davidson," the young man said. "I met you briefly after an incident at the Louvre last summer. As I recall, you were doing something in the fountain."

"Right. I'd dropped my spectacles." Johann edged away from him. He had briefly encountered the man after the inspector questioned Iris about the murder of Monsieur Anctil, curator of the Renaissance collections. As Johann recalled, he'd been fishing out one of the little clockwork butterfly spy devices from where he'd knocked it so the sound of its distress whistle would be dampened, quite literally.

"How is Mademoiselle McTavish? She seemed quite the sensible young lady, not one to be permanently affected by having witnessed such a horrible thing as a man's death from poison in front of her."

Now Johann was halfway up the walk to the theatre entrance, but the man's words made him pause, although he'd said something similar to her at the time. He'd later regretted his harsh words once he got to know her better. "She is quite well. I'll tell her you asked for her. Well, er, I'm sure you're busy." He gestured to the tearful woman who gave a statement to one of the gendarmes and the mass of clothing that looked like a fallen crow on the sidewalk just beyond the fence.

"Yes, I'm investigating a crime of a rather random nature." Davidson inclined his head toward the same scene. "And it's the second one I find you at in rather strange circumstances, so I would say I am doing my job."

"I had nothing to do with it," Johann told him. "I was inside rehearsing with the rest of the orchestra when I heard the scream."

"And so you ran from a rehearsal to see what it was? Was the music that boring?"

"There's nothing wrong with the music."

Johann didn't want to reveal his concerns to the inspector. Besides, what would he tell him, that a ghost had been sighted at the theatre, and they thought he was up to no good? Or that Mademoiselle St. Jean had experienced something strange, apparently having no recollection of leaving her scripts in a trail from the stage to the star's dressing room or locking herself in...with the key.

"I'm afraid I must return to my rehearsal," Johann said. "If you want me to come to the station and make a statement later, I can. Isn't this out of your jurisdiction?"

"All of Paris is my jurisdiction, as I am the city's chief inspector. And I've been meaning to return to this place, particularly since I was made aware that you and Mademoiselle McTavish are in residence, so I will call on you later." He touched the rim of his hat and turned to join his colleagues, who now questioned witnesses.

When Johann walked through the theatre door, the warmth almost felt bruising to his cheeks and fingers, but it was nothing compared to Madame St. Jean's clutching his right biceps.

"What did the inspector want?" she asked. She let him go and smoothed her skirts.

I've never seen her this agitated. "He wanted to know why I was outside in my shirtsleeves in this weather."

"As long as he does not return," she said and moved to the nearest window, but she stood behind a curtain.

"Why?"

"I am Romany, and Marie being half-Romany and without a father is another count against us. I pay my taxes and for their silly licenses, but they always watch us."

"Unfortunately, he's going to return to ask me about what I saw, and I think he may want to talk to Iris. He was the detective on Anctil's murder case, and I suspect it is still unsolved."

She drew herself up. "Then when he does stop by, I count on you to get rid of him as soon as you are able."

"What did you see?" Johann asked.

"Nothing, but I'm sure what happened will be in the papers later today."

Johann tried to make a joke to calm her. "If I'd known this was such a rough neighborhood—"

"It's not, Maestro. And don't forget what you owe me." She turned and left.

Ah, well, it's not the first time a woman has walked away from me in a huff.

When Johann returned to the auditorium, he found it empty, the other musicians having gone home. His instrument sat where he'd left it, but underneath was a note—*"Do not concern yourself with Mademoiselle St. Jean. She is quite sane. Trust that her guide is watching out for her and leave her be."*

"Her guide?" He looked around, again with that feeling that

the skin between his shoulder blades twitched under some sort of scrutiny, but the theatre was empty.

"YOU DID IT." Iris gestured to the fake lighting system, now dark. Edward had hung back when the others ran out to investigate the scream, and she elected to stay with him. "You figured out how to make aether power it."

"It's not powering it. It's lighting it. Steam is still required to power the motor that directs the gas through the system." Edward had pleaded exhaustion and now sat at the table and toyed with a small screwdriver. The aether isolation device also stood dark, so the only light came from the flickering gas lamps on the wall. With the curtains drawn, the atelier felt cozy and almost claustrophobic.

"So why can't we open the curtains?" Iris moved toward the window. She half hoped Edward would stand to stop her, at least hold her arm in that gentle way of his.

He's solved his problem, so he can get back to courting me now. Or doesn't he want to?

"This is going to sound crazy. Well, more crazy than usual." He did stand, and Iris tried not to appear too eager for him to be beside her. He walked past her and peered through a narrow space in the curtains, and she sucked in her stomach to keep her shoulders from obviously slumping around the ache in her chest.

"Is something out there?" She kept her tone neutral.

"A raven, but not a normal one. This one is steam-powered and seems to have some sort of camera inside it. Johann thinks it's a Clockwork Guild invention, but it's not their usual kind of device."

"You're sure it's steam-powered?"

"We only got a brief glimpse of it. Hopefully we closed the

curtains before it took a picture of us or the aether devices, but yes. Johann said it seemed to breathe fire, and I figured it out."

A year ago, Iris would have dismissed the raven he described as the ravings of a madman who had been working too hard, but that was before she'd become intimately acquainted with the clockwork spy butterflies. She still automatically looked twice at any flash of gold or brass.

With Edward at the window, Iris glanced at the screwdriver he'd been fidgeting with, and the tips of her fingers tingled as it called to her to read it. She hesitated. Edward had some sense of what she could do, although she didn't know to what degree he understood what objects told her. Either way, he didn't like it when she invaded his privacy. But he hadn't been talking to her, and she needed to know how he was mentally. The specter of the nervous breakdown he'd had in the past hovered in the back of her mind. She hadn't witnessed it firsthand, but Johann Bledsoe had described it in sufficient detail that she knew she didn't want Edward to have another one.

I'll try one more thing, and if that doesn't work, I'll do it.

"How are you doing?" she asked and joined him at the window. He glanced at her but didn't shift his gaze from outside for more than a moment.

"What do you mean?"

"I've hardly seen you, and I know that's partially my fault— I've been in exams and studying a lot—but I've missed you." She reminded herself to breathe in the seconds that stretched before his reply.

"I'm all right. Working hard too."

But have you missed me? She wasn't going to ask him, lead him along or do all the work for him. *You're such a genius, you figure out how to continue the conversation.*

Finally he asked, "And how are you? Do you have your exam results yet?"

All right, that's a start, although I wish he'd said he missed me too.

Lucille's words came back to her—that she would always come second to his work—and she stalked away from the window.

"They went well, I think. They'll post marks at the end of next week."

Now she stood within reach of the screwdriver. *Has he been thinking of me at all?*

He returned to watching for, well, whatever he was worried about. Iris placed a finger on the tool and mentally directed it to tell her what he'd been feeling and thinking. Profound fatigue overlying anxiety—no surprise there—and a resigned feeling of hopelessness and dark expectations. *That's unexpected.* But she couldn't confront him about it, not now that they were talking. Sort of talking. And the only impression of her was of her bright, fake smile. Seeing it from his perspective made her heart collapse into her stomach—she looked like her mother had when humoring her capricious daughter, but Iris could always see the lack of genuineness.

Iris closed her eyes and clasped her hands together. She didn't know what he wanted, what he truly needed.

That's my theme, failing those who love me.

Hands on her upper arms startled her, and she leaned back into him. She tried not to notice that he smelled like he'd been in the laboratory for long hours or to feel the aching tiredness that radiated through his clothing. He must be exhausted if she could feel it from the material, which typically didn't harbor impressions like hard substances did.

"In your studies, have you found anything that might be helpful?"

The frustration in his voice negated the comfort in his hands. "What do you mean?"

He stepped away and gestured to the aether isolation

device, which was hooked up to a small engine. "We have the frequency to stabilize it, or rather the range of frequencies and tones in which it will not fade. We're still missing something that will help us convert it to a power source."

"You want me to help you?" Iris didn't know whether to be thrilled he wanted to include her or upset that he wanted her mind rather than, well, the rest of her.

"I *need* you to help me. And I need to sleep."

He stumbled out of the atelier. Iris thought about reading another object, but she didn't know which he had touched most recently and which ones O'Connell had, and she had no desire to invade the Irishman's privacy. She peeked out of the window, but all she saw was snow falling from the sky.

8

____

héâtre Bohème Townhouse, 2 December 1870
Marie stayed on the front stoop and watched Doctor Radcliffe dart through the crowd around the fallen man. Some of them looked askance at his dark skin, but the intense expression in his gray eyes moved them out of the way. Patrick O'Connell followed behind him, as always, and eliminated any other obstacles. Maestro Bledsoe ran from the front of the theatre, and Marie shook her head, bemused. Now he was the one without a cloak, but she hung back, the impulse to play the role of *premiere femme* trying to take over. The muscles in her face settled into a haughty expression, and her shoulders straightened as if to show off her figure.

She closed her eyes. *I am Marie St. Jean. I am not a premiere femme. I am an ordinary but haunted girl.*

What had Iris said about a dangerous spirit in the theatre? Could it be the same one who had appeared to her? Or who she thought appeared to her. Sometimes she couldn't distinguish between her dreams and reality. But why would she have been napping in Corinne's—*no, my*—dressing room?

Not mine. I am not Henriette.

She knew what would help, what always did. She would go underground and visit the one person who always saw through her, perhaps the only one who knew her core self, although he would never answer her questions. Still, being down there near him placed her firmly in herself, not one of her roles. Unfortunately the special entrance she needed to the underground was in the theatre, and the crowd stood between her and it.

The gendarmerie appeared as well as a tall man in a nondescript dark suit and hat. Something about him said he was important, and she followed her instinct to draw back and pull her hood over her head. Now he intercepted Bledsoe, and they walked toward the theatre's front entrance.

This was her chance. She slipped down the stairs and walk, then across the street to avoid the crowd. One of the gendarmes questioned Radcliffe, who gestured as he wiped his bloody hands on a rag. O'Connell stood by a distraught woman, whose degree of distress made Marie guess she'd been with the murdered man. Another man in a dark suit questioned her under O'Connell's watchful eye, and Marie shook her head. The Irishman had an interesting mix of being attracted to high-drama situations and sometimes causing them, but with a surprising amount of tenderness. She thought he'd be good for a young lady who needed both excitement and gentle handling in the future.

Snow fell in small and then larger flakes, obscuring the tableau. Marie crossed again at the corner and walked down the block before ducking down the alley she'd chased Corinne through the day before. Or had tried to chase her.

Now, the portico door or the rear door? Which is least likely to bring me in contact with Maman? *Probably the portico door—she's likely hiding out from the inspector in the bowels of the theatre.*

She turned and slunk through the carriage lane and to the side door under the portico. The door opened to reveal Lucille.

"Stupid *fille*, what are you doing out there? He will see you."

She grabbed Marie and pulled her into the theatre and the cloak room.

"Who? The man you were looking for earlier?" Marie extracted herself from her mother's grasp and rubbed her arm.

"*Non*, the inspector. He has been here before."

"Why?" Marie was accustomed to Lucille's high drama, but the woman seemed thoroughly frightened this time. She even spoke in a mix of French and English, which she only did when particularly perturbed.

"Because of things you and I would rather not speak of. Why are you not back at the townhouse as I instructed Mademoiselle McTavish?"

Marie opened her mouth and closed it before her inner *premiere femme* could say, "Because I am an actress, and I belong in the theatre." She clenched her left fist and started her litany, but her mother's lips drew back in a satisfied smirk.

"Because you cannot stay away. Because you were born to be Fantastique."

"No, I have other business." *And this is why I don't tell you things.*

"With Monsieur Bledsoe?"

Marie's thoughts aligned with her mother's apparent suspicions, and the remainder of the cold from outside melted from her cheeks. She couldn't tell her mother of her true intentions, but she didn't want to lie outright. "That is my affair, not yours."

"If you are to make another grave mistake that will take you away from me, I have a right to know. Are you interested in the maestro?"

Once set on a path, Lucille wouldn't let go. Marie sighed. "I find him handsome and interesting. I may even enjoy being in his company, but I am well aware he has made his share of mistakes, and I have no desire to help him pay for them."

"*Bien.*" Lucille released her grip on Marie's arm, and they walked into the front hall. Lucille drew a curtain back, glanced outside, and let the material fall back into place with a heavy snap. "They are still out there." A wrinkle of indecision appeared on her forehead, an unusual expression.

"What were you so concerned about earlier?" Marie asked. "Why did you chase us out of the theatre? Is it safe to go through there now?"

She almost asked about the strange man who appeared to her in her dressing room, but she still was unsure if it was real or if she had dreamed the whole thing from the tortured mind of the Henriette character. That was the problem with playing someone whose brain ended up being addled by opium.

"The devil inside or the angel of justice outside," Lucille said, and her shoulders slumped. "At least there is the chance the devil sleeps."

"I'd probably find his company more interesting." Marie turned to go, but Lucille put a hand on her shoulder.

"You are well aware that sometimes good intentions end up badly. Keep that in mind and be careful. A strong man can only protect you to a certain point."

She let go, and Marie entered the theatre itself. A lone figure sat on the stage and played the violin with a touching, mournful air: Maestro Bledsoe.

Merde. That's what I get for implying my interest to my mother. I should've known it would work out for me to see him.

But something in the music tugged at her, and she stood behind a pillar and listened to it. The expression of the notes made her homesick for something, but she didn't know what.

A piece of paper fluttered down from the balcony above her. Marie looked up but couldn't see who had dropped it. She picked it up and shoved it in the pocket in her cloak.

Sometimes the wanderlust in Johann subsided just enough

for him to feel a twinge of homesickness. The snow outside made him think of how his family home would look now at the beginning of the holiday season. Perhaps a light dusting would give the peaks and sharp-angled roofs a glittering edge, or a heavier fall would make the old hall look like a dowager trimmed in white fur—dignified and elegant, but also potentially deadly.

His mouth twisted into an almost-grin at the association. One never escaped a conversation with his grandmother, the dowager Marchioness, without some sort of scar. Typically for him it included a hint or direct statement of what a disappointment he was to the family, a dreamer rather than a doer like his older brother.

A fluttering movement caught the corner of his eye, and he looked up to see Marie standing in the back of the theatre, something clutched in her hand. Whatever it was disappeared into her cloak pocket, and her expression distracted him from curiosity about what she'd caught, if anything. Longing warred with confusion on her face.

"Mademoiselle?" he asked. "Are you all right?"

"That music," she said and put a hand to her middle between her heart and her stomach. "It made me homesick for something, but it doesn't make sense. This is my home, such as it is, but now I miss...something. What were you playing?"

Johann had spoken with hundreds and played before thousands, but he'd never told his secret. His gut said he could trust her even if he wasn't trustworthy himself. What would it be like if he was, if he could bear open his heart to someone else? He'd never wanted to, and the idea struck him as strange, but accustomed to going with his impulses, he stepped into that space between fear and trust.

"It's my own composition. I call it *Winter*."

She moved closer, and the amused lift of her cheeks

became apparent when she stepped into the light cast by the lamps in the orchestra pit. "Original title."

He put his violin on its stand. "You mock me, Mademoiselle?"

Her smile vanished, and now her cheeks reddened. "Oh, no! It was lovely, but it needs a name that's less bleak and more poetic, maybe *Blossoms Under Snow*?"

He liked seeing her blush and wondered if she was one of those women whose flush covered her entire torso if it was deep enough. He sent a *desist* thought to his groin, but it bounced the notion back with the urge to keep her talking and blushing. "I can't use a word like *Blossoms* in a composition title. I'm far too manly for that—it would make me appear weak."

"Then how about icy shards? That shouldn't challenge your masculinity." The temperature in her tone matched that of the hypothetical ice.

What had he said? It figured he would get himself in trouble before long. What did she want?

The answer came to him, then—to be respected for who she was. And he saw her as a very strong woman. But he didn't know what to say to get himself out of this mess. He only knew one thing—he didn't want her to leave angry.

"Forgive me," he said and took her hand. That was always a safe bet, much safer than the ones that had ended him up in this mess, the ones he'd taken to escape his father's influence.

"For...?" She wouldn't look at him, and she snatched her hand away.

"For being an ass. I'm too good at it. I didn't mean to imply that womanliness was the opposite of strength. In truth, you and Iris are two of the strongest people I know."

"Iris? You are on such intimate terms with her?"

"Miss McTavish, then. Yes, we've been working together to help Edward, and no, nothing improper has occurred between us. We're...friends."

"You're not accustomed to being friends with women." Her statement was almost a question.

"Not typically. I've not treated them well in the past, I fear."

What was she doing to him to make him want to confess and clear his conscience to make room for... For what? He certainly had no desire to be tied down to anyone. As soon as he got this little problem with the Clockwork Guild worked out, he planned to continue the adventure they'd started, perhaps even to the Ottoman Empire and beyond, and he wasn't afraid to go on alone.

She drew back, but she didn't leave. "Why the sudden burst of honesty?"

"It was the music. It is a piece about my home, and I play it when I miss it."

She took a seat on the front row, and he joined her but sat with a proper seat between them.

"Where is home for you?" she asked. "I know you're from England, from near that little village where Cobb's train picked you up, but not much else about you."

The sentiment hung between them—other than that he had an apparent gambling problem.

"Ossfield Manor," he said. "It's one of the noble estates in the countryside, beside Edward's family estate. We grew up together."

"So your father is..."

"A marquess."

"So you're a noble son?" Her face expressed amused disbelief. "I should have guessed."

"A second son. And how so?" He looked at his hands, his fingers calloused from his long years playing music. "These don't look like a nobleman's."

"No, but you have the air of a spoiled brat about you sometimes, although you have a good balance of loyalty, at least to your friends."

Now he was truly offended. "Mademoiselle, you wound me. I'm not a spoiled brat by any means. In fact, the money I lost was completely my own, not my father's."

"But couldn't he have helped you?"

That was the point, for him to refuse. But all he said was, "He didn't want to. In fact, he sent me away in disgrace and told me he didn't want to ever see me again."

"So why did you do it, gamble so much away you've made trouble for yourself?"

He'd never been able to explain to Edward, who did what he wanted and whose family had long given up on trying to push him into any sort of role he didn't care for, but Johann recognized that Marie seemed to struggle with a reluctance similar to his. He took a deep breath and pushed his father's disapproving face out of his mind.

"It's family tradition for second and third sons to go into some sort of trade or role that would help the running of the estate, whether it's a magistrate, some other local office, or even a businessman who can help broker the estate's goods. No useless army commissions or clergy vocations for the Bledsoes, especially since those require an investment of some sort."

"So they pressured you?"

"It wasn't pressure so much as lifelong training. 'Make yourself useful' was my parents' refrain from my childhood, and art and music are the most useless trades of all."

"Even though you're disciplined enough to have made it work for you. I heard of you long before I met you."

He jumped on the chance to distract her from her line of questioning so he wouldn't have to tell her about the stupidest thing he'd done. "Was I what you expected?"

"Not at all."

"Oh?" He moved to the seat next to her. "And what did you expect?"

She shrugged and pulled her cloak around her. He took the hand that was on her lap and kissed the back of it.

"Monsieur, you presume. And you haven't said how your family drove you to gamble."

But she didn't draw her hand back, and he trailed kisses from the delicate soft skin between her index and middle knuckles down to her wrist. Now he was close enough to see the blush did extend down her neck, and he wished she wasn't wearing a cloak, that he could see more of her chest and the delicate pink she would turn when she thought of him kissing other things, for that particular maneuver hadn't failed him yet. When he reached her wrist, he allowed one tooth to lightly graze her skin before the final kiss. She shifted, her breath quickened, and he wondered what unladylike sensations he made her feel.

"Marie!" Lucille's call drew them both to their feet like marionettes jerked to attention.

"I have to go." Marie drew her hood over her head and disappeared through the door beside the stage.

He sat to allow the evidence of his ungentlemanly feelings toward her subside and smiled. He might have told her more than he had any other woman, but he still hadn't revealed the extent of his juvenile stupidity even if she did make him fuzzy in the head like a young buck. He'd always liked actresses and hadn't hesitated to bed them, but he promised himself he would be careful with her.

It's always best to not bite or sleep with the hand that feeds you... or her daughter.

He returned to the orchestra pit and picked up his violin. He hadn't seen anyone in there, but he found a note when he opened his case.

You may think Mademoiselle St. Jean is another of your games, but she is not for you. Stay away from her, or your true nature shall be revealed.

9

____

Théâtre Bohème, *2 December 1870*

Marie walked quickly, every step a delightful torture due to the sensations at her core and between her thighs.

Mon dieu, *what was that about?*

The answer came before she wanted it to: it was her usual pattern. Due to her stupid talent, men saw in her what they wanted. Johann Bledsoe liked actresses—she'd read that in Cobb's dossier on him—and she was playing a woman who had been caught up in the same great passion she inspired, at least in the sensationalized version of the Hector/Henriette story *Light Fantastique* told.

She had to stop due to her tears obscuring her vision in the dim passage. There was no point in tripping over her own disappointment and twisting an ankle or worse—she was deep enough in the bowels of the theatre now that no one would hear her calling, and it was possible that they wouldn't find her for days if she injured herself.

It had felt like an honest conversation, two people deciding to trust each other just a little, but as with everything in the theatre, it was an illusion. The only real part was that she might find herself attaching more to her idea of him. He had an artist's soul—that much was apparent, and it was enough to keep drawing her down a destructive path like water in the inexorable groove of the sewer.

That's a lovely image, and trying to find the good, pure part of a man beneath all his merde *has never gotten me anywhere.*

She stopped her mind from following that notion and paused between two set pieces. She glanced around to make sure no one saw her. The cool air and quiet settled around her, and the smells of musty wood and decaying paper and paint did nothing to dispel the feeling of being in a tomb.

Where old sets go to die, and now I descend into Hades, she thought for the hundredth time before pulling open a trap door and allowing her foot to find the first of the narrow steps in the darkness.

Unlike the wooden stairs leading from her most-used sewer passage to the other end of the theatre basement, these were of stone, and she wondered again who had built them and for what purpose. She'd asked Zokar when he gave her directions as to how to find his camp, but he'd only told her that they were there before the theatre and probably extended farther toward the surface to a long-destroyed church or monument. That was the most logical explanation for why she always had to walk through a city of the dead to reach him.

Her torch was in its customary place at the bottom of the stairs, as was the little tin of matches that always held just two —one to light the torch and another in case the first didn't work. It was all he'd allow her to keep there, and if neither lit, she wasn't meant to visit him that day. She wondered if he somehow manipulated them or the torch to keep her from coming at inconvenient times. There was nothing she'd put past him, and she thanked whatever god might be listening that he was on her side.

The torch lit with the first match, and the words scrawled along the walls, souvenirs from when the passage was used as a prison during one of the uprisings, seemed to jump out at her. Most were pleas to God or other supplications, but she paused at one and traced it with her finger, her usual ritual.

But I loved him.

They echoed her own feelings of betrayal and frustration, and she wondered what woman—or man, which she allowed the possibility for since she'd known enough actors—had scratched the words so deep she still hadn't found the bottom of their despair with her fingertips.

The passageway led her deeper underground, and the walls took on a natural stone look.

Although she knew the bones had not been disturbed in a long time, she always held her breath and tiptoed through. She stayed alert for the rattling noise that would indicate they came to life like in the cautionary tales about girls who would get lost in the catacombs and fall prey to angry ghosts. Marie had started exploring the underground areas around the theatre as soon as she could get enough time away from her watchful mother and give her governesses the slip. She had a good sense of direction and soon figured out what passages led where and which were dead ends or too full of sewage at certain times of the year. Lucille never approved of these explorations, and keeping an eye on her daughter was one of the primary motivations for allowing Marie to start acting.

Now through the catacombs, Marie had to focus on the scratches on the walls again. They seemed random here, but she knew how to discern their patterns. She didn't know how Zokar did it, how he changed the way she reached his camp every time, but she'd found out once that following her previous trail and not following the lines in the strange language on the walls would lead her to one of those dead ends or disgusting sewers. One time she'd needed to bathe in citrus water for a week before she felt like she shed the smell just from being near it.

Finally a warm glow at the end of a tunnel so long she felt she must have gotten something wrong told her she was close. She inhaled the scents of wood smoke and food cooked with spices that made her feel warm all the way from her nose to her stomach, which growled. Her little ham and cheese roll hadn't lasted long, and her mouth watered.

As always, Zokar was there to welcome her with a warm embrace. His wife Saphira offered a bowl of hearty beef stewed with those wonderful spices.

"I could hear your stomach a mile away," he said, and she felt his words rumble through his barrel chest. His full black beard was streaked with more gray than the last time she'd seen him, but his face looked just the same, as did Saphira's.

"What's the news?" Marie asked him and followed him back to the fire in front of his tent, one of many in the large cavern that seemed to be natural, even to the vent at the top that drew the smoke. It always felt backwards to ask him what was going on since he lived underground and she on the surface, but he was always more informed.

Out of necessity, he'd told her.

She was so used to seeing him jovial that when a scowl crossed his face, she stepped back and nearly tripped over a goat pen. He steadied her elbow, and Saphira only shook her head. She never spoke, having come from Romania, where her tongue had been cut out for a supposed lie—a common punishment inflicted on the Romany who lived there as servants and then as slaves. She'd been one of the lucky ones to escape, and Marie was always conscious that her heritage made her vulnerable to scapegoating and the unjust punishments that came with it.

"What's the word on the siege?" he asked and sat with a

heavy sigh on one of the makeshift chairs, a crate covered in blankets.

Marie settled on the one next to it. "It's a stalemate. Some supplies are able to come in through the underground and airships, but not nearly enough, and I fear the people will riot soon."

He nodded. "And the theatre? Is Lucille having theft problems?"

"No, *Maman* hasn't mentioned any. She is doing well, her usual self. I don't know what her network is telling her, but she doesn't seem to be too worried. She's busy with the start of the next production."

He chuckled and shook his head. "Lucille will proceed with her plans no matter what silly army dares to disrupt her."

Marie wanted to ask why he was always so concerned with her mother, and she'd formed a theory through the years, but he always evaded her questions. Now she had more pressing things on her mind, but she had to tread carefully. Zokar and Saphira didn't ever admit to being able to work magic, and they became offended if anyone asked.

"I'm the female lead of the play," she said.

Zokar drew his brows together but didn't say anything, just waited for her to continue.

"And I'm worried that I'm not going to be able to keep myself from slipping too deeply into the role." She looked into his coal black eyes for some sympathy, some sign of understanding.

"Did Lucille not train you how to manage your talent on the stage?"

Marie relaxed slightly and handed her now-empty bowl to Saphira. Previously, if she had brought up her troubles, he would only offer her empty assurances.

"I am afraid if I tell her what I can do, she will draw me

further into it and make me keep going with it. All I want is to escape, but I tried that and it didn't work."

"No, you came back." He shook his head again. "Silly girl. Your good heart will be your downfall."

"But I don't even know if I have a good heart. I don't know what kind of heart I have, what kind of person I am, and I won't know until I can live my own life."

"And what of a young man? A family? Children?" Zokar gestured to the camp.

Marie knew that half the people there were related to him by blood or marriage. Somehow he knew her better than most, so she could be honest with him. "I think that's something I want someday. A normal life. But I don't seem to attract or be attracted to normal men." She rubbed the back of the hand Maestro Bledsoe had kissed, and the memory and resulting sensation made her shift on her hard seat.

"That's another problem."

"Yes, but I need help with the stage thing first. Do you have any...advice?"

Zokar and Saphira exchanged looks, and Saphira shook her head.

"You are not ready for some truths yet, *cherie*, and I need you to help me first."

Marie squashed her disappointment, but she nodded. "I owe you much, not least for saving my life when I got lost down here all those years ago. What do you need?"

"Only for you to keep an ear out. I know your mother has her spies. Perhaps you can help find something that has been lost. Or has wandered off."

A goat bleated, and Marie asked, "An animal?"

"Not quite. I've been working on an automaton that can think and act like a man."

Marie shuddered. "Why?" *Real men are trouble enough. Why do we need fake ones?*

"Because we have jobs that need to be done, and our numbers are getting less and less with our inability to live openly. Young people are leaving the camps, some in disgrace, and some with their own reasons."

"Can I see it? The automaton?"

"That's the problem. It's either wandered off or gone missing. Since its trail went cold, I cannot find it, but something as wondrous as that will not stay hidden for long. I need to find it before the *gadze* government does and tries to turn it to non-peaceful purposes."

"I'll do my best." Marie stood. "Thank you." She thought about what she had seen in the hall and in her dressing room, but she wanted something solid before she told Zokar anything or at least to be able to tell him where to look. The theatre and its myriad hidden passages was a big place.

Zokar hugged her again. "Any time, little one. I will walk you back to the stairs."

JOHANN LEFT THE THEATRE. The strange notes left in his violin case unnerved him more than he wanted to admit. Did they have anything to do with Frederic the jealous violin player? If so, why didn't the man want to confront him openly? That was how Johann preferred to do things—air grievances and sort them out, either with words or with fists. He'd gotten good at fighting without damaging his hands.

These French are crazy.

With his thoughts as tightly wrapped around him as his cloak, he didn't see the dark figure that approached him until he ran into it.

"Oh, Maestro, I didn't see you. This snow is falling hard."

"Doctor Radcliffe, I apologize." Johann stepped back a pace. "I hope I didn't injure you."

"Not at all. I was just seeing if there was anything on the sidewalk I might have missed after the earlier tragedy, but I think Inspector Davidson and his men picked up what little there was to find."

They walked back toward the townhouse, but Radcliffe hesitated before they turned on to the walk leading up to the front steps. "May we speak privately elsewhere?" he asked.

"Of course. Where did you have in mind?"

"Follow me." Radcliffe led him to a clinic a few blocks away and unlocked the door. "Several of the city's doctors fled before the Prussians boxed us in," he explained. "One of them left this space, so I moved in."

Johann stripped his gloves and cloak and hung the latter on a hook by a stove in the main room, which Radcliffe added coal to and stirred back to life. Thankfully the office was still warm from the morning. "I knew you were doing something to occupy yourself, but I didn't pay much attention to what."

"Yes, you've been busy with keeping out of sight and making sure Professor Bailey stays stable."

There was no judgment in his tone, only observation, and Johann wondered how much the doctor had noticed. Like had he seen how Johann looked at Marie, or how she looked back at him? He thought he could still taste her skin on his lips, especially the salty dew that came to it when he made her blush all the way down to her—

"Would you like some tea?" Radcliffe asked. "I have the good English stuff."

Johann blinked to clear the memory of the desire in her hazel eyes from his brain. "Tea would be perfect. How did you get it, and what are you using for water? I thought it was regulated at this point."

"Some of my patients can't pay in money because they're using it for the goods smuggled in on the airships, so we barter." Radcliffe filled a kettle from a bucket in the corner. "I get water from the pump down the road once a day. Boiling it seems the best way to approach it at this point. At least the Prussians haven't figured out how to block it at its source yet. Paris is a canny old city."

"Right." Johann stood by the stove and warmed his hands. The temperature seemed to have dropped several degrees while he was in the theatre, and the chill stayed with him.

Or maybe Mademoiselle St. Jean had warmed his blood.

Radcliffe's next words cooled him.

"I saw you speaking with the inspector. Do you know him?"

"Not very well," Johann said. "We encountered each other last summer after the incident at the Louvre."

"Right, the belladonna poisoning." Radcliffe had figured out the means, but the culprit was still at large as far as anyone knew. They all had determined it had something to do with the neo-Pythagoreans, a slippery cult. "He recognized you?"

Johann allowed his frustration to tighten his lips into a frown. "Apparently my new coiffure and beard are not enough to deter the observant."

"You're good at deluding yourself." Again, that neutral tone, but Radcliffe's words stung.

"Yes, I know you pride yourself on your expertise on all things mind-related. You could have said something before. I could have gone to a barber and had my hair dyed."

Radcliffe rubbed his own beard. "Short of surgery to change your facial features, I don't know that any disguise would have worked for you. You have a certain way of carrying yourself that makes you easy to pick out."

"You're not helping."

"What do you know of the victim of today's stabbing?" Radcliffe asked.

"That's a random change of subject. Nothing, other than it was a man."

"It was a man of about your height with your coloring and

light-colored hair and beard. He also had a certain swagger to him according to the witnesses who had walked behind him for a few blocks. They said he managed to block the sidewalk with his lady friend no matter how hard they tried to get around him, but it wasn't intentional."

"You're saying that I block sidewalks and am an inconsiderate ass?" But he knew it was partially true—he tended to walk as though he was the only one on the path, and he expected others to get out of the way.

Radcliffe spoke slowly as if laying out the pieces of a puzzle on a table between them. "I'm saying that the murder victim resembled you in some uncanny ways, and your disguise isn't terribly effective, not for those who know you. We also know the Clockwork Guild and the neo-Pythagoreans are not above violence in their means."

Now the stove couldn't dispel the chill that slithered between Johann's shoulder blades. "So you're thinking the target was me."

Radcliffe nodded. "And I wonder how comfortable you'd be with bringing this knowledge to the inspector."

"Not terribly. Madame St. Jean seems to feel he'll cause trouble for her because of her Romany background even though she's a law-abiding citizen." He shook his head. "Why would she be afraid if she's done nothing wrong?"

"Those who are different become scapegoats in troubling times such as these. So far the city is limping along with what the airships can bring in, but resources will run out eventually, and the people will turn on each other starting with those who they perceive as other. She probably doesn't want to draw attention to herself beyond what she already does."

Radcliffe stared into space as he talked, and Johann wondered if he spoke from experience.

"Then we should look into things on our own and see if

there is another explanation, bring that to the inspector and deter him from looking into those of us at the theatre."

The doctor produced a piece of paper from his pocket. "I recorded all the witness names I overheard once the gendarmes left as well as what I could remember of their addresses."

Johann raised his eyebrows and scanned the list. "You have a good memory. There's a lot of detail here."

Radcliffe shrugged. "It's helpful, but sometimes it's good to forget."

The water in the kettle boiled, and Radcliffe made the tea. "I'm aware that you have had some liaisons since coming to Paris. Did Madame Cinsault happen to be one of them?"

Johann sighed. "Would you believe me if I told you I didn't know because there have been so many?"

The look Radcliffe gave him said he did believe him although he didn't want to. "Perhaps you should make a list of the ones you can remember dallying with, and we can see if there are any areas of intersection."

Johann opened his mouth, but he didn't expect the words that came out on a tide of an unfamiliar emotion—regret? "Just please don't tell Mademoiselle St. Jean."

"For your safety, you probably should, but I will leave that up to your discretion. Now, where do you want to start?"

Johann gazed into his tea. "Do I truly have to reveal all this to you?"

"Do you want to endanger Madame after all she's done for us? And Mademoiselle? There are consequences for not being careful, you know."

It's because of Mademoiselle that I don't want others to know how wanton I've been. It was a new experience for him, considering the potential results of his actions. But as reluctant as he was, he knew it was necessary. "Madame LeFleur first caught my eye when she walked by the theatre one rainy Sunday afternoon..."

He thought he heard Radcliffe mumble something like, "And here we go."

"But it was her daughter, Mademoiselle Elise, who *truly* caught my eye."

10

héâtre Bohème, 2 December 1870

Once back in the theatre, Marie shut the door of the dressing room behind her and lit one of the lamps. Someone had cleaned Corinne's things out of there, and so the furniture and dressing table stood bare except for a few lamps and pillows, similar to how it had looked when Marie was the primary occupant of the star's dressing room.

That was long ago, and I have more pressing things to think about.

She lit the other two lamps so that the small room blazed with light. After placing her cloak on a hook by the door, she rolled up her sleeves and walked to the wall of the room that was a mirror.

From where she stood, it looked like an ordinary mirror, somewhat tarnished in places because of its age. She held one of the lamps up close to it, but she didn't see any evidence that it could be a one-way window. Cobb had had one on his airship between his office and the dining room, from where he could watch and listen to his guests after they thought he had retired to his suite, which was directly below his office and accessible via a secret passage behind the closet. He never trusted the Clockwork Guild's listening devices and preferred what he heard with his own ears over inscribed information.

Marie shook her head to dislodge the memory, which highlighted to her that she knew many of Cobb's secrets. It was strange that he'd left her alone, even stranger he'd let her go from his employ, but the oddness of the circumstances hadn't occurred to her before now. She'd been too focused on evading her mother's attempts to force her back on the stage.

"And now I am back on the stage in more ways than one," she murmured. She examined the edges of the mirror and the wall around it for wood dust, scratches, gaps or any other sign it could be moved and had been recently. There was nothing.

"*Bien.* I was dreaming, then. Zokar's automaton must have wandered off on its own."

Perturbed at the idea that an automaton could come to life and move on its own but comforted that the mirror couldn't possibly be a door to a secret passage, Marie reached into the pocket of her cloak and extracted the paper that had fallen from the balcony earlier. She saw it was a newspaper clipping with the headline, *"Scientist, Musician Disappear on Continent Under Mysterious Circumstances."*

It was dated two months earlier in October and detailed how brilliant scientist Professor Edward Bailey and talented musician Johann Bledsoe had gone on an expedition funded by an American but hadn't returned. The only connection to their whereabouts, a Miss Iris McTavish, had reappeared briefly for her father's funeral but had remained close-lipped regarding where the young men were, only meeting privately with their families to assure the concerned parents of their sons' safety. Still, the reporter said, some sort of foul play was suspected, and if Miss McTavish were to return without the young men, she would face questioning from the authorities about them and the mysterious death of Lord Jeremy Scott, who had met a tragic end in Italy that summer.

Hiding from Cobb means hiding from everyone. It hardly seems fair.

The sense of entrapment Marie felt when she really considered her circumstances cinched further and made for a too-tight belt around her spirit. Suddenly weak, she sank to the chaise lounge and clutched her stomach, where the invisible belt felt real. She blinked to clear her vision, which had gone foggy, but it only continued to cloud, and the mirror shimmered to her left. She twisted sideways to look at it, but her head lolled back, the muscles in her neck collapsing as the familiar smell filled the room again.

Cobb's tobacco.

She struggled to move, to escape.

"Come now, darlin' don't hurt yourself." Gentle hands repositioned Marie's head and smoothed her hair back.

"You're no ghost," she whispered. All she could see was a shadowy form above her. Light gleamed off his face, a metal mask. "Who are you? Zokar's automaton?"

"I'm whoever you need me to be. You were telling me an interesting story earlier today. What happened the next night when you went to meet Cobb for dinner at his hotel?"

Marie's tongue tripped out the story as if it moved on its own accord.

~

17 MAY 1868

Marie put her heart into the performance that night because in spite of the complication of having lost her traveling papers—and she suspected she had help in losing them because she knew she'd kept them hidden in a safe place—she intended it to be her last.

It was the closing night of the play as well, which leant a certain energy to the performance. At the end of the play, the audience rose to its feet, stamping and applauding, and she bowed and snatched a rose out of the air on the way up. She held hands with her costar, an older actor named Maurice, who had played the man Marie's character had fallen in love with and become obsessed with, and bowed again. After five curtain calls, she said goodbye to the rest of the cast and made her way to her dressing room, where her mother waited for her.

Instead of looking pleased at the record receipts from the performance, Lucille glowered at the large bouquet of flowers on Marie's dressing table. Mostly hothouse flowers, the bouquet was obviously expensive but still tasteful. Her heart fluttered as her eyes analyzed the contained extravagance of the flowers and design of the vase. Even after only a brief encounter, she recognized Parnaby Cobb's style.

"Who is this from?" Lucille demanded.

"I don't know, *Maman*. They must have arrived during the final act after my last costume change." Marie hated to disturb the bouquet, but she dug through it until she found a small envelope that contained a card. "It must have slipped down when it was delivered."

"Or someone didn't want it to be found by anyone but you."

Marie tried to buy some time by reassembling the bouquet so it looked mostly like it had before. The fragrance of the flowers filled the room with sweetness and a sharp green odor from the crushed leaves. Not able to put it off anymore, Marie opened the card and found only a number—the room where she was to meet Cobb?

"It's from an admirer."

Lucille held out her hand.

"A secret admirer," Marie told her and held the card away from her.

Before Lucille could demand anything further, the other actresses from the play rushed into the room *en masse.*

"Marie, you were brilliant!" Janelle, who had played the maid who facilitated the meetings between Marie's ingénue and Maurice's dirty old man, gushed. "You may have to fend off old Maurice's advances after that performance. I think he believes you are truly in love with him. Oh, are those from him?"

Marie snuck a look at Lucille. During the play, Marie had become the ingénue—or she felt like she had—and the words of love she spoke were real in the moment. She was glad the performances were at an end because she could avoid Maurice until everything got back to normal, as it always did except for her feeling like she missed a sliver of her soul.

Corinne, who had played the betrayed wife, sniffed. "They're lovely, but if Maurice could afford those, you need to be paying the rest of us more, Madame."

She didn't offer a compliment, but she never did. Playing a character jealous of Marie's wouldn't have been too much of a stretch for her. Every time she came into Marie's dressing room, Corinne had some sort of backhanded or sly remark and looked around the room with the air of one who surveyed a piece of property she intended to own. Tonight Marie didn't mind. She didn't care if Corinne moved in the following day because she fully intended not to need the dressing room again. But now she needed to get rid of all of them so she could retrieve her papers and complete her disappearance.

"Thank you all for your kind words," she said, avoiding looking at Corinne, "but I am exhausted and developing a headache." And she would soon with all of them whizzing around the flowers like bees or a clockwork butterfly she had once seen. It had moved with more purpose than its natural brethren.

The girls filed out after offering final words of congratulations, leaving Marie with Lucille.

"You are not getting a headache," Lucille said.

"Is that a command or an observation?"

"Let me see the card that came with the flowers. I doubt Maurice sent them, and there were men in the audience who looked at you like they wanted to be next in line for seduction."

"Don't be ridiculous," Marie told her. "I was acting. They know that."

"There is a thin border between acting and perceived intention. I am your mother. It is my duty to protect you."

"There isn't a name on the card." There, that wasn't a lie.

"I can see if I recognize the handwriting. Men frequently send letters requesting to meet you."

"They...what?" This was news to Marie. Were any of them potential suitors? Had Lucille kept her daughter from the possibility of settling into a normal life so she could exploit Marie's talent on the stage?

"You have a wonderful talent, to make people believe what you are, beyond any actress I have ever seen. It's marvelous but could put you in danger."

More than you know. "What do the men write to you, *Maman*?"

"I have known others with abilities like yours," Lucille said. "I have tried to raise you as a normal Parisian girl, but you are different. You need to speak to me of such things."

"I don't know what you're talking about." Again, an evasion. She certainly never felt like she had a normal upbringing. Most girls her age were being trotted out for potential husbands. She was being put on stage, although she had never objected, only wondered. But as for confiding in her mother—absolutely not. Lucille would only want Marie to develop her talents further at the cost of her sanity. That was why she needed to get away, to spend time in an unfamiliar place among people who didn't know her so she could figure out who she was. As young as she was, she was mature enough to know she needed to determine her own identity before she could think about loving someone.

"You can deny all you want, but I know what I see. And you need to give me the card."

"No." Marie held it over the flame of one of the lamps until the heat made her drop it. The paper burned and shriveled, but not before the ink ignited and the number stood out in glowing lines like a scrawled address in hell.

"What did it say?" The lamp flames flared, but the rest of the room darkened except for Lucille's eyes, which gathered and reflected the flames.

"I hate it when you do that," Marie snapped. "Stop trying your witch tricks—you know your illusions don't work on me."

"You think you are clever, but you're just a stupid head-strong girl." The lamps and the light returned to normal, and Lucille looked old and tired for the first time Marie could remember.

"I know what I'm doing."

"Oh, do you? Do you think I don't know what it's like to be young and passionate, to be driven by your desires? It takes more effort than you know to construct your life to minimize the mistakes of the past. I don't want you to suffer like I have."

"Now you are being dramatic." Marie grabbed her cloak off the hook. "I'm going for a walk."

"Don't insult me with your lies. You are going to meet someone."

"If I am, it's none of your business. I have the right to a normal life, *Maman*."

Feeling exhilarated with a twinge of guilt at having finally told her mother what she truly wanted, even in a roundabout way, Marie made her way through the theatre and to the side door. She was and wasn't surprised to see a coach waiting there with two matched beautiful gray horses harnessed to it.

"You're Mademoiselle St. Jean?" the coachman asked, his flat American accent coming through his clumsy French, a better calling card than a physical token would have been.

"*Oui.*" In the dim light, the brass accents on the coach glinted rather than shone, but it still gave the vehicle an air of controlled extravagance. When the coachman handed her into it, Marie found the interior to be just as elegant with plush seats, but so dim it took her eyes several moments to adjust, and it was difficult to discern object from shadow, particularly as the coach rolled away.

One of the shadows detached itself from the side of the carriage and put its hand over her mouth before she could scream.

11

———

T héâtre Bohème Townhouse, 2 December 1870

Iris had just gotten the last of her notes off the floor and organized when Marie stumbled into their room. She reached out, and Iris rushed to help her to her bed. She wore no cloak, and her face was flushed like she ran from some sort of nightmare.

"Where have you been?" Iris asked and wrinkled her nose. "Have you been smoking opium to get into character?"

Marie shook her head so hard she almost fell over on to her bed. "No, there is a ghost in my dressing room."

"A what?"

"A ghost who knows all my secrets. Or he will soon. He makes me talk and talk even though I don't want to."

Iris put a hand on her friend's shoulder and drew back from her fever-hot skin. "Really, Marie, if you're seeing ghosts, you need to lay off the tobacco. Or have you become an opium addict?" Iris knelt in front of her friend and searched her face for the telltale signs of recent opium use. "Whatever you're doing to get into the character of Henriette during the opium nightmare part of the play, it's not worth losing your health over. Or are you ill?"

"Just let me sleep. And ignore anything I might say. And don't tell my mother."

Before Iris could say anything in reply, Marie rolled over and breathed heavily.

After finding Marie's cheek hot, Iris ran down the stairs. She searched for Radcliffe, whom she found just coming in the front door with Johann Bledsoe. She stopped short on the stairs when she saw the look on the doctor's face, which was of bemused shock.

"Are you sure it didn't have anything to do with her? I treated her fiancé, who is a jealous sort," Radcliffe said as they hung up their hats and cloaks on the coat rack by the front door.

"I don't know how he would have found out," Bledsoe replied. "We were discreet. It's a good thing Lucille doesn't keep many servants, makes it easy to get in and out without too much notice." He looked up, and his eyes widened when he saw Iris, who stood with her mouth agape.

Were they discussing the maestro's female conquests with the air of two men talking about where they could easiest go for a stroll? It seemed a rather indecent conversation to just be having, and indeed, both of them looked like they'd been caught at something naughty from the guilty looks they exchanged.

"Mademoiselle," Johann said with a bow. "I didn't see you up there. Have you taken to welcoming visitors to the house from the stairs?"

Radcliffe looked at him, and then to Iris with an apologetic shrug. "Forgive us, Mademoiselle. We were not as careful as we should have been with regard to the potential for innocent ears to overhear us."

There was that innocent comment again, that assumption she wasn't ready for certain pieces of knowledge. "Although I'm not experienced in the ways of the world, I'm aware of them," she said with a bite to her tone. "And if you're quite finished talking about the maestro's activities, I need your help. Marie is ill."

Both men rushed to the stairs and bumped into each other at the bottom just below where Iris stood. She held her hand out just short of Bledsoe's chest. "Although you're quite familiar with female anatomy, Maestro, I believe Doctor Radcliffe will be more helpful in this situation."

Bledsoe had the grace to look abashed, but he still followed Iris and the doctor up the stairs. Iris tried to shoot him "go away" looks. Either he ignored her, or she needed to develop fiercer facial expressions.

"What's wrong with her?" Radcliffe asked.

Iris relayed Marie's strange behavior and comments as well as her observations about Marie's temperature.

"Did she seem ill this morning?" he asked. "She appeared fine at lunch, if somewhat perturbed that she's had to take the role."

"No, she seemed all right. Well, as much as she could be with the pressure Madame St. Jean puts on her." She dropped her voice so no one would overhear. "Do you think she's hysterical?"

"She doesn't seem the sort to develop hysteria suddenly," the doctor said. "Let me examine her, and I'll ask you more questions if needed. Would you accompany me into the room?"

"Of course." As close-knit as their group was, Iris appreciated the doctor's discretion, at least where she and Marie were concerned.

"I'll come too," Bledsoe said. "You may need me to help move her."

When Iris opened the door, the smell of the tobacco hit her

with a strange intensity and familiarity. Radcliffe sniffed the air, as did Bledsoe.

"That's an unusual blend," the musician said. "But I feel like I've smelled it before. Has she taken up smoking to deal with the pressure of being on stage?"

"She said no." Iris watched Radcliffe as he listened to Marie's breathing and took her pulse. He also opened her eyelids and had Iris hold a lamp nearby so he could check the color of Marie's eyeballs. The light made her murmur in protest but not wake.

"Her pulse and breathing are fine, and her color is good. Keep a cool cloth on her head tonight, and let me know if her condition worsens. Oh, and once we step out, loosen her corset or get it off her if you can. The more air she can get into her lungs the better to clear out whatever put her in this state."

"So you think it's a substance and not an illness?" Iris bunched the fabric of her skirts in her hands. *Not more poison. I can't watch someone else die in front of me, especially not my first true friend.* "Who would have done this to her? Surely you don't believe her talk of ghosts." She pressed her lips together before she said more because she wasn't sure she could explain her comment. She sent a pleading look to Bledsoe.

The maestro sat on the chair beside Marie's bed and smoothed her hair back. She muttered something and moved her hands as if to bat his away.

"I doubt she needs your help, Maestro," Iris said more sharply than she intended. "Even if you are an expert in corset removal."

"He's probably your best chance of getting it off her," Radcliffe said and coughed. "But by all means, try on your own first."

Him and his dry humor. Iris shooed the maestro away from the bed and took his place on the chair. She first unlaced and removed Marie's boots, which even in her drugged state, Marie had been careful to leave dangling over the edge of the bed. She then covered Marie with a sheet so the men wouldn't inadvertently see too much of her and unbuttoned Marie's blouse. Marie didn't like help getting dressed, so she used a front lace corset. That should have made the process easier, but when Iris tried to untie the laces, Marie rolled on her side, and Iris couldn't get her to roll back for long enough to use both hands to undo the devil of a knot. She found she needed an extra hand.

"Need help?" Bledsoe asked.

"Unfortunately, yes. I suppose you're proficient at undoing tough knots one-handed."

"I've been known to untie a few, but why don't I hold her in position while you do it?"

"Right." Iris's neck felt like it was aflame with the embarrassment at having suggested he undress her friend. Of course having him hold her would be best.

With Bledsoe's gentle help and under Radcliffe's watchful eye, Iris got Marie undressed sufficiently that her clothing wouldn't restrict her breath or movement, and she hoped she managed to keep the wanton musician from seeing too much. She was also thankful Lucille didn't come in and find them.

There was one unexpected visitor at the end of the process, when Iris finally got a cool cloth placed on Marie's forehead.

Edward walked in, took one sniff, and asked, "Is she all right? And why does it smell like Parnaby Cobb's tobacco in here?"

Edward felt much better after a good nap and a shave, much more like himself than he had in several months. When he heard the commotion downstairs, his first thought was that one of the steam ravens had gotten in, and he was almost relieved to find that the problem was more human in nature.

Iris sat on a chair by Marie's bed. Pins barely contained her white-blonde hair, and she looked somewhat disheveled, but she maintained a certain angel of mercy look. The thought made him clench at the bottom of his heart-well, the familiar sting of guilt unfurling there. She had been so kind and patient with him, but he knew there was a countdown to their time together, that he would eventually hurt and destroy her.

He shook his head. He had sworn to himself that he wouldn't let these thoughts intrude, that he would enjoy his first meal with others in many days—or had it been weeks?—but something kept him anchored to the past and experiences he'd rather forget. A smell teased his nose, and the memories connected to each other with the inevitable momentum of a boulder rolling down a hill and setting others in motion—the fateful meeting at the Department of Aetherics, the airship, and then Rome, that horrible morning in the underground temple. Of course whether it was relevant or not, all his memories ended up with him looking at Jeremy Scott's grotesquely burned face, his eye sockets and teeth leering at him accusingly.

You did this. You betrayed your beloved science to eliminate me as a rival. Is this what you will do with everything you love, distort and destroy it?

"Edward?" It was Iris, and she stood with a hand on his arm. Her eyes looked tired. They always seemed that way now. "What did you say about Cobb's tobacco smoke?"

"I thought I smelled it. Probably a trick of my imagination."

Johann wrinkled his nose. "Tobacco smoke, yes, but why Cobb's? Doesn't it all smell alike?"

"No." Edward sniffed the air again. "It's all a little different depending on where it's grown. Cobb flavored a specific blend."

"Are you sure it's his?"

Edward's mind clawed for purchase—what made him think he could speak with any expertise on this matter? He wasn't certain of anything right now, only that he had to get the Eros Element to work with the theatre lighting system. So much of everything else was unknown. If there was anything he'd learned in the past few months, it was how much he didn't know about life and people and—he looked at Iris—women.

"No, maybe it just smells similar. But what's wrong with her?" Seeing Marie lying there... She looked broken. Is that what would happen to Iris—that she would break too—from something he did?

"I don't know." Radcliffe paced the room. "I can't determine what she's been given to make her unarousable."

"Not Belladonna," Johann said. "She'll make it, right?"

"I hope so."

Edward's hands shook, and he shoved them in his jacket pockets before Iris could notice his trembling. The image of her lying broken on a bed pushed at the edge of his awareness. "I need to go."

He bolted from the room and down the stairs to the receiving parlor. Lucille was just coming in the front door.

"Ah, Professor, it is good to see you out and about, at least outside of the atelier."

"Marie's sick," he said.

Lucille's skin paled, leaving her wrinkles deeply shadowed. She moved toward the stairs. "What is wrong with her?"

Iris met Lucille at the top of the stairs and filled her in in low tones. She shot Edward a regretful look and followed Lucille from view. Edward turned toward the fire.

"Are you all right?"

Edward started. There, in the back of the room, sat Patrick O'Connell. The large Irishman seemed less intimidating with his bulk folded into one of Lucille's wingback chairs. He held a book in his lap, but the lamp beside him was off.

"Isn't it dark to be reading?" Edward asked, fixated on this detail. Nothing seemed to make sense outside of the atelier, and he felt the need to return to it, like an itch in his soul. But no, he'd come out for Iris, and he would stay out until they could have a nice, normal meal.

"Just thinking."

Edward had become accustomed to the Irishman's laconic tendencies in the time they worked together, but in the past few weeks, he'd become more terse.

"Thinking about what?"

O'Connell shook his head. "None of your concern." But his voice held a heaviness with which Edward was intimately familiar.

"You're lonely," Edward said.

"We all are." He pushed himself out of the chair. "If Miss St. Jean is ill, we might be on our own to find dinner. You want to grab something? I know of a cafe that still has fresh meat."

Edward shook his head. "I'll stay here, thanks, in case Iris needs me."

"Suit yourself."

O'Connell walked out of the front door, leaving Edward to wonder what he'd meant. *We're all going stir-crazy here at the theatre and atelier. This siege needs to be over so we can leave.*

But England seemed far away with fairytale remoteness, and he knew that even if he were to return, his life would never be the same.

~

CARRIAGE IN PARIS, *17 May 1868*

Marie struggled in the carriage against the hands that held her across her chest and over her mouth.

"I'm not going to hurt you, Mademoiselle," a male voice said in her ear. "But I have a favor to ask you."

Marie stopped struggling. A favor? Who did this person think he was, that he could trap her and ask her a *favor*? She found some strength and wrenched her head to the side.

"You can unhand me. Coachman!" she yelled.

The coach pulled to the side, but instead of releasing her, the hand across her chest moved lower so it was beneath her cloak, and the hand that had covered her face disappeared, but she felt cold metal against the back of her neck.

"If the coachman finds me, you'll be paralyzed or dead before you can say anything. I recommend you make up something to get rid of him."

Marie couldn't remember what she said to the coachman to get him to start driving again, but the journey resumed. She suspected the coachman must know there was someone else in his coach and that they were in collaboration. That made her feel in even more danger. Plus she hadn't seen the man in the carriage—where had he hidden? But she had also gotten in without checking. It was a mistake she wouldn't make again.

The knife disappeared, but she knew it was there somewhere. She sought back through the roles she had played. Surely there must be one she could draw on for this situation. Ah, there, Marguerite the Spy from one of her early plays. Never mind that Marguerite was also a femme fatale—Marie didn't need to seduce anyone at the moment, just to escape.

"You have my attention," she said with a resigned sigh a la Marguerite. "And I am bored with these games. What do you want?"

The seat behind her drew back a couple of inches, and she suspected her new attitude made her captor wary. "Cobb has something of yours that you want back. You know what kind of man he is, or you will soon. I'm looking for something he stole from me as well."

"That is not my concern, Monsieur. If you want help

retrieving an object, then you're better off hiring a thief than an actress."

A low chuckle. "The rumors about you are true. Let me guess, Marguerite the Spy? The way you speak, it's as if you're her."

Marie would have been shocked if she hadn't taken on Marguerite to the degree she had. Part of her screamed at her to do anything she could to escape from the man in the carriage, not only because of the knife but because he knew what she could do.

He spoke like a gentleman even though he acted like a thug, and she latched on to that. If she could appeal to his nobler nature... "You have me at a disadvantage, Monsieur. Who are *they* and what have they said about me that makes you think I can help you?"

"That you are capable of not only playing a role but becoming that role even more than the best actress to cross the stage in decades. That you bring crowds to their feet and make men fall in love with you on sight. That you can make anyone believe anything about you."

"This still doesn't tell me how you think I can aid you or why I should."

"If you help me retrieve what I've lost, I will aid you with your quest to get what you want from Cobb. Remember, I know what you are, and I might be able to help."

Marie kept her breathing even over the excitement that warred with caution in her chest. Someone outside the theatre did know who she was and what she could do. And as she'd feared, they wanted her to use her talent in a way she wasn't comfortable with, at least that was what she suspected. Right now she needed it to get out of this situation. What would Marguerite do? Right, get more information for something she could use against her captor.

"How can you help me? It seems you're more in need of me

than I am of you. Why else would you hide in the carriage and threaten me?"

"It was the only way to get to you between your mother's watchful eyes—and she has them all over the city—and Cobb's guards. This is the coachman's last day in Cobb's employ, and he owed me a favor. I know these things about Cobb's household and servants. That's how I can help you."

"I will consider your offer."

"Then I will leave you with this one caution—you think you're clever enough to avoid becoming ensnared by Cobb, but he collects beautiful and unusual things that he feels he can turn to his purposes. He has no intention of letting you go."

The carriage slowed, and the strange man slipped out at a corner. Marie leaned back against the seat, but her shoulders wouldn't relax. She knew to sift through the man's words for the grain of truth in what he said, but she was afraid that he'd been accurate in one thing—she was playing a deadly game with Cobb, and her freedom was the prize. It remained to be seen who would hold it in the end.

12

———

Théâtre Bohème Townhouse, 3 December 1870

Marie woke to Lucille's cool hand on her forehead and sat upright.

The man in the carriage—I've heard his voice again. Or have I?

The memory faded like fog, and the wisps slipped through her mental fingers. Plus she had other pressing matters to deal with, like where was she? She found herself disrobed and in her bed at the townhouse, although she couldn't recall how she got there or what had happened to her clothing.

Iris stood just behind her mother, and shadows highlighted the dark blue of Iris's eyes.

"What happened?" Marie asked.

Lucille moved her hand from Marie's forehead to under her chin so she could look into Marie's eyes. "It looks like you were drugged with something. Do you remember anything?"

"I was in the dressing room looking for a secret passage, and…" She pulled her head back from her mother's hand. "I just remember dreaming after that. Did I fall asleep? How did I get here?"

Lucille looked at Iris, who shrugged and said, "You came in

mumbling about something and went to bed. We couldn't wake you."

"'We?'"

"Yes, Doctor Radcliffe and Maestro Bledsoe came to my assistance."

"Did they help you...?" Marie gestured to her corsetless torso, now only covered by a shift that was thin enough for her aureoles and the dark patch of hair between her thighs to be visible.

"Yes, but I made sure you stayed covered as best I could."

The thought of the maestro's hands on her made Marie blush and remember their kiss in the theatre.

Too bad I wasn't awake for my disrobing.

"What did you dream?" Lucille asked.

Marie couldn't take the hurt in her mother's eyes that would come if she told her she dreamed of the shame of years ago. Why were these things coming back now? She'd been back at the theatre for months. She also couldn't tell Lucille she'd been to see Zokar.

Oh, right, the automaton. In the dressing room.

But the thoughts slid away from her, and she couldn't make them connect to her state and her dreams. There was only one tangible thing left, the smell of Cobb's pipe tobacco that clung to her hair and what little clothing she had on, and it made her stomach turn.

"I'm going to be ill," she said. Lucille handed her a chamber pot, more decorative now since the townhouse had been fully plumbed for several years, but nothing came up, either from her stomach or her memory.

There was something else, a man's voice. Why is that important?

"Rest now," Lucille said. "I cannot give you anything to make you feel better since I don't know what's been done to you. Sleep as best you can." She smoothed Marie's hair back from her forehead and left.

Iris didn't, however, and took Lucille's place at the edge of the bed.

"Are you sure that's all you remember?" Iris asked. "You can tell me. I know your relationship with Lucille is complicated."

Marie turned her face toward the window, now dark from what she could see through the gaps between the curtains. "Old shames. I couldn't tell her because I already hurt her badly when it happened."

"You mean with Cobb."

She's quick. "Yes. What happened all those years ago. She doesn't know the truth, but there's no point bringing it all up again. She didn't believe me when I tried to explain it before."

"What did happen? You've never told me the whole story."

Marie looked at Iris, who gazed back at her with tired eyes. Their dark blue depths still had an innocence Marie didn't want to sully, particularly since her own had been taken so violently. "I'm too tired now. We'll have to talk later."

"I understand." But her tone said she was disappointed, and Marie wished she could take her words back, but then she would be caught in a lie.

"We'll talk sometime," she promised.

Iris nodded and left Marie to the darkness and her dark thoughts. The irony of the one detail she needed escaping her memory when the rest of them crowded in made her want to weep. She slipped again into sleep.

AT ORCHESTRA REHEARSAL later that morning, Johann tried to catch Frederic alone during the first break, but the French violinist evaded him with slippery persistence. About halfway through the practice, Lucille appeared at the back of the auditorium with a tall man who had deep-set eyes and a wild mane of dark hair tinged with gray. He dwarfed the petite

Lucille, although she stood straight at her full height. She signaled it was time to stop, so Johann gave the orchestra a break.

"Maestro Bledsoe, this is Hamish Fouré," Lucille said with a big smile once Johann joined them. "He is the conductor, just in on last night's airship."

"I apologize for not coming sooner," Fouré said. "Getting in and out of Paris is unusually complicated these days." His deep voice had an interesting burr to it, and Johann recognized his accent as Scottish. Although he couldn't remember meeting the man, there was something familiar about him.

"I appreciate you taking the risk to conduct the performance," Johann told him. "Your dedication to your commitments is admirable."

"When Lucille told me earlier this year what she planned in honor of Hector and how she wanted to combine the drama of his music and his life, I couldn't say no. We all suffer for our art."

The way Lucille looked up at the conductor made Johann wonder if there was another reason he'd risked life and limb to come into Paris. "Your name is French but your accent Scottish."

Fouré dismissed the contradiction with a shrug. "I've lived abroad for many years, and I'm a half-breed. My father was French, my mother Scottish, and I spent most of my time growing up with her family. I only come to Paris for very special reasons." He looked down at Lucille, and Johann couldn't believe it, but the indomitable woman blushed.

"Well, then, I'll step back and allow you to take your rightful place at the conductor's podium," Johann said. He caught sight of Frederic standing at the back of the auditorium alone reading a pamphlet. "Excuse me."

He tried to edge along the side aisle, but the other violinist looked up, and their eyes met. Frederic's lips drew up into a smirk, and he turned and walked out of the theatre. Johann cursed under his breath and followed him.

Damn him, I'm going to make him tell me what he meant. If the Clockwork Guild is watching me, I need to know.

Johann found the theatre lobby empty, but again, the feeling of eyes following him made him pause. He took a deep breath and looked around for the source of the feeling.

Everything has a logical explanation, as Edward and Radcliffe keep saying.

He walked toward the water closets on the far side of the lobby near the cloak room, and the feeling intensified. A breeze blew the curtains nearest him, and he snatched them aside only to be met by a blast of cold air through a broken windowpane. He looked down to see a rock at his feet along with shards of glass. A note was tied to the rock, the scrawled words legible in spite of melted snow—*"Prussian Gypsy go home."*

"Bastards!" Now Frederic stood beside Johann.

Concern for Marie outweighed Johann's anxiety about the Clockwork Guild. "What do you know of this? And were you watching me?"

"This happens every so often." Frederic gestured to the mess and the rock. "Usually when the people in the neighborhood aren't feeling safe. Lucille ignores them or gives the arrondissement free tickets to the performances."

"So she placates them so she doesn't have to involve the police."

"She is a powerful woman, but her influence only goes so far. As for whether I was watching you, I suspect you have encountered our theatre spirit."

"Now you're joking."

"He is no joke, Maestro. I heard he scared Corinne off. It's best not to get on his bad side. Things happen."

"What sorts of things?"

"He will leave notes, and if you do not heed them, then he

becomes destructive. There are accidents." Frederic shrugged as if to say he didn't know how *accidental* the accidents were.

Johann shook his head. "And is he behind this vandalism? The note?"

"*Non.* In fact, the last time something like this happened, those who did it found themselves accidentally in the path of a runaway carriage. One of them lost a leg."

Johann wondered how his fellow violinist could speak of something so horrible in such a casual manner, which then reminded him of why he came out to the lobby in the first place. "How did you hear of me, and who is looking for me?"

With deliberate movements, Frederic opened and looked at his pocket watch. "I'm sure our conductor is ready for us to resume, and we should tell Madame she will need a new window."

"Who have you told about me?"

"Oh, no one important." Frederic turned to face him fully. "And I will continue to keep my mouth shut on one condition."

"You want to be concertmaster. Fine with me."

"*Non,* that is not it. As much as it pains me to admit, you have talent. No, my condition is that you stay away from Mademoiselle St. Jean. I fully intend to court her and convince her to stay here in Paris." With that, he turned on his heel and walked back into the auditorium.

"Well, *merde,*" Johann muttered.

A piece of paper fluttered down from the ceiling, and he looked up to see a shadow disappear into a space between the top of the box office and the ceiling. He picked up the missive that had almost landed on his head and read, "*You have now been warned away from Mademoiselle twice. You had best heed the warnings, lest a fate worse than death befall you.*"

He crumpled the note up and put it in his pocket before returning to the auditorium. Again, the feeling of being watched followed him until he passed through the door.

MARIE WOKE to the feeling one has when it has snowed, and the light coming through the window is extra bright, promising that the drab and dreary scenery of yesterday would be smothered in a fresh new layer of beauty. She'd slept soundly and dreamlessly, for which she was thankful. Her head didn't ache, exactly, but the inside of her skull had a strange hollowed-out feeling like something had been scooped from her brain.

When Marie opened her eyes, she saw Iris, who sat at the desk surrounded by piles of paper, a plate with the tail end of a croissant perched atop one of them and a mug beside her. She didn't look bright and fresh. Quite the opposite, in fact.

"Are you all right?" Marie asked.

Iris raised her shadowed eyes to Marie and propped her head on one hand. "I should ask you. Do you remember anything?"

"No? Fragments, maybe. You saying you kept me covered while I undressed." She felt the heat spread over her face, neck and chest at the vague memory of a man's gentle but strong hands supporting her.

A slight smile, which didn't do much to liven Iris's pale face, appeared. "Something like that."

"Did you sleep at all?" Marie sat and swung her legs over the side of the bed. Her feet found her slippers, and someone had put her robe over the end of the bed. The air had a crisp, cold feeling. *Yes, it must have snowed.* But the window was frosted over, and she couldn't see outside.

"A little here and there. I kept waking to make sure you were breathing."

"I'm sorry." Marie couldn't think of what else to say. She felt even less in control of her reality than when a role took over her person.

"You would do the same for me." A slight lift of Iris's tone on *me* made her statement into a hint of a question.

"I would. I have. In Rome. That morning when I woke, the first thing I noticed was that I couldn't hear you breathing. I thought something horrible had happened to you."

Marie turned from the distress on Iris's face.

I shouldn't have brought up that morning. But she asked.

She walked to the other window, the one with the window seat, and looked outside. Yes, there was a layer of sparkling white over everything, and she drank in the beauty. Even the gargoyles on the theatre wore little white berets and appeared less fierce.

"Are you hungry?" Iris asked. "It's almost lunchtime."

Dread pierced Marie's gut. "And then this afternoon, a read-through."

"Lucille may not make you."

Marie shook her head. "No, she will. She'll know I'm feeling better. I can't hide anything from her."

"Then I'll help you dress. Pick out something warm. We're conserving coal."

Marie looked out of the window again. Less smoke from chimneys than she would have expected streaked the sky. That was the downside of the snow—the cold weather would stretch the city's coal reserves. The beauty of winter might hasten the inevitable rioting in the streets, and then what?

We might all be Prussian by Christmas.

13

Lucille had taken the news of her broken window with surprising calm, but Johann surmised the presence of Maestro Fouré might have something to do with it. Or the fact that Fouré said he would cover the cost of replacing it while posturing like it had been *his* theatre damaged. Johann wondered at his own sudden possessiveness—it was not like he planned to stick around long-term—but he also didn't like what the vandalism meant about the tenor of the neighborhood toward Lucille and Marie.

On his way back to the townhouse at lunch, Johann caught sight of Lucille talking to a street urchin, and he suspected that through her network of informants, she would know the perpetrators by teatime. At least he hoped she would. Now he had to decide on his own course of action. Woken by fevered dreams of the enticingly bare shoulders of Marie St. Jean—and strangely, his dreams wouldn't show him more than that— Johann had grabbed a quick breakfast off the sideboard that morning and headed out to walk in the lightening dawn and cool his... Well, something needed to be cooled.

He slipped out with Radcliffe, who headed to his clinic early, and they agreed to meet that afternoon to start their investigation by speaking with the widow of the previous day's attack.

Now as he mounted the steps of the townhouse, Johann wondered whether he should let Radcliffe speak with the widow alone so he could tail Frederic and determine who his contact was. But the Clockwork Guild was canny enough they wouldn't be obvious and likely communicated with the other violinist through more covert means. Notes dropped from the auditorium balcony, perhaps? But hadn't Marie gotten one? Surely the theatre spirit, or whoever was trying to make everyone believe in one, wasn't part of the Guild.

He put his cloak on a hook in the small cloakroom just beside the front door and mounted the stairs to the living space. His head spinning with trying to sort out the possibilities—really, Edward's scientific mind was better with complex problems than Johann's musician one—Johann barely registered the cheer that occurred when he walked into the dining room. He blinked the problems of the day away to see Patrick O'Connell clap Edward on the back and almost knock him over, Iris's happy expression, and—was she here?—Marie looking pale but pleased.

"What's going on?" Johann asked.

"Patrick finished converting the theatre lighting system, at least the main part, for the aether," Edward said. "We'll be ready to start testing tomorrow. And I owe it all to you. Well, most of it."

"Why?" Johann flinched away from the gazes of the others. Formerly he would have lapped up the attention, but after the months of hard looks subsequent to the revelation in Rome that his gambling had put the others' lives in danger, he steeled himself for the inevitable turn of the tide from approval to distrust. He pushed the image of his father shaking his head in disappointment out of his mind.

"Something you said on Thursday. It made me see what I needed to do to make it all work. I'd been spinning my wheels on a different sort of problem and got stuck."

Edward admitting a mistake—that was something Johann thought he'd never see. Well, if his friend could grow beyond his misfit foibles, Johann could too, starting with not taking more credit than he deserved. He couldn't help but sneak a look at Marie to see if she paid attention.

"I can't take credit for your genius, *mon ami*." He shook Edward's hand. "And congratulations. I hope this brings you the sort of knowledge you seek."

"It's progress. The more I learn about it, the closer I get to finding out how to turn it into energy."

"I have an idea of somewhere I can search for clues," Iris said. "The Louvre has some ancient texts and carvings from the Ottoman Empire. Some of the illustrations resemble the style of the stuccoes in the Porta Maggiore temple. It's worth a further look."

Johann didn't miss the shadow that passed over Edward's face or the trembling hand he put in his pocket.

"That would be grand," Edward told Iris with a forced smile.

She put a hand on his cheek. "I'm sorry. I can't believe I spoke so thoughtlessly."

Radcliffe stepped forward from where he'd been talking to O'Connell but apparently had an eye and ears on the conversation. "There are some schools of thought that you should avoid what might distress you," he said. "I, for one, believe you should face it until it doesn't."

Edward took Iris's hand and kissed it. "I know you want what's best for me. Now if you will excuse me, I'm tired again. Those weeks in the lab exhausted me."

He went up the stairs, to his room, Johann presumed, but the suspicious and sad look on Iris's face told Johann she thought the same he did—Edward was avoiding any further conversation.

"I could tell he didn't want to ask me to look, but he did, and so I did," she said to Marie. Then she turned to Johann. "Is this what happened last time with his breakdown?"

Johann tried to remember, but the paleness in Marie's cheeks made him pause. "Should you be up? You look exhausted."

She wouldn't meet his eyes. "Still recovering from whatever happened yesterday. And I have a read-through this afternoon."

"I'm sure Madame would allow you to rest if you needed." He wanted to ask what had happened and if the ghost had done something to her. It was maddening—how could he be expected to stay away from her if she was going to be harmed?

"No." Marie finally met his gaze with a spark in her own. "I'm not backing down from this."

"It's not worth it if you make yourself ill." *Or someone else does.*

"I won't fail her again. Now if you'll excuse me." She left in a swirl of skirts, and Johann turned to Iris.

"I don't suppose I can scare you off as well?"

She pursed her lips into a small smile. "No, I'm more determined. But please, you'll tell me if you remember anything useful, won't you? How did he come out of it before?"

"He threw himself into his work. That's the one constant with Edward—when he's working he's happy."

"Oh." She looked down at her hands. "I was hoping..."

He would have lifted her chin to look at him again, but he wouldn't make such an improper gesture with witnesses, no matter how close they'd all become. He had to settle with addressing the wisps of white-blonde hair at her temple.

"Remember what I told you."

"I'll remember. But it's tough." Something sparkled on her cheek, and Johann looked at Radcliffe and O'Connell, half-hoping for rescue and half-fearing they would think he'd made her cry.

"He has more friends this time. That will help."

Now she looked up at him, and the fierce Iris he remembered from their previous trip to Paris appeared. "But I can't see if I'm on the right track with my research if he won't talk about it."

Marie reappeared, wearing her cloak and pulling on her gloves. Johann picked up evidence of cosmetics, but at least some of the color in her face seemed to be her own.

"Then you'll have to act more independently," Marie said. "Think of what your father would have done. From what you've said, he didn't allow others to interfere with his work, intentionally or not."

"Right." Iris sighed, but she held her shoulders straighter. "Then it's off to the Louvre for me. Perhaps Monsieur Firmin will be in since we're between terms, and he can give me direction."

"Just be careful," Johann said. "You don't want to let him know what you're looking for, exactly."

The look Iris and Marie gave him told Johann his admonishment was unnecessary, but he'd spent enough time with academic types to know that sometimes their enthusiasm got away with their tongues.

"I have all too clear a memory of what can happen to someone who knows too much," Iris said. "Remember poor Monsieur Anctil."

"I do. All too well. As does Inspector Davidson, and he remembers you too. He was at the murder scene yesterday and may want to speak with you."

"Why?" Iris held out her hands. "I don't have anything to add to his investigation. I didn't even witness what happened."

"He sees some sort of pattern, apparently. Guilt by association." Johann didn't miss how Marie drew back into herself when he'd mentioned the inspector. He wanted to protect her from...

Well, he didn't know what. But if she felt threatened, he needed to make her secure, particularly so they could finish what the kiss in the theatre had started. But if it would put her in harm's way... He shoved that problem to the back of his mind and returned his attention to Iris.

"I'll be careful what I say to him, don't worry." She looked at Marie, who held out Iris's cloak while avoiding meeting Johann's gaze. "If he can find me."

She took her cloak, and the two women walked out into the bright sunlight.

"Are you ready?" Radcliffe asked.

Johann fixed himself a quick sandwich of the same variety of meats and cheeses they'd had the day before and the day before that and... "Any word on the situation outside the city?"

"More of the same," Patrick told him. "Any progress made by the French is erased by the next day, but the Prussians aren't advancing, either. They're focused on strangling the city."

"At least it happened after the growing season when cellars were full," Radcliffe added, "but I'm seeing more and more nutrition-related problems, so something isn't coming in that needs to."

Whereas before he'd been glad that Lucille St. Jean had stocked her pantry and the townhouse's cellar with foods that would last the winter, he now wondered if it would make her even more of a target. At least her maid Claudette seemed loyal.

Indeed, the girl gave him a shy smile when she entered to clean up the remainders of lunch, of which there weren't much. He grinned back at her and gave his smile that extra push that seemed to attract the ladies, although he couldn't explain how.

Claudette glanced away, but her neck under her chignon was pink, so he knew she'd noticed.

Radcliffe cleared his throat. Johann finished his sandwich, and they left. When he glanced behind him to say something to Patrick, Johann saw Claudette watched him.

MARIE SAID goodbye to Iris and walked into the theatre lobby. The musicians had finished their rehearsals, but a few of them still lingered, including—*merde*—Frederic.

"Ah, Mademoiselle," he said and held both hands out to her. "I was hoping you would appear. I hear you are to do the read-through this afternoon?"

"Yes." Marie clutched her script with both hands and edged away from him. "If you'll excuse me."

He stepped in her way, and she had to draw up short lest she appear to fall into his waiting arms. *That was a nasty trick.*

"I just wanted to invite you to join me for dinner this evening," he murmured so close his steamy breath stirred the curls that had escaped from her chignon.

She stepped back and wiped a hand across her temple to rid herself of his residue. "I'm afraid I'm unavailable."

"Are you seeing Maestro Bledsoe?" he asked.

Marie drew back from his bluntness. "That is none of your business. But I've not been feeling well, if you must know. I plan to return to bed once I'm done here."

Now Frederic was all attentiveness. "Oh, then let me help you to the stage."

"I can make it, thank you."

Marie dodged his hand, which seemed determined to take her elbow. *I should at least be polite to him. No need to make an enemy.* But after the dreams brought on by the ghost—or her own nervousness about the role she was going to have to play, she wasn't sure which—she couldn't stand the thought of a man touching her. Aside from Maestro Bledsoe, whom she knew only wanted what she was willing to give him. Frederic had always wanted more, and she didn't trust him.

"Ah, Marie!" The booming voice caught her attention and made Frederic draw back. She looked up to see her mother's friend and suspected paramour Hamish Fouré. He took her hand and kissed the back of it. "You look as lovely as ever. How are you, my dear? Come, let us catch up as I escort you to the stage. We best not keep your mother waiting."

"Until later, Mademoiselle," Frederic said. "I'm sure I will see you again soon."

Once out of earshot, Fouré asked, "Was that little man bothering you?"

Marie couldn't explain it, but she felt strangely at ease with Fouré. He was like Zokar, an older gentleman who never looked at her inappropriately and whom she felt she could trust. To a point. All men could be trusted to a certain extent, but each had a limit to his dependability.

"He has wanted to marry me since I was sixteen," she said with a sigh. She almost added that he was the last person she wanted to see her as Henriette—the idealized woman—but she'd never spoken of her talent with Fouré, although she'd often wanted to.

"Well, you are a beautiful girl, but I can see you do not feel a mutual attraction."

"Not at all." She smoothed her face before the wrinkles around her nose from her disgusted expression stuck, as her mother had often threatened.

Panic shot through Marie's gut when she laid eyes on the stage. But then another thrill, this time of exhilaration. She remembered how it had felt, especially at the beginning, when the world had been limited to the boards and the curtains. It had been an escape from the messiness of life because everyone had their place and their role, and all was predictable. They moved back and forth and interacted with mechanical precision, but with passion and the magic of looking through someone else's eyes and speaking with their tongue, at least for a few hours.

She hadn't always hated it, not until the emptiness overtook her after her first play, and she felt like a slice had been carved from her soul to compensate for the total immersion she had experienced. It seemed unfair. She liked being the best at something, finally having Lucille's approval.

A thought occurred to her, then—would she want to act if she could use her talent but didn't have to pay the price?

Is that possible?

She brought her attention back to the stage and the actors sitting in a circle. There were eight, two of them women. Marie recognized Janelle, who had been in a different theatre's production when Marie and the others had arrived back in Paris.

She's all grown up now.

The other woman didn't interact with the others, but rather looked around and gave smiles in response to comments but didn't say much herself. Her straight hair, of a nondescript color between blonde and mousy brown, slid from its pins. She had to keep tucking stray strands into place, and her nose was too long for beauty but shy of exotic.

She looks like she belongs at the front of a schoolroom, not on stage. But Marie stopped that uncharitable train of thought. She hadn't thought much of Iris's delicate beauty at first, dismissing her as a frail English miss until she'd gotten to know her.

That was one of the few advantages working for Cobb had afforded her—the experience to know that there were all kinds of people in the world, and one could never make assumptions because appearances were often cultivated. Still...

"Do you know that actress?" she asked Fouré. "The blonde?"

His brows drew together as he squinted to see who she was talking about. "That's Leigh Sellers. She's English, I recognize her from home. I wonder what she's doing here—she was quite the hit in London."

I wonder if she'd be willing to take over the role. Marie knew Janelle didn't quite have the presence for Henriette, but perhaps Leigh would prove her initial impressions wrong, particularly as she already had some notoriety.

Henri, who was to play Hector Berlioz's character, stood when he caught sight of her. "Ah, and there is our Henriette."

Marie stopped just shy of the stage stairs and waited for the familiar feeling of something welling up from her center and covering her over to start, but nothing happened.

"Are you all right?" Fouré asked.

"I don't know." Marie was glad for his supportive hand on her elbow because she was so surprised she would have collapsed otherwise.

"Lucille mentioned you weren't feeling well. Perhaps you shouldn't do this today."

"No, no, I'm fine."

But am I? I don't know whether to be glad or unhappy.

She thanked Fouré for escorting her and ascended the steps to take her place in the circle. Lucille appeared from backstage and took the last empty chair.

"Now," she said. "Let us begin. We will go straight through. Henri, you have just seen the woman with whom you fall instantly madly in love. Go."

Marie automatically flinched from Henri's direct gaze, but confusion flickered over his features. She guessed how he must feel. He'd been in her last production and had heard the rumors of poor old Maurice, who had supposedly gone mad afterward. She'd heard the rumors from overseas and felt badly, but what could she have done?

"Henri?" Lucille asked.

"Ah, right." He cleared his throat and started his lines.

When it came to be Marie's turn to speak, she again waited for the role to take her over, but it didn't. She felt it try to edge in, but she fought it and instead drew on her stage training, which she found to be rusty. She found herself tripping over words and messing up phrasing that should have come naturally, but exhilaration bloomed in her chest—this was her, not some phantom trying to overcome her.

"This is not what I expected," Leigh Sellers said when they took a break after the second act.

By that point, Marie was sweating. Since when was acting so exhausting? *Since I have to actually put effort into it.* "The first time actors come together can be rough," she said.

"Marie, come here." Lucille gestured for her to come backstage. "We need to talk."

Oh, here we go...

"My child, what has happened to you?" Lucille asked and put a hand on Marie's cheek. "Where is your gift?"

"I'm fine, *Maman*." For the first time in years, Marie felt challenged on the stage, and she liked it.

"*Non*, you are not *fine*." Lucille elongated the *I* sound into a nasal tone like the Americans used. "You have lost your presence. How am I to fill the seats if you are not acting at the top of your potential?"

The exhilaration Marie had felt at the thought of finally being a real actress twisted into anger. "Perhaps this is my true potential. At least I'm not going to lose part of myself to this."

"If something is worth pursuing, it is worth giving yourself fully to. Now, do you want to keep this role, or shall I give it to Mademoiselle Sellers? She asked to move into it after Corinne left, but I wanted you to have it. Not because you are my daughter, but because you are a talented actress. Or has all that time with that American warped your talent?"

Marie flinched at the accusation and all the layers beneath it. She glanced at Leigh, who appeared to study the script but who snuck sideways looks at her and Lucille.

No way is she going to steal my part.

Marie narrowed her eyes, and Leigh returned her attention to her script. *Good.* Marie wanted the chance to see if she could be a real actress without losing part of her soul.

"No, I will keep it. Perhaps I'm just rusty."

Lucille nodded and banged her stick on the floor. "*Bien.* You will continue, but do not be afraid of it."

Marie watched Lucille walk back onstage and took some deep breaths. A piece of paper fluttered down to her, but when she glanced up, she couldn't see anything or anyone moving on the catwalk overhead.

"*The effects of the smoke should be wearing off, so if you choose, you can resume your talent,*" the note read. "*If you would like to learn to control it, you need to trust me. I can help you do so without substances, but you need a disciplined mind and heart.*"

A chill skimmed over Marie's neck and shoulders, and she felt the stirring deep inside that meant the role was there waiting for her to call upon it. Could she master her talent, use it without allowing it to eat away at her? Her mother obviously expected her to, but the question was, did she want to?

What do I really want?

She'd always thought she wanted a normal life, but she recognized she made that choice out of fear of losing herself. She remembered her first play and the joy she'd taken in being someone else in the ultimate game of make-believe. Then, after she became the star, she reveled in the adulation of the audience after she allowed them to be transported to a different place and time for a few hours. There had always been that soul-fracturing emptiness after. But could she have everything, the stage and her soul? She wasn't sure if whoever it was heard her, but she held the note up to the shadows and said one word.

"Yes."

A draught stirred the ropes, and a blast of cold air made Marie shiver.

Merde, *what have I done?*

14

———

Maison Cinsault, *3 December 1870*

Johann and Radcliffe arrived at the house of the newly widowed Madame Cinsault after a long, chilly walk in the snow. Neither man said much, and Johann wondered what Radcliffe's thoughts turned to. He had seemed restless that day.

"Something bothering you?" Johann finally asked. The icy sunlight had given way to more snow, and it swirled around them and gave the sensation of walking in a private cocoon.

"Since the siege began, it's been difficult to get news of the outside world. I'm concerned about how the war at home is going."

"Right, the War Between the States."

"Or the un-Civil war," Radcliffe replied with a wry smile.

"Is your young lady still in Vienna?"

"That's the other problem—I don't know. If she's returned to Boston, my friends at home would tell me, but the post isn't coming through, at least not much of it."

Johann found himself interested, if only to take his mind off his own problems. He'd often found that if something worried him, his mind would sort it out if he left it alone.

"Do you still think that the E.E. will be able to help her?"

"Now this is where I'm thoroughly perplexed," Radcliffe said. "I know the professor was already having problems before last summer's expedition, but it seems to me he should be better by now. Better than he is, anyway."

"It took him a long time to get over Lily," Johann pointed out. "And he didn't kill anyone that time."

"Right, but I've also noticed Patrick slipping back into some old habits, ones he's worked on changing since we met."

They arrived at the Cinsaults' house, and Johann knocked on the door. A butler opened it and looked them up and down.

"Madame is not receiving visitors," he said.

"We just have a few questions for her," Johann said. "We're with the theatre."

"Madame does not want her husband's murder turned into a play. You English do that enough with your own crimes. There's no reason to bring that filthy, disrespectful habit here."

"It's not like that," Johann told him and stuck his boot in the door when the butler tried to close it. "We're trying to figure out what happened. Would you please tell her that Maestro Sable and Doctor Radcliffe are here to see her? The doctor assisted Monsieur Cinsault, or tried to."

"I will tell her. Wait here." He shut the front door on them, leaving them to rub their hands and stamp their feet in the cold.

"Bloody French," Johann cursed under his breath.

"You didn't really think this through, did you?" Radcliffe asked. "I thought you had a plan for how to get in."

"Plans are a waste of time. Ah."

The front door opened, and the butler, with an even more aggrieved expression, stood aside for them to enter.

"Madame will speak to the doctor," he said. "You, Maestro, are not to say a word."

Intrigued, Johann responded, "I will respect Madame's wishes."

The butler led them into a parlor, where Madame Cinsault sat. Although at the older end of middle-aged and dressed in unflattering black satin, she still had the almond-shaped eyes and long neck of a classic French beauty. Her gray-streaked dark hair was pulled back in a twist, and she studied the two men with a look that made Johann feel like a side of beef in a butcher's window. He guessed what the motive in the murder had been, but he waited for Radcliffe to speak.

"We are very sorry to intrude on you during this difficult time," Radcliffe said.

Madame Cinsault waved away his apology and fixed her gaze on Johann. He noted the absence of any sign that she'd been crying.

"You are probably wondering why I don't want you to say anything, Maestro Sable." Her voice was pitched low in a seductive purr. "That's because if you were to speak and be intelligent, I would fall again into the kind of temptation that killed my husband. Luckily for Doctor Radcliffe, I have a policy against dallying with men who know more about my insides than I do."

Johann had to bite his lip not to reply or give her a charming smile, as that devil inside him wanted to do. The kiss he'd shared with Marie flashed into his brain.

"And what temptation was that, Madame?" Radcliffe asked. He looked relieved.

"The kind that makes me recognize you as dark and exotic, Doctor. I do thank you for your assistance to my late husband, but you know as well as I that there was nothing to be done for him."

"Do you know who killed him?"

She dropped her gaze, and her dark lashes lay thick on her creamy cheek. "I might. I don't know."

"How?"

She glanced back up at him. "It's an old story, Doctor. Love begets jealousy, and crimes of passion occur."

"So your lover killed him?"

She shrugged. "I am telling you this to clear my conscience because I know you are not the police. Inspector Davidson has already been around, you see. As for which of my lovers it could have been, I don't know who had the nerve to wield the knife."

Johann turned his head to hide a smile. He recognized her need to be in control and knew she would choose men who wouldn't challenge her too much.

"Did anyone indicate they wanted to?"

She laughed, and the sound coiled in Johann's center and made him want to grin in response. *I am not interested, I am not interested.* He wanted to respond to the invitation in her eyes, so he focused on what he found off-putting about her, which was pretty much everything except what she pulled out of him.

"Oh, they all did when I told them I was too comfortable to leave him for them, but I knew they wouldn't. Or I thought I did."

"Did your husband know about the affairs?" Radcliffe asked. His gray eyes were serious, and sweat beaded along his hairline. Johann wondered if he, too, felt whatever surrounded Madame Cinsault. The temperature in the parlor certainly didn't warrant perspiration. Like most of Paris, this household conserved its coal. The air was barely warm enough to take the worst edge off the cold.

"Of course. He had his own indiscretions." Now her eyes glistened. "We had a thoroughly comfortable arrangement, gentlemen. I will be honest with you and tell you I mourn that as much as I mourn him, probably more, for now society's dictates of a widow's behavior will limit me."

Radcliffe wiped his brow with a handkerchief. "Do you think one of your husband's mistress's husbands could have killed him?"

She shrugged again with classic French *je ne sais quoi*. "I suppose it's possible. I wish I could help you there, gentlemen, but he was discreet, as I was, so I can't give you any information as to who he was dallying with. As long as we were both home for dinner, it didn't matter. If you would like to look through his things, be my guest. I didn't allow the inspector to do so."

Johann guessed Inspector Davidson didn't respond to her the way she wanted. In spite of her obvious charm with whatever enhanced it, Johann had also lost the initial pull of attraction to her. There was too much of a sense of a spider sitting in the middle of its web waiting for its next prey. And a man had died, either directly or indirectly because of her.

The butler showed them to Monsieur Cinsault's chamber, which consisted of a sitting room and bedroom. He hovered at the door, likely to ensure they didn't steal anything.

"You're more versed with this sort of thing than I am," Radcliffe murmured. "What exactly should we look for?" His words puffed from his mouth—the chamber had obviously not been heated since its occupant was killed.

Johann rubbed his hands together and then gave up and put on his gloves. "Tokens from women, I suppose, although they're more likely to receive gifts than give them. Letters as well. If he and Madame had an understanding, he wouldn't have worried about her finding them."

They looked through the room as quickly as they could—it was bitter cold—but didn't come up with anything. Then Radcliffe asked to see the study, but that, too, was a chill, dead end. Soon they stood in the snow that had piled on the front step.

It's almost more comfortable out here away from that strange woman.

Not that he was one to not appreciate a willing female, but something about her put him off. *Yes, she's too good at playing the game. I prefer women who are more honest. Or innocent.*

Now that wasn't a comfortable thought. He put it away, and they walked toward the street in silence. Once they stepped on to the sidewalk, Johann relaxed, and Radcliffe's shoulders lost some of the protective hunch they'd had.

"What a strange house," the doctor said. "I'd heard the upper class French were looser about certain things than the Americans and certainly the English, but that was creepy."

"I agree."

Before Johann could say anything else, a voice from behind them asked, "Did you learn anything, gentlemen?"

Johann turned to see Inspector Davidson, and he did not look pleased to see them there.

AFTER SHE LET herself into the staff entrance with her student keys, Iris found herself keeping to the walls like a rodent anxious not to be seen. As with many of the museums, the Louvre was closed to the public to conserve coal during the siege. It lacked more than it held due to the most valuable objects having been taken out of Paris or hidden underground in case of Prussian shelling. Now boxes of arms and ammunition lined the walls where cases had once held displays of precious artifacts.

The lack of either people or the ticks and clanks of the steam heating system made for a thick layer of silence, like dust in a room that hadn't been opened for years. She stopped, took a breath and straightened her shoulders. Monsieur Firmin, who ran the *Ecole d'Archaeologie* and who was also head of the classical collections at the Louvre had said the students could visit to do their own research during the break with what little was left, but they should either bring their own coal for heat or expect to be chilled. Being English, Iris didn't mind the cold so much, and thanks to Madame St. Jean's generosity, she had comfortable clothing.

Or as comfortable as possible. Something about the cold in the museum seeped through her many layers.

Iris flexed her fingers, which tingled with the familiar desire to touch the objects around her and sense what previous handlers had thought and felt, usually just impressions. A few things gave her sharp enough images and emotions to propel her into past scenes, and she'd had to learn to be careful when she was with others not to go into a trance as she followed the threads of memory into the past. She wasn't entirely convinced that objects were only solid, dumb masses, at least not all of them, not the way they held on to the memories, sometimes the spirits, of their creators or what they represented.

In the Classics storeroom in the basement, she nodded to the waving *kore* statue, which had since been verified as having been sculpted during a later period in memory of a beloved slave girl who had perished in the Roman arena. Iris had known those facts already but had enjoyed the challenge of proving intellectually what her touch-sense told her.

Well, aside from the ire of the other students, who had deemed her a showoff and a teacher's pet. Indeed, it had been a hard lesson that she should keep her enthusiasm and knowledge, of which she had more than the other students even beyond her unusual talent, to herself. Her father had trained her well, and now she was happy to be alone at the museum so she could fully revel in her abilities.

Or was she? The air carried the sharp-edged scent of smoke, and she sniffed, turning her head in different directions to determine where it came from. Although she didn't desire to speak to anyone, she needed to make sure the fire was of the friendly, contained sort and not the rambling destructive kind. She followed her nose to a hall lined with offices, where light shone under only one door. She squinted to assess its quality. She didn't realize her curiosity had carried her to stand in front of the office in question until she heard a voice say, "Who's out there?"

Iris recognized the gruff tones and replied, "It's me, Iris McTavish, Monsieur Firmin."

"Have you come to do me in, then, like poor Anctil? You'd better open the door and be done with it."

Iris wanted to turn and flee, but she knew that would be disrespectful, no matter how she didn't appreciate his attempts at humor. She didn't find his jokes about her role in the former curator of the Renaissance collection's death funny, but she didn't know how to tell him, either.

Perhaps he's grieving and this is how he's dealing with it.

She opened the door and walked in to find the fire thankfully contained in the grate and Monsieur Firmin sitting behind his desk with what looked like an ancient manuscript in front of him. She couldn't see the writing clearly enough to tell, but it looked like one of the near Eastern ones. *Possibly a form of Greek.*

Iris didn't think she'd ever seen Monsieur Firmin smile, and his face held an even deeper scowl than his customary one. The electric lamp on his desk cast the planes of his already severe features into harsher relief, and Iris thought an impression might make a good beginning of a grimacing ceremonial mask.

"Don't just stand there," he said in English. "Go warm up by the fire. If you're going to freeze to death trying to leap to the head of the class, you won't do it on my watch."

"Thank you," she said because it was the only logical thing to reply, and she wasn't going to refuse the warmth. She stood in front of the fire and held her hands out. The tingling in her fingers told her she'd been colder than she recognized.

"*De rien*. I expected that you, of all of them, would be silly enough to come to the museum in the cold. Is our current state of besiegement not exciting enough for you, Mademoiselle, that you feel the need to dig into the drama of the past during your time off?"

Might as well talk to him. It is nice and warm here, and I'm going to have to ask him where to look for what I'm seeking. But I can at least be honest, and maybe he'll tell me how I did on my exams.

"I don't find it exciting at all. As much as I like living in Paris, I don't enjoy being trapped."

A sharp bark of laughter escaped him. "And what do the young know about being trapped? You use that word so freely. Trapped in a promise, in a relationship, in a situation you don't know enough about to get out of."

Iris glanced over her shoulder at him and saw he studied her. She kept her expression perplexed with little effort. *No reason to let him know his barb hit home. What do I know of what's going on with Edward? And do I want to get out of it? No, I won't betray him, and I do love him.*

"Your eyes give you away, Mademoiselle. What are you here to avoid? An awkward situation at home? A young man who won't give you the attention you want?"

The heat in Iris's cheeks had nothing to do with the fire, and her eyes stung, but not from smoke. She moved away from the hearth toward the door.

"As much as I respect your knowledge, Monsieur, I do not have any wish to be insulted."

"I have seen only a few young women with your intelligence, Mademoiselle. Most of them have been lured away from promising careers by a young man who they felt could give them more. If I insult you, it is to awaken you to the fact that *les hommes* will try to convince you they are more important than the science you pursue. Any science, really."

He doesn't know Edward. "I don't see that as my problem, Monsieur."

"Then why are you here? The snow outside is thick for so early in the season, and the rest of the museum feels like a Scandinavian ice tomb."

Iris had to laugh at his sour expression, and she reminded himself that at his age, he probably felt the cold in his joints. Her father had just started complaining the winter before he died in spite of being in apparent good health.

No reason to refuse help because I'm irritated. But I'll show Johann I'm capable of doing this without revealing too much. Not that he's the soul of discretion.

"I'm here to get ahead with my studies of artifacts from the classical period in the Byzantine Empire. We've mostly looked at Greek and Roman objects, and I didn't see a near Eastern course in the catalog. While I know it was part of the Roman Empire at one point, I also appreciate the other cultural differences and influences and would like to know more."

"That's because we don't have enough for one." His frown deepened. "We've been waiting for Madame Dieulafoy to send back her finds from the area."

"Will she come here?" Iris couldn't help but ask about her idol, who, she noted, employed her husband and took *him* along on expeditions, not the other way around.

"I imagine she will return to Paris at some point, yes, but we never know exactly what Madame Dieulafoy will do," Monsieur Firmin said with a shake of his head. "She is a free spirit, and the exception to the rule I mentioned earlier."

"Then it's all the more important that I study up on that area of the world," Iris pointed out. "You'll need help when things come in."

Firmin's scowl rearranged itself into something resembling

a smile. "You are a determined young woman. Very well, I will show you where to start."

"*Merci.*"

He rose from his seat slowly, again reminding Iris that he was an old man, took a book from his shelves, and moved to the door. She turned to follow him, but something tugged at the edge of her senses. She stilled. The last time that had happened, she had discovered a clue to her father's death and a note he left for her. The pull directed her to the manuscript he had been studying.

"Monsieur Firmin, if I may ask, what were you looking at when I came in?" She had to rush to catch up with him.

"It's an ancient Byzantine manuscript. Nothing relevant to what you want to know, just some records of crops and agricultural transactions."

Something about his posture said he was lying to her, but she didn't challenge him. She decided she would look at it on her own when she had the chance. Not that her Greek was that strong, especially not from an area of the world where other languages strongly influenced it, but items made of cloth or paper typically didn't hold impressions. That this one seemingly did and wanted her to read it intrigued her.

He brought her to the classical gallery with the waving statue. After he turned on the electric lights, which did nothing to increase the temperature, he pointed to a glass case covered in cloth.

"In that case are some typical Byzantine pottery examples, but they have not yet been labeled. Your job is to do so by period and type." He handed the book to her.

Iris placed the book on a nearby table and removed the cloth. The glass lids weren't locked, and it looked like someone had gone in and smashed the pottery so that all that remained were shards, which lay about like large chunks of clay confetti. She looked at Monsieur Firmin questioningly.

"What happened?" she asked.

"They arrived here like this in a large box. I would like to get my hands on whatever workmen dropped it."

"Me too." The enormity of the task ahead made Iris's stomach twist. "They can't be identified until they're reconstructed. I can see some features, but shape is impossible."

"Then you have a puzzle to keep you occupied. Good luck."

He left, and Iris turned to the case. *Big hairy ox's bollocks! He just wants me out of his hair, or what's left of it.*

She picked up a potsherd, noting its texture and colors. It gave off faint impressions, but it seemed to have been handled and moved a lot since arriving in Europe. She would have to seriously focus to dig far back enough to see its original shape and function.

How to do this? Well, without using too much energy. If I were to put all these together with just my touch-sense, I would end up with a huge headache and in bed for a week.

Iris glanced at the door, where Monsieur Firmin watched her. With a wave, he disappeared.

That was the first genuine smile I've seen on the man this year. He's expecting me to fail.

With renewed determination, she flexed her fingers and set to trying to get some idea of which shards went together.

If this is what it takes to obtain access to the materials I need, then so be it. Edward's not the only one who can throw himself into work.

15

O*utside Maison Cinsault, 3 Dec 1870*

"How long have you been here?" Johann asked Inspector Davidson. The darkness of the clouds overhead mirrored Davidson's expression, and Johann steeled himself against the disapproval inherent there.

See? This is why I don't make myself useful. Damned if I do, damned if I don't. He looks a self-righteous sort.

"Long enough," was Davidson's reply. He spoke with clipped words, like he picked up each one with tweezers and hurled it at them. "And did you glean anything interesting from Madame Cinsault, or did you merely influence a witness to be less welcoming on my return visit?"

"I'm sure she'd enjoy it regardless," Johann muttered.

If Davidson heard him, he ignored him. "I need to talk to the two of you anyway. My coach is parked around the corner. It's still cold inside, but it's outside of the wind."

"Are you offering us a ride?" Radcliffe asked.

Johann glared at his companion. "You want to take him up on it?"

"It's beastly cold out here." Indeed, the doctor looked

miserable. Johann recalled how Radcliffe had seemed perfectly content in the furnace that was Rome that summer, unusual if he considered Radcliffe as being from Boston.

But was he? Johann had never asked, just assumed. Either way, he would deal with Davidson's questions to get out of the cold for a bit.

"Come, gentlemen, I promise nothing untoward will befall you." With a strange smirk, he gestured for them to follow.

They found his carriage around the corner, as promised. Johann admitted to some relief once he climbed in out of the swirling snow and biting wind.

"This weather isn't good," Davidson said and rapped on the wall between him and the carriage driver. "The city is already short on coal, and this will make it run out sooner. I fear our men will not be able to outlast the Prussians with the fear of riots."

"Won't the people prefer a coal shortage to the Prussian yoke or reparations?" Radcliffe asked.

"For many of them, slavery is a mere concept, not a reality," Davidson replied. "Cold is real to them."

Radcliffe straightened, and Johann raised his eyebrows. He and the others deliberately didn't refer to the doctor's dark skin and the ancestry it implied.

"I meant no offense," Davidson said and held his hand palm-down. "Perhaps we should steer toward safer subjects."

"Yes," Radcliffe said. "Let's. What do you want to know?"

"What did you observe about the scene yesterday?" Davidson asked.

Radcliffe related how he had rushed into the crowd and found Monsieur Cinsault lying on the sidewalk bleeding from his wounds.

"What sort of weapon do you think was used?" Davidson asked.

"Something long and sharp enough to go through all those layers of winter clothes."

"So it was a planned act," Johann said. "Who carries a knife like that around?"

"There are certain professions, and I expect more men to be armed with the Prussians pushing at the gates," Davidson noted. "But you make a good point."

Johann arched an eyebrow at the pun, but Davidson seemed not to realize he'd made one.

"You're a battlefield doctor, correct?" Davidson asked Radcliffe.

"Yes."

"So you've seen all kinds of injuries inflicted by blades."

"You could say that," Radcliffe frowned. "What are you getting at?"

"Only that you're in a unique position to be able to answer my next question. Did the wounds seem to be professionally inflicted or aimed by an amateur?"

"One of them was in the left kidney, so between the location and the speed of the attack, I would say the stabber knew what he was doing."

"My thoughts as well," Davidson said and looked out of the window. "From what witnesses said, the stabber ran up behind him, got him in the kidney, pulled the knife out, and then when Cinsault fell, stabbed him again in the chest. So the question remains, who wanted Monsieur Cinsault dead to the degree they were willing to hire an assassin or someone equally adept at knife-wielding?"

"And what kind of assassin inflicts a second wound after a fatal one?" Johann asked. It was terribly exciting watching the detective piecing it all together. Then he remembered the widow sitting in the middle of her web mourning the loss of her convenient lifestyle more than her husband, and he felt doubly sorry for the poor dead sod.

"Perhaps he wasn't sure he'd met his mark through all the winter clothing, as Doctor Radcliffe suggested," the detective said. "That makes more sense for the context—it makes no sense for someone who knew what he was doing to attack there, in front of the theatre, unless he was trying to send a message." He glanced at Johann.

Or was trying to confirm the identity of the victim.

A chill slid down Johann's spine, and he recalled the strange raven. "A message?"

Like the Clockwork Guild is watching me, and they're willing to do anything to obtain what I owe them.

Davidson's voice startled Johann from his panicked thoughts. "As for you, Maestro, why did you run into the fray in your shirtsleeves?"

At least he didn't have to come up with a clever answer for that question. He could tell the unvarnished truth. "I heard the scream and was concerned it might have been one of the women in our group."

"But it wasn't."

"No, thank God."

"And what would you have done, unarmed and without even a coat?" Davidson shook his head. "I admire your chivalrous instincts, but you could have caught your death of cold, not to mention you were too late to do anything."

With the inspector's proclamation of Johann's uselessness— or was it impotence?—the carriage slowed, and Davidson said, "And here we are. Please give Miss McTavish my regards and tell her I shall call on her tomorrow."

With that, he let Johann and Radcliffe out. They stood and watched the carriage drive away.

"That was odd," Johann said.

"Not really," Radcliffe replied. "You gave him the information he wanted, which was to eliminate you as being connected to the stabbing."

"Why would he think I was?"

"Perhaps it had something to do with Monsieur Anctil's murder. You do seem to have rotten luck with showing up around people being killed, and he's obviously looking for a connection."

"Yes, he said as much yesterday." The chill slid back up Johann's back. They turned and walked toward the townhouse's front door.

"You may have more to do with this than you recognize. Remember what we talked about yesterday."

"Then why aren't you afraid around me?" He didn't want to admit he had similar fears, and he certainly wasn't going to mention the Clockwork Guild, the source of his shame.

"I've faced worse." With that, Radcliffe pushed his way through the front door.

Johann shivered on the doorstep, reluctant to enter. What did he deserve of the warmth and camaraderie that awaited within? Only mere crumbs of it, if that. He had put the others in danger before—was it to be so again? If that was the case, he vowed to leave before something happened to any of them. But he needed more information.

When he glanced over his shoulder, he saw a dark shape in a tree. It was impossible to see through the snow in the dusky light, but he thought it might have glowing eyes. Instead of going inside, he decided to take a walk to clear his mind and draw the steam raven—if that was what it was—away.

MARIE LEFT the theatre during a break in the snow. The others had already gone, taking advantage of the brief respite from the flakes falling from the sky and blowing on to unprotected skin and into the creases between collars and necks. Sometimes the snow felt like it had a mind of its own and was determined to make people, her in particular, as uncomfortable as possible.

The branches of the trees stretched toward the darkening sky, the flickering street lamps gilding the snow gathered on the branches. Marie liked the winter, when the trees were naked and showed their true forms. She wished it was as easy for her.

"Mademoiselle!"

Marie turned to see Janelle come up behind her.

"What are you doing here still? I thought you'd already left. This isn't the kind of weather to be dawdling in, and I almost just locked you in the theatre."

Janelle bit her lip and looked away, a girlish gesture in spite of the womanly curves she had acquired in the previous two years.

"I wanted to talk to you," Janelle said. "I don't live far from here."

"All right." Marie turned to go back into the theatre, but she hesitated. What if whatever had stolen Zokar's automaton lurked in there waiting to peel more memories from her brain? She took some satisfaction in locking the door. "I'll walk with you to your flat. I could use the exercise."

"Aren't you afraid to be out alone after dark? They say women shouldn't be, especially not now during the siege with desperate men about."

The role of Marguerite the Spy tugged at the edges of Marie's spirit. She shrugged it and Janelle's concern off. "There are ways to get around that others don't know. I'll be fine. What do you want to know about?"

In spite of brushing off Janelle's concern, Marie watched the shadows between the street lamps and under the trees, sparse as they were, as they walked.

"I just wanted to know—" Janelle stopped and coughed. "I mean, you have such a stage presence. I've never seen anyone act like you do, not even Mademoiselle Sellers, as good as she is."

"Even after today?" Marie couldn't help but ask. She'd managed to keep Henriette from taking over until the very end. Now in the chill air, she felt like it melted off her and left her soul as bare and exposed as the trees.

"Everyone has a rough day, and the others were accustomed to Corinne, so they were off rhythm. I have faith that Fantastique will have a triumphant return to the stage of the Théâtre Bohème."

"You're assuming she wants to."

Janelle turned her wide-eyed gaze to Marie. "Why wouldn't she? I mean you? You were the greatest actress. That's why I want you to teach me."

Marie turned away from Janelle's innocent request, and a moving shadow caught her eye.

"Are we close to your place?" she asked.

"Yes, Mademoiselle. Just around the corner."

"I think we're being followed."

Janelle turned to look behind them, but Marie stopped her with a hand on her arm. "Don't let on that we know. Just walk normally."

Marie felt the role of the female spy coming over her. It felt like her cheekbones grew higher and a cool glint came to her eye. Not that she could see it, but her eyelids narrowed of their own accord. She knew whoever looked at her would see a cold woman, someone not to be interfered with.

"Mademoiselle, I'm nervous," Janelle said. "I don't want to show them my lodging."

Marie fought the urge to snap at Janelle to be quiet—the girl at least was thinking cautiously. "Then if we're almost there, you go around the corner to your place, and I'll deal with them. Can you make it?"

Janelle nodded.

"Then go."

She didn't have to tell Janelle to walk quickly. The girl disappeared around the corner, and Marie heard a door open and shut. She turned to face whoever had followed them.

"Pleasant evening, Mademoiselle St. Jean." The sneering American accent destroyed the melody of the French words.

"There's no need to waste time with pleasantries," Marie addressed the two men who faced her on the sidewalk and blocked her from returning from where she came. "What do you want?"

"We work for someone who's an old friend," the same man said, switching to speaking English. "He wants you to come with us, Miss. And what he wants, he gets."

They must mean Cobb. He knows Mother wouldn't let me out of her sight long enough to see him. But what is he doing in Paris? And how did he get through the siege lines? The Blooming Senator must be flying again.

"I'm not interested in seeing your employer," she said and drew the aura of the spy around her. "If he wants to meet up with me, he can make an appointment like everyone else. I'm busy."

The two men moved closer, and the larger one, who hadn't spoken, grabbed her upper arm.

"He's not interested in being like everyone else."

"Is there a problem, Mademoiselle?"

Again, Marie was relieved to hear the voice of Maestro Johann Bledsoe, but dismay made her huff.

What is he doing here? I don't want him to get hurt.

16

P*aris, 3 December, 1870*
Johann turned the corner and saw two men manhandling Marie. Without thinking, he sauntered over and put himself in the middle of the dangerous situation. For a second, he was distracted. Marie should have been panicked, but her face showed haughty contempt, and she almost didn't look like herself.

"I have the situation under control," she said and jerked her chin for him to go.

Like hell.

"Are you quite certain? That thug has his hand around your arm."

"Quite."

With movements that blurred beneath the streetlamps, Marie kicked the man in the knee, and, startled, he let go. She hit him with the flat of her palm in the nose, and he staggered back, clutching his face, blood streaming from under his hands. The other one made a grab for her, but Johann caught his arm and swung him around into a nearby tree. Johann took her hand, and they ran in the direction he'd come from, back toward the theatre. Once they reached a busier area where more people strolled, they stopped and assumed a more normal pace, but he noticed her hand on his arm trembled.

"Are you all right?" he asked. "You were, well, fantastic. You almost didn't look like you."

"Thanks, I think." She looked at him with wide hazel eyes, back to the Marie he knew. After their kiss the day before, his mind would only call her Marie, not Mademoiselle St. Jean, as would be proper. But he didn't want to do proper things to her, no matter what sort of warnings he got.

"Who were they?"

She looked around as if to make sure they hadn't been followed. Johann was almost certain they hadn't been—he recognized the crooks' type, hired thugs who would only do easy jobs.

"I think Parnaby Cobb might be in town. They said their boss was an old friend and wanted to see me."

"If his airship had landed in Paris, there would have been a stir. People are desperate for news of the outside."

"People are sneaking in and out, and he is particularly resourceful when there's something he wants but desires to stay out of public attention."

She clung to his arm, which he didn't mind.

"Why not just send you a card?" he asked. "Make a proper visit if he wanted to see you?" Not that he wanted Parnaby Cobb to whisk her away, as he apparently had done before.

"My mother hates him for what he did. If he stepped foot near the theatre, she would make sure he regretted it. No, he knew I could get away from his men. This is a message that he hasn't forgotten me."

Johann placed a hand over hers and squeezed. "You have friends now. We won't let him harm you."

"Thank you." But she sounded doubtful.

They turned the corner on to the block with the theatre,

where one of the trees sported a red glow near the top. Johann stopped short, tugging Marie back with him.

"What is it?" she asked.

He pointed to the tree, which was in the park across the street. "Look up there."

She squinted slightly. "I see a red glow. Is that a bird?"

"It's a raven, but it's not an ordinary one. It's steam-powered, and it has a camera at the back of its beak."

The look she gave him said she thought his next destination might be Bedlam. "Are you sure?"

"Edward saw it too. It's been following me this evening. I'd prefer to stay out of its sight."

"We can go around the block and use the alley behind the theatre to get to the servants' entrance."

"That will work."

They did as she suggested, and Johann kept glancing over his shoulder for the red glow.

Now it was her turn to ask, "Where did it come from? Why is it following you?" Instead of fear, her voice held a note of breathless excitement that he could identify with.

Perhaps that's how Cobb lured her away—she wanted more excitement in her life. I can understand, but what's more exciting than the stage? All right, traveling the world would be, but at what cost?

"I don't know." He dragged his mind back to the present and away from the fears that she would leave again if given the chance. Which was stupid—he was going to head out as soon as Edward got to a place of stability, assuming he could figure out what to do with the specter of the Clockwork Guild debt hanging over him.

He recalled the note he'd found in his violin case. "The raven isn't the only strange thing. Someone left me a note when I stepped out of the theatre yesterday warning me away from you. I thought it might have been your friend LeClerc."

Marie looked up at him again, this time with a slight lift to one eyebrow. "I doubt Frederic would feel he needs to leave you notes. He's direct enough on his own."

"I agree. Someone's been dropping notes on to others in the theatre. LeClerc got one. You did too."

She didn't answer him, only said, "Turn here."

"What was it?" Johann pressed. "Was it a note warning you away from me?"

"No, it was a newspaper article from September. From an English paper. If Iris goes back, she'll need to be with the two of you to prove she's innocent of something happening to you."

"My family knows I'm on the continent." Johann had made sure to telegraph them occasionally with brief updates so his grandmother wouldn't worry. While he'd always thought of her as the Dowager Dragon, he knew she did what she did out of love.

His father, on the other hand...

Was that a ploy to get him to return and assume his rightful place as the lackey in the family hierarchy?

"I have the article in my dressing room in the theatre," Marie murmured. "I didn't want Iris to find it and be upset. Of course it brings up her possible role in Jeremy Scott's death."

"Of course," Johann said with a sigh. "It's amazing how some things just won't go away. Here?"

They emerged on the street that ran beside the building on the other side of the theatre, an abandoned church that was mostly used for storage. Johann didn't know what kind of storage, only that he'd sometimes seen soldiers moving crates in and out of it. He scanned the scraggly trees that struggled for sunlight along this avenue and didn't see anything.

"I think it's clear," he said.

"Good, let's go."

They made sure no carriages, steamcarts or horses came along—the street was empty—and darted across. The same alley Marie had chased Corinne down enveloped them. It again concentrated what little breeze there was into an icy spike. Johann drew her closer. Just to keep her from getting too cold, of course.

"Careful," Marie said. "Sometimes there's ice because the drainage isn't great." Her words held an undertone of affection for a familiar place, or maybe she was happy to be close against his side and was warning him because she was concerned for his safety.

He chose to believe the latter. For the first time, he wondered what it would be like to have a traveling companion. An agreeable one without Edward's foibles and with certain assets Edward lacked. And by God, the girl could take care of herself. *No helpless damsel here.* He had to admit the attraction of a woman who could hold her own and wouldn't require constant attention or rescuing.

Could she be the ideal woman for him? The thought disturbed and intrigued him at the same time.

They reached the servants' entrance to the townhouse and paused. Johann didn't want to let Marie go, and she didn't seem to want to be released, either.

"We should go in," she said.

"We should," he agreed. Neither of them moved.

A colder gust of wind blew through the alley, and Johann turned and drew Marie to his chest. Even through all the layers, he could feel the curve of her waist. She looked up at him, and at that moment, she was all he wanted. It seemed that a rosy glow illuminated her face, and the urge to kiss her again, this time sweetly on the lips, overcame him. He bowed his head, inviting her to meet his lips with her own. Her eyes heavy-lidded, she stretched toward him.

A drift of snow plopped on top of them, knocking Johann's hat off and smacking him on the back of the head with its icy hand.

. . .

MARIE DREW BACK WITH A GASP, the face full of snow the opposite of the warm kiss she'd expected. She wiped it from her eyes and off her cheeks. Bledsoe brushed it off the top of his head and neck, but he shivered, and she guessed a trickle or two of ice-cold water had made it under his collar.

"Did your mother arrange for that?" he asked, his customary mask—that was to say, a lopsided grin, returned. He leaned over to retrieve his hat.

Marie looked up, but she couldn't see anyone on the roof above them. Not that she expected to—it was too steep to climb safely.

"I wouldn't put it past her." She opened the servants' door with one of the keys on the theatre key ring.

The light in the kitchen illuminated the now wet and sorry state of their attire even under their cloaks, which they shed as soon as they entered.

That's not the only part of me wet and unhappy. Marie had so badly wanted that kiss, but she knew it was for the better that it hadn't happened. The maestro's charm had been in full force in the alley, and the Henriette role Marie had been fighting all day emerged to meet it. Had they kissed, Marie would have always wondered who was kissing who and if he really meant it.

He's a scoundrel and not to be trusted.

As if he'd heard her thoughts, he suggested, "You should get out of that soggy blouse."

"Excuse me?"

"Not here," he said and then looked away. "I mean, you don't want to get sick."

"I'm sure that's exactly what you meant." Getting a face full of wet snow made her cross, and she shivered.

"You're being impossible. I got dumped on too."

"Fine." She took two purposeful steps toward the stairs and

then turned around. "But remember you were the one who wasn't acting like a gentleman."

"And I'm sure my attempt wouldn't have been your first kiss." He shot back. He ran a finger behind his collar.

"How dare you?" He was right, but Marie wasn't going to let him get away with saying such things.

"Perhaps you should go. And change." He spoke deliberately, and she guessed he was holding his temper.

"Perhaps you should too. More than just your clothing." And with that, she stalked up the stairs and into the back hallway. She took the servants' stairs to the floor with the bed chambers—no reason to run into anyone and have to explain where she was and what she was doing when the snow fell on her.

How did that happen? It wasn't snowing, and it's not the right temperature for it to melt.

When she arrived in her bed chamber, she found the window open, and a cold breeze had strewn Iris's notes all over the room. However, she found a piece of paper on her bed that didn't look like the rest of them. It was a note in strange handwriting:

A truly disciplined woman does not allow her passion to run away with her in an alley. Good thing the snow was there to cool you off. If you want to control your talent, you need to control yourself, Mademoiselle.

Respectfully, The Spirit of the Bohème

"*Merde*," Marie muttered. "He has a point."

She vowed to stay away from the violinist, no matter how much she wanted his promised kiss.

17

____

Théâtre Bohème, 4 December 1870

The next morning, Marie stepped into the crisp air of the alley behind the townhouse. Since it was Sunday, the street was quiet, and she knew the chances of her being disturbed were minimal. She had a ghost to find and give a piece of her mind. She didn't care whether it was a true specter or a man pretending to be one—he had gone too far with the snow on her face and the note in her bedchamber.

The more she'd thought about it, the angrier she became, and sleep had eluded her much of the night. She'd been manipulated enough by her mother. She wasn't going to take it from anyone else.

In the light of day, the snow from the roof lay scattered on the ground even after the morning's deliveries, which were fewer and fewer as the siege went on. When she looked up, she had to squint but thought she could make out the gap in the snow on the roof. The pattern convinced her that someone had shoved it off, although she still didn't know how a man could traverse it safely. Perhaps if he had a wire and pulley like they used in the theatre?

How dare he?

Now truly furious, Marie entered the theatre through the back entrance so no one would intercept her. She made her way to her dressing room and propped the door open in case the spirit decided to play his usual tricks with his smoke and the mirror, which she knew had to move somehow.

Yet another mystery. As much as I don't want to, I'm going to have to talk to Maman *about it.*

The discouragement the thought brought her cut through her anger for a moment. Obviously the spirit was connected to what had happened with Cobb somehow. Otherwise, why would he be so interested in the details? But revealing the strange goings on to her mother would bring up bad memories and reopen old wounds.

Marie glanced around the room to see if anything had changed and saw another newspaper clipping and a photograph had joined the article that mentioned Iris and the script for *Light Fantastique* on the dressing table.

"English Inspector Investigates Murder in Rue Saint-Tomas."

The new article was from the previous day's paper and detailed what had happened in front of the theatre. The photograph was dark, but Marie could make out Bledsoe, Radcliffe, and a man standing in front of a nice but nondescript carriage. The man's features were familiar to her.

"You recognize the third man?"

The voice came from all over in the dressing room, not just behind the mirror, and the door slammed shut.

Marie jumped, panic shooting through her. In spite of her resolve to stand her moral ground and confront the spirit for the snow incident, Marie's heart whirred like one of the little clockwork butterflies that had followed them the previous summer. She placed the photograph back on the dressing table and backed toward the door.

Just talk so he pays attention to what you're saying, not what you're doing. The bit of advice floated into her brain from sometime in the past.

"I don't know," she said. "He looks familiar." A memory she had tried to suppress came back to her, of her failure to take on the role of spy.

No, I have to stay in the present.

She reached the door and found it to be locked from the outside. "Let me out. I'm not playing your games anymore."

"He is Inspector Henry Davidson," the ghost said. "Do you know him?"

"I already told you he looks familiar." The memory of her first conversation with the inspector tried to shove into her brain, but she kept her face neutral. *Concentrate on the situation at hand.* "And do we have to talk about him? I have a bone to pick with you about the face full of snow I got yesterday evening."

A low chuckle. "I was just reminding you of the deal we made, Mademoiselle. You must have more discipline than that if we are to work together on managing your talent."

"What I do outside of the theatre is my affair, not yours, *casse couille.*"

"And you are sharp-tongued like your mother."

Marie's left eyebrow tried to rise before she got control of her expression. "And what do you know of her? Have you spoken to her?"

"I observe everything that happens in this theatre."

Marie thought she caught something in the spirit's tone that indicated he recognized his slip. *So he has talked to her.*

"The question, Mademoiselle, is whether you are serious about managing what happens to you on the stage. And dare I say, off stage as well? I have seen you wandering with the tale of your struggles to maintain your sense of self and sanity written on your face as your feet take you where the role does."

Marie crossed her arms against the shiver his words

brought. That was what had happened before she saw him the first time. "Keep talking." As she listened, she tried to pay careful attention to his voice so she could figure out why it sounded so familiar. She also tried to trace his accent—American, but from which part?

How does he know so much? Yes, he's observant, but we actors are an eccentric lot.

"Great talent comes with a price. I can help you minimize the cost, but I require compensation."

"Trust an American to put it in terms of money." Marie couldn't help the twist at the corner of her mouth—now he reminded her of Cobb. "But I prefer that to you attempting to control what I do and who I see."

Another chuckle. "That is your soul's price, not mine. How are you to learn to control the role erupting from inside you if you allow other impulses to drive you? No, Mademoiselle, discipline in all things first."

Merde, *he's right. If I indulge my desires, how can I possibly contain this talent, which is its own urge? No, I must practice discipline, as he said.*

She sighed her frustration and allowed her arms and shoulders to relax. "Fine. Where do we start?"

"There is an alkaloid in the smoke I use that helps control the part of the brain from whence these impulses arise. First we use that so your mind knows what it feels like to drive your talent."

"But it also loosens my tongue and brings up vivid memories I would rather not relive."

"And that, Mademoiselle, is my price. Shall we begin today's treatment?"

Marie opened her mouth, but she couldn't agree right away. Yes, she wanted to control her acting talent to keep the roles from overtaking her and eating away at her soul, but she didn't want to reveal too much of the past, and she disliked not being the one to drive her words.

"Why are you doing this?" she asked. "Why help me? What do you want?"

"Because I know you are the greatest actress of this era, and I want this theatre to thrive. Otherwise, this poor old spirit will be without a home."

She didn't believe him, but he had made one slip with his comment about her mother. If she cooperated, he would make others, and she could find out who he was and what he truly wanted. Then she could finally make up to her mother her mistakes of two years previously and not have to bring up old wounds to do so. She didn't know exactly how she would accomplish that, but she knew it was all connected somehow. She would only need to cooperate to a point to get the information she needed.

I'm thinking like a spy.

She sniffed and caught the smell of the smoke, but without Cobb's tobacco in it. She strolled to the fainting couch and reclined on it, making sure her head and neck were in a comfortable position.

"Now tell me about Inspector Davidson."

Hotel Auberge, 17 May 1868

Marie alighted from the carriage, still shaken from her encounter with the man who had pulled a knife on her.

Focus on getting your traveling papers back. Obtaining them had cost her most of the francs she'd managed to squirrel away and hide from her mother's ever watchful gaze, not to mention the trouble of managing the meetings and appointments with government officials to receive them. She wondered again how they'd ended up on top of the dressing table and not in the secret drawer. Sometimes her talent made her do things she didn't remember, which was one more reason she needed to get away from this place and figure out who she really was. Then maybe she could balance everything and keep from losing her mind.

She walked into the hotel lobby and noted immediately the difference between it and that of the theatre. Whereas the theatre was red-carpeted and dark wood-paneled, the hotel lobby was like being inside a golden egg. A crystal chandelier shimmered above gray-streaked marble floors. All the wood was light, and the accents brass. The people there, mostly foreigners, generally ignored her. Marie straightened her shoulders and allowed herself to take the first deep breath since leaving the theatre.

"Mademoiselle St. Jean?"

Marie's breath ended in a hitch as she turned to see who had spoken her name. The man didn't look like a servant, and although his accent was good, she picked up that he was not a Parisian.

"*Oui?*"

"A word before your meeting?" he asked in English, and she picked up he was himself British.

"I'm sorry, but I really have to go. I'm already late."

"I will only take a moment of your time, and it is an urgent matter."

"You and everyone else." But she followed him to the restaurant, where he led her to a table in the corner.

He held up two fingers to the waiter.

"I don't feel I should have alcohol this evening, Monsieur."

"Not to worry. They know me here. I've ordered us some tea. You'll need the extra alertness when dealing with Cobb."

Marie raised her eyebrows. "How do you know?" It then occurred to her she shouldn't have confirmed her errand.

He shrugged and waited to answer until after the waiter

brought the tea service with scones. Marie's stomach growled— she hadn't eaten since that afternoon.

"Please." He gestured to the pastries. "I've had dinner and am not hungry, so help yourself."

She buttered a scone. "While I appreciate this hospitality, Monsieur, I must ask you to state your business. I cannot afford to miss this appointment."

"I don't want to alarm you, Mademoiselle, but I do feel it necessary to warn you that with Parnaby Cobb, things are not what they seem."

Now she gave him a look she'd often seen on her mother's face. "Don't take me for a fool. I had already gathered that for myself."

"Then you know you are being drawn into a dangerous game."

"Yes, that has been made quite clear." *Although I do prefer tea and scones to a knife at my throat.* "What, specifically, do you want me to look out for?"

"I appreciate your directness, but I don't want to put you in additional danger by revealing why I am interested in Cobb and his affairs. Just trust your instincts and make note of anything that seems unusual."

Marie finished her scone and stood. "Is there anything else?"

"Yes. I won't give you my name, but if you are in any sort of danger, I can be reached at the Hotel LaVue down the street. Ask for the Englishman. They'll know who to look for."

Marie nodded and walked out of the restaurant. Now she had two men interested in using her to get at Cobb. What had the man done to deserve such attention?

That matters not. I just need to get my papers and not worry about the rest of it. I'm not interested in these games, even if Marguerite the Spy would be.

But as she crossed the lobby, she felt the role coming over her again and smiled with the confidence of a *femme fatale.*

MARIE AWOKE on the chaise lounge but waited before opening her eyes. She listened to determine whether anyone was in there with her, but her ears picked up only the scrabbling of something behind the mirror.

Wait, something behind the mirror?

Marie moved as quietly as she could, but whatever it was heard her and skittered off. Had it been any day but Sunday with the theatre being as quiet as it was, she wouldn't have noticed it among the various other sounds, but the quality of the noise confirmed her certainty there must be a space back there large enough to lead from a secret passage.

But which one?

If she could figure that out, she could possibly entrap her spirit and find out what he really wanted and why he insisted on digging up uncomfortable memories.

And then I wouldn't have to involve Maman.

She turned from the mirror to see the script lying on the desk. She'd memorized the first few scenes but knew she had a lot more lines to learn. Doing that was more difficult this time around too.

I'm out of practice.

She shoved aside the thought that there could be a price to not using her strange talent equal to the trouble of allowing it to take over. Previously, the lines sprang to mind when she needed them with a minimum of prior effort on her part. Now they slipped away almost as soon as she memorized them, or thought she did.

With a sigh, she placed the newspaper clippings in a drawer

and turned up the lamp. She'd just gotten settled on the chaise when a knock on the door interrupted her.

"*Entrée,*" she called.

The door opened to reveal Frederic. He carried his violin case, and he glanced around the room. His shoulders dipped before he assumed his typical assertive stance.

"You are alone?" he asked.

As far as I know... Marie gestured to the empty room. "I don't see anyone here, do you?"

"Monsieur Bledsoe—" Frederic shook his head, and the little she could see of his neck below his ears turned pink. "I am sorry, Mademoiselle. I did not mean to impugn your reputation."

Marie wanted to box his ears but kept her hands balled in her lap. "You implied enough. And if you were truly concerned for my reputation, you wouldn't stand here in my dressing room without a chaperon. And what are you doing here? *Maman* gives everyone Sundays off."

Marie thought she heard the low rumble of laughter. Frederic seemed not to notice.

"Mademoiselle, please believe me, I only have your best interests at heart." The desperate edge to his tone kept her from making the sharp retort that wanted to fly from her tongue.

"Then what do you want? You shouldn't be here."

"But I had to catch you alone, and I remembered from before how you like to be alone in the theatre when you are learning your parts."

Marie allowed a sigh to escape her in a huff. Again, she felt pulled in two different directions—away from her past and toward a true career on the stage.

"Please believe me," Frederic continued, his eyes wide and desperate. "There is something you must know."

She lowered her voice. "I don't know if I'm truly alone."

Now he looked at her like he wasn't sure she had full command of her sanity. "What do you mean? You just said..."

"The walls have ears. Come, let's go outside."

This is insane, going into the alley with him, but he seems serious.

Once outside, she drew her cloak around her and looked at Frederic. "What did you need to tell me?"

"It's about Maestro Bledsoe."

Marie held up a hand. "I know you dislike him because of his apparent interest in me, but I can assure you, there is no understanding or arrangement between us."

Especially not after last night and what he implied.

"*Non*, Mademoiselle, if he were merely a rival for your affections, I would not feel the need to warn you thus."

Remembering Bledsoe's comment and now faced with Frederic's statement made her snap, "Oh? Are my affections worth so little that they can be handed back and forth like a mere trifle?"

Frederic rubbed his temple with the hand that wasn't carrying his violin. "That wasn't what I meant. If I were only competing for your heart, I would have no trouble with him."

"That's not much better." Marie crossed her arms and rubbed them. It really was beastly cold outside, and of course the alley concentrated the wind. She only hoped the uncomfortable conditions kept others from listening to them, and she glanced up to where a gap in the snow on the roof showed nothing watched from there. She almost wished something would dump some snow on Frederic to cool *his* ardor.

"Please listen. Your beauty has me so flustered, I'm not speaking with my customary eloquence."

Marie decided not to interrupt him again, not because of his attempt at charm, but so she could return to the relative warmth of inside. She nodded for him to continue.

"Maestro Bledsoe puts all of us in danger. He has gotten

mixed up in a most dangerous situation. He owes money to some ruthless men, and they will stop at nothing to see him pay or punished."

"Is that all?" The words escaped Marie. *I can't let on that I know Bledsoe's secret. But how does Frederic know?*

"All?" He gripped her arm and put his face so close to hers she had to try not to breathe in the steam he exhaled. "Do you not understand—he doesn't care for the rest of you, not your mother or Professor Bailey or Mademoiselle McTavish or the dark doctor or his friend. He is only concerned with himself. With movement at the front, there is no telling what will happen once regular commerce resumes."

"My mother has the situation well under control."

"Or does she? Please heed my warning, Mademoiselle. Your mother needs to make him leave once the siege lifts and regular transportation resumes, for as long as he is here in the city, you are in danger. *We* are in danger. I should not even be telling you this."

Frederic looked over his shoulder, but Marie didn't see anything.

"I will see you tomorrow. Please, just keep your distance from him. And if anyone asks, you did not hear about his disgrace from me."

"Very well, I didn't."

Which is the truth since I already knew.

He pecked her on the cheek before she could duck and stalked off too quickly for it to be a regular walk but not fast enough for it to be an undignified run. Marie watched him go, and she couldn't help but frown.

What did he mean? And how does he know the maestro's secret?

18

L ouvre, *4 December 1870*

Iris left early to go to the museum in spite of a dull ache at the base of her skull and feeling like she'd drunk too much wine the night before. Which she hadn't, but she recognized she stretched her talents to their limits. If the Louvre was as deserted as it had been on Saturday, it should be truly empty on Sunday, and hopefully she would be able to concentrate enough to finish sorting the potsherds. When she arrived at the Classics storage gallery, she found Firmin waiting for her, and he wasn't alone.

"I believe you remember Inspector Davidson," he said. "He was here last summer after Anctil—"

"Mademoiselle." The inspector tipped his hat with one hand. He held a briefcase in the other.

Firmin cleared his throat and glanced sideways at the inspector. "Have you been involved somehow in another tragedy?"

Bollocks, not now. Not when I need him to think of me as a competent student, not a troublemaker.

"I have not," Iris said and turned to face Davidson. "What is the nature of your visit, Inspector?"

"I have a few questions for you about the murder two days ago in front of the Théâtre Bohème."

Firmin raised both his eyebrows. "I thought so."

"I don't know anything about it," Iris replied as sweetly as she could around the tension in her jaw from trying not to clench her teeth.

"May we borrow an office?" Davidson asked Firmin. "It's beastly cold in here."

As previously, something about the way Davidson spoke made Iris wonder if he might be English, not French, even beyond his very Anglo last name.

"Well, we are trying to conserve coal like everyone else. Surely the Prussians will be driven off by this weather."

"According to the report from the emperor's high command, their supply lines have been harried by your countrymen outside Paris, so they are getting restless. He expects something to happen soon, so be ready."

"So it will either be riots over coal and food or an invasion," Iris said. Both men looked at her like they were surprised she entered the conversation.

Davidson spoke first. "Yes, Mademoiselle. You should be careful not to be out after dark and to not walk unescorted."

Piqued that he hadn't considered her statement, Iris walked ahead of them.

They arrived at Monsieur Firmin's office, and he unlocked it. "I arrived early due to a bit of insomnia and had a fire going earlier. It should still be warm, at least more so than the galleries."

The sight of the old manuscript on Firmin's desk made Iris's fingers itch to touch it, but she contained her excitement.

"I have some business to attend to in the Renaissance

wing," Firmin told them. "If I have not returned by the time you finish, just close the door behind you."

Iris almost protested that it wasn't proper to leave her, a young woman, alone with a young man like Inspector Davidson, but if Firmin left, she would have the opportunity to touch-read the manuscript, so she just nodded.

Davidson poked at the smoldering coals. "This is certainly more comfortable than that gallery. How do you work in there all day? By the way, do you mind if we switch to English? As much as I speak French, I find it exhausting before I've had my morning tea, and I wanted to catch you before you started your work."

"That's fine. How did you know I would be here?"

"I had one of my men follow you yesterday."

Heat bloomed in Iris's cheeks. She hadn't noticed someone following her, but then, she'd also been caught up in her own thoughts.

I really do need to pay more attention.

"That's why I warned you to be careful," he added. "I know you're an intelligent and capable young woman, but scholars tend to be more aware of their internal world than what's going on around them."

Like Edward. Think of Edward, not how much I enjoy how Inspector Davidson speaks to me like an equal, at least when he's not with Firmin.

He smiled and removed his hat. Without the stern expression, he was actually somewhat good-looking in a wholesome English way.

Iris ignored the throb of homesickness and asked, "You had some questions for me?" She drifted nearer the desk, drawn by the manuscript.

"Please, have a seat. This won't take long, but I'd like you to be comfortable. I noticed there were no chairs in the gallery."

And he's considerate. Or maybe he's trying to make me let my guard down.

She sat on one of the chairs in front of the desk. He pulled another one over, and she scooted back to ensure their knees wouldn't touch. This close, she could see his eyes were light brown with a touch of gold, and they looked tired. That more than anything made her soften slightly toward him—they were all worn out with the constant threat of the siege from without and civil unrest within the city. Plus he had to try and maintain order amidst all of it.

Still, what is a young man from London doing on the Paris police force, as an inspector of all things?

"Now about what happened at the theatre." He was all business again. "What do you remember?"

"Nothing, really." She flexed her hands palm-up. "We were in the townhouse and heard a scream outside. Doctor Radcliffe ran out to assist, Mister O'Connell right behind him. Mademoiselle St. Jean left after they did."

"And you didn't follow them?"

"No, I was talking with my—" What was Edward? Certainly not her fiancé. "My friend, Professor Bailey."

"He must be a good friend if you stayed with him rather than run outside to see what happened. Or are screams that commonplace around the Théâtre Bohème?"

"I didn't feel like putting on my cloak and gloves." As soon as the words left her mouth, Iris recognized how stupid she sounded. Or lazy. Either way, not the way to get the inspector to think well of her so he'd leave her alone.

"So let me see if I understand this," he said. "A man dies in front of you last summer, and then another one on the sidewalk in front of the theatre where you're essentially living, and you don't seem to be affected by either."

"You underestimate me, Inspector. Some women don't show their feelings outwardly, at least not as much as others. I was greatly upset by Monsieur Anctil's death. Perhaps I didn't want to relive it, and so I didn't go outside to view the spectacle with the others."

"That presumes you know what the spectacle was. No, you were avoiding it for some reason. What were you doing in the townhouse with Professor Bailey?"

For a moment, Iris thought he implied she and Edward had taken the opportunity to steal some caresses outside of the watchful eyes of others, but he didn't look like a man having lewd thoughts.

"It's none of your business, Inspector."

"Perhaps it is." He placed the suitcase on a chair and drew forth a folder. "I have a copy of your traveling papers issued by the French embassy in England last summer. At first, they seemed unremarkable, but then I noticed the clerk's name who signed them. This is a young man we've been watching closely."

"Why? And how are you watching him from Paris?"

"You're a smart young woman. Surely you've wondered why an Englishman is on the Paris police force." His challenging grin almost made him look boyish, and Iris felt herself smile in response.

"Perhaps."

He laid the folder on the desk away from the ancient manuscript and opened it. "This particular clerk was found to have ties to an American entrepreneur. I believe you've met him, Parnaby Cobb."

"Yes." Iris wasn't going to lie to him. "But isn't it normal for businessmen to have ties in travel offices?"

"Not this particular one. You see, this clerk was in charge of approving papers for Frenchmen in England to travel to the United States, not the continent. He acted outside his jurisdiction, which is unusual, but we wouldn't have caught it if we hadn't been watching him."

Iris felt like Davidson was trying to imply something, but she wasn't getting it. "So why were you watching Cobb?"

"Have you heard of an organization called the Clockwork Guild?"

"That's impossible," Iris blurted out. "He can't be connected with them. They attacked our airship, Cobb's airship."

"But did you actually see the fight, or did you head straight to the escape compartment?"

"I didn't witness the battle, but Johann Bledsoe and Marie St. Jean did, at least some of it." Iris tried to keep her brain from remembering the fall afterward. Her stomach still got a funny floaty feeling when she thought of it.

"I'll get to Mademoiselle St. Jean in a moment. The point is that Parnaby Cobb has suspected ties to the Clockwork Guild, which has been implicated in many tragedies and which may be active in the city undermining the French defense against the Prussians."

"But why? None of this makes sense. They attacked Cobb's ship to get at Maestro Bledsoe." Iris bit her lip. She didn't mean to implicate him, but she had the sense of discovering a larger piece of a complicated fresco or painting whereas she'd only seen a corner of it before.

"Do you know why?"

"Something about a gambling debt. He hasn't spoken much of it. What are you really after, Inspector?"

"I need to know what Cobb sent you on a mission for. You must have found it because the Department of Aetherics at Huntington University got a generous donation from him, and you're able to afford the Ecole Archaeologie."

"Why do you want to know that? I don't see how it's relevant."

Davidson flipped to a page with two photographs. One was of Monsieur Anctil's body. The other was a large man in a cloak lying face-up on the sidewalk.

"Don't you see how you're in danger, Miss McTavish? I refuse to believe your proximity to these two deaths was coincidental."

Iris turned from the bulging, staring eyes of the corpses to the manuscript, which enticed her as a more pleasant diversion.

Not now.

"I suspect from what Professor Bailey did that Cobb was looking for an alternate power source to coal. Did you find one?"

Not really. Iris didn't trust her tongue, so she only shook her head.

A hand on her shoulder made her turn, startled, and she found Davidson's face inches from hers.

"I'm trying to protect you, Miss McTavish. Please believe that. The Guild isn't afraid to kill, and although your friends seem to think them dormant, they're sneakier than you suspect. My advice to you is not to trust anyone with whatever secret you've discovered. But if you do decide to trust me, you know where to find me." He placed the folder back in the briefcase, pressed a card into her hand, put his hat on, and left.

Iris sank into one of the chairs in front of the desk, Davidson's card barely held between her thumb and forefinger.

Cobb working for or with the Clockwork Guild? *Impossible!* Or was it? He did want them to find an alternate power source to coal, which powered steam machines and factories. The devices that had edged the clockworks into near obscurity. And she knew from studying ancient history and espionage that often secret societies' members didn't all know about each other.

Big hairy ox's bollocks. This means he's not as out of the picture as we thought he was.

~

Johann waited for Iris to leave before he exited as well. He needed a long walk in the snow followed by some practice time alone in the theatre to deal with the sexual frustration that had tormented him all night. He preferred to call his unrest that rather than guilt over what he'd said and the knowledge that Marie's parting shot—that he needed to change, all of him—had hit home.

But what if he didn't want to? What if he liked how he was? He'd gotten that message enough from his father and brothers, that he wasn't good enough because he didn't value the same things they did.

Consequently, when a rag picker approached Johann and tugged on his coat, he almost snapped at the girl. He caught himself and instead gave her a franc so she could at least get something to eat. She curtsied and handed him a note before melting away into the sparse crowd in front of the theatre.

Why are all these people here?

Johann looked around and saw several people pointing to a plume of smoke to the east.

"What is it?" he asked a man nearby.

"There was an explosion, Monsieur. We are not sure what it means. Perhaps they are fighting?"

"Well, it is a battlefront." *And Davidson said to be alert for signs of...something.*

"*Oui*, and we are wondering should we defend ourselves? The army has stored munitions in the church. Perhaps we should help ourselves to them, for we cannot count on the soldiers to protect our families. You are young and strong—come help us!"

Indeed, several of the men were now arguing and gesturing to the church. Johann was almost relieved to see Inspector Davidson's carriage roll up. The inspector stepped out and held his hands up, immediately taking control of the crowd.

"There is nothing to worry about," he said. "The French

army has made a decisive strike against the Prussians and seem to be pushing them back. Go back to your homes and wait for word on progress."

Another vehicle, this time a steamcoach, rolled up, and several national guardsmen exited and took positions around the church. The crowd grumbled but dispersed.

"As for you, Maestro, you should probably stay in the theatre or townhouse. Or..." Davidson plucked the note from Johann's fingers. "Or you should perhaps go visit Madame Cinsault, as she requests."

Johann took the note back. "Hasn't anyone told you it's impolite to read someone else's mail?"

Davidson grinned. "Come, I'll give you a ride. The city is tense, and a man walking along with something as valuable as your violin is at risk."

Dammit, he had a point. "Very well."

They climbed into the carriage, which moved after Davidson tapped on the ceiling. "Of course I count on you to pass along any information Madame gives you," Davidson said, now in English with a perfect upper-class accent. "As a show of our good faith in each other, of course."

"I'll pass along anything useful," Johann replied. "Although I suspect you're investigating more than the murder."

"I'll determine what's useful, and yes. You can ask Miss McTavish and Mademoiselle St. Jean, but you will find that our purposes are much more in alignment than you realize."

"How so?"

Davidson patted the briefcase on the bench next to him. "For example, I know you are several thousand pounds in debt to the Clockwork Guild, and you are currently trying—and failing—to hide from their agents."

"Are you one of them?" Johann asked. He steeled himself. *This is it, the end. He's going to finish me. And what if Cinsault was murdered because of his resemblance to me?*

"No, quite the contrary. I've been tasked with investigating them and other secret organizations that have global reach."

Johann deflated at the words *global reach*. "Meaning I can't ever escape them, so I may as well cooperate with you."

The inspector smiled with a cat's grin. "Precisely. I had my eye on Monsieur Cinsault even before his untimely death, although I'm not sure which society he was involved with. I need you to gain access to his papers. Madame allowed me to look around his study, but I couldn't do so thoroughly with the butler watching me as closely as he did, and I still lack a warrant. The judges are tied up with looting crimes."

Johann also suspected that the English-born inspector might have trouble getting the judge's ear, but he didn't say anything. The smoke in the sky appeared farther away in spite of them moving east.

"That's a good sign," Johann said.

"Possibly. The Prussians aren't going to be beaten so easily, I fear. Stay alert for word of a counterattack and panic in the streets."

"Right. You sound hopeful about the possibility. Has the hunt for secret organizations not been exciting enough for you?" Johann bit his tongue, but too late. He couldn't help but tweak Davidson, especially now that he knew what the man was—a spy.

Davidson gave him a look of pure English condescension. "I'm ready for this stalemate to be over, as I'm sure you are. Although if you want to make your move on Mademoiselle St. Jean, you had best get to it."

"What do you mean by that? Surely you don't have designs on her."

"She would likely not be pleased at your phrasing. But no, I don't. She has been getting a lot of attention lately. Haven't you noticed the ravens?"

"Of course."

"We've observed that they tend to follow only two of you around—you and her."

They pulled up to the gate in front of the Cinsault estate. Johann looked around at the large houses with their walls that were more for show than actual function. Or were they? "You'll wait here?"

"For as long as I can. Try not to delay any more than you have to, but be thorough."

Johann shook his head at the contradictory instructions but shook the inspector's hand. "I appreciate any help you can give me with the Guild," he said, although he hated to ask for help getting himself out of a sticky situation.

"And I appreciate your assistance with this investigation."

Johann walked up to the front door, and this time the butler let him right in.

19

M*aison Cinsault, 4 December 1870*
Johann found Madame Cinsault in her husband's study. Unlike the previous week, it was relatively warm with a fire in the grate. Madame stood by one of the windows and barely turned to acknowledge him when he entered.

"Ah, Maestro," she said. "I'm glad you could come."

As a connoisseur of women's voices and tones—mostly so he could know when he was in trouble—Johann picked up that she spoke not with flirtatious intent but with a panicked edge.

"Is something wrong, Madame?"

"Come see." She gestured for him to join her at the window. Once he stood beside her, she traced a shape that had been etched on the outside of the window.

Johann felt the same sort of rush when he stepped on stage and knew his father and brothers were in the audience. In other words, he knew things had just made a drastic turn for the worst. There, beneath Madame's manicured nail, was a square inside a circle, the same symbol that was on the paper Monsieur Anctil gave Iris before he died. She'd later explained to him that it was a Pythagorean symbol showing the merging of the heavenly and earthly realms.

"Have you seen this before?" Johann asked. He glanced toward the door and was glad not to see the butler.

At this point, she cannot trust anyone, but at least we now know which secret society Cinsault was involved with.

"Yes, on some of my husband's letters. He kept those hidden from me, but I knew where he put them. I read them to ensure I knew what he was up to."

"What did they say?"

"They were written in some sort of code. I can find them for you."

She walked to the large desk and bent over, giving him a nice view of her décolletage. He turned back to the window and studied the symbol, which was barely visible against the snow outside.

"When did this appear?"

"Last night." She sounded mildly annoyed, so he turned back to her and gave her the admiring glance she seemed to want.

Johann imagined the fingering for the Symphonie Fantastique overture melody to keep himself calm while she dug around under the desk. They knew less about the neo-Pythagoreans than the Clockwork Guild, and the neo-Pythagoreans seemed more mysterious and ruthless. They had gotten away with murdering poor Anctil, after all.

"It's a well-hidden compartment," she told him. Finally she said, "Aha!" and something clicked.

"These are his secret letters," she said and handed him a bundle of them. "Please take them. I'm frightened."

"Was there something else that made you feel threatened?"

She reached into her décolletage and pulled out a slip of paper. "This."

He read the note, which was in a different handwriting

from what he'd received in the theatre—thank goodness—but it had a certain familiarity.

Know you are being watched. Do not let your guard down for a moment lest you meet a fate worse than Monsieur's.

"This has gone beyond a jealous lover's motives," he said.

She nodded and turned back toward the window. "Whatever Alain was involved with, he was obviously in beyond what he could handle." She clenched a fist. "And he put both our lives and comfort in danger."

Johann had no doubt that if she could resurrect her poor husband and chastise him for what he'd done, she would. Still, he couldn't help but comment, "I think he got the worse end of the deal."

She looked at him with a slight lift to one corner of her mouth. "So you feel he has been sufficiently punished for his actions?"

"I would say being dead is enough."

"Ah, yes, but dead men are unable to regret."

The butler reappeared and with a bow announced a visitor. Johann stepped back from view of the door, but there was nowhere for him to hide.

The Marquis de Monceau strode in and walked directly to Madame, giving her a passionate kiss.

And here's our first suspect. His dark brown hair was pulled back into a simple ribbon, and he wore an outdated velvet coat that would have looked ridiculous on anyone but him.

Johann tried to gather his wits about him—what was he doing here? And why was he kissing her like that? One would think a lover would be more discreet with someone else in the room. Johann hadn't seen the marquis since the previous summer, when Iris had broken one of the marquis's statues after it attacked her and he had then essentially run them out of the city.

The marquis stepped back and looked at her. She gasped

and waved a hand in Johann's direction, but the nobleman didn't seem to notice.

"Ah, Daphne, I am greatly disheartened by your husband's death."

Johann decided to rescue her by clearing his throat and throwing himself from the proverbial crepe pan into the fire. "You certainly don't look disheartened. Or is that how you greet all your female friends?"

The marquis sighed with exaggerated shoulder slump. "You as well? Daphne, you promised me you'd be discreet about us and tell me if you wanted to bring a third party into our games."

"No!" Johann and Madame said at the same time.

"I tried to tell you," the widow said, "but you just came in without giving me the chance. Where is that butler? He should have told you I have company."

"He said you were alone."

"He was trying to make sure you were distracted." Johann dashed to the nearest window and saw the top of the butler's head over the wall. "I suspect he is up to no good, Madame. You should go somewhere safe."

"But where?"

"Come to my townhouse," the marquis said. "It is very secure. You know I do everything to ensure the safety of my treasures." He glared at Johann. "Unless my guests do something destructive to them."

"I had nothing to do with that," Johann said but quickly added, "and I'm sure Mademoiselle McTavish also meant no harm. She said what happened was an accident. But this is irrelevant. You should take Madame and go."

"We will speak further of this," the marquis told him. "I did not know you were in the city. I'd heard rumors, but I knew you would not be able to resist performing, so when I didn't hear of you on stage, I thought they must be false."

"Well, surprise."

The marquis tapped a finger on his lips. "You may make up for the damage, or try to, by giving me and Madame a private concert this afternoon. Would that suit you, Daphne?"

She smiled, and Johann tried not to groan. He hoped the private concert would be of the musical type, but by now he had enough of an idea what the marquis and Madame would be up to.

"I'm afraid I'm in rehearsal for a show," Johann said. "As you said, can't resist the stage forever."

"Ah, but as you know, I can make your life miserable here in the city. This afternoon, my townhouse, at two o'clock. You may go."

Johann tucked the letters into his waistcoat and bowed to Madame. "*A bientot*, then."

The curve of her lips suggested a lizard about to snatch a bug, and he tried not to dash too quickly out of the office. He wished he had some way to tell the detective to apprehend the butler and was relieved to see Davidson talking to the man when he reached the sidewalk.

MARIE WASN'T sure what to do once Frederic left. She knew she needed to learn her lines, but she was reluctant to go into the theatre, where memories piled on top of each other, both courtesy of the ghost and of her own mind. She walked through the alley to the side street and looked along the deserted boulevard, quiet for this time of day, even on a Sunday morning. Typically there would be some traffic—church-goers who hadn't given up their faith like their government had given up on them.

Then it hit her. She had walked outside without looking at the sky.

Marie stalked as quickly as her skirts would allow to the front of the church next door to the theatre. Between its yard and the theatre and townhouse's front gardens, there was space enough to see in either direction, especially since the trees had lost their leaves. The national guardsmen didn't give her any notice beyond approving gazes. There, in the east, was a plume of smoke.

But what does it mean?

She looked around to see if someone, anyone, was outside, but the street remained deserted. The naked trees reached their branches toward each other and quivered in the breeze. A sense of aloneness and exposure descended on her, and she fled to the nearest structure, the church.

The front door had long been barred once the priests left and the military moved in, but Marie knew of a secret door between it and the theatre. At one point, it had been the continuation of a secret passage before the alley had been cut and the portico built. As there wasn't an obvious entrance, there were no guards there. It looked like masons had shored up the entrance with brick, but Marie pressed two of them, and it swung inward with a creak.

Gratified that no one had apparently used the door recently and fearful someone might have heard it, Marie inched it closed to minimize the noise. The slick cool of the church enveloped her, and she closed her eyes to allow them to adjust to the gloom. The room she stood in had formerly been the sacristy and held the scents of dry stone with a lingering smoky and herbal overtone of incense.

Marie opened her eyes when her nose caught the whiff of something more acrid.

That's not incense.

She knew the army was using the church for storage, but she hadn't made the connection until now. She wandered into the nave and saw that where there had formerly been pews, there were stacked boxes of guns and barrels of gunpowder.

Marie put her hand to her stomach at the thought, *This place is a bomb.* She could only imagine what would happen if someone lit a fuse in here—it would take out the church and the theatre and possibly the townhouse. Whereas the possibility was remote if the French held the city, if the Prussians managed to invade, they'd want to seize it. And the French would rather blow up their own city than let the enemy have more weapons.

A hard edge let Marie know that her thoughts had driven her to back into a large crate, and she steadied it. Not that it needed support—she did—and her mind whirled through the possible meanings of the morning's quiet and what they could mean for her own family's safety. Not just hers and Lucille's but also Iris and Edward, Patrick O'Connell and the doctor, and even the detestable Bledsoe who counted her previous kisses against her.

Where is he, anyway?

She hadn't seen him leave that morning, but he wasn't there for breakfast. Neither was Iris.

Oh, God, Iris.

Had she gone to the museum? What if fighting or riots broke out in the street and she was trapped?

Calculation and strategy replaced panic. *First thing, see who's at the townhouse and if anyone has any news.*

With that course decided, she slipped back out of the church, careful to ensure the secret door clicked locked behind her. She walked into the alley and almost into a national guardsman, who looked about her age.

"Best be careful, Mademoiselle," he told her. "The peasants in the area want to get at what's in the church."

"Spiritual solace?" she asked with a bright, innocent smile she'd used often enough it didn't prompt any one role to appear.

He chuckled. "Solace of some kind, that's certain. Best get

home. Things are heating up outside the city, and the emperor wants everyone to be safe."

Or out of the way where they can't see his mistakes. But Marie only nodded and turned toward the servant's entrance of the theatre.

"Wait, Mademoiselle." He took her hand and kissed the back of it. "But if you would like to offer me some comfort, we change shifts at six. I saw you in the alley with the violinist earlier."

Marie snatched her hand back. "You have mistaken me for a different kind of woman, Monsieur."

He held up his hands. "I did not mean to insult you." He rubbed his eyes. "I'm sorry, I'm stupid about this sort of thing."

"Yes, you are." She stalked away before she said anything else to him that could come back against her later and tried to convince herself the cold wind explained the tears that bubbled up from the ashamed place inside her.

A shadow overhead made her glance at the sky and gasp. The airship passed so quickly she wasn't sure if she'd seen it, and it was too high up to hear, but it left behind a vapor trail. She lifted her skirts and ran to the townhouse.

Once Davidson left, Iris turned to the manuscript on Monsieur Firmin's desk. It continued to push at her, and she held back to prepare her mind for whatever it might assault her with. She typically had to reach with her mind to penetrate the fog of thoughts around an object, not defend against the sensations. She tried to push away the memories of the first time an object had been so insistent. The poison holder that contained the last note her father wrote to her had called to her like that, but with more frightening insistence. She later came to find it was from the danger she was in.

No time to dwell on useless memories. I have to concentrate on what I'm doing now, not that I won't be having Christmas in the house in Huntington Village with Father and Cook and Sophie, that traitor. All right, maybe I won't miss her that much.

The betrayal of her beloved maid, who had served Iris's mother since childhood and then assisted with Iris's care, still stung. She'd seen Sophie at Jeremy Scott's funeral, all traces of affection erased from her beautiful face when Iris told her she had a maid of sorts and had learned to do for herself, and no, she didn't want Sophie to come to Paris with her. Rejecting her had felt like a victory at the time, but now emptiness replaced vindication. Iris was in a place that could soon turn into a war zone. Sophie was safe in England with her husband.

Iris sat and buried her face in her hands. *What am I doing here? Am I here because I want to be or because I can't go home? Sometimes dreams don't come true the way you want or expect them to.*

She wiped her eyes with the heels of her hands and sniffled the last of her sorrow away. Whatever her feelings, she had a job to do, and she felt that there was some sort of significance to the manuscript on Monsieur Firmin's desk. Whatever her emotional outburst meant, it was good she'd at least had the space for it here. She never knew when she might be interrupted at the townhouse, and it was typically never by who she wanted to disturb her. Perhaps Edward would be more accessible now that he'd solved the aether light problem, and she'd help him get to the next step however she could.

Iris locked the door and removed her gloves. One of the coals in the fireplace shifted. The crunch, hiss and shower of sparks made her jump, but she was determined to proceed no matter how spooked she felt. With a deep breath, she sat and filled and emptied her lungs a few times. She inhaled focus to her fingertips and mentally placed barriers on the exhale, trying to find the balance she needed to best approach actually touching the manuscript.

When she felt as prepared as possible, she closed her eyes and touched the ends of her thumbs, index fingers, and third fingers to the parchment. She had the sensation of spinning, or at least the dizzy feeling that comes after, and for a minute all she could see was smoke. Then she smelled the burning, and her vision cleared to show her a series of fires in a grain storehouse. She clutched the manuscript with both hands and detected a voice in her ear.

"Run, flee now! They mustn't find it. If they do, they'll use the eternal flame for the perverted aims of their gods. At least they are burning the key, the fools."

Hands shoved her, and her feet skidded along water-covered flagstones before finding purchase. Bucket brigades had formed, but one by one they gave up and fell away, following Iris—or whoever she inhabited—out of the building. She held the rolled up parchment to her heart but could still feel its pounding through her thin breastbone and the scroll in her fingers. Now outside, she attempted to clear the after-images from her eyes and found herself in a temple courtyard.

A giant stepped in her way, and Iris recognized the armor of a Varangian guard. From the perspective she looked at him, she guessed she was small, child-sized. But why would such an important document be entrusted to a child?

"What do you have there, little one?" the guard said and held out a hand the size of a ham hock.

Iris ducked around his arm, but he caught her by the hair. A vigorous shake of her head left him with a chunk of it and her free but with blood running down her neck. She ran and ran until her lungs and heart felt like one organ desperate for air and tight with terror that they wouldn't get enough. Her eyes stung, and the insides of her nose and mouth had a bitter taste that drove her to crave water, but she dared not stop. No one detained her, although crowds gathered at corners or wherever they could see the flames and then the glow of the temple.

Finally, in an area with narrow streets the perfect size for her and the rats, she slowed and made her way to a house just below the city gates.

An older woman opened the door and pulled the child in. "I heard your footsteps. What is happening?"

"The temple is burning. They set fire to the granary." They moved to sit at a table, but the child wouldn't release the scroll even when the woman reached for it. Giving it up would mean letting go of the life she'd known to that point, which although it was harsh, was at least familiar. Iris couldn't blame her.

The older woman shook her head and sucked her teeth, or at least the few she had left. Iris knew that was a sign of disrespect toward whoever would commit such sacrilege, but her eyes were drawn to an almost faded tattoo on the woman's wrist rather than her interesting face. The symbol was a square inside a circle, and her heart resumed its hummingbird thrumming. Her modern aware self noted it, that it was a Pythagorean symbol. She waited for the woman to speak, to give her further instructions.

"They are getting desperate," she finally said and opened her hands.

"But why are the granary records so important?" Iris asked. She cheered the child on, happy that the trauma of the fire hadn't dampened her curiosity and had increased her caution. "Especially with the grain burned and the temple next to go."

"Because they are more than they seem, little one. The scholars are very close to finding what they seek, and the emperor knows. He wants to snatch it away before they can use it against them to make a fire that will not burn out."

"There is no such thing." The child's certainty came through with a sense of wonder. Could the scrolls with the long lists of numbers really give a clue to such things?

"Not yet, there isn't. And when there is, Constantinople will be the first to burn." Now her teeth showed their rot when she cackled.

Iris backed away. She didn't want Constantinople to burn—she had family there. That was where she'd lived before the priests had come and snatched her up to become a page destined to be a temple concubine. She wasn't sure what a concubine was, exactly, only that they ate better food than the priests, slept late and ordered the pages around.

The woman lunged for her, but Iris slipped away easier than she had from the guard and ran outside. She was soon lost in the maze of streets.

Iris lifted her fingers from the pages, which she now knew had once been a scroll, and opened her eyes. It took her a moment to recognize her surroundings, but Monsieur Firmin's voice jolted her back to the present.

"I knew your father, Mademoiselle McTavish. He had a very unusual talent, and I suspect you do as well."

20

héâtre *Bohème, 4 December 1870*

"It's getting stuck somewhere around here," Patrick O'Connell said.

Edward looked up from the main console. "Let me see." He wiped his hands on the rag he kept nearby, not because he'd soiled his hands, but due to needing to feel like he didn't have any oily residue on his fingers. Even the smallest amount could interfere with the flow of aether through the various chambers. It was yet one more fascinating thing about the substance, but he felt no closer to figuring out how to turn it to a power source, which had been their original mission.

He walked to where O'Connell stood and mentally mapped out the connections between the central console, which looked like the top part of an organ with its various stops plus levers and dials, and the place where the flow of the aether gas had stopped.

"It looks like it's clear, but it won't pass through." O'Connell pressed his lips in a tight line, and his eyes were red-rimmed. Of all of them, he seemed most affected by being stuck in Paris. Strangely, being vigilant to the Irishman's moods made Edward less conscious of his own doubts, which plagued him at night especially.

Edward put a jeweler's scope to his eye and bent to the glass tube that carried the gas. He could barely see into the brass fitting, which was at a corner, but it did look as though there was ample space for it to pass through.

"Is the hydrogen passing?"

"Aye."

Edward stepped back and surveyed the area. One of the things he loved and hated about aether was how unpredictable it could be. Working with O'Connell had given him a new respect for the nuts-and-bolts of producing and directing the substance as well as the equipment they used and the need to look at the whole picture. If he'd done that in Rome, stepped back to look at the whole situation before he acted...

He pressed his hand to the wall to force himself to stay in the present and felt a slight vibration.

"The orchestra isn't rehearsing, but something is causing this. Perhaps the vibration of life in the city?" he mused. "And there's something about the vibrations, particularly how they're moving through this corner. Do we have any buffering material for the joint?"

O'Connell handed him a plug of putty, which Edward molded between the brass joint and the wall.

"That seems to have done it." O'Connell shook his head and rubbed his eyes. "That's the strangest stuff I've ever dealt with, Professor."

"It definitely has its quirks. How far does it go now? This might be the key to having it spread throughout the theatre system. I wish the siege would lift so we could get the rubber tubing. The glass and brass are too sensitive to outside noise."

They worked methodically to find areas that needed buffering. When the vibration in the walls ceased, they had to as well.

"How far did we get?" Edward asked. There seemed to be

miles and miles of tubing. Some of it had been replaced with rubber, but not nearly enough.

"About a fifth of the way, I estimate." O'Connell's jaw cracked with a large yawn.

"What have you been doing?" Edward asked. "At night, I mean."

O'Connell gave him a measuring look. "I'm doing my part to supplement our income so Madame doesn't have to cover all our expenses while we get this set up. Don't worry about the tubing, I've got some coming."

Edward almost asked, "But how?" Some of O'Connell's absences clicked into place. "You're helping the privateers, the ones with the airships."

O'Connell grinned. "A brawny lad like me can always get work unloading, especially since I know how to work quickly, and making emergency repairs."

"So that's why you're always so tired." Edward paused. "And how you're getting first crack at the beer and liquor. That's brilliant." He didn't drink alcohol, well, not much, but he appreciated the benefits for those who did, as long as they didn't go overboard. And with supplies running low, every sip was appreciated.

"We do what we need to survive." This time O'Connell caught Edward's eye and held his gaze. "Even if sometimes we go farther than we mean to."

Edward looked down at the eyepiece he turned over in his hands, and his stomach made turns that echoed the motion of the instrument. "I don't want to talk about what happened in Rome."

"You need to talk to Chadwick about it. You need to know what your brain is trying to do to deal with it. Besides throwing you off."

The eyepiece dropped from Edward's trembling fingers, and he caught it with his shoe to keep the lenses from shattering. It rolled into a corner, and O'Connell picked it up before Edward could reach for it. Edward knelt on the floor, his skin tingling with the memory of the aether burns, which had somehow been healed in that moment through Iris's intervention. He'd never believed in any deities, but he knew they exacted a price. Perhaps he was paying his.

"Is it my brain or Fate trying to punish me for what I caused to happen, what I did to another man?"

"At least you didn't call him innocent. You saw the bruises on Iris's arm—he wasn't going to be gentle with her."

O'Connell helped Edward to stand.

"Haven't you done anything you regret, that you'll regret forever?" Edward asked.

"Aye. But you can't dwell on it. We do what we need to do and then move on. Iris loves you. Focus on her." Patrick gestured to the console and the tubing. "And what you're doing for the theatre."

Edward nodded, but doubt still sat like a heavy fog in his middle. It seemed that everyone was doing something useful but him, even if he was trying to help with the theatre's lighting.

No, he was selfishly experimenting while the others contributed to lessening the burden on Madame St. Jean, who had taken them all in.

He knew his true self now, that he was a ruthless charlatan undeserving of love. When he had converted the theatre system and had taken the next step toward converting aether to energy, he would do them all a favor and step off the stage.

Permanently.

Johann approached Davidson and the Cinsault butler. When

the man saw Johann, he tried to run, but Davidson thought quickly and tripped him.

"I won't say anything, I won't," he mumbled and looked around him as though there were spy devices on the ground. Davidson reached down to haul him to his feet, but he shuddered and lay still, his mouth foaming.

"*Merde,*" Davidson said and rolled the man over. "He must have had a poison capsule in his mouth."

Part of the butler's wrist showed between his sleeve and glove, and the inspector frowned. He knelt and separated the two items of clothing, revealing a tattoo of a square inside a circle.

"The sign of the neo-Pythagoreans," Johann said. "There was one on the office window too, and a threat toward Madame Cinsault."

"What did Madame say to you? Did she give you anything?"

Before Johann could answer, a steamcart driven by a gendarme rolled up, and two more got out from inside.

"You're needed at the station, Inspector," the tallest one said. "Do we need to arrest this man?" He looked Johann up and down like he was a suspicious person.

And perhaps I am, considering I stand here with a dead man at my feet.

"No, but your timing is fortuitous. You're needed here. This poor gentleman should be taken to the morgue, and I have to talk to the maestro. I will take him back to the Théâtre Bohème and then return to headquarters."

The gendarme tipped his hat, and Davidson and Johann climbed into his carriage.

"What did the butler say to you?" Johann asked. "I'm guessing he wasn't asking for the time."

"No, he was telling me to watch out for you because you had stolen something from Madame Cinsault." Davidson held out a hand.

Johann handed over the letters. "Here. If they're going to get people killed, I don't want to have anything to do with them."

Davidson took them and flipped through, looking at the return addresses. With each one that passed, his left eyebrow crawled higher on his forehead. "I know these names, all prominent merchants."

"It wouldn't be the first time rich men have gotten entangled in a cult."

"And it appears Cinsault was the ringleader. I will need to study these more carefully, and I'll let you know if I need anything further from you."

So you use me and then you cut me out? I don't think so.

"Now wait a minute. That's not why I agreed to cooperate with you." Johann reached to snatch the letters back, but Davidson moved too quickly, and all Johann could grab was one. He put it in his overcoat pocket.

"Return that immediately. You agreed to cooperate with me for protection from the Clockwork Guild."

"And for information to protect my friends. Give me the rest of the letters."

"Now Maestro Bledsoe, be reasonable. This is a police investigation. You need to cooperate with it even if we do find your friends are involved somehow."

"Only if you promise not to do anything to Lucille St. Jean or her daughter, regardless of what you find."

Now both Davidson's eyebrows made a run for his hairline. "If they are in any way culpable for the crimes around the theatre, I cannot promise their immunity."

"My friends are not involved. I promise you that. In fact, they're in danger. You probably have a report somewhere showing the theatre was vandalized."

"I've heard no such thing. Your Madame St. Jean involves us as little as possible. She must have friends in high places for the Théâtre Bohème to not be used as a hospital as the others are."

"Regardless, you keep me apprised of the investigation, and I'll give you the letter."

"What if that is the one with the clue that will solve the case?"

Johann crossed his arms. "You'll have to look at the others first."

"Fine." Davidson sat back with a huff. "You're incorrigible. If there's another murder because of your antics and the delay they're causing, I will prosecute you as well as the one who wields the knife."

"Go ahead." The carriage slowed. "Oh, and if the Clockwork Guild has anything to do with this, I count on you letting me know."

"I will return later for the letter, and I will have a warrant for its seizure."

The carriage stopped in front of the theatre, and Johann climbed out. He'd barely set foot on the ground when the door slammed behind him, and the carriage huffed away. Johann patted his pocket.

"Now let's see what you're going to tell us before the good inspector returns for you."

A motion in the sky made him look up, and he saw an airship floating high above the city.

What in the...? I thought those were only flying at night.

He walked into the townhouse and straight into Marie. He held her to keep her from falling and felt a jolt to his core.

MARIE RAN through the kitchen and into the front hall, where she smacked into something that was both hard and soft. Hands on her waist steadied her.

"Easy now."

Damn. It was Maestro Bledsoe. She stepped back, but he didn't release her.

Relief at seeing him safe collided with the memory that she was still angry with him and made the questions spill out of her. "What are you doing here? Where have you been? Did you see the airship? What does it mean?"

She took a breath to ask him something else, and he effectively shut her up by drawing her in and fastening his mouth on hers. She closed her eyes and melted into his embrace. His tongue met hers, and her anxieties ran out of her, leaving her clinging to him for support. He broke the kiss first but didn't let her go.

"Now, one at a time. Yes, I saw the airship. I don't know what it means, but I have on good authority the French are pushing the Prussians back, and we should be prepared for anything in case they rally. Perhaps it was doing reconnaissance?"

Marie half-heard what he said and half-processed the kiss. Her mind flipped through the roles she could/should be playing at the moment, but panic over seeing the airship and knowing what was happening overwhelmed her. Yes, she wanted the siege to end, but after having seen what was in the church...

"Hey," Johann said and tilted her chin up so her gaze met his. "What's wrong?"

"The church next door, it's full of—"

"Guns and gunpowder. Yes, I know. So do the people in the neighborhood. That's why it's being guarded."

"One careless mistake and the theatre and we could be destroyed."

He gave her a searching look. "I've been around Edward enough to know when someone's using anxiety over one thing to cover up another. What are you really afraid of, Marie?"

Her mouth dropped open, and she stepped completely away from him. "How dare you? I've already told you. Do you think I'm lying?"

"No, I think you're afraid to admit something."

"And why should I trust you?" She drew her cloak around her to make up for the warmth lost when she moved away from him. Part of her wanted to confide in him—artist to artist, of course—but the ghost's admonishments and Frederic's warnings played in her head.

It's too big a risk.

"I've learned from my mistakes," he said, his expression serious. "Please believe me when I tell you that I'm trying to help you because I..." He trailed off, his gaze focused behind her.

Marie turned to see her mother standing on the landing.

"Madame," he said.

Lucille inclined her head. "Please excuse us, Monsieur. I need to talk to my daughter."

21

---

ouvre, 4 December 1870

Louvre, 4 December 1870
        Iris snatched her hand back from the manuscript, and her mind tripped over possible explanations for what she was doing. Monsieur Firmin's expression had never held warmth, but now he studied her with feral curiosity like she was an exotic object worthy of study.

"How long have you been there?" she asked and recognized how guilty the question made her sound.

"Long enough. I've only seen one other person approach objects like you do. I watched you yesterday with the potsherds. You have talent and a good understanding of how to categorize them. You approached the examination and sorting with excellent logic, but you were particularly fascinating when you got stuck."

Iris clasped her hands in front of her and willed her expression to stay neutral. "I didn't see you watching me, Monsieur." She kept her gaze on him but attended to the path to the door in her peripheral vision.

"There is a storeroom on the second floor with a window

that opens on to the gallery you were in. I would be a poor professor if I did not keep an eye on my students, wouldn't I?"

He moved to block the door, and she knew she couldn't get out from behind the desk and make it to the door before he did.

"Tell me what the manuscript told you, Mademoiselle."

"What are you going to do to me?"

Firmin held his hands in front of him, palms up. "I am unarmed, as you can see. I only require your assistance with some objects that have been giving me particular trouble."

There was something in his demeanor she didn't trust, and she recalled their previous conversation about female archaeologists. Now his words took on a different meaning—had the desire to get away from Firmin driven the women into the arms of other men?

"You will merely be ensuring you obtain your degree. Credit will go to the school, as it should."

"You mean it will go to you."

"You are a student still, Mademoiselle. There will be time for you to get credit for your discoveries later, provided you can demonstrate you made them." His smile held a sordid glee.

"And how would I do that?" Iris saw her future spooling out. She knew he would come up with some way to keep her under his influence so he could continue to use her unique talent for his own benefit.

"Well, you do need access to sites and materials. I have a wide network of colleagues who could help you."

"Or hinder me."

He shrugged and gestured to the manuscript. "The choice is yours, starting with now. What did the manuscript tell you? I have been poring over the numbers, and they simply do not make sense for what it supposedly is."

"It was stolen from a burning temple. I didn't get much further other than to see how it was lost."

"But what do the numbers mean?" He leaned over the desk and towered over her.

"I can't say."

"Can't or won't?"

Iris pressed her lips together.

"If you do not cooperate, Mademoiselle, I cannot guarantee your being able to continue the program."

Whereas Iris was sure he exaggerated his influence previously, now she knew he made a real threat. Plus she needed access to it to get the information to Edward.

"I will tell you if you will translate it for me," she said.

"Very well."

"It's apparently some sort of esoteric formula for a fire that will not burn out."

"Apollo's flame," he said. "Supposedly derived from a certain mythical element the Pythagoreans believed in. The manuscript was discovered in Alexandria, but we suspect it originated in the temple of Apollo Smintheus."

Iris saw herself and Firmin engaged in an interesting dance and reminded herself that he didn't know they'd found the Eros Element or were experimenting with it.

"What is it?" she asked. "Or them."

Now he snapped into lecture mode. "The Eros Element is a mythical power source, and Apollo's Flame is its expression. These numbers might hide the notations a scientist of old made when doing his or her experiments. They would have been illegal in that region at that time. But I cannot translate them for you, Mademoiselle, for I lack the key to whatever the code is."

"Oh." Iris couldn't hide her disappointment.

"I'm going to do something I rarely do. Since we are in a siege situation and the museum may be looted in spite of my best efforts, I am going to allow you to take the manuscript with you so you can practice the translation. Perhaps your young mind can decipher what mine is missing."

"Oh!"

He stood behind the desk, gently picked up one end of the scroll, rolled it up and placed it in a leather satchel, which he handed to her along with a book he plucked from the shelf. She slung the strap over one shoulder and clutched the book to her chest.

"I don't have to tell you to be extremely careful with this."

"I will," she said, hardly daring to breathe as though any unnecessary motion would cause the manuscript to crumble.

"Now go and find somewhere safe. I will stay here at the museum and do my best to guard its treasures."

A chill crawled along Iris's spine. "Is the fighting that bad, then?"

"Not yet, but the situation is volatile in the city. I'll send you home in the museum's carriage."

"Thank you." Iris moved toward the door.

"Oh, and Mademoiselle?"

"Yes?"

"If you're right about what the manuscript contains, it could be a great boon for science and for France, perhaps even lead to a weapon that will end this siege. Remember this is where you had the opportunity to hone your archaeological skills, not England."

Iris nodded and forced her lips to lift in what she hoped was a convincing smile. She felt like a favored pet, not a respected scientist, and she knew whatever she discovered would help make Firmin's career, not hers. Still, she would play along to help Edward with his quest. He didn't have any such demand for divided loyalty.

No, sadly science is his first love, above Mother England or me. I will not be jealous of it. But what will this mean for England? I don't trust that the French government, whether it's the emperor or someone else, won't turn this against my own country and people.

She exited the museum with a heavy heart because she knew she'd never be able to return.

MARIE FOLLOWED Lucille to her office in the townhouse, which had once been the main housekeeper's before Lucille had decided all she needed was a maid and cook, and she could just as easily keep an eye on two people herself. Lucille sat behind the large desk and motioned for Marie to sit in one of the chairs in front of it. She looked around. As per usual, everything was in meticulous order.

If only life could be ordered like one's office. God knows I've tried.

"It has come to my attention that you've been using some sort of substance to smother your talent," Lucille said and fixed Marie with her black gaze.

Marie raised her eyebrows, neither confirming the accusation nor lying about it. *She's talking to me like a manager, not like a mother.*

"I should have put the signs together sooner, but I was preoccupied with the different challenges inherent in this upcoming performance, particularly at this time."

Marie allowed a snort to escape. "The city could be under attack and you're worried about how I'm managing my acting ability? Aren't there more important things to worry about, like the store of arms in the church next door that could blow us all to bits if the wrong people get hold of it?"

Lucille narrowed her eyes. "This is a matter of equal gravity. Do you know what will happen if you smother your talent, kill it completely?"

Is that possible? She found herself simultaneously horrified and thrilled at the thought.

"I know what will happen if I don't." The memory of Bledsoe's kiss pushed its way into her mind, distracting her. Had he kissed her or the idealized woman? She hadn't felt like she played a role, and she had had a dose of whatever was in the ghost's smoke that morning. Could he have kissed her, Marie, and not who he thought she was?

Her mother's words pulled her back to the matter at hand.

"You are afraid you lose part of yourself with every role. You fear you will never discover who you truly are."

When faced with a direct question, Marie had to tell the truth. Plus this was no time for lies, not with the possibility that this could be their last conversation. "Yes, precisely."

"Has it ever occurred to you, *cherie*, that this problem does not come from your talent, but from some other issue deep inside you?"

This time Marie didn't have an answer, either stated or thought. After a minute, she asked, "Are you saying there's something seriously wrong with me?"

"*Non*, I am saying that the answers you seek are not so far from you, and running away will only make it harder to find them, as will trying to deny something that is an integral part of you."

Marie leaned forward. "Then tell me how to control it, how to keep the roles from taking over."

Lucille took one of her hands. "It is something you can only find out for yourself, for it is different for everyone. But you must be careful of those who offer you easy answers. You will find that there is no such thing as easy, and the price is too great."

"You speak in riddles." Marie slumped back. "Answer me one question, then. Who is the man in the metal mask who lurks behind the mirror in my dressing room?"

Lucille's face went from olive to ashen. "I was afraid he had returned, but I hoped I was wrong."

"That's not an answer." But the expression on Lucille's face and her coloring made Marie think to when the last time she'd seen Doctor Radcliffe was and how quickly she could fetch him if her mother was to collapse.

"He once offered me an easy solution to a very difficult problem, and I was fool enough to take it. I don't know exactly who he is, but he is likely trying to harm you to get to me. You need to not have anything more to do with him, Marie."

"Tell me how to get to the passage behind the dressing room, then. Let me discover where his lair is and flush him out."

"I will take care of him." Lucille stood. "I forbid you to have anything to do with him. Focus on Maestro Bledsoe—he is accustomed to being one thing and acting another. Ask how he manages it."

A knock on the door forestalled anything else she was going to say. A little boy with wide eyes and curly dark hair handed her a note. He looked familiar.

"I told him never to contact me here," Lucille murmured.

"He said it's important, Madame."

Lucille dashed out of the office, leaving Marie sitting bewildered in her chair. So her suspicions were correct—Lucille did know the theatre spirit. But how? Was he helping Marie so he could get at Lucille?

Dammit, why are there always more questions than answers? And what did she mean about Maestro Bledsoe?

The identity of the boy struck her—she'd seen him in Zokar's cave. With the questions whirring around in her head like clockwork butterflies, Marie rushed into the corridor, but the child and Lucille had disappeared.

WHEN CHADWICK LOCKED up his clinic to return to the townhouse for lunch, he noticed the streets were strangely quiet and looked up at the sky, where he saw the vapor trail of an airship overhead. It was of course too high up to see if it had any identifying colors or markings to say whether it was French or Prussian, but it did point his gaze to a plume of smoke on the horizon to the east.

That explains why no one has come in today. He'd risen early and slipped away while it was still dark, preferring to worship at the altar of science than that of a god who had taken everything from him. Although it shocked a lot of his clientele, he was open on Sunday to accommodate those who had to work the other six days.

He arrived back at the townhouse in time to see Iris McTavish alight from a carriage. She had a satchel at her hip, its strap across her chest, and clutched a textbook to her chest. She, too, glanced up at the sky and squinted, then caught sight of him when she looked straight.

"Ah, Doctor Radcliffe, a word?"

He nodded but didn't say anything. Something about her reminded him of Claire, and it caught him off-guard in moments like these, rendering him speechless and breathless with grief until he could recover control over himself. He hadn't been able to put a finger on what, precisely, about her made him react like this. Perhaps it was her curiosity mixed with kindness and passion to make the world a better place. That was where the resemblance ended, and he thankfully wasn't attracted to Iris like he'd been to Claire. One shattered heart was enough for a lifetime.

He'd heard Claire was studying analysis in Austria after having been treated in Vienna, but he didn't know when or if she would be mentally whole enough to see him.

Iris didn't seem to notice his reticence. "I was wondering if I could borrow your knowledge of ancient languages," she said.

"Monsieur Firmin has perhaps given me the next piece to our puzzle as to how to harness the power of the E.E."

She grinned like a proud student, but a shadow flickered through her dark blue eyes.

"And what kind of pressure did he put on you?" Chadwick forced himself to keep his demeanor relaxed in spite of the protective urge she prompted.

"You're a reasonable man, so I can say this to you." She paused before ascending the front steps. "He hopes it will end up being a weapon to help the French against the Prussians, but I doubt they will stop there."

Now the twist of panic in Chadwick's gut was for a different reason. "And they could pass it along to the Confederates, giving them the advantage in the war in the States."

"I'm sorry," Iris said and put a hand on his arm. "Of course. Your family and people are in more immediate danger than mine."

"That's all right." He patted her hand and escorted her up the stairs. "It's easy to forget about other wars when you're in the middle of a battlefield. Can you delay your work? Keep the knowledge out of Firmin's hands?"

She wouldn't meet his eyes. "There are reasons—very good ones—he thinks I can solve this riddle before anyone else can."

"Like what?"

She stepped aside so he could open the door for her. "It's too hard to explain, especially to a man of science."

With that cryptic remark, she rushed upstairs toward her and Marie's room, but Madame St. Jean stopped her on the landing.

"There is fighting, and we do not know if shelling will start. Grab what you need, and we will go to the theatre so we can escape underground if need be."

22

Théâtre Bohème, 4 December 1870

Weighed down by his and Edward's valises, Johann almost tripped over the messenger in the livery of the Marquis de Monceau, who waited for him in front of the theatre.

"The marquis said to remind you of your appointment with him at two."

"Are you insane?" Johann asked. "There's fighting and fear of shelling. You should be somewhere safe."

The man bowed and handed him a message. "The marquis says he still expects you to play for him this afternoon. He has sent me to guide you."

"Please give him my regrets, but surely he understands the situation has changed."

"He said not to take no for an answer and that Madame has something further to tell you."

Johann cursed under his breath. *It's not like we're completely safe in the theatre. A well-placed mortar could bring it down upon our heads even if we're underground, and there is the question of the explosives in the church next door.*

"Very well. Let me deliver these, and I will come with you."

He found Edward and Patrick O'Connell under the stage.

"I grabbed some of your things from the atelier," he told Edward. "And Doctor Radcliffe packed a bag for you as well, O'Connell."

"What's going on?" Patrick asked.

Johann heard him, but the haunted look on Edward's face delayed his answer. He knew it was pointless to ask if Edward was all right—he never admitted to fatigue when he was in the middle of a project—so he asked, "How far have the two of you gotten?"

"We're about halfway there," Edward said and rubbed his sleeve across his eyes, leaving a smudge across his temple.

"I keep telling him he needs to rest, but he won't stop." The Irishman sounded both admiring and annoyed. "What brings you down here with luggage? Does Madame expect us to move in until the lighting system is completed?"

"Oh, right." Johann turned to face O'Connell, who looked as exhausted as Edward, perhaps more so. "The French are mounting an offensive, and there's fear of shelling from the Prussians in reprisal."

"Well, at least something's happening," O'Connell grumbled.

Johann bit back his retort. He only wanted to deliver the items and be on his way.

"Here are Edward's and my bags. Will you bring them to wherever Madame wants us to settle in?"

"Aye. Where are you going?"

"To play for the Marquis de Monceau at his townhouse," Johann said with unconcealed frustration. "Apparently he feels that the Prussians wouldn't dare interrupt his afternoon entertainment with something so rude as a shell through his roof, and he could still make a lot of trouble for me once this situation has ended."

Patrick nodded, and Edward only turned back to the tube he was placing some sort of putty around.

"Be careful," Patrick said.

"Right, I'll tell the Prussians to aim elsewhere," Johann told him. He took his leave and ran into Marie in the vestibule. He tried to tip his hat and brush past her, but she stopped him.

"Why is the marquis's man standing outside?" she asked. "Surely you're not going to accompany him."

Johann wanted to kiss her again, but he held back. He'd seen some men slap a hysterical woman, but he preferred his own methods. Plus she wasn't panicked now, only concerned, and it loosened something inside him to think she was worried about his safety.

"I'm afraid I have to. I don't want him making trouble for me or for your or your mother, and you know he will if he doesn't get what he wants."

"Then please be careful." She stood on tiptoe and kissed his cheek. Then she hurried off.

The imprint of her lips warmed his face until he reached the marquis's townhouse, where the impression of the kiss melted off in spite of the warmth inside.

AFTER JOHANN LEFT, Edward turned back to the joint he was buffering, but Patrick's hand on his arm stopped.

"I think we're far enough along to test the footlights, see if they'll give people a rosy glow from below." He grinned, and Edward had the sense he'd said something vaguely dirty.

Speaking of dirty... Edward wiped his hands on a rag that may have been white at one point but now matched the dingy state of his and Patrick's clothing. Contorting into and squeezing through small spaces in the old building certainly made his work more challenging than it had been at the university, but he didn't feel like he could ever return to those pristine halls of his previous life.

"It may be a good opportunity to get the others' minds off the situation, as much as that can happen," Patrick said.

Edward heard the subtext—*and get you out of your head, which you've been ridiculously stuck in all day.*

"Fine. We should probably take a break, anyway."

When they emerged from underneath the stage, Edward carrying his and Johann's bags, they found the others gathered in the theatre along with Maestro Fouré, whom Edward had met briefly the day before.

"And how is the work coming?" Lucille asked as though they weren't in danger of the roof exploding over their heads at any moment. Only the way she twisted her skirt around one fist gave away her state of agitation.

"It's coming," Patrick told her. "We're ready to test the foot-lights if you're interested in watching. Perhaps you and Mademoiselle could stand on stage so we can check the intensity of the lights."

"I'll go downstairs and turn it on," Edward offered. He felt Iris's gaze on him and felt the urge to escape her and her expectations.

"No, I'll go. You stand up here and observe. You're more precise than I am."

Patrick disappeared, leaving Edward with the others. Marie and her mother walked on stage, but Marie looked oddly uncomfortable in spite of being a renowned actress.

"Do you think she's all right?" Iris asked him. Somehow she'd snuck over to stand next to him.

"I suppose so." Edward didn't know what to think.

The theatre was plunged into darkness for a heart-stopping moment, and Iris's hand found his.

"Is this part of the demonstration?" she whispered.

"Yes, it's the only way to get a true measure of the light quality without interference from any other sources."

The foot of the stage took on a glow so slight it was impossible to tell whether it was really there or an after-image.

"Like the moon."

He wasn't sure she said the words, but they brought him back to that horrible morning in Rome. He snatched his hand back.

"What's wrong?" Iris asked.

"Why did you say that?"

"Say what? I only asked if the darkness was part of the demonstration."

The glow increased, and Lucille's and Marie's shapes took form.

"Why did you say the thing about the moon? You know it's going to bring on bad memories."

"I didn't say anything."

He felt her hand on his arm, and he jerked away. "Don't touch me."

The light grew, and with the part of his mind that still took scientific note of what was happening, Edward saw Marie had tears running down her face, and Lucille looked angry. Still, they both looked younger and more attractive in the gentle rose-peach glow of the aether lighting.

"Edward, please, look at me." Iris had tears in her voice.

Edward couldn't look at her now, not when he knew he'd hurt her. It must have been his imagination, the thing about the moon. She wouldn't deliberately do something to distress him. It was his fault—he was the bad person, the one who should have been lying dead under the altar in the temple under the Porta Maggiore in Rome.

The theatre filled with murmurs and snappishness, and the scientist part of Edward's brain took note of that—what was going on? His lungs struggled to pull in the thick air, and he broke away from Iris's seeking reassurance. His panic carried him from the theatre into the lobby, where the windows let in icy light and the air felt less solid. He could breathe again even without the aid of a paper bag and took gulps of air.

It was when he stopped to breathe normally that a single gunshot crackled through the silence and brought it tumbling around him followed by screams that rent the air like shattered glass.

"Useless child, too cowardly to use your gifts or take the marvelous opportunities offered to you. Why did I even bother letting you on this stage?"

The words hissed in Lucille's familiar tones of contempt cut Marie through her middle. Why was her mother speaking to her like this now? She thought they had reached some sort of understanding, or at least that Lucille had spoken her piece, but no, she had to submit Marie to a verbal stabbing as they stood on the stage, in front of everyone but invisible in the dark.

A tingling sensation overtook her, similar to when a role fought to control her, but made of restlessness, like ants crawling under her skin. Then the tears came, unbidden but needed to release the grief, wash away the disappointment she would always have in herself...and that her mother would always have toward her. She'd never get rid of her past mistakes, but at least she could release the pressure around them.

Sometimes.

Marie wiped her eyes and pinpointed the source of the rosy-peach glow that surrounded her as the footlights. The light grew brighter, and whispers floated in the darkness beyond. She drew her eyebrows together like frowning would clarify the words, but she only heard the bickering rhythm.

That's odd. Has something happened?

She glanced toward Lucille, who looked away with a pained expression. Marie left the stage and walked up the side aisle. Now that the glow wasn't in her face, she saw Radcliffe engaged in some sort of discussion with Iris, but there was no sign of Edward. Iris shook her head and rushed up the aisle on the opposite side.

Wasn't Edward supposed to be observing? Where is he? Iris's concern for Edward came through their link.

A pressure at the back of her skull made Marie lift her skirts and trot to meet Iris in the lobby. When she opened the door of the theatre, the noise of a gunshot split her awareness in two. With one side of her mind, she took stock to make sure none of the windows had been pierced and Iris was safe. She and Edward stood away from the windows, which thankfully seemed whole. With that settled, Marguerite the Spy took over so quickly Marie was barely aware of the changes in her.

She stopped, remembering her mother's words that she had more control over the roles than she recognized.

I will give you expression, but you need to let me lead. She imagined herself and Marguerite in a waltz with Marie dressed and leading like a man.

She edged to the nearest window and, careful to stay as much behind the curtains as possible, peeked out. Two national guardsmen knelt by a supine figure on the sidewalk and gestured for the gathering crowd to return to their homes.

It was the violin case beside the injured man that made Marie forget caution and run out the front door of the theatre. She shed Marguerite like a cloak, panic replacing the role.

"Johann?" she cried.

But no, the man had light brown hair, not blond. He lifted his head.

"You must lay back, Monsieur." One of the guards held a rag over a spot on his abdomen.

The ashen color of Frederic's face and stream of blood

flowing from the corner of his mouth told Marie that the guard's attention was futile.

"Do you know this man, Mademoiselle?" the other one asked. His bushy eyebrows tilted in sympathy.

"Yes, he is a friend."

The guard moved aside so Marie could kneel beside Frederic. She took his hand, but he turned his face away.

"You come too late, Marie. I am finished."

"What were you doing out here, you stupid man?" she asked. Relief that it wasn't Bledsoe lying in front of her turned to guilt. Yes, Frederic was annoying, but he didn't deserve to die.

He turned back toward her and took his hand from hers. "I came to ensure you and Madame were safe."

Now the guilt turned to sorrow and choked Marie with its bittersweetness. "You didn't have to do that. We're fine. We can escape underground if we need to."

"I also need to give you this." He reached into his pocket and pressed something into her hand. "Do not look at it now. Just take it."

Marie took the packet of paper with something hard inside and slipped it into the hidden pocket in her skirt. She looked up when a hand squeezed her shoulder, and she saw Iris stood beside her along with the others. Radcliffe ushered the other guard away and examined the wound. He looked at Marie and shook his head.

Marie took Frederic's hand and tried to smile encouragement, but the tightness in her throat muscles wouldn't allow much expression. She'd done this on stage, knelt by a dying lover, but her previous roles retreated from her, leaving her emotionally naked.

One line did float into her mind.

"You'll be fine. Just take a little rest."

Frederic coughed. "This will be more than a little rest, Mademoiselle, and I will be far from fine. Ah, if only you had accepted my proposals." He tried to chuckle, but he grimaced instead. "I see that rake Bledsoe has abandoned you, so I am doubly sorry to leave you."

Marie knew that Bledsoe had a good reason for leaving them, but she felt his absence. Not that there was anything either he or Frederic could do against a Prussian mortar.

"Never mind him. Just tell me who did this to you."

He coughed again, and more blood oozed from his mouth. "I did not see them, and the street was deserted."

Marie looked up. Radcliffe spoke to the two guardsmen a little distance away, so she knew he was already questioning witnesses.

"I will find out who did this, and I will avenge you."

"Do not worry about revenge," he whispered. "For they have only put me out of my greatest misery at you not loving me."

Frederic's eyes fluttered closed, and Marie kissed him on the forehead. He took a last rattling breath and lay still.

A vibration in the air heralded the hum of airship motors. Strong hands pulled Marie away from Frederic. Her mind had gone numb, her body stiff. This couldn't have happened, could it? She would walk off stage now, and everything would be normal.

"Pick her up, Patrick, she's in shock."

Radcliffe's voice—his doctor voice, she called it, when he was taking charge—came to her as though he stood at the back of the theatre. The ground left her feet, and she found warmth and softness to one side, cold and regret on the other. Not that she hadn't loved Frederic—she couldn't force that emotion—but that she hadn't been kinder to him.

Just before they entered the theatre, she looked up and saw three airships flying in formation overhead. They were low enough for her to see they were unmarked.

"Privateers doing reconnaissance," O'Connell muttered.

"For who?" Iris asked.

"For whoever is paying them the most."

Pieces of paper fluttered down from the sky, and Iris grabbed one midair. They entered the warmth of the lobby, but Marie felt cold all over. She glanced up to the little balcony over the box office and saw a glint of light off metal, but then it was gone.

23

arquis de Monceau's Townhouse, 4 Dec 1870

When Johann was shown into the drawing room, he expected to see the Marquis de Monceau and Madame Cinsault in some sort of state of *déshabillé*, but only the marquis met him, and thankfully the nobleman was fully clothed.

"No Madame?" Johann couldn't resist saying.

The marquis poured himself a generous glass of brandy and held up the decanter, his eyebrows asking the question.

"Please," Johann said. He set his violin case by the chaise and joined the marquis at the bar.

"To the emperor. May his bladder stone drag him to hell for getting us into this mess," the marquis said.

Johann clinked his glass to his host's. "And to your health."

"And yours as well."

The brandy slid with surprising smoothness down Johann's throat. "You've gotten into your cellar. I thought you only brought this stuff out for special occasions."

The marquis's shoulders slumped, or they seemed to. Today he wore a coat of purple, and he displayed his signature style of combining the fashion of the previous century with modern conventions. After what Iris had discovered in his chateau, the marquis's odd taste in clothing that straddled centuries made more sense.

"I'm afraid I've gotten word that Daphne might be in more danger, so she is in hiding somewhere safe."

"Not here?"

The marquis only shrugged. "I need to know if I can trust you before I reveal her whereabouts to you."

Previously Johann would have been happy to follow the strange steps of this dance of secrets and revelations, but he wanted to be away and with his friends in the theatre. And Marie, if he were to be honest. He wanted to do something to quell the panic in her eyes.

"I don't care where Madame Cinsault ended up. Her butler is lying in the city morgue, so keeping her hidden seems a prudent course."

"That is sad news but not unexpected. I never trusted the fellow." The marquis gestured for Johann to take a seat in a wingback armchair by the fire and sat in the one beside it. He slumped back and took another gulp.

Johann took the seat that had been indicated for him. "He had an interesting tattoo on his wrist. A square inside a circle. Have you seen the symbol before?"

"You know I have." Now he sounded peevish.

"No, I didn't know. Where?"

"It was marked on the crates that brought my statues to me, the *kouros* including the one Mademoiselle McTavish damaged."

"Ah, right, you mentioned you wanted to talk about that."

The afternoon light coming through the window showed the lines around the marquis's eyes and mouth, particularly when he deepened them with a scowl.

"Things have been happening in my library. It seems that

whatever she did, she started something sinister. That's how I ended up in my townhouse even though it's the dead of winter —I can't stand being there anymore."

An icy drop of anxiety dripped from the back of Johann's skull and down his spine. He remembered Iris and Marie talking about some sort of force in the chateau on their way to the fateful party, but he'd been focused on his performance and had only half-listened.

"What sort of things?" His irreverent side wanted to ask if the strange occurrences had interfered with the marquis's ability to bring ladies in there and have them swoon in his arms when the statues started moving. If so, that would explain why he was so grumpy.

"You know they move, that they were supposedly part of some larger piece. Some of them have started moving singly, and two of them turn their heads."

"While you're looking at them?" Johann tried to remember if the statues had separate pieces for head and body.

"While I'm out of the library, but when I return, their faces are turned toward the door as though they were expecting something. Maybe me." He drained his glass. "And then at night, when I walk by the door, I hear whispers. You probably think I'm insane."

"No..." Johann had seen stranger. "But I do wonder how you think Miss McTavish could have possibly started all of it."

"What was she looking for? Really looking for, not your cover story. I've done some digging and found your travel permits requested by that American Parnaby Cobb. Americans don't get involved in anything unless there's something in it for them."

Johann studied the fire. How much to tell him? He and the marquis had been friends for years. In spite of the marquis's temper and having been run out of town by him the previous summer, Johann felt he could trust him to a point. He selected his words as a debutante might choose desserts at a dance—carefully and for maximum satisfaction.

"The American wanted us to look into something even he wasn't sure existed. Some sort of substance from ancient times."

"The Eros Element. Yes, I've come across mention of it in my studies."

Damn. "Well, that's what we were supposed to search for, and so Miss McTavish was acting as our archaeologist in her father's absence."

The marquis gave him a piercing look unmuddled by the brandy. "That explains her interest, but not what happened. And did you find it?"

"We came close, but we didn't find exactly what Cobb had us look for. He fired us when we were in Rome."

"So what's happening in my house has something to do with the Eros Element and Mademoiselle McTavish." He leaned back, and the chair's winged protrusion obscured his face. Johann wanted to see him to try and guess his thoughts, but he waited. Typically the marquis thought out loud.

"And this symbol has something to do with it. That's why you're interested in Madame Cinsault. And here I thought she was another of your conquests."

"Not exactly." Johann smiled. He wouldn't mention Marie to the marquis. She was his alone, and he surprised himself with his thought that she wasn't a conquest—at least not in his usual sense.

"Will it help you to succeed on your mission if I can get you out of Paris?"

Now Johann did lean forward to see if the marquis was serious. He looked straight ahead, a strange expression on his face, and the fire flickered in his eyes with diabolical light.

"I'm sure we will need to leave at some point, but Mademoiselle has her studies to consider." He wouldn't mention the aether light experiment, although he guessed Edward and

Patrick had made as much progress on that as they would, at least with regard to harnessing its luminous power.

The marquis waved his hand. "The Ecole was one of the emperor's pet projects. It won't reconvene next semester—that toad Firmin knows but won't tell his students until after they pay their tuition and he can disappear with it. His time at the Louvre is done once the emperor is, and there is a strong current of revolution. Anyone who is intelligent will leave Paris once the siege is over before all hell breaks loose."

"And you won't try to stop Firmin?"

"Who says I haven't? But I have to tread carefully. He's the type of man who will do something desperate and dangerous when he's cornered."

"Then I will pass along your generous offer to the others," Johann said. "Although I'm not sure how you plan to get us out when the city is locked down tight and airship space is outrageously expensive, not to mention dangerous."

"There is a favor I would ask in return. Once you leave and satisfy your mission, bring Mademoiselle back and have her reverse whatever happened in my house."

"You don't want her to do that before we leave?" Johann asked and then mentally kicked himself.

"No, I shall wait until after the siege is over to ensure that my house survives. If it does not, then I will determine a different price."

Should I agree? Johann pondered his half-full brandy snifter. *Regardless of whether the Prussians invade or not, the emperor's time is done, and this city does have a history of violence and chaos with its governmental transitions.*

"I cannot speak for Mademoiselle, but I will bring your offer to her."

"Good." The marquis stood, and Johann did as well. "I look forward to hearing from you."

Johann left his brandy on a side table and picked up his violin. "I trust you no longer need my services this afternoon?"

"No, even the sound of violin music makes me anxious after that night. Be careful. Oh, and take a bottle of the brandy. I suspect you'll need it."

Johann bit back his reply, that he had no control over where the Prussians aimed their shells and instead bowed and thanked the marquis for the gift. The butler let him out, and the coachman awaited him. He hated to be the one to break the news to Iris—she'd worked so hard at her classes—but he would see if she'd withdraw before she paid her tuition for the next semester.

It seems ridiculously difficult to find an honest man in Paris.

MARIE WATCHED the guardsmen leave with Frederic's body. Maestro Fouré had arrived during the commotion—another man to make sure they were safe but who couldn't do anything about the situation. He, Lucille and Iris tried to get Marie to come farther inside into the theatre, but she refused. She had to know Johann was safe. Yes, she could acknowledge the desire as irrational—what was he to her, or her to him?—but she couldn't sit still in the semi-dark and wait. At least this way she could watch outside for his return.

A woman caught her attention. Not that it was difficult to spot her—the streets were generally deserted, people hiding in their basements and other underground places, and she also wore bright blue, which made her stand out and identified her as a streetwalker.

She must be trying to solicit the guardsmen. Stupid at a time like this, but I have to admire her persistence.

But the woman seemed to try to avoid the attention of the guards around the church and instead would pause in front of the theatre, look at it, and shake her head. She then walked to the end of the block, turned around, and repeated the process.

Marie was about to go out and ask the prostitute what she wanted—none had been so brazen as to approach the theatre before—when the marquis's carriage pulled to the end of the drive and to the side portico. She ran to unlock the door and meet Johann, who emerged with his violin and a bottle of brandy. The label indicated it was from the marquis's private collection. She halted before she flung herself into his arms. His hands were full, and irritation replaced relief at seeing him safe.

Has he been drinking and relaxing while the rest of us have been dealing with murder and fear?

"A present from the marquis?"

"One of a few. This one doesn't have any strings attached, at least I think it doesn't."

Now Marie's curiosity piqued. "What else did he give you? And has he forgiven Iris for breaking his statue?"

She knew Iris had acted in self-defense, and she still wondered how Iris had managed to pull an object from the past to smash something in the present.

"He's tied the incident to a different problem." He handed her the bottle. "Take a swig. This is going to get complicated."

She took the brandy but didn't open it. "We should probably talk to the others. And I have something to tell you—Frederic is dead."

She couldn't help the tears that pushed their way out of the corners of her eyes. How was he dead? She wouldn't miss him that much, but his murder was another sign of the world gone awry.

And the danger of her talent. Would he have returned if she'd not been playing the ideal woman?

The look Johann gave her made her wish she'd kept the

stupid tears where they belonged. It was the sympathetic expression one usually had for a new widow.

"I'm sorry for your loss," he said, and he appeared to retreat into himself. "What happened?"

"He was shot on the front walk. He was coming to make sure we were safe." The irritated edge leeched into her tone in spite of her efforts to keep her voice neutral.

"Of course." His chest puffed and deflated with a sigh. "Then we definitely have to talk, to plan. It's becoming too dangerous here."

The others also greeted Bledsoe with the coolness of emotional exhaustion. Edward had disappeared with Patrick into the lower parts of the theatre to continue working on the lighting system, as everyone had agreed that it gave those on stage a most flattering glow. Iris sat with a large book and a lantern, Lucille with a script, Fouré with a score, and Radcliffe with a scowl.

"Where have you been?" he asked.

"With the Marquis de Monceau," Johann said.

"What's the word outside? Any news of the battle?"

"None, although I suspect Inspector Davidson will be here at some point. He seems pretty well-informed. I need to talk to all of you about something."

A rustling in the balcony made Marie look up, and she saw the light glint off something metal.

"We should probably go somewhere else," she said and lowered her voice. "Somewhere below."

Iris looked up but didn't question her, just nodded. "That might be wise."

"Very well," Radcliffe said. "Madame? Maestro?"

"We will stay here and wait for word of the battle," Fouré said and put an arm around Lucille.

Marie allowed her forehead to wrinkle in surprise but didn't say anything. *Might as well let someone have some fun. Or perhaps it's a life-or-death situation tryst. Either way, I'm fine with it, surprisingly. There's something right about the two of them.*

Now if only she could find that rightness with someone herself. And she'd have to be more careful with Johann. He was in even more danger than Frederic had been but likely under the same influence.

"Very well, lead the way," Iris told her.

Marie led Johann, Iris, and Radcliffe through the backstage area, down to the dressing rooms, and even farther down to where they could hear Edward and Patrick discussing the next step of the lighting system conversion. Her companions followed her down one more level to where old set pieces were stored. Iris sneezed.

"I would think that you of all people wouldn't be bothered by a little dust," Johann, teased. "I thought ancient dirt was your specialty."

"Ancient dust doesn't get stirred up quite like the modern stuff does," she said and sniffed primly. "Do either of you have a handkerchief?"

Radcliffe gave her his. Marie glanced at the wooden set pieces that portrayed parts of a street scene, lampposts and a brick wall. Something odd about the surface behind them caught her attention. She brushed past Johann and lifted her lantern to examine the bricks.

"What is it?" Johann asked.

"There's something back there."

"It's just a crack," he said.

"No, it's like the one at the church." She pressed one of the bricks with her left hand and stepped on a slightly protruding one. The wall swung inward with a smooth, silent movement.

"Someone's been using that," Radcliffe said. "It's in good repair if it moves that quietly."

"I wonder..." Marie turned to face them. "I need to see where this leads. I'll explain in a bit, but please wait here."

Marie headed for the crack in the wall, but Radcliffe held her back.

"Wait," he said. "There are other things to discuss before you go after him."

She raised an eyebrow in surprise but nodded. "Very well, then. This way leads to the underground. I have friends there who will give us space to talk unmolested."

"Are they trustworthy?" Radcliffe asked.

"I trust them with my life." *And I have more questions for them. Like what was the Roma boy doing bringing a message to Maman?*

Although she had a lantern, Marie checked the match tin. It was full, so she guessed Zokar had information for her. She couldn't tell him exactly where the automaton was, but she could give him a place to search, especially now that she was mostly sure of the entrance to the spirit's special set of secret passages.

The inscription of "But I loved him" seemed all the more tragic now that she knew exactly what Johann thought of her. Or who he thought she was, a woman who had been kissed too much but was also ideal. She wondered which opinion of her would win or if they would combine to make her into an actress to be toyed with but not taken seriously.

Then Radcliffe had to keep tugging at Iris to keep her attention on the task at hand. Occasionally they passed human-shaped shadows in alcoves and corners, refugees from the surface, more than Marie had seen previously. They seemed as uninclined to bother the group as Marie was to disturb them. The bones showing through the skin and the gauntness of the faces she could see told the tale of starvation, the poor who couldn't afford to provision themselves and who were the first to lose the strength to struggle for access to what the government could give them.

One small family group had a fire with a small carcass

roasting over it—rat. In fact, the typical scurryings and scratch-ings were absent, replaced by the sounds of humans who had been reduced to living like animals.

A hand on the small of Marie's back startled her. Johann kept her close and glared about, daring anyone to bother her. She would have been amused if he'd been guarding her, not who he thought she was. A glance behind her told her Iris and Radcliffe kept up with them. Iris did look wistfully at the inscriptions and then the patterns of bones as they passed through the ossuary but didn't stop. Marie promised herself she would bring Iris back when all this was over and Paris was free again.

When they came to the fork in the path, Marie looked for the scratches that would tell her which way to take, but the wall had been plastered over.

What is this? She ran her fingers over the smooth surface and felt it was still damp. Could someone have found out how she traveled down here and had her directions obliterated? Were Zokar and Saphira and their family safe?

"What is it?" Johann asked.

"This is where they tell me how to come, how to find them." Marie swallowed around the itch of panic in her chest.

"Who are they?" Radcliffe asked.

"My friends. The Roma."

Some of the shadows detached from the walls, and the lamplight reflected in warning flashes off drawn knives.

Radcliffe drew a gun, but they were outnumbered.

"The four of you need to come with us," the leader said in softly accented French. "Someone wants to have a word with you."

"*Merde,*" Marie breathed.

24

héâtre Bohème, Sunday 4 December 1870

Edward emerged from the gloom of the theatre to the dusk of late afternoon. The theatre and lobby had been deserted, and he surmised that either the battle was over and the siege broken or resumed, or the others had descended into hiding somewhere below. He figured that if they had to go farther below, they would have told him and Patrick. So that meant siege as usual with the typical chance of shelling because if it had been over, there would be celebration in the streets.

So here he was getting some fresh air and natural light. In his university days, which felt like ancient history, he'd sometimes found that taking a walk could give him new perspective on a problem. He and Patrick had almost gotten the lighting system updated to run with the aether. All they lacked were some parts that were supposedly coming in on that night's airship, but who knew how reliable that would be?

But beyond their immediate task, he felt there was a missing piece of the puzzle. Well, more than one. The biggest one—how could they convert the Eros Element from light to power? That was their original mission, and aside from his darkest moments, he felt he could not rest until he'd solved that particular problem. But something tickled the back of his brain about what he'd seen and experienced in the theatre.

"Excuse me, Monsieur?" It was a young woman dressed in bright blue. He must have been tangled in his thoughts if he missed her walking up to him because even in the twilight, her dress shone against the drab background of the Parisian winter. The color of her garment and the degree of cosmetics revealed her profession.

"I'm not interested. Please leave me be."

She didn't duck her head as prostitutes typically did when he dismissed them, and she wouldn't let him move past her. Instead she plucked at his sleeve. "Please listen to me, Monsieur. I have seen something horrible."

Her eyes widened in desperate imploring, so Edward nodded with a sigh. "Fine. What is it? You do realize the city is at war, so horrible things are bound to happen."

"A man was killed earlier today, right there in front of the theatre."

"Yes, I know."

"But listen, Monsieur. I saw who did it."

It was a smaller piece of the puzzle, but it got Edward's attention. "All right, I'm listening."

She took his hand and tugged him to the side of the theatre that was away from the church and the guardsmen who would occasionally glance their way with smirks. She pulled him behind a tree.

"What are you doing?" he asked. "They'll think we—"

"Let them. It was one of them who did it, who shot the violinist."

"Are you sure?"

She glanced over her shoulder. "Please believe me, Monsieur. I was walking along here—I left my patron's house around lunchtime and missed the news of the battle. I saw the violinist coming the opposite direction. Then something changed about the atmosphere, and I thought we were going to be blown to bits by a Prussian mortar, but it was a different kind of feeling."

"What kind?"

"I felt angry." She looked down. "I wasn't always like this, a fallen woman. I once was a dancer, but an injury on stage ended my career. I thought I had accepted my lot, for men are willing to pay me, or they were when they had money before the siege, but I was overtaken with a feeling of unfairness. I wanted to hurt those who hurt me, and I would have attacked one of the guardsmen—they're the worst clients, smelly, brutish, and rough—but one of them raised his musket and shot the violinist. I screamed before I could help it. I was afraid they would shoot me too, so I hid."

"Did the others not do anything?"

"The other two on this side of the church were arguing with each other and did not see him until after. Then they took him away."

Edward's mind sorted through her story. She couldn't be telling the truth, could she? But he had heard screaming, so it must have been her. "And what happened after that?"

"The feeling, like a fog, lifted from my brain, and I would have gone to the fallen man, but another young woman came from the theatre, and two other guardsmen came to the man's aid. I wanted to tell her what happened, but I couldn't work up the courage to go into the theatre. Madame St. Jean has not been kind to those like me who approach her, even if it is for honest work."

Her tale matched up with what he had seen and, more disturbingly, what he'd felt. He would have attributed the irrational anger to the escalation of danger in the siege situation, but then it should have started earlier and lasted longer. No, it had to be something else, and the only temporal match was the use of the lighting system.

And it had been during the original demonstration that the other man had been murdered in front of the theatre.

Edward steadied himself with a hand against the tree, heedless of the icy bark.

It wasn't possible, was it? Could the use of the Eros Element at certain frequencies led to behavior change, an inflaming of certain passions? But what was the connection of the guardsman to the violinist? Or was it a random act of violence against someone of perceived privilege?

The questions erupted through his brain faster than he could catch them.

"I'm sorry," he said. "I must go. I have to record this data."

"Data?" the woman pursed her lips in confusion. "What do you mean?"

"I can't explain. Thank you for coming forward. Please do not tell anyone else about this."

She held her hand out. "And how much is my silence worth to you? After what I've seen, I'm going to have to go to a different part of town, start over, lest the guardsman find me and shoot me too."

He gave her all the money he had, which wasn't much, and she tucked it away and disappeared. He leaned against the tree, comforted by its steadiness.

The substance was named the Eros Element. The Eros of legend prompted people to do irrational things by shooting them with his arrows. But it couldn't be possible. What sort of scientific principle was at work here?

The fact that the action of the Eros Element might be beyond science frightened him even more than its possible uses.

Marie thought she recognized one of the men from her attack on the street. The character of Marguerite the Spy snapped into place like a favorite jacket, and she surveyed their attackers through heavy-lidded eyes.

"Really, gentlemen, is all this drama necessary?" she asked.

Iris hid a surprised laugh behind one glove, and Marie caught Radcliffe giving her a look of almost clinical measurement, but the one she was most concerned about was Johann. She could handle the situation if he would stay quiet, but she knew that would be a challenge for him. She laid a finger on his arm and found his muscles tight and ready for action.

"You wouldn't come with us up top, so we had to find you down here. Nice of you to walk right into our temporary home."

Marie glanced around. *That explains why they plastered over the scratches—they knew others would be coming through here and didn't want to chance discovery. I wonder if Zokar and Saphira have moved.*

A prick of anxiety that she'd lost her friends to the crowding of the underground passages before she could say goodbye stabbed through the barrier the role tried to place between her true self and her pretend self, and she balanced the two in her awareness. Now if only she could get rid of the thugs.

"If this is your home, your decorating leaves much to be desired. But then, you're not French, so you don't know any better." *Keep bantering until you come up with a plan.*

The shadows behind the erstwhile kidnappers shifted, and in a moment they found themselves surrounded by men familiar to Marie from Zokar's camp. These men carried handguns and longer knives.

"The leader is expecting you," one of them said with a wink. "He's wondering why you're running late."

"As you can see, I've been detained." Relief washed the role away, and Marie gave the one who spoke a smile that was hers alone.

"No harm meant, Mademoiselle."

The way the leader of the thugs sneered through her title, that he knew she wasn't a Miss but rather a Mistress, told Marie he must come from Cobb. Lack of respect from his men, or rather respecting her only because she'd been his plaything, had been one of the most irksome parts of working for him. And one of the things she would never tell her mother, although she knew Lucille suspected.

Cobb's hired hands sheathed their knives and sauntered down one of the passages. Their attitude confirmed their employer.

"Friends of yours?" the young Roma man asked.

"Hardly, but I'm not going to be able to avoid them forever. Although if I'm going to have to deal with Cobb, I'd rather do so on my terms, not his."

The Roma men surrounded them and ushered them down a different passage, not one Marie recognized. They took so many twists and turns she knew she wouldn't be able to find her own way out. Johann put a possessive hand on her waist, and she almost moved away but thought better of it.

Might as well enjoy his attention while it lasts, even if he does see me as just another actress to use. Like Cobb did.

"Are you sure they work for Cobb?" Iris asked and interrupted the bitter train Marie's thoughts wanted to take. "How did he find us?"

"He and my mother have one disturbing thing in common —they know how to get information." *And they know how to use me for their own ends.*

With that heartening thought weighing down her mind, Marie almost missed the savory smells of the camp that always felt like a homecoming.

"What is that?" Johann asked and sniffed the air. "That

smells amazing. How are they able to get spices and goat meat with the rationing?"

The leader glanced behind him with a scowl. "We are not taking more than anyone else in Paris, Monsieur. We have had to fight for everything we have, and we knew to conserve our own resources when the siege started rather than act like those who thought it would be over in a month."

Instead of his usual genial expression, Zokar greeted Marie and the others with a frown.

"You brought more than just her," he said to the man who had led them through the underground. "What are these *gadze* doing here?"

"I'm sorry, Zokar," Marie told him. "They're with me. Your men helped us to escape a trap."

"They're good men."

The individuals in question disappeared into the even more crowded encampment. Marie wondered again why Zokar never suggested she allow herself to be courted by one of them. Zokar led them to his tent, where Saphira stood over a pot of something savory-smelling. When they approached, she started ladling the stew into bowls.

"Oh, we couldn't," Iris said. "Please keep the food to feed you and your family."

Saphira ignored her and held out a bowl.

"It's fine," Marie told her. "Hospitality is very important to them. Just take it."

"Thank you," Iris said, and Saphira nodded with a smile.

Soon they were all seated around the little fire, and Zokar looked each of them over. His gaze lingered overly long on Johann, whose genial expression faltered under the intense scrutiny.

"Are you an honorable man?" Zokar asked.

Johann straightened, and Marie held her breath. Would he make one of his typical smart remarks?

"I've made mistakes in my past," he said, "but I'm trying to move past them."

Zokar smiled, but the skin around his eyes creased with sorrow. "I cannot fault a man who admits his mistakes. I have made plenty of mine in my own time, but you will find that the goddess gives us second chances, more than we deserve." He looked at Marie, then glanced away.

Marie had the sense that there was something very obvious she was missing, but Zokar interrupted her mental puzzling with a question.

"And what have you found out about my automaton?" he asked. "It's still missing, and we haven't found a trace of it."

"I think it may be in the theatre," Marie told him.

"The metal mask you've been dreaming about," Iris said. "Is that an automaton? Is that what locked you in your dressing room?"

"No, that's someone different, but I suspect he's taken the automaton and has disassembled at least the head. Otherwise I don't know where he could have gotten the metal for the mask."

"Who is that?" Zokar asked. "Lucille wouldn't allow such pranks, at least not—"

Saphira gave him a sharp look, and he cleared his throat.

"How do you know my mother?" Marie asked. "You've never given me a straight answer."

Radcliffe cocked his head, his gray eyes on Zokar's face. "I think, but no... It could be an ethnic characteristic."

"Your dark friend seems to be approaching the answer, so I will tell you," Zokar said. "Yes, Lucille is my sister. You, Marie, are my niece."

~

EDWARD RECALLED a conversation they'd had in the carriage on the way to the train from Paris to Rome wherein the doctor had admonished Patrick about how there was no such thing as magic, just things that science couldn't explain yet.

When he sought out the Irishman after his confusingly informative walk, he found him dressed in dark clothing and pulling a dark cap low over his eyes.

"Where are you going?"

"The airships are coming in at different times since they have to avoid the Prussian patrols, so we have to be ready all night."

"Are you sure they'll be landing tonight?"

O'Connell shrugged. "Don't know, but we have to be ready to unload in case they do come. Even if the siege is over, we need that rubber tubing."

"I need to talk to you about something. It's important."

"Then put on your darkest clothes and follow me. I have a hat you can wear. Chad packed an extra one."

Edward found a dark set of work clothes and put on his cloak, which had a hood he could pull over his head. Patrick nodded approval, and they set off into the dusk.

"Are you all right with a bit of a walk?" Patrick asked.

"That's fine." The idea of sneaking around after dark exhilarated Edward. "As long as we can talk."

"We work together all day, and you barely say anything outside of what's needed for the system. Why the urgency now?"

"You have a point, and it has something to do with the E.E. Do you remember last summer when we were in the carriage on the way to the train to Rome, and Iris and Marie were telling us about what had happened at the marquis's chateau?"

"Aye."

"And Doctor Radcliffe told you there's no such thing as magic, just things that science hasn't explained yet."

"Aye. What's your point?"

"Well, we don't know much about the science of how the

mind works." Walking through an icy Parisian night was a far cry from the lecture halls Edward had been accustomed to, but it was easier to talk about such things when he couldn't see his audience's face. Patrick walked ahead of him but obviously could hear him.

"Yes, that's why we've gotten sucked into this strange predicament," Patrick said. "Chad wants to know how to fix Claire's mind."

"And there are electric treatments that have helped melancholics in asylums."

"Right, but they don't help anyone else. Believe me, he's pursued that line of thinking. It's a dead end."

"Well, since we've been working with the E.E., what have you noticed about your own emotions and experiences? Mentally, I mean."

Patrick walked so long without answering that Edward thought the Irishman hadn't heard the question or had been offended by it.

"I'm sorry," Edward said. "I'm always saying the wrong things these days. Forget I asked."

Patrick wheeled around so suddenly Edward stepped back.

"No, that's it. You're brilliant." He grabbed Edward by the shoulders. "I thought it was that I wasn't sleeping, but I couldn't sleep, and I've felt things that didn't make sense, always when we had been running the system. Oh, thank God, I'm not going insane with this crazy situation!"

Edward's hood slipped off, and he pulled it back on, hopefully before anyone saw his face.

"Don't you see?" Patrick clapped him on the back. "That means you're not crazy, either. That melancholia over what happened in Rome—it's not you. You don't have to feel so guilty over what happened."

Edward coughed and shook his head. "I have to take

responsibility for what I did, even if some of my feelings about it aren't my own. But maybe..."

"What is it?" Patrick asked. He started walking again, and Edward trotted to catch up.

"Maybe in that moment when I made the decision to destabilize the E.E. and injure Scott—I didn't want to kill him, just make sure he wouldn't hurt Iris again—maybe I wasn't thinking like myself but was under the influence of Eros."

"You have a point."

"But what does this mean for our project? We can't have people in the theatre feeling illogical things."

"How much theatre have you seen? Of course we can. That's what the arts are about, helping people feel things they might not otherwise."

"I don't want it to be dangerous. It won't do Madame St. Jean any good if audience members start trying to kill each other."

"Then we need to adjust the frequency."

"No, we need to stop the experiment, take time to get our own heads on straight."

Patrick held up a hand. "We need to be quiet now. We're getting close."

Edward wondered if there was a true need for silence or if Patrick wanted to stop the conversation. Either way, he knew they still had things to discuss. If use of the Eros Element was potentially dangerous, they needed to know how to deal with it.

Why does every answer come with a host of new questions?

25

——————

Roma Camp, 4 December 1870

"What do you mean you're my uncle?" Marie stood and caught Saphira's bowl—now empty—before it shattered on the ground. She straightened and looked Zokar in the face, searching for some sort of clue. "Why didn't you tell me?"

Saphira took the bowl, and the look she gave her husband said that she, too, thought the revelation ill-timed, but Marie didn't know if it was because she wanted Marie to know all along or if she still wanted Marie to be ignorant of the fact they were family.

Family!

All along, since childhood, Marie had wanted a normal life and to be part of a family, and here hers was, hiding below the surface like the roles that overtook her that lived below her skin.

Or was this another role? No, the betrayal that welled up from the center of her chest was all too real.

"Why did you keep this a secret?" Marie asked, interrupting

whatever silent communication occurred between her aunt and uncle.

My aunt and uncle. How could I not have known?

"Lucille asked it of me," Zokar said. "But the time for secrets is over. Once the siege ends, we are moving on to a safer place. There are already murmurings of violence to come to the city even if the Prussians do not conquer it. And if they do, it will likely go badly for us."

A warm hand on Marie's arm made her stop and take a breath before speaking. She sorted through her thoughts to choose which would be best to express. "But why didn't *Maman* want me to know about you? Why did she keep me from you?"

Zokar's face blurred like the painting she'd seen from one of the avant garde artists, where images were hinted at through a haze that reminded her of a rained-on windowpane, and she rubbed the tears from her eyes.

Johann tugged her to sit beside him, and she leaned against him. Something crackled in his waistcoat.

"She wanted to raise you as a Parisian girl, not as Roma, although she couldn't completely escape her heritage," Zokar said. "And as I said, I made mistakes. I allowed her to be exiled from the camp for becoming pregnant by an outsider."

"She said she chose Marie's father and that it was some sort of arrangement," Iris said. "She made it sound intentional."

"As you've probably noticed, Mademoiselle, Lucille creates her own reality, her own memories, to suit how she thinks things should have been."

So what does she think of me, then? Marie accepted a cup of wine from Saphira, who motioned for her to drink it. It had an herbal taste skimming along the top of the typical fruit and alcohol flavors.

"Are you medicating me?" she asked.

"It is an old remedy to calm a fussy child, but with an adult enhancement," Zokar said. "This must be quite a shock for you. She is only trying to help."

Marie put the cup beside her. She needed to keep her wits about her, and now wonder replaced betrayal and gave her a sense of deep peace and calm. *She had family!* It wasn't normal family, but what about her life was typical? Not much.

"So do you know who my father is?" Marie asked. She had often wondered, often suspected different men in her mother's life, including Maestro Fouré, but her mother was tight-lipped about that part of her past.

"That is a question for your mother. Perhaps now that you know about us, she will tell you about him. She may act like she forgets her heritage beyond what it takes away from her, but she must feel the flow of time changing and know that secrets between friends and family are not helpful."

"Speaking of which," Radcliffe said. He picked up Marie's cup and sniffed it. "May I have the recipe for this? I work with soldiers and am always looking for calming remedies that do not involve opium."

Saphira nodded vigorously.

"She would have been a doctor like you had her tongue not been cut out," Zokar said.

"How did you know I'm a physician?"

"We know about all of you at the theatre and that the professor and the Irishman are doing something to the lighting system. We also know that the violinist here is hiding from someone and that Mademoiselle needs to learn that the best education is in the field and away from greedy administrators."

"Well, then." Iris stood, and Marie was surprised to see the shimmering in her eyes from fought-back tears. "You don't know everything. You don't know I won't be able to go back."

"You have a tremendous gift. You will find a use for it that will help others as well as yourself."

"Why can't you go back?" Marie asked at the same time Radcliffe inquired, "What gift?"

A commotion interrupted the conversation, and the guards brought in another person.

"*Merde,*" Marie whispered. It was Inspector Davidson.

EDWARD PULLED his cloak around him and slipped through the darkness behind Patrick toward the airfield, which was near the now unused Gare du Nord. The streets had an empty feel, possibly due to being in an industrial section filled with factories that had been converted to manufacture munitions and which ran shortened hours due to lack of materials. Warehouses surrounded the large field, one of a dozen in the city.

A bird call floated through the night, and it took Edward a minute to remember that all the birds had flown for the winter or had ended up on Parisian plates as pigeons replaced chickens. Patrick stopped and whistled back.

"What does it mean?" Edward whispered.

Patrick held up a hand—quiet.

Edward shifted from foot to foot. The damp cold made him wish for Madame St. Jean's hearth, although the townhouse fires would be out tonight with everyone in the theatre. But surely the Prussians wouldn't shell at night, would they? He guessed it didn't matter what they hit—or when—as long as they knew they were destroying something along with Parisian morale.

Another bird call came from a different direction. It didn't sound all that different from the first one, but Patrick headed toward one of the warehouses, and another man joined them. They didn't say anything, just nodded to each other. Edward couldn't see the newcomer's face, but a silent conversation of facial expressions and head-jerks ensued. He guessed Patrick vouched for him, although he certainly didn't know why or what use he would be. His weeks working in the atelier had atrophied the muscle he had, and he was already feeling the exhaustion of over-exerting himself.

They slipped into one of the warehouses, which was empty. A fire burned in the middle, and a group of men huddled around it.

"Who's he?" one of them asked.

"The professor," Patrick said. He shook hands all around, as did Edward, although no one gave their names.

"What's the load tonight?" Patrick asked.

"Not food," one of the men said. His wiriness spoke of a high metabolism.

"Too bad, I was looking forward to some frites with my rat," one of the others said.

"There's an outgoing," the first man, the one who'd asked Edward's identity, said. "Some hoity toity with his mistress."

"Hopefully she doesn't have too much padding in her—" One of the others held his hands in front of him to indicate large breasts. "There's a big load of mail tonight."

Edward kept silent. He'd learned long before to not say anything when men talked about women. His lack of experience made him useless in such conversations, and displaying his ignorance would only get him mocked. Unfortunately sometimes staying quiet drew as much attention as saying stupid things.

"So what's the professor think?" the first man to speak asked. "If he's a professor, he should be able to figure out how to manage the load, see if the lady needs some help with balance." He made an underhand grabbing motion. "There are some things that need hands-on adjustment, not math, eh Professor?"

The other men roared, and Edward squirmed. He knew he should say something witty, prove himself in this hierarchy, but he found the banter disgusting. Sure, Iris didn't have a huge décolletage, but he couldn't imagine treating her so crudely, even in her absence.

"I prefer calculations with a gentle touch," Edward said.

"No reason to bruise the goods," Patrick jumped in.

The man's grin folded into a scowl, but the other men laughed, and the one Edward had identified as the leader clapped Edward on the back.

"Oh, this one's a charmer."

The light tinging of a bell made the smiles disappear, and roughened hands drew caps down over serious expressions. Patrick gestured for Edward to follow him.

"Just stay out of the way," he said. "And watch Louis, the one you put in his place. I won't say he didn't have it coming, but he's known for his slow-burn temper and ability to wait for revenge."

"I will."

The foreman joined them and held up a hand before they exited the warehouse. "Since the professor here has demonstrated he knows how to handle the lady, he can help her board the airship. Red, watch him."

"Aye," Patrick said. "He's getting you out of the way," he told Edward.

When they walked into the night, the cold air smacked Edward in the face. The temperature must have dropped ten degrees during the brief time they were in the warehouse. Then he noticed the carriage, an understated affair, but he'd seen it when he emerged earlier from the theatre.

"Is that Monceau's?" he asked Patrick. "It looks familiar."

"Yes. Remember, focus on the lady and stay out of the way."

The driver and footman assisted the two passengers out of the carriage and unloaded the luggage. Then they all stood aside while the foreman drove the carriage and horses away.

"Is he storing them?" Edward asked.

"No, they're using them to pay for passage and airfield fees. The servants will go with them."

"Then why do they need my help?"

"They don't, but stay near them in case they do."

A change in air pressure and wind tone heralded the arrival of the all-black airship. Edward lost track of his charges as he watched it, or tried to—it was hard to make out where its outlines blurred into the night beyond in the darkness. It landed with a less than graceful bump.

The marquis, dressed uncharacteristically somberly from what Edward recalled of Johann's descriptions of the man, turned to Edward.

"You're with the group at the Bohème," he said.

Edward didn't know what to say. He wasn't going to lie, but Patrick's warnings of secrecy and the enforced anonymity he'd observed among the others came to mind.

"That's fine, I understand if you don't want to speak to me. Just please give my apologies to Maestro Bledsoe but tell him the captain of this ship and her sister vessel are aware of my promise to him."

"I will," Edward said.

Edward followed the servants, the marquis and his friend, a woman sheathed in several veils, to the airship but did not board because a steward, also dressed all in black, met them at the gangplank. Being near the ship made him queasy as he remembered their not-so-gentle exit from the last one he'd been on.

The crew, including Patrick, carried boxes and bags up and down a different gangplank, and the whole loading and unloading operation was over in a very efficient manner. Patrick's hand on Edward's shoulder drew him back as the walkways were drawn back into the hull and the ropes loosed. The airship lifted straight up and disappeared into the moonless dark.

"Now what?" Edward asked.

"Tonight the crew splits up the liquor and disappears back where they came. And we have our tubing."

A bright light overhead seared Edward's vision, and he rubbed his eyes. Patrick grabbed him and dragged him back into the warehouse.

"What—?" He blinked to clear the afterimage. "What happened? What was that?"

But he remembered Marie's warning from their first airship trip, that a small flame could ignite the hydrogen in the balloon and cause disaster. Objects landed on the asphalt and grass outside with sickening thuds, and the cool air took on a serrated smoky feel.

Patrick's normally ruddy face had lost all color, confirming Edward's suspicions.

"Go back to the theatre," Patrick said. "You're in no shape for rescue and salvage."

The door opened, letting in a plume of smoke, and the foreman stumbled in. "Won't be any rescue from that," he said and took off his cap. The others did likewise.

"Take your friend back to the theatre," Louis told Patrick. "I can tell he doesn't have the stomach for what we'll have to do."

The foreman took charge. "Louis, Henri, make sure the burning is confined to the field and not spreading. Then we'll figure out what we can save."

Edward noted his words—what, not who.

"We don't need you," the foreman told Patrick and shoved a box of something that clinked at him. Edward suspected the Frenchman wasn't telling the truth, but Patrick didn't argue. He nodded, put his cap back on his head, and gestured for Edward to follow him out of the back of the warehouse.

"The crew on the ship was French," he said. "Let them mourn them and their nobleman."

Edward looked up at the sky when they reached the wide

boulevard. The moon split the clouds for a moment, but it was long enough for him to see some sort of device with a white canopy floating down from the sky. The moonlight disappeared before he could point it out to Patrick, but he suspected there had been at least one survivor from the airship disaster.

26

___

*R*oma Camp, *4 December 1870*

Johann felt Marie stiffen when she saw Inspector Davidson. Iris also sat straighter, and her face assumed her customary mask, an expression he called neutral academic because Edward had a similar one.

Has she spoken to Davidson yet?

"Ah, good, I was hoping to find you here," the inspector said and waved to them. Johann felt the suspicious gazes of the other people in the camp follow Davidson and flick back and forth between him and them. Even Zokar lost some of his wistful geniality he'd had once he revealed to Marie he was her uncle.

Welcome to the mixed blessing that is family.

"You know this man?" Zokar asked.

"He has been annoyingly present as of late," Johann said.

"I heard that," the inspector told him. "I'm glad I have all of you gathered here. Oh, hello Doctor Radcliffe."

"Inspector."

He sat on a makeshift bench beside Radcliffe and accepted a bowl of stew from Saphira.

"Now wait a minute," Zokar said. "My men brought you in because they caught you nosing around. This isn't a social visit."

Saphira shrugged and gestured for the inspector to eat. Zokar huffed and went to speak with his men.

"Delicious, thank you. As for what I was doing here, I'd heard rumors that one of my targets had made a camp down here, so I was trying to find it. My men and I split up to search, and I got lost."

"We are aware of who you are and what you do, that you're not a typical policeman."

Marie looked around. "I don't know what you're talking about. I thought you investigated murders."

"Only the ones that have particularly strange characteristics. But as I have said to your colleagues, I am part of a team of counterespionage agents with interest in international organizations like the Clockwork Guild and cults like the neo-Pythagoreans. You will not be surprised to know that your former employer Parnaby Cobb has been mixed up with the Clockwork Guild."

"But how? They attacked his airship. And I knew a lot about his affairs, and there was never anything remotely hinting that he was associated with them. In fact, we had to look for and remove their spy devices frequently."

"As an actress, you are a mistress of making people believe in something made-up. Would you consider that the battle was a carefully choreographed illusion?"

"And the camera ravens?" Johann asked.

"I am still not sure whose devices those are. There is something strange going on at the theatre."

"Wait a second." Marie glanced around at everyone. "So everyone knew what you do except me?"

"He only told me today at the Louvre," Iris said.

"And me at the Cinsault house." Johann tried not to move

too much lest the crinkle of the letter in his waistcoat give its presence away. Although perhaps Davidson wouldn't be so eager to confiscate it when he was so outnumbered.

They all looked at Radcliffe.

"He just asked me to keep an eye on things at the theatre clinic and let him know if anything strange came in," he said. "This is the first I'm hearing of his broader purpose."

"So why are you happy we're all gathered here?" Iris asked. "Do you have news for us?"

"Only a couple of items, and I was hoping you all could help me with a puzzle."

Zokar approached them. "There has been an airship crash."

Davidson rose. "Where?"

"At the Gare du Nord field. No survivors."

"I should go, but I will come to the theatre tomorrow provided that the Prussians don't start shelling."

"They may," Zokar told him. "News from the front is that whatever gains the French army made didn't last, and it's back to siege as usual."

"We should go as well." Marie stood, as did the others. The letter crackled when Johann moved, and Davidson raised an eyebrow.

"I will be particularly interested in what you have to say, Maestro, seeing as you're the primary suspect in the murder of Frederic LeClerc."

MARIE SAID goodbye to Zokar and Saphira. Her mind still tripped over the words *uncle* and *aunt*. Those were words she'd always reserved for other people's families. Like Johann's. But it seemed his family, like all others, had its problems.

"What do we do now?" Iris asked once they traversed the

tunnels. "We're back to facing a problem that's bigger than all of us, and it seems that Cobb has found us again."

"Yes, he's tried to get to me twice now." Marie held up the lantern to illuminate a fork and the scratches on the wall, unmarred here, told her which branch to take to get out. She wished the pattern to all their problems was as clear.

"We need to do something to get rid of him, or at least get him to leave you alone," Johann said.

"And you can't have him leading the Clockwork Guild to you," Marie responded, reminding herself that he tended to act with his own interests in mind.

"Plus there's the murder of Monsieur Cinsault," Radcliffe pointed out. "And now Frederic LeClerc."

"And Cinsault was also somehow involved in the neo-Pythagoreans," Johann said and pulled a letter from his waistcoat. "I need to look at this before Davidson takes it back. This is the one I was able to keep from the bunch Madame Cinsault gave me."

"Right," Iris added. "There's also the question of whether to trust Davidson. Let's stop and look at that here. We seem to be alone."

Johann pulled the letter from its envelope, and Marie illuminated it with her lantern.

"Lafitte. I know that name. The family are theatre patrons, very protective of their daughter."

"Then we have a problem because this is signed by Amelie Lafitte," Radcliffe, who apparently read faster than any of them, said. "It's about a meeting of students to study the ancient rules of trade and she's inviting Monsieur to come and speak to them about his expertise in applying those principles to modern times."

"It's perhaps in code," Iris remarked. "Trade could mean the activities of the cult."

"Likely," Radcliffe agreed. "You'd need her to confirm that."

"Good luck getting close to her," Marie said. "She has one of the strictest fathers in Paris."

Johann's rueful expression told her that he thought of his own childhood. "All the more reason she's seeking to engage in something rebellious like dabbling in the secrets of an ancient and deadly cult."

"You said her family are theatre patrons." Iris looked at Marie. "Could you see what information you have on them? Perhaps your mother would know of them, both because of the theatre and because of her network."

"I'm not talking to Lucille." Marie turned and illuminated the passage ahead of them. "She hid the fact that we have family right here in Paris from me. I can't trust anything she says."

"But if we can draw this connection, we can shift the blame for the murder elsewhere," Radcliffe pointed out. "And Davidson won't look as closely at the theatre anymore, at least not for that killing. Frederic LeClerc is another matter."

Johann followed Marie. "Obviously it wasn't me. I was with the marquis all afternoon, and he and his servants saw me. They can vouch I was at his townhouse at the time of the killing."

"Right."

Now that they had reached the more crowded part of the underground, they fell silent, each wrapped up in his or her thoughts. They remained that way until they reached the theatre.

Marie looked up the stairs. That way her mother and the theatre spirit waited for her, but if she were to remain underground, there was no telling when Cobb's men would try again and bring enough others with them that she would have no choice but to go with them or risk her friends harm.

"Are you all right?" Iris asked.

"I suppose. I'm going to put this out and go to the top of the stairs and open the door for us." She extinguished the lantern and placed it where she had found it then did as she said.

She looked lingeringly at the place where she knew the ghost's tunnel might be and promised herself she would return later when she knew he wasn't there. How she'd know that she wasn't sure yet, but she guessed he didn't stay in the secret passages all the time. He had to eat like normal people.

Not that he's exactly normal.

They found Lucille, Fouré, Edward and Patrick in the auditorium. Marie thought it was just the dim lighting at first, but no, Edward's and Patrick's skin was smudged, and a chemical smoky odor made her wrinkle her nose.

Edward stood, and Iris ran into his arms.

"What happened to you?"

They explained about the airship crash and the fate of its noble passengers and the marquis's servants.

"*Merde,*" Marie said. "There goes the maestro's alibi."

"And our ticket out of Paris," Johann said.

"He said to tell you the captain of the sister airship knew of his promise to you," Edward said. "And there was a woman, a prostitute, that saw one of the guardsmen shoot LeClerc."

Marie recalled the woman in the blue dress. "I think I saw her. Where is she now?"

"I gave her all my money, and she said she would go to a different part of Paris."

Marie slumped into a chair. "We'll never find her."

"And as for the airship," Patrick said, "until they know why this one blew up, they're not going to fly any more in or out, I'm certain of it. If the Prussians have found a way..."

"And they've been trying," Fouré said. "They know that what comes in, even if it's not enough to feed the millions here, is keeping the city from surrendering, as is the mail and news from elsewhere."

"Then why are you here?" Marie asked and stood to face

him. "Our small production isn't anything more than a diversion. It's not going to make a difference for anyone, not in any meaningful way. Our theatre would be better used as a hospital like the others."

"What are you really angry about, *Cherie*?" Lucille asked.

"Don't call me that. Don't call me your dear one. I know that Zokar is my uncle, that you told him to keep me away and lie to me so I wouldn't know. Why? Why did you want to keep me all to yourself?"

Lucille paled under her olive complexion. "You have been communicating with him."

"Yes, he rescued me one day when I got lost in the underground. He's how I know my way down there. Why didn't you want me to talk to him?"

"It is something that you wouldn't understand," Lucille said. "I do not bring up your disgrace, and I hope you will give me the courtesy of allowing me to not reveal mine."

Marie forced herself to ignore the stricken expression on her mother's face. "What disgrace? You haven't done anything shameful."

"You need to tell her," Fouré said. "You need to not have any more secrets."

Lucille turned to him. "I did not ask your opinion."

"You never have, my dear, and it has caused me regret as well. And that is why I am here," he said. "I had to make sure that the love of my life and my daughter were safe in this siege."

A hardness under her derriere made Marie realize that her knees had given out, and she'd plopped gracelessly on the floor. Although she'd suspected, hearing the truth shocked her, and it joined the rest of the tension of the day in knocking her down.

"You're my father?" she asked. Johann offered her a hand up, but she batted it away. She grabbed the chair next to her and hauled herself up.

The room spun, but she refused the support of anyone near

her. She careened down the aisle and through the door beside the stage, heedless of obstacles. She ran to her dressing room, slamming the door.

She had an aunt and uncle.

She had a father, a man she already respected and who seemed to make her mother happy. But her mother hadn't said anything to her, only left her to suspect and wonder where she had come from. Well, now she knew.

"Well, well, what a lovely little family reunion you were having," the ghost said. "Why'd you leave, darlin'? Too much emotion even for you? Or whoever you are at the moment?"

His words startled her but also made her stop and see what role had overtaken her.

"For me, I suppose. I'm not being anyone right now, just Marie St. Jean... Fouré."

"He hasn't claimed you, though, has he?"

"No, but my mother wanted his relationship to me kept a secret, so he couldn't."

Childhood taunts came back to her, the cruelty of children to a girl without a father or even the memory of one. Now that she thought about it, that had been the first time she'd allowed a role to overtake her, that of not caring when faced with cruelty.

Emotions battled back and forth like the French and Prussians outside the city walls. Joy at finding her family, connecting with others related to her and who could understand her on a blood level warred with anger at her mother for keeping those connections from her for so long. And then there was concern for Johann—the French rumor mill loved nothing better than the drama of a love triangle that came to a violent end. With the city being on the edge of a riot or worse, a violent takeover by a radical group that felt the emperor wasn't doing a good enough job, the police might bow to public opinion to keep things quiet.

And underneath it all, fear and shame that her mistake with Cobb still wouldn't leave her be, that he wanted to see her for some reason. She knew he would want her under his control again, possibly to spy for him on whatever Edward was doing, but also because she knew so many of his secrets. His letting her go to Paris had been part of his game all along.

"What are you thinking, Mademoiselle?" The ghost sang behind the mirror. "Why does a frown mar that beauty?"

"You're not funny," Marie told him. "And you have secrets too. I don't believe you care so much for the welfare of this theatre."

"Ah, but you have met me in the past. Do you not remember?"

"You know I don't."

"I know you don't." A wheezing giggle. "Of course you don't. Most people do not, for I am the invisible hand of death."

"Now who's being dramatic?" She teased him but swallowed around the flame of anxiety that he was becoming unhinged. Plus, the memory of a knife at the back of her neck flashed through her brain.

Could it be the man in the carriage? But I never saw his face clearly.

"Ah, but you need my cooperation. Whose raven do you think it was that kept you and the maestro from sharing a kiss in the alley with some well-timed snowfall? And who captured a photo of him trying that could doom him in the eyes of the police?"

The memory-feel of the icy snow spread from Marie's face to her extremities, and her heart thudded through it. "You wouldn't."

"Oh, but I would, for I need you to be tough and disciplined, Mademoiselle *Premiere Femme*. It is what *Maman* wants, after all, regardless of who *Pere* happens to be."

Disgusted, Marie fled from his demented laughter.

I have made a deal with the devil.

She encountered Iris in the hall.

"Oh good, there you are. Is that where you've been hiding? Who were you talking to?"

"The spirit of the theatre."

"The one who trapped you and who smokes Parnaby Cobb's tobacco brand?"

"Yes." Marie admired Iris's ability to put everything in a succinct and logical way.

Perhaps he used to work for Cobb. That's how he has the tobacco blend. That will help narrow down who he is and therefore what he wants.

Iris gestured for Marie to follow her. "The battle is over, so we're back to siege as usual. Everyone's gone back to the town-house." She put a hand on Marie's arm. "Join us if you're up for it. I know you've had some shocks."

"Lead the way. We all have pieces of the puzzle and need to put them together somehow."

On the way, she racked her memory for when she had met the ghost previously. So many Americans worked for Cobb.

This is impossible. But he did let slip one thing—the ravens are his.

27

—————

Théâtre Bohème, 4 December 1870

Iris and Marie exited the theatre through the back. Iris kept the lamp shielded to the point that they could only see a few feet in front of them and pondered how the threat of the Prussians and the uncertainty around the airship crash made them all feel like they needed to scurry and hide like rodents trying to avoid a large cat.

"Ooof," Marie said and stumbled. She caught herself, but her legs got tangled in her skirt, and she landed on her derriere. "Twice in one night. That's gonna be sore tomorrow."

"Are you all right? What did you trip over?"

Iris helped Marie to her feet, and in the lamplight, the large bundle of cloth resolved into the body of a man. A man with chestnut hair and aristocratic cheekbones who gazed at the sky with a surprised and horrified expression.

"Edward?" Iris whispered. Her soul collapsed somewhere around her middle, and she backed into the wall, her hand over her mouth. "No, it can't be."

Marie reached toward her. "It's not him. I thought so too, at first, but Edward would never go out so unshaven."

Iris directed the light toward the man's face and saw the lips were too thick and the nose too long to be Edward, but he did have a strong resemblance. Now she was thankful she had the wall to support her so she wouldn't collapse in relief.

Marie felt at the man's neck for a pulse. "Whoever he is, he's really dead."

"Poor chap." Iris's almost grief made her sensitive to the fact that someone would be waiting at home for this young man and would wonder what had happened to him.

"We're going to have to summon Davidson, aren't we?" Marie asked with a sigh.

"'Fraid so." They left the body in the alley. Although they didn't say that the murderer could be lying in wait, both of them rushed to the back of the townhouse, Marie stiffly, and the keys jingled with her trembling as she opened the servants' entrance door.

The first thing Iris saw once they left the cloakroom was Edward standing at the stove heating up milk to put in his tea. He and Radcliffe spoke in low tones.

"Enjoy it while you can," Radcliffe said. "Cream has been reserved for the children, and I suspect milk will be next to be held apart for the sick and young."

This damn siege. Why can't it be over? But then wishing so means I want fighting to happen, and there will be more death, more widows.

With a sob, Iris flung herself into Edward's arms. He still smelled of smoke and fear, but she didn't care. He was warm and alive and—

"What? What is it?"

She relished the tender tone in his voice, and they clung together, both having looked in the face of death.

"I thought I'd lost you," Iris said. She looked up into his bright blue eyes. "Please don't leave the townhouse by yourself. It's not safe."

"Explain?" he asked Marie.

"She had a scare," Marie said. "There's a man in the alley who looks like you. He's dead."

"I'll take a look." Radcliffe rushed out.

Edward frowned, but in a puzzled way, not a fearful one. His next words confused Iris more than his expression. "How? We haven't been running the aether lighting system. This doesn't make sense."

Iris drew back. "What do you mean? What does that have to do with anything?" *Is he going mad?*

"It's one of the things we need to talk about, preferably before Davidson arrives. You see, my dear, Patrick and I might be accidental murderers."

THEY GATHERED in the receiving parlor since they expected Davidson to arrive momentarily. Lucille had sent a message for him to the nearest pneumatic tube delivery station in the old Gare du Nord. She now waited in her office for a reply. Marie noted how tired everyone looked with an extra layer of exhaustion on top of the wear of the siege.

No one likes to be trapped.

"He's not going to like being interrupted at the crash site," Johann said.

"True," Lucille replied. "He may not come."

"We can only hope," Marie muttered. "Is it possible that the man fell from the airship?"

Radcliffe shook his head. "Not unless they stabbed him from behind first. His injuries are similar to those of Monsieur Cinsault."

"What did you mean that you're an accidental murderer?" Marie asked Edward.

Edward and Patrick exchanged glances. "It doesn't make sense to me," Edward admitted.

Marie kept her expression neutral so a hysterical giggle wouldn't escape.

He doesn't like saying those words. For him everything should be orderly, but it's not, is it? Nothing is.

"He thinks that when we run the aether lighting system, it affects how people feel and behave," Patrick explained. "The way I've been feeling since we've been working with it, I can see it."

"The first murder, Cinsault," Iris said. "That was when you were demonstrating it in the atelier."

"And Frederic when we were testing it in the footlights," Marie added. She didn't look at Johann. She couldn't, not now that she knew the spirit would leave evidence of their almost-kiss where the inspector could find it and seal the case for his guilt.

"But what about this one?" Edward asked. "We haven't been running the lighting system, not since earlier. Could he have been out there that long?"

"No," Radcliffe said. "The body was too warm to have been lying in an icy alley all day."

"So what does this mean for the theatre?" Lucille asked. She held up a message. "The inspector will be here as soon as he can. He requested we stay put so he can question us. Bah, as if any of us are going anywhere with the Prussians at our gates and a murderer—or three—afoot."

"We shouldn't use the system, obviously," Edward said. "Not until we know we can do so safely."

"But if it has that large of an effect, shouldn't more people have been killed?" Iris asked. "What's the vulnerability?"

"Madame Cinsault said that she had lovers," Johann pointed out. "Perhaps romantic jealousy plays a part?"

"But that then points back to you as a guilty party even though we know you weren't here," Marie said.

"Maybe you weren't Frederic's only project," he said. "Maybe it was another jealous lover."

"The guardsman did try to invite me to, well, something." Marie swallowed the lump of disgust that rose when she thought of how he'd propositioned her.

Radcliffe poked at the small fire in the grate, more to do something than to adjust the position of the coals, Marie thought. "But then how do the neo-Pythagoreans fit into this? Is it possible that it's the same murderer, someone trained to kill?" he asked.

"That's a different motive entirely," Edward agreed. "But could the Eros Element have caused him to act before he planned on it?"

"This is all speculation," Lucille said. "Do I or do I not have a lighting system for the theatre?"

"What does it matter?" Marie asked. "With the situation as it is, there's no point in putting on a production."

"It matters a great deal, *Cherie*." Lucille held up a gilt-edged envelope. "The empress herself has asked that we go on with our opening night this week to lift the spirits of the Parisians after the failure of the sortie battle and the airship tragedy."

"We cannot use the aether lighting," Edward said. "It's too dangerous. Even if it causes one person in the audience to do something rash, it's not worth someone getting hurt."

"I agree with you," Radcliffe said. "But it is your opinion that matters, Madame."

"The light was so lovely on Marie's face. Could you not adjust it so it is safe?"

Edward and Patrick looked at each other.

Marie felt the role trying to overcome her, the idealized woman. The kind of woman a man would kill for without truly understanding her because of what she represented to him, not because of who she truly was. Part of her wanted to take the stage again, to prove she could do it, but she feared she couldn't control her gift without the spirit's help, and after their last conversation... Well, he seemed to be losing touch with his sanity, and she didn't trust him.

But could she trust herself to balance the role and her true self? Being onstage had always caused her gift to manifest most strongly, so she didn't trust her little moments of victory to this point.

No, it's too dangerous. She tried to press in her mind, *Say no, say no, say no. Tell her the show cannot proceed because you can't undo your adjustments that quickly. I cannot go back in that theatre.*

But if I don't, then the spirit will not get what he wants, which is information.

"I think we can do it," Edward said. "We have copious notes and could bring it back to a frequency that won't light the stage as well but shouldn't be in that dangerous realm."

"Aye," Patrick said. "I can look in my journal, see when I was feeling like myself, and we can cross-reference."

A knock on the door told them the inspector had arrived. He had dark circles under his eyes, and he gratefully accepted a cup of tea from Iris.

"Thank you. It's been a very long day. I take it you've heard the battle is over and the siege is resumed as it was."

"Yes," Radcliffe said.

"Have someone listening out just in case. With the return of the stalemate, the Prussians might start shelling to cause Paris to capitulate. Our informants tell us that consumption is making its way through their lines. Now tell me about that unfortunate chap in the alley. My men are questioning the national guardsmen outside the church now to see if they heard or saw anything. Do you think your, er, friends down below could shed any light on what happened or one of your informants, Madame?"

"Everyone was staying in, including my staff."

And my uncle. Marie's thoughts took on that hysterical edge again. It all seemed so surreal, like what happened on the stage was more solid and predictable than real life.

There's definitely something to be said for scripted surprise.

"And now the letter, Maestro." Davidson's fatigue showed around his eyes, but his manner was as incisive as ever. Johann handed over the now-crumpled missive. "I trust that you will not do anything hasty."

"We're working toward the same end, Inspector."

"We'll see." He handed his now-empty teacup back to Iris and stood. He swayed on his feet before gaining his balance and rubbed his eyes. "With this new murder... Just tread carefully, and I expect you to share any information you may obtain."

Marie kept her expression neutral and avoided making eye contact with any of the others. What would the inspector think about the Eros Element being the culprit? He likely wouldn't believe them, and then they'd all be arrested.

"Try to get some sleep, Inspector," Lucille told him.

"Right. No rest for the weary." With a tip of his hat to the ladies, he was off.

"What are we going to do?" Iris asked after he left.

"What I told him to do." Lucille shooed them out of the room. "Get some sleep. No one can solve problems when their brain is exhausted."

They complied, but when Marie turned to wave to the gentlemen, she caught Johann's small smile before he turned. Her stomach flipped, and she felt an answering grin on her own face. Perhaps they would dream of each other and not of airship crashes or murders.

One can only hope since we cannot interact otherwise.

THEY ALL SLEPT LATE the next morning, but then it was off to rehearsals as usual.

"Hey," Johann said as he and Marie put on their cloaks in the room off the kitchen, "are you all right? You've been avoiding me." He brushed a curl away from her face. "I just wanted to see how you are after the revelations of yesterday."

She ducked her head away from his almost-caress. "I'm fine."

He dropped his hand to his side although his fingers wanted to gently turn her face up to his and claim a kiss. Why did she seem so soft and encouraging one moment and so cold a day later? "You don't seem fine. Are you and your mother not speaking?"

"I'm not talking to her until she's ready to tell me the entire truth. I feel that she's withholding some crucial piece of information from me so she can continue to dangle my mistakes over my head."

"You keep blaming her for you not being able to escape the past, but is there something you're holding on to?"

She scowled up at him. "That's rich from the man who won't tell how he got in such a difficult situation with the Clockwork Guild. We all have secrets, Monsieur."

"I'll tell you mine if you tell me yours." He kept his tone playful, but his heart beat a staccato retreat rhythm in his chest.

She'll think I'm a fool, but if it helps her to move forward and heal, it's worth it.

"I've got to take care of something," she said. She glanced around, then put both hands behind his head and tugged his face to hers. He didn't resist and wrapped her in his arms, meeting her lips with his. He regretted his previous insult to her, that he wouldn't be her first kiss, but he decided to be her first amazing one. Not that it would be difficult—she brought up a depth of passion from him he'd never experienced, although she was far from his first kiss too.

She pulled away and laid her head on his chest. His heart felt like it wanted to beat through his ribs to be closer to her. There were other parts that wanted to be closer to her, and he hoped she couldn't feel them through her skirts.

"I'm sorry," she said and pulled away. "I... I don't know what I feel, but whatever I do, it's irrelevant until I take care of something."

Something threaded through her voice, a plaintive undercurrent. This time he did give in to the urge to put a hand under her cheek and turn her face toward him.

"What are you going to do? You're not going to put yourself in danger, are you?"

She swallowed, the motion of her throat muscles like the flutter of a desperate bird. "It's the spirit of the theatre. He's the one who controls the ravens, and one took a picture of our almost kiss in the alley."

Johann put the pieces together in his head. "He's still trying to keep us apart, isn't he? What does he want with you?"

"I don't know." She placed a hand over his and turned her cheek to kiss his palm. "But I'm going to find out. It's time for Marguerite the Spy to have a performance."

"There's a difference between playing a role and truly taking action," he said.

"Not for me. It's time to make this gift into something useful. Don't follow me."

With those cryptic words, she left, and a gust of wind slammed the door in his face. When he pushed it open again, she'd disappeared into the swirling snow.

"Well, *merde*," he said and put his hat on. He thought about the rehearsal, how the orchestra needed him with the other first violin dead, but he couldn't shake the feeling Marie needed him more.

I've taken bigger gambles than this.

He plunged into the whiteness and followed Marie into the theatre. He crept toward her dressing room, ears alert for the sound of voices and speaking, but when he arrived, he found someone already stood outside the door.

28

———

T *héâtre Bohème, 5 December 1870*

Marie headed straight for her dressing room. She allowed the role of Marguerite the Spy to overtake her because she would need her wits about her for this confrontation. She'd tossed and turned all night, feeling like the answer to the ghost's identity was just beyond her reach. She'd met him. She knew she'd met him other than in the carriage. His voice teased her between dreams of Johann's kisses and her actually being aware of him removing her corset and clothing. Somehow finding out who her father was made her feel more legitimate, like she might have a chance at a family and a normal life, and although she knew she shouldn't be attracted to the musician, he was the one her heart turned to.

"*Merde,*" she muttered. He had secrets too, and she still wasn't sure he wouldn't flit off once the siege was over, particularly since he still had his debt to the Clockwork Guild to worry about. But they could figure that out later. First she needed to find the ghost's lair and destroy the pictures of her and Johann. To do that, she needed to ensure the spirit wouldn't interrupt them. How she would get him to go away and give her a chance to seek his lair…

That she would leave to Marguerite.

Before she could snap into her role, she found the rehearsal schedule on the dressing table.

She cursed again under her breath. Lucille had reversed the timing. The actors were to have the theatre in the mornings and then the musicians in the afternoon. Which meant…

A knock on her door startled her. "Marie? It's Janelle. Your *Maman* says you're needed in the theatre *toute suite.*"

The role of Marguerite fell away like a heavy gown. "Tell her I'll be there in a minute."

A low laugh made her look toward the mirror. "You are wanted onstage, Henriette. But can you handle the role on your own?"

"Are you offering the smoke again?" Marie asked. She placed a hand over her nose and mouth. "Because I do not want it. I want to tackle the stage without help."

"Ah, you are a brave woman. I wish I could watch you, but I need to spend the time in my workshop so I can monitor the musicians this afternoon. I'm concerned about the lack of first violins."

"Joh—Maestro Bledsoe can handle it."

"You're on a first-name basis with him now?"

"It was a slip. We are informal in my group, as you must have observed."

"You're right. If it wasn't for the accents, one would think you're all American, not just the dark fellow."

Marie almost asked him why he was so invested in the performance but decided not to. She wanted more for him to be away from his lair that afternoon so she could find those damn photos.

CHADWICK SAW Johann rush out of the townhouse and decided to follow him. They needed to talk with Amelie Lafitte. His instincts told him there was another aspect to the situation, but he didn't know what to make of Marie's tale of the spirit of the theatre, and he was still skeptical of the influence of the Eros Element. Part of it was not daring to hope, true, but he was a man of science, and all they had was anecdotal evidence thus far. There was the strange night when she had collapsed in her bed and had been impossible to wake.

He found Johann walking out of the hallway that held most of the dressing rooms, including Marie's, preceded by one of the young actresses. Radcliffe had helped her with an upset stomach the month before, and she smiled shyly at him but had eyes only for the musician.

"What are you doing here?" Johann asked.

"Following you," Radcliffe admitted. "Trying to keep you out of trouble. Whatever she's doing, it's her battle, not yours. Besides," he added in a low tone so only the two of them could hear him, "isn't it best you stay away from her lest you place more suspicion on yourself and cause more trouble for her?"

Johann's blue-green gaze snapped to Radcliffe's gray eyes, and he reminded himself to try and keep the bitterness from his tone. If only he'd followed his own advice. But then he wouldn't be in Europe in the middle of this fascinating mess and possibly within reach of something that could help Claire. For if the Eros Element could manipulate emotions, perhaps he could help her to not react badly when she saw him, and they could rediscover...

What? The prejudice that had landed them in this predicament in the first place. But he could at least give her back to her mother.

Lack of scientific method, dammit. There's no point in hoping. Get your mind back where it needs to be.

"You wouldn't let the woman you love go off into danger on

her own," Johann said, then stopped. His startled look said he hadn't allowed that word to trip off his tongue while talking about a woman very often, maybe ever.

"She'll be rehearsing this morning. Madame switched the schedule. You give her too little credit for being able to keep her daughter out of trouble."

Indeed, Marie emerged from her dressing room looking determined but without one of her many expressions that gave her the air of being a completely different person. Chadwick wondered if it was a side effect of their work with the Eros Element, but even before they'd discovered it, when he first met her in that little village in the north of France, she'd convinced him she was nothing more than a maid. Even with his belief that everyone was more than others assumed them to be, it had taken effort to not allow his gaze to slide past her, almost like he fought some force.

Marie nodded to Johann but didn't say anything. The musician followed her with his gaze until she disappeared, his mouth set like when he played a particularly difficult passage.

"Ahem," Chadwick said. "Perhaps we should try our luck with Mademoiselle Lafitte before you have to rehearse this afternoon."

The streets had more people on them than when the battle raged, but everyone watched the sky, where airships flew by every so often.

"That's new." Johann sidestepped a woman who seemed convinced it was more important to look up than where she was going.

"Something's changed." Indeed, the air was charged with the heavy thickness of expectation, an imminent change of tide. "Perhaps the countryside is coming to the city's aid. I doubt the Prussians would have been able to build that many in so short a time."

Johann coughed. "Never underestimate Prussian inventive-ness. They're only flying over, not landing."

Chadwick looked at him, surprised he didn't attach some sort of remark about Prussian actresses to his comment about inventiveness. Perhaps he was changing. "They're staying out of cannon range, so they must be French."

They arrived at the address on the letter, which was within easy walking distance of the theatre. That made sense since the family was patrons. The Parisians did love their neighbor-hoods, which reminded Chadwick of the way Southerners stuck to their small towns, both with their almost blind patrio-tism for governments that may or may not have their best inter-ests at heart.

A butler answered the door, and Chadwick was quick to introduce himself as a doctor, and Johann gave his assumed name of Monsieur Sable.

"Oh, are you here to see to Mademoiselle?" the man asked. His skin had a gray tinge to it, which Chadwick diagnosed as emotional distress rather than illness, an entire household under strain.

"Yes," Chadwick said. He didn't like to lie, but he also didn't want to pass up the opportunity to speak to the young woman in private.

The butler showed them to a parlor, where Mademoiselle Lafitte lay on a chaise in a pose of classic hysteria, her blonde curls in disarray over the pillow behind her. She moaned and thrashed, and her mother clung tightly to her hand.

"Doctor Chadwick Radcliffe," the butler said.

"Please don't stand," Chadwick said. "What happened?"

"You are American," Madame said, and rubbed her eyes with her free hand. "Are we in such a bad state that we have to depend on foreign doctors?"

"Yes, since so many of your French ones have abandoned

you. May I examine the patient? You can stay with her. In fact, I would prefer you do so. What happened?"

"Two days ago, she went to a meeting with the students." She said *students* with the inflection of one who was talking about an infestation of rats or insects. "Her father is too indulgent to let her do such things. When she returned, she was very quiet, would not speak to anyone that evening, and then the next morning, this."

Chadwick and Johann exchanged glances. That was the meeting referred to in the letter.

"We are doomed," Amelie moaned. "We must leave."

"We cannot leave, *Cherie*," her mother said. "Not with you like this."

Chadwick felt the girl's forehead and lifted her eyelids. There was no sign of illness or injury, not even of intoxication of some sort, but something about her behavior reminded him of what had happened to Marie.

Amelie opened her eyes, saw Radcliffe, and drew back.

"Don't let him near me, *Maman*! Don't let the dark man take me."

Madame Lafitte stood but didn't let go of her daughter's hand. "You must leave. You are making her more upset."

"Try to keep her as calm as you can. I have seen something similar recently and will let you know when I find something to help."

Madame nodded. "Very well. I would like her to be better in time for us to see the new show at the Bohème. Is it true that Fantastique will be taking the stage again? Amelie greatly admires her."

"Yes, and I was thinking she may be helpful if she were to come speak with your daughter. Perhaps a familiar face will bring her out of whatever this is."

"Very well."

The butler showed them out.

"What are you thinking?" Johann asked.

"We need to find out what happened at that meeting. Marie is the best one to do that."

"Because the girl admires her?"

"That and other things." Chadwick wanted to test his hunch. If what he suspected was true, it would add one more piece to the puzzle that was the Théâtre Bohème. "Have you noticed how she tends to take on roles and get into them more than any other actress you've seen?"

"Yes, but she's very talented."

"Just pay attention to her."

"Oh, believe me, I have no trouble doing that."

JOHANN WOULD NEVER HAVE GUESSED he'd miss Frederic. If there was a way the other violinist could sabotage him as stand-mate, he'd found it. From altering his bowing technique so it created a certain disharmony coming from Johann's direction to refusing to find a rhythm with regard to turning the pages, there had been an annoyance every few minutes.

But Frederic's behavior didn't compare to the hatred the other musicians directed at Johann after Frederic's death. It was a true French coldness, a frosty politeness that pushed Johann away more effectively than harsh words could have. He straightened his shoulders and sat with his back to the rest of the violins, although he could still hear whispers behind him.

Even worse, Maestro Fouré frowned in his direction frequently. When the conductor called their first break, he gestured for Johann to join him. They walked to the backstage area, and Fouré looked at Johann from under his thick gray brows.

"Now that you know about the relationship between Mademoiselle St. Jean and me, I hope you will feel comfortable telling me anything," the conductor said. "Although I have been unable to be a true father to her—and please believe me when I say her mother felt that was in her best interest, so I believe her—I do love her as a daughter and want her to be happy."

"I didn't kill LeClerc." Johann ensured he looked straight at the conductor when he said it to leave no doubt that he told the truth.

"I didn't think you killed him directly, but I wonder if it's possible your attention made him a target."

"How so? Do you think I have friends who are that powerful?"

"No, but you have enemies who may want you out of the way, and the government is running out of money to pay the guardsmen."

Johann exhaled too sharply for it to be a breath, but not hard enough for it to be an exasperated sigh. "I'm never going to escape from that mistake, am I?"

"You can solve your problems with the Guild, but it will not be easy, and the success of this performance will be key."

A small, unfamiliar sensation burst in Johann's chest— hope. If he could clear his debt, he could pursue Marie. "I'm willing to do anything."

"Those are the words of a desperate man." Fouré frowned. "Or one in love. Tell me, do you love my daughter?"

Although the declaration had snuck out from Johann's lips that morning, the words now caught in his throat. He knew he did, but as for how she felt about him—well, he didn't want to gamble his reputation in case she made a fool of him.

"I feel very strongly for her," he said and felt the emotional barrier snap back into place between him and Fouré.

"So now you're being cautious? You are still young and stupid, Maestro, if you don't know what's worth betting on."

"I've learned a few things over the past year." Johann

refused to let the older man's gaze wither him like his father's had.

"One more thing. Marie is a headstrong girl. Don't let her go into danger by herself."

"Trust me, I'm trying not to. But what did you mean about the first performance?"

"If it goes well, Lucille might give everyone a bonus. I am willing to give mine to you for your freedom."

Johann didn't know what to say. His father would never do anything so generous, especially not to help Johann out of a mistake.

"Thank you."

"You're welcome. Now remember what I said about keeping Marie out of danger. She's more like her mother than she would like to admit."

29

T héâtre Bohème, 5 December 1870

Marie found herself the subject of curious gazes when she reached the backstage area.

"Are you going to be able to perform?" Leigh Sellers asked. "I know all the lines if you're not comfortable."

Marie allowed the *premiere femme* role to overtake her, but she felt that she held it rather than it grasping her. "Your attempt to sound helpful shows that you're trying to be a good actress, but I'm not going to take you up on your most kind and *generous* offer."

Leigh humphed and stalked off. Marie glanced around, and the other actors looked away.

"It is good to see you back," Janelle whispered. "Leigh was sure she would be able to steal your role."

"She can try, but she won't succeed."

Throughout rehearsal, Marie felt like the role she played reflected facets of her own personality and experiences. It still tried to overtake her, and she let it to a certain extent, but she did not allow it full control. The only problem—when she struggled with the balance, she forgot her lines. By lunchtime, she was frustrated enough to feel relief when Lucille called for an end to their work for the day.

"Be sure you are prepared tomorrow," she told Marie.

Marie went to her dressing room to see if the ghost was still lurking about. If not, she would sneak into his lair. She was studying her script when a knock startled her.

"*Entree!*"

The door opened, and Doctor Chadwick Radcliffe walked in.

"They said I would find you here. How are you settling in to the life of the *premiere femme* of the Théâtre Bohème?"

It took a moment for her to process his words. She was startled to see him there, and he just didn't fit in those surroundings. Her mind placed him in the infirmary, not the actors' hall.

"Fine, I suppose. To what do I owe the pleasure of your visit?" Although she wasn't sure it was a pleasure. "If you're concerned as to my mental state, I'm fine." *I think.*

"I'll get right to the point so I don't disturb you further." He gestured to the chair in front of the dressing table, and she nodded for him to take a seat. He settled in and placed his hat on his lap. She noted how precise his movements were, no motion wasted.

"Does this have something to do with Amelie Lafitte?"

He smiled, his teeth white against his skin. "Yes, and we need your help and your talent to move us along."

Marie shifted to hide the shock of anxiety his words produced, both from the fact she was having difficulty managing her talent and because the way he looked at her and his words at the townhouse made her wonder if he suspected what she could do.

"I'm not sure I follow, Doctor."

"Maestro Bledsoe and I spoke with Mademoiselle Lafitte. She is quite mad, or seems to be, but her mother said she admires you. We hoped you might be able to reach her mind, find out what happened to her."

A draught came through the room from somewhere, and Marie pulled her shawl around her shoulders.

"I can go tomorrow. I need to work on my script." *And find the ghost's lair.*

"I would caution you not to wait too long lest the young lady go further into her hysterical state before you can speak with her."

"And you're sure I can help?"

He gave her a measured look that made her wonder what he really wanted to say. Finally, he told her, "You have certain charms that make you very convincing. I've heard of your talent as an actress, and I look forward to seeing it in the upcoming production."

"You overestimate my ability. I'm not finding this one as easy."

The skeptical lift to his eyebrows told her he didn't believe her, and she tilted her head. The motion brought on the sense of a mask molding her face from the inside out, and she found herself back in the character of Marguerite the Spy.

No, no, no, I don't want this right now.

"Are you all right, Mademoiselle?"

"I'm well enough." Even her voice took on a smoother, huskier tone. "Continue."

"You know how Inspector Davidson is interested in the theatre, even more now that he is involved in the murder investigations and is curious about what we were doing for Cobb."

"Yes."

"You don't want him to poke around too much, however."

"No, I don't. I don't trust him."

"Then help us solve this, and perhaps you can also help clear Bledsoe's name."

The thought intrigued Marie, but she wasn't sure if it was

because she truly wanted to find out or if she acted from the impulses of the spy character who seemed determined to inhabit her body at the moment. However, she felt more in control of whatever it was, like she could push it away if she needed.

Perhaps the spirit's concoction or training or whatever is working.

"Very well, I will help you."

"Good. Please let me know when you think you'll be able to visit her."

"I'll have a messenger bring a request over today."

He stood and bowed slightly. "Thank you for your assistance, Mademoiselle."

She inclined her head, and just before he closed the door, she heard him say, "Uncanny."

Once he left, she closed her eyes and focused on letting go of the part, visualizing it peeling away from her from her head downward.

"You are improving, Mademoiselle." The spirit's voice flowed around her, but she thought she could pinpoint the source from—of course—the direction of the mirror.

"Oh, you're still here?"

"Only just returned to check in on you."

"Then I will bid you *au revoir*. I cannot concentrate on my lines knowing that someone watches me."

She rose and moved toward the door. The low laugh that followed her made her shoulders tighten.

"You mock me, Monsieur?"

"Try as you might to escape me, you will find that our futures are more intertwined than you may think."

"I'm not in the habit of responding to vague threats, especially from men who try to manipulate me."

With that, she exited the room and closed the door behind her. Once in the hallway, she realized she'd forgotten her script.

I'm not going back in there. This may be a good time to send that message.

The feeling of being watched followed her until she left that floor and ascended to the auditorium level. She only hoped that meant she drew the spirit away from her dressing room and his hideout.

Johann saw Marie skirt along the edge of the auditorium and disappear into the administrative wing, her expression determined. Maestro Fouré inclined his head in that direction. Johann nodded, and when the conductor called a break, he placed his violin in its case and went to search for Marie.

He found her in Lucille's theatre office giving a message to a young man.

"And bring me the reply when you get one," she told him. He jerked his chin to his chest once and was off.

"What was that about?" Johann asked.

"Doctor Radcliffe asked that I help you with Amelie Lafitte."

In the watery sunlight coming through the window, her face looked pinched and pale.

"You don't have to. I'm sure the inspector will manage to blunder his way into the relevant information."

Her laugh brought some color to her cheeks and loosened the tension in his chest.

"He's not so bad. He only wants to do his job, as we all do. Speaking of which..." She stood. "I must go back to my script."

"Which isn't in here."

"No, it's not. It's in my dressing room."

"I'll walk you down."

She pressed her lips together, but she nodded. "Thank you."

When they reached the dressing room, she opened the door and said, "Goodbye for now, then."

"*Au revoir.*" He followed his impulse to lean in and kiss her on the cheek. "Happy studying."

She shut the door in his face.

He rubbed his nose and shook his head. There was something odd—odder than usual—about her behavior. He walked away but waited at the end of the hall behind a lintel where he could watch for her without her seeing him. After a few minutes, she opened her door, looked around, and went the other way toward the stairs to the basement. He followed her and caught up to her just as she reached the two old set pieces she had paused between on their trip down to the Roma camp.

"Wait," he said.

She whirled around. "What are you doing here?"

Johann looked at the dark rectangle and the pale determination on Marie's face. There was a spark in her eyes, of the excitement at being on the cusp of an adventure, and he knew there was an answering one in his. "You're not going down there alone. I'm coming too."

She opened her mouth as though to protest, and he clenched his jaw, ready to argue. She shrugged. "Suit yourself."

Johann tried to take the lantern and lead, but Marie held it from him. "I'll go first. I know how these corridors typically go, and this way I can see if it connects to any of the paths I already know. Move quietly, don't speak and listen for the sound of anyone following us."

"Aye, captain."

She rolled her eyes but didn't say anything. He followed her into the gloom, which seemed to swallow the lantern light such that they could only see a few feet in front of them.

"Are you sure that light is bright enough?"

"Hush! We mustn't talk lest he hear us. I have no doubt he

has ways of listening even though he's supposed to be observing the musicians."

Johann wanted to ask who *he* was, but he complied with her instructions and kept alert for the sound of anyone following them. After a few twists and turns and a slight climb, the lantern light bounced off a wall of glass.

"Aha," Marie breathed, then turned to her right. She gestured for him to follow her, and they went through another labyrinth of passages until they came to a dead end and a trap door.

"Help me open it," she mouthed.

"Are you sure about this?"

She nodded and set the lantern on the floor. They pulled at the door, and it opened slowly. Instead of descending the ladder, Marie shone the lantern into what looked like a workshop. Various mechanical and clockwork parts lay strewn on a table, and Johann caught his breath when he saw two of the steam-powered ravens.

Who is this, and why has he been spying on me?

They looked at each other with astonished expressions that turned to panicked ones when a voice behind them said, "And how do you like my toy shop, Mademoiselle? I warned you to stay away from this man."

Merde, *he tricked me. He wasn't interested in the musicians.*

Marie straightened and stood, as did Johann. Now that she could see him more clearly in the lamplight, she took note of the spirit and saw he was solid and not at all ghost-like. Not that this came as a surprise—she'd known he was human. But she was glad to directly confront him directly even if it was at the wrong end of a gun.

A metal mask covered the man's face, but it was topped with a mane of curly dark hair. He wore evening dress and a cape, but instead of black, it was of a material of the sort of color that blended into the shadows. Marie recalled Radcliffe's saying that there had been an inventor Patrick worked with who was working on such a substance but who had gone mad from the chemicals and grief over his lost love and disappeared. Could this be the insane inventor of the Union? And had she met him before with Cobb?

"So you've found the entrance to my workshop," he said. "And therefore of my humble quarters. You know I cannot allow you to leave now that you know my secrets."

"You're not a very good ghost if you're going to confirm all the rumors about you. Spirits like you are supposed to be more subtle," Johann said.

"Ah, and as for you, Maestro, I did tell you to stay away from Mademoiselle." He gestured with the steam pistol, and the red indicator on the butt made the shadows appear to whirl around him. "You first, Maestro. And don't try anything funny in the workshop."

Johann preceded Marie down the ladder and then helped her when her dress caught. The spirit climbed down it with the nimbleness of an arachnid, always keeping the gun trained on them.

"As for what to do with the two of you, I shall have to ponder that. Into the chamber with you."

"The chamber?" Marie asked.

"Yes, I had it built for just such an occasion." He opened a door on the other side of the workshop and ushered them through before locking it behind them. A chain hung from the ceiling, and Marie pulled it. A bulb illuminated the chamber and gave her the feeling of being in the midst of a crowd, for the room was paneled with mirrors that reflected their images in each direction.

Everywhere Marie turned, she saw her face, but it seemed to her that in each panel, she looked slightly different. In one she appeared confused. In another, angry. In a third, frightened. And in the final one, she swallowed against the paleness, the sense of stark truth that with everything reflected to her externally, she was empty inside.

"Are you all right?" Johann asked.

"It's the mirrors. There's something strange about them."

"Yes, but look at the bulbs. Or bulb. I think there's just one." He pointed to it, and Marie recognized the three-tube structure of the ones Cobb used on his train and what he'd had installed in the theatre when he pretended to try to make nice with her mother.

"They're Cobb's," she whispered into Johann's ear. "The spirit must be his inventor, the one Radcliffe talked about."

"Now, now, no secrets, Mademoiselle. That's not very entertaining for me."

"I'm not trying to entertain you," she snapped.

"Then you're not going to be a very interesting captive. And I know you have such a range of talent. How do you like my mirrors? They each have a different coating and surface texture to give you an altered appearance. Of course when I built the chamber, I anticipated it would just be for you, after this upcoming performance."

"Why?"

"Because your mother owes me, and I was going to take that which is most precious to her. But don't worry, Mademoiselle, that will all be made clear in time. Meanwhile, I need for you to tell me what happened with Cobb once you met with him. Enough of the preamble."

A slight odor came to Marie's nose, that of Cobb's tobacco, and she knew that wasn't all the spirit pumped into the room. "No," she said. "I won't tell you anything unless you release Maestro Bledsoe."

"Marie, no," Johann said. "I won't leave you here. This man is mad."

"I'm mad?" The spirit's voice floated into the chamber again. "Or perhaps you are to think you had a chance with her. You do realize she's spoiled goods."

"Oh, now that's unnecessary," Marie said. She struggled to keep her eyes open and slumped against one of the mirrors. Johann caught her and lowered her to the ground, where he supported her torso to recline against his.

I have to do something, keep him from pulling the information out of me. It's my only bargaining chip.

She thought about the mirrors, the facets of herself, and how the different roles pulled from her own characteristics. If there was anything everyone agreed upon, it was her stubbornness. What role had she played that meant she was focused and stubborn?

The ingenue, the one that drove Maurice mad. No, I can't do that one. I can't manipulate Johann like that.

"Do what you need to do," he said. The weight on her head told her he was also slumping.

"You can try to get me to talk," Marie heard herself saying, her voice younger and lighter, "but I refuse to do so on the grounds that I am my own woman, and I will not be manipulated by a man."

30

———

héâtre Bohème, 5 December 1870

Pay attention, Radcliffe had said. Johann couldn't be sure because he recognized he was under the influence of some sort of substance, but Marie felt lighter, and she sounded younger with all the stubbornness of a typical teen. Johann's mind drifted to the past in spite of his wanting to listen to the conversation. He remembered that attitude well from his own younger sister Lizbeth. She was probably married off by now to someone who would help increase the fortunes of the estate or its influence or—

"Very well, Mademoiselle," the spirit said and broke through Johann's fog of memory and resentment. "You can stay there in the chamber while I see how the orchestra is getting on without Maestro Bledsoe, but be aware I will be back, and I will discover your secrets. I need something in your memories, and I refuse to think I have brought you along on this journey for nothing."

Cool air blasted into the chamber, and Johann's eyelids released their vacuum-like grip on each other.

Edward would be proud of my scientific observations.

He dragged his lids open and ignored the urge to look around at the crowd of reflections. Only one thing mattered to him.

Marie appeared pale, and with her eyes closed and lips slightly pursed, she seemed young and innocent. He'd bedded many actresses, and they'd all had a hardness to them, but Marie was all soft strength, not bitter brittleness, no matter what she'd been through. He suspected that when—*if*, he corrected himself; he couldn't presume her feelings, and her willingness meant everything to him—they did come together, he would lose himself, his heart, to her. Her kisses, more addictive than opium, had shown him that, but he was willing to trust himself to her. Now if only he could get her to trust him.

He leaned over and kissed her. "Wake up, sleeping beauty. We have to figure out how to get out of here."

"Mmmm." She kissed him back and reached her arms around his neck. He buried his hands in her hair and ignored the ping of hairpins falling out. Why did actresses need so many pins in their hair? He relished the silky smoothness of it on his hands and wrists and the welcome openness of her mouth. He moved to pull her more firmly on top of him, and the light went out.

Marie pulled away and asked. "What happened?"

Johann moved his hands to the sides of her face to keep contact with her and enjoy the contours of her high cheekbones and the curve of her jaw. "I don't know whether that was intentional or accidental. Either way, it will be more difficult to get out of here if we can't see."

"It would be impossible anyway. He's too good with building things." She slumped against him, and he stroked her hair.

"There has to be something we can do. That I can do."

She turned over and laid her head on his chest. "You can

accept my offer to take your freedom and leave. The ghost doesn't care about you, only me."

"Never. I'm not leaving without you."

He tangled his fingers in her softly curling tresses, and she rewarded him with a contented sigh.

"You don't want me, anyway. As he said, I'm damaged goods, and I don't even know who I am half the time."

Her tone was jesting, but the undercurrent of despair to her words echoed his own hopelessness about his family situation and what happened with the Clockwork Guild. He closed his eyes, not that it mattered in the dark, but he had to shove away the wall that rose between his mouth and heart.

"I never told you about what happened to put me in debt with the Clockwork Guild."

An almost imperceptible shift in her posture told him he'd surprised her.

"No. You're very good at avoiding the topic."

"Because I'm ashamed of what happened. I told you about my father and my brother, how they pressured me to go into something sensible to help the estate."

"Yes, and how your musical talent wasn't useful to them. Such a waste."

He kissed the top of her head. "Even after I succeeded, the pressure didn't stop. He kept telling me I was foolish, that I could still take control of parts of the estate my brother wasn't interested in. As if I should be honored to take his leftovers."

"And you couldn't leave."

"No, not completely. You more than anyone know how hard it is to escape the influence of an overbearing parent, no matter how far away you are."

She made an unladylike sound. "What in the world gives you that idea?"

He laughed. "You've picked up Iris's expression. But yes, he started to use his influence to keep me from getting paying musical jobs, and he cut off what little income I was getting from my one corner of our property. I had to show him I was too irresponsible to manage the estate. First I made sure my own reputation as a rake would keep his business associates from taking me seriously, but it backfired."

"Let me guess—that helped you with them."

He wanted to kiss away the despair in her voice, but he continued. "Yes, some of them had the nerve to ask for introductions to some of my friends. Most men are cads."

"That I also know too well."

"So then I had to show I wasn't to be trusted with money, and I started gambling." Saying the words made his stomach turn like he'd eaten a bad cream puff. How could he have been so stupid? "And once you enter that world, you cannot leave it unless you go far away or die. I thought I controlled my risk, but I drank too much one night and overshot, although whiskey had never affected me like that before."

"Was that the first time you'd gambled with the Clockwork Guild?"

"Yes, it was a secret club. I had only just gained entrance."

Marie pulled away, and he reached for her, only to find she leaned up so she could turn her face to his. She kissed him on the lips, but instead of passion, it held sympathy.

"That's how he snared you. Cobb, I mean. He knew he had to get to you to get to Edward and go after the Eros Element."

"And everything was choreographed from that point on." Although he hated the man, Johann had to admire Cobb. The American was even more ruthless than Johann's father and a much better puppet master. Perhaps he was even involved to some extent in the siege of Paris, although that seemed to stretch the boundaries of possibility.

"So what do we do?" Marie asked. "We can't escape Cobb if we can't get out of this mess. You have to go get help."

Johann held her tight to him. "And I told you, I'm not going to leave you. I trust you with my secret. Whatever you have to tell the madman, it will not change my opinion of you. I love you, Marie, no matter what you've done, and we'll get out of this together."

MARIE SCOOTED out of Johann's arms. "That's not you talking, that's whatever was in the smoke." Her heartbeat fluttered in her throat like a caged bird that feels the door might be opening to freedom. But at what cost? Yes, he'd revealed his past to her, and she sympathized, but he'd only gone too far with his money, not his body and self. Plus he had used other women, other actresses, to do so.

The old doubts crept in. Did he truly love *her* or was he attracted to who he thought she was because he was picking up on her talent? And what about when the siege lifted? Even if he wanted to stay, he would have to continue to run from the Guild until he could scrape up enough money to pay them back.

Her mind whirled like a panicked bird now banging back and forth between the bars of hope and despair.

That doesn't even make sense. But what does it matter?

The muffled thunk of a door closing somewhere outside the chamber made her still, and the hiss of gas alerted her to cover her eyes before the bulb illuminated the chamber with a thousand flickering, mocking lights. Although weak, they made her scrunch her eyes behind her hands.

"So I find the two of you not in each others' arms," the ghost said. "That's promising, for the orchestra isn't the same without your expert leadership, Maestro. I am willing to let you go in exchange for something."

"I'm not leaving without her," Johann said simultaneously with Marie asking, "What?"

They glared at each other.

The ghost's low chuckle echoed through the room. "And so

we disagree. I will release him if you tell me about that first fateful meeting with Cobb."

"I will do what you ask if he can go," Marie said and then mouthed, *"Get help."*

"No," Johann grasped her arms and whispered, "What if he gases you again and you don't wake up? I saw you that one night. I was terrified you wouldn't come out of it."

His words brought Marie back to the vision of that episode. Whereas her memories previously had had the fog of trauma obscuring them from full recollections, having dreamed it brought back all the details and confirmed her suspicion now that she had her memory and the man side-by-side.

"The man in the carriage!" She turned to where she thought the voice came from, although it was difficult to pinpoint exactly. "You were the man in Cobb's carriage, the one who wanted my help getting something back from him. What was it? Was it some sort of design for a machine?"

"Ah, Mademoiselle, you have found me out." A light flickered behind one of the mirrors, showing the man, still masked. Johann reared a hand back to smash it, but Marie caught it and twisted it behind his arm.

"I forgot about your strength," he ground out. "You can let off a little."

A bitter laugh bubbled up from her gut. "Most people do. You won't do anyone any good if you can't play."

Johann struggled against her grip. "But he's just on the other side of the glass. I can get to him."

"No, let's bargain," she said. "I think I know what he wants."

"And what is that, Mademoiselle?" The spirit sneered through the words.

"That night in the hotel, I looked through Cobb's things," she said.

"And do you recall what you saw?" Now the man sounded interested.

"No, not in any great detail. I remember the evening's events more than the setting."

"You need to go into the memory. If you do, I will release you."

Johann turned, and Marie let him go. "Send her to her dressing room and let me be there with her."

"No," Marie said. *I can keep him from knowing the full extent of my shame. It's bad enough the spirit will find out.*

"Yes," Johann said. "That way I can make sure he doesn't kidnap you while you are insensible."

"I am willing if you are, Mademoiselle. I trust your word."

Marie nodded. "I'll cooperate."

A mirror on the other side of the chamber lowered, and a dark square joined their reflections and that of the inventor. Her lamp sat just beyond.

"That goes back to the passage you came through and to your dressing room. Go on. I will follow with my revolver in case you think about running."

Marie didn't waste any time. She grabbed Johann's hand and dragged him through the corridor after picking up the lamp, which gave off a weak glow.

"Do you think he'll allow us to escape?" Johann murmured.

"I don't know." Then a terrifying notion occurred to her. "I only hope that Edward and Mister O'Connell aren't working on the aether lighting system. The inventor is already unpredictable."

Johann squeezed her hand. "I won't leave you, no matter what."

They reached a wall of glass, and Marie saw her dressing room just beyond. She looked behind her and saw the spirit with his gun in one hand and a strange-looking lantern in the other. He set the lantern on the floor and moved a lever on the wall, which caused the glass pane to lower soundlessly to the floor. Before she and Johann stepped through, the spirit handed Johann a mask.

"It will filter out the smoke for you, Monsieur."

"Thank you."

They walked into the dressing room, and Johann headed for the door, but the ghost's voice stilled him.

"Don't even think of it, Monsieur. This glass is not bullet-proof, and she will perish if you try to escape before I get what I need."

"I gave my word," Marie added. "He can trust me."

The brief hunch that came to Johann's shoulders told Marie that he'd taken her words the wrong way, that he thought she implied he wasn't trustworthy. With a sigh, she laid on the chaise lounge.

"Please come sit beside me," she said. He pulled the stool over from the dressing table and sat beside her, her hand in his.

This time when she smelled the smoke and the familiar feelings of lethargy overtook her, she had an anchor to the present and to safety, at least until she revealed her shame.

31

1 *7 May 1868, Hotel Auberge, 17 May 1868*

Armed with her role of Marguerite the Spy, femme fatale and deadly assassin, Marie ascended in the lift, barely acknowledging the operator. She had a goal, a mission. The warnings she'd received about Cobb swirled in the back of her mind, but her role gave her confidence she could handle him. Men fell at her feet at the theatre, after all, and gave her whatever she wanted. Why should this one be different?

She knocked, and Cobb opened the door. Every part of her body that his gaze fell on felt like something horrible and grasping raked over it. It required all her willpower and Marguerite's confidence to not shudder.

"You look lovely," he said and stepped aside. His hotel suite had a parlor, where a pull-in table held silver-domed dishes."

Simultaneously anxious and relieved, Marie asked, "No servants?" *Or witnesses.*

He took her cloak. His hands lingered on her shoulders longer than needed, and his breath tickled her ear. "I thought you wanted to speak to me in private."

Marie thought she heard the lock on the suite door click

from the outside but quelled the panicked urge to test it. If it was, indeed, locked, she would have to escape with her wits, and for once she was glad to have the role on board. She focused on the mission, or missions, she had been given and walked around the room, pretending to be awed by the sumptuous surroundings but really searching for signs Cobb had been involved in smuggling or had something he shouldn't. Not that either man had given her anything specific to look for.

There was a drafting table in the corner, where Marie saw a drawing of something mechanical. A quick look at the table told her that her own papers weren't there, and she pressed her lips against the frustrated sigh that wanted to escape.

"What's this?" she asked. She picked up the large piece of paper, and whatever it was seemed to look back at her. It reminded her of a drawing she'd seen in a museum by DaVinci, but instead of multiple views of muscles and the male parts, it had numbers, lines, rods, and gears.

"Nothing for you to worry about." Cobb took it away and rolled it up. "May I pour you a drink?"

Marguerite and Marie both said, "No, thank you."

"Oh, but I insist. I ordered this especially for you."

He pulled a bottle of wine out of a bucket, and Marie was relieved to see the cork still in it. He opened it and poured some of the golden liquid in a glass.

"To our friendship," he said. "And I have a proposition for you."

The sip Marie had just taken turned bitter at the back of her mouth, but Marguerite stretched her lips into a knowing smile.

"And what would that be?"

He pulled a chair out for her, and she sat at the table. He lifted the domed covers off the dishes. "I read the papers you're so eager to retrieve."

"And?"

"I believe I can help you with your goal of traveling the world in a way that would be mutually advantageous to us both."

The food smelled heavenly—creamy and with an expert mix of herbs—but she'd lost what little appetite she had. Marguerite told her this would be the perfect role, the opportunity to get closer to Cobb's affairs and investigate his wrongdoing. Marie told Marguerite to shush, that she only wanted to get her documents back so she'd have the freedom to choose her own path.

Don't anger him until you have your papers in hand.

"How so?" she asked and took a bite of quail.

"I recognize that you think you need a break from the stage. It happens sometimes with particularly talented people, they need to step away from their vocation and mature in other ways, but the danger is that you'll find something you think is comfortable and never return."

"I can determine my own needs, thank you."

"Ah, but trust me as someone older and wiser who has seen much wonderful potential go to waste. I propose that you come work for me on my airship. You're smart, and you have the singular ability of being very convincing in whatever role you choose, so you can be my eyes and ears in places where a man can't go."

Marie swirled her wine and pretended to consider, but one thing she and Marguerite agreed—she needed to get out of there with her papers, but he wasn't going to let her go easily. "Although your offer is tempting, I cannot accept it."

"I will pay you generously, if it's money you're worried about. Much more than you make as an actress."

"Thank you, but I'm afraid I have to go. My papers?" She held out a hand.

"Allow me to convince you further." He took her documents from his waistcoat. She saw her autograph scrawled across the outside. Instead of giving them to her, he walked to the fireplace, which was lit against the late spring chill. Too late she realized what he was about to do and had only half-risen when he threw them into the flames.

"No!" She ran to the fireplace and grabbed the poker, but the letters had already been mostly consumed. The ink from her autograph blazed in a flash, and then they were all gone.

"No," she whispered. Tears smeared the flames into a wall of light, and she turned away. She clenched the poker, and Marguerite whispered to her to put it to good use, take her revenge, and run. Cursing her lack of innate ruthlessness, Marie dropped it, fell to her knees, and sobbed into her hands.

A gentle hand stroked her hair. "There, now. I can take you to places you've only dreamed of."

She wobbled to her feet and rubbed her eyes with her hands to clear the tears. "I don't want to go anywhere with you. I'll find a way myself." She grabbed her shawl and stalked to the door.

"I wouldn't leave just yet, Mademoiselle." He lowered his voice. "A photographer and reporter are waiting outside this room, and two more are in the lobby. All of them have received tips that famed actress Fantastique is having a torrid affair with an American entrepreneur, and you know the press has been looking for evidence that you're a wildcat in bed like every other actress. Do you want to give the papers something to squawk over in the morning? It would kill your mother."

Marie stilled with her hand on the knob. "I do not take kindly to being blackmailed, Monsieur."

"I'm only trying to convince you of what's best for you. Leave with me tonight."

"And that wouldn't be as scandalous, to just disappear?"

"No one would have to know. You're between shows, so it will be weeks before anyone misses you. You can even say goodbye to your mother, although you don't need to pick up anything. We can get clothing made for you easily."

Part of her wanted to tell him to shove off, that she would weather the scandal, but a bigger part of her wanted to escape. If she could only make it out of France, she could start over. Especially if he were to pay her well. And she could help the handsome detective and escape from the man in the carriage.

"Very well, Monsieur."

"Good. Shall we seal our arrangement with a kiss?"

Marie held out her hand. He kissed the back of it.

"And now shall we finish dinner? The baked Alaska here is delightful, they say."

Marie took her seat at the table. Cobb acted the gentleman that night, but she was too naive. Soon the circumstances of her employment included more than she'd been led to believe, and by the time she returned to France, her reputation was thoroughly ruined, as was her innocence.

Théâtre Bohème, 5 December 1870

Johann was a cad. He'd been called that many a time by many a woman, but this was the first occasion he felt it. Even in her trance, Marie's face showed the strain of the memory, what her attempt at independence cost her. He breathed through the mask, which smelled of something acrid, but whatever it was, it kept him from falling into the past like she had.

When they'd started on this strange journey, he'd only seen her as a maid and then as an actress who could be treated like the others. None of them had ever indicated to him that they were anything but willing to bed him, the famous musician, but he now wondered if that was because he'd never looked for shadows behind their eyes or had mistaken the cynical twist of their mouths for flirtatiousness. And he certainly hadn't tried to know them better, to discover the courage that led them to choose their own paths or the tragedy that had forced them into their lifestyles.

Now he stroked Marie's hand and willed for her to come out of the nightmare.

"Have you found what you were looking for?" he asked the spirit behind the mirror.

"Yes. As I thought, Cobb stole the plan for my automaton. I had never received confirmation until now."

"How do you know it was yours?" Johann asked.

"Because of what she described. I was inspired by Leonardo DaVinci's Vitruvian man, and so that's how I drew out my plan."

Marie stirred, and Johann directed his attention to her face. Some color came back to her cheeks, and anger at the spirit flooded through him. Was that one detail worth risking Marie's health and forcing her back through the worst experience of her life?

"And you couldn't just draw another one?"

"If a composer loses a symphony, can he just write another one? If a novelist loses their book, can they just produce another one with the same elegance and inspiration? No." Now the spirit's voice echoed around him as its volume reached agitated levels. "No, Monsieur, I could not *just draw another one*, for he also had my developmental notes, and no matter how hard I tried, I could not reproduce the genius of the first attempt."

Or you were smoking something when you drew it the first time and couldn't remember what you did. Johann didn't voice the words, but he'd met composers who swore they couldn't create without opium or some other substance to help them. The memory of their erratic behavior and less than clear logic made him bite his tongue over his thoughts. The spirit still held a gun, after all.

"Will she be all right? How long will it take for her to come out of this?"

"You can remove the mask. I have doused the Persian lamp."

Johann decided to wait until Marie was fully aware in case there was something in the air still. He'd already spilled his secrets, but he wanted to be able to move if the spirit decided to take Marie with him. Not that he could stop a bullet, but perhaps he could wrest the gun away or—

I am a true fool. I have no plan, no good one, anyway.

"She is beautiful when she sleeps, isn't she?"

Johann stood between Marie and the mirror, or at least as much as he could. "Yes, but she is spoken for."

"Brave words, monsieur, considering I'm the one with the weapon. But you are powerless—she will not be with you unless I give her leave to do so."

"She is her own woman!" Now Johann tore off the mask and stalked to the mirror, but Marie's whisper stopped him.

"Johann, please don't."

He took another step.

"Oh, please come closer, Monsieur, so I can get a clear shot with my camera if not my gun. The violinist in the actress's dressing room shall be a juicy tidbit for the papers, particularly if he is found murdered there."

"You wouldn't dare. That would ruin the theatre. You got what you came for. Why pursue this further?"

"My business is not finished with Madame St. Jean. Until it is, I cannot allow her daughter her freedom, but you may feel free to court her under my watch here to make sure nothing improper happens. You know her judgment isn't sound. Just beware she is a tricky one and can take on many faces."

"There's no need to insult her."

"Johann, don't worry about me, just come back," Marie

pleaded. She half-sat and leaned precariously toward him. He dashed back to support her before she fell.

"And remember, Monsieur, Mademoiselle, if you try to escape, my ravens will catch you or the Prussians will chase you back in or shoot your airship down. Your lives are mine for the foreseeable future."

The spirit's laughter faded, presumably as he walked back down the hidden corridor.

Johann helped Marie to sit fully, but his hands, which he was ashamed to think had supported many women in various states of reclining, felt clumsy. Once she sat, he moved away. He didn't want her to think he put her in the same category as the actresses he'd used in his campaign to prove his irresponsible nature.

"So now that you know, are you disgusted and disappointed in me too?" she asked. Perhaps the smoke left a rasp in her voice, but Johann suspected he heard the tears she fought back. Her dark locks fell about her shoulders, and this new look, the disheveled tangle, made her seem young and vulnerable.

He sat next to her and took her hands so he wouldn't give in to the temptation to bury his hands in her hair and revel in its silkiness. "Absolutely not. We've both made mistakes that we're not proud of."

She tried to smile, but tears fell on to their joined hands, and she collapsed against him. He held her while she sobbed.

"I just want to get away," she whispered once she'd calmed.

"I know you did."

"No, now. There's nothing for me here, but we're trapped."

"Hey," he said and lifted her chin. He couldn't resist kissing her. "We'll get out of this. The siege can't last forever, and I have the marquis's promise even if he is no longer alive."

She nodded, and he was glad she didn't mention the airship. The spirit might try to shoot it down himself. He captured her mouth again, and she opened to him, running her fingers through his hair. He grasped her and pulled her to him.

A squawk and thunk made them jump and pull apart, and Johann saw a red glow behind the mirror.

"We're being watched," he said. He wished he could throw something at the raven.

"Yes. Help me to the townhouse. I need to sleep without dreams after that."

"Good luck." He knew his dreams would be tantalizing and filled with her. At least the spirit couldn't get to them there. He thought.

32

———

$\mathbf{M}$*aison LaFitte, 6 December 1870*
When Marie woke the next morning, she found a ribbon and a thimble in her slippers, which had been placed at the foot of the bed.

Ah, right, the feast of St. Nicholas. I wish he had brought us an end to the siege. I feel restless enough to expand and float away on my own.

She couldn't help but check around and behind her as she dressed. She'd slept later than the rest of the household, and when she went down for breakfast, she found a single roll instead of the usual variety of baked goods on the sideboard. It was one more reminder that Parisians would soon literally be tightening their belts as supplies inside the city ran out. She ate quickly and was finishing her tea—coffee was completely gone—when a knock on the front door echoed through the house and startled her. She heard Claudette answer the door, and soon the maid appeared.

"It's a boy," Claudette told her.

"Thank you. Where is everyone?"

"At the theatre, except Mademoiselle McTavish, who is in

the atelier. She says it's easier to spread her research materials out up there, and she's English so she doesn't mind the cold."

"She's tougher than she looks."

I'm not so sure I am. When Marie thought about what she'd revealed to the spirit and Johann, shame twisted her insides. She could have said she got caught up in the femme fatale role, but she didn't want to lie even if it meant admitting she'd joined Parnaby Cobb's collection of beautiful things in exchange for what she thought was freedom.

But that was a different time, and she'd figure out what to do with Johann when she saw him again. Thankfully that wasn't an imminent worry. "Bring the boy up."

The urchin she'd given the message to the day before walked into the dining room. He kept his eyes straight ahead, and Marie admired his focus.

"Madame Lafitte says to come as soon as you are able, Mademoiselle. Her daughter is doing worse."

Marie gave the boy a coin and hesitated before she dismissed him. She noted the hollowness of his cheeks, the thinness of the ankles and wrists sticking out from the too-small clothing. The siege was taking its toll on the poor first, but she wondered how long it would be before they all felt its effects on a deeper level.

"Claudette, take him to the kitchen. I'm sure our cook can find something for him."

"You're very kind, Mademoiselle," he said with a bow. Marie took note of him, thinking he would be a good addition to the theatre company with how he carried himself. Then she stopped—she needed to get away, not become more involved.

In the front hall, she wrapped herself in her cloak and walked into the cold. She hoped the air would sharpen her focus—they'd be going into dress rehearsals soon, but parts of the script still slid through her mind and refused to catch in memory. Plus Radcliffe's words had disturbed her. Did he know about her ability? He seemed a man of science, but then the Eros Element and its emotional effects had bent all their concepts of reality and possibility.

The Lafitte house stood sturdy and gray, not huge and ostentatious, but also larger than the average Parisian home. Marie recalled that Monsieur Lafitte was a merchant, although he hadn't done quite as well as Cinsault. But it seemed that they had something in common—members of their household who were involved with a dangerous cult.

The butler raised his eyebrows when he saw Marie, and she braced herself for the inevitable searching look, the rumor-fueled sniff of judgment, but he only nodded and gestured for her to follow him.

Amelie lay in a parlor that would be cheery and well-lit when the sun was out, but the gloom outside and the half-drawn curtains gave it a somber air. Marie recognized Madame Lafitte, who rose to greet her. All she saw of Amelie was a tangle of blonde curls over the end of the chaise.

"Come, let us speak before she awakens."

She led Marie into a dining room, where the curtains did lay open to let in the gray light outside.

"When I saw your message, I didn't dare to hope that you would actually come," Madame said. The tension around her mouth drew lines of strain down her pretty face.

"I'm not sure what I'm supposed to do, but I hope I can help in some small way."

"Your leaving was a blow to all of us, not just your mother and the theatre. Amelie always admired you, always looked forward to your performances. I hope that seeing you will bring her back to an easier time."

Marie maintained her composure, but inside the all too familiar strain of guilt twisted her stomach, particularly as she had just relived how stupid she'd been. "You don't mean just the siege."

"No, although that's been hard. Like most, we didn't anticipate it would last so long. Amelie felt betrayed when you ran off and became involved with a group of students. We thought she was just going to lectures, but those turned into rallies, and then, after the republicans failed to topple the emperor, something darker."

Madame Lafitte picked up a pamphlet from a sideboard, and Marie recognized the symbol, a square inside a circle.

"I found this in her cloak pocket. It's all nonsense to me, but I know it has something to do with her condition."

Marie opened it. The language looked familiar, but she didn't understand the words. *Iris or Radcliffe might be able to translate it.* "May I keep it?"

"Yes. She brought that back with her three nights ago. She has not been the same since."

A moan from the parlor startled Marie with its soul-aching depth. Madame paled.

"She is awake. Come. I pray that you will be able to help her."

She led Marie to Amelie, who lay with one arm over her eyes. The room smelled of sweat and old perfume, but Marie caught a whiff of something that tickled her brain with its familiarity. It briefly brought her back to a different parlor in a different time, but the flash of memory was gone before she could grasp it.

"Look who's come to see you," Madame said. "It's Fantastique."

Marie no longer cringed at her stage name, but she wasn't sure what she was supposed to do. She searched the roles that came to mind, but arrived at *la premiere femme* Fantastique, which she was surprised to find didn't feel like a role, but rather was part of her.

"Mademoiselle Lafitte? Amelie?" Marie sat on the stool beside the chaise and took one of the girl's hands. She remem bered Amelie as a girl with wide blue eyes in a delicate pretty face. Her features had grown into lovely young womanhood, but her eyes held a haunted look that went well beyond her years.

What did you see?

"Fantastique, you are here!" The girl's voice was hoarse, and Marie tried not to flinch from the smell of her breath.

"Yes, I've come to help you." Marie stroked her hand. "Tell me about your favorite play."

Amelie shook her head, and when she saw her mother, she closed her eyes. "Leave us, *Maman*. I must speak with Fantastique alone. The rose opens, and the thorns will dance."

"Very well, but I will be in the next room if you need me." To Marie, she whispered when she passed, "This is the sort of nonsense she's been saying."

Amelie struggled to sit, and Marie placed pillows behind her. She took both Marie's hands and squeezed with a strength beyond her frail appearance.

"You know of what I speak. You have seen it, the spirit, in action. It is awakened with the song of the spheres, and it waits to bask in the light of the eternal flame."

"What are you talking about?" Marie swallowed against the terror the memory brought up, of being trapped in the statue's arms at the Marquis de Monceau's house. Could it have had something to do with the immolation of the airship he'd tried to escape on?

"It was stirring, waiting, but it has been released, and it seeks the minds of weak men to possess. It has consumed many, and only I escaped to tell the tale, to give the warning."

Marie hoped the feverish glint to the girl's eyes meant she had only imagined horrors, but she suspected something had happened. "What do you mean, only you escaped?"

"Tell the inspector to check the church. There is more than one means of mass death in there."

"I've been in there. There's nothing but weapons."

"There wasn't until the other night. The painting, Mademoiselle. Eros and Psyche. Their wings moved, and it was too much for them."

The chill that overtook Marie had nothing to do with the temperature of the room. She recalled hearing the rustling of the wings when the statues came to life.

"But the National Guard was keeping people out."

"Many of them are students and don't see the reasoning in the government regulations. Stop arguing with me and listen! It may not be today or tomorrow, but it awakens." She shrieked with laughter. "And when it does, all will dance to its tune, flesh men and mechanical ones."

Madame Lafitte came in and shooed Marie out. "She is getting agitated. Please tell Doctor Radcliffe to hurry with his cure for her."

"I'm sure he is doing his best, but I will pass along the message and tell him what happened."

Once outside, she breathed the cool air in with relief, but it did nothing to loosen the tightness of dread in her stomach.

What is happening? Is the Eros Element causing other effects Edward didn't anticipate?

Iris opened the blinds of the atelier to let in the sunshine, which she hoped would help to warm the room. She'd left Marie asleep, and Johann had avoided her at breakfast before she could ask what happened to make Marie so exhausted and Johann so serious. Had they engaged in the kind of improper activities she would supposedly find out about when her innocence wasn't in danger? But both of them seemed experienced in that way—at least that was what they projected—so Iris wasn't quite sure what to think. She only knew that something of serious import had occurred.

But Johann and Marie weren't her main concern. She needed to continue to read the manuscript Monsieur Firmin had entrusted to her. Even if she couldn't understand all the words, she could continue to get images of the history. She needed to find out where the temple page had gone with the document and how it had come to the Louvre.

Iris spread the bound pages, which she now knew had once been scrolled on the table in front of her, in the spot where Edward had placed his tools. They both did similar things, she mused, to try and figure out the world and how it worked. His ability to engage in complex mental calculations and observations seemed no less mysterious to her than her own talent.

She took off her gloves and closed her eyes. The pages drew her fingertips to them like magnets to metal shavings, and the paper took on a soft quality, not brittle as it looked.

THE VISION DROPPED her into the page's labored escape from the peasant woman who lived by the wall. She first became aware of running downhill and a cool breeze tinged of salt and fish guts. To Iris, it would have been an unpleasant smell, but to the girl's nose it smelled like a far-away home.

Wooden slats replaced the stone streets, and she slowed to quiet her steps. The blaze from the temple, although at the top of the hill that housed the city, illuminated the docks in an eerie muted light. Sailors gathered in small groups, gesturing and pointing, and arguments rose in a dozen languages around her. She listened for one that sounded familiar and headed in the direction of the shouting in her dialect. She searched for familiar faces among the men and spotted one with a square-cut beard. He wasn't from her country, but she knew the merchant, who was a friend of her father's.

"Menelaus," she said with a gasp.

He looked down at her, startled. "What? Fausta, is that you?"

She nodded, and her knees gave way beneath her. He scooped her up and threw his cloak around her.

"What have you there?" one of the others asked. "That wharf rat's a little young for you, don't you think?"

"She's a chieftain's daughter. Have some respect." He ushered her aboard a nearby ship. "What's happening at the temple? Aren't you goddess-promised?"

Fausta nodded. Tears of relief stung her smoke-chapped cheeks. "It's burning. I don't know what started it, but the emperor's guards are up there. I think they're looking for this."

She handed him the scroll. He unrolled it, and his heavy brows drew in. "They're granary records, but something's not right. These can't be the measures. There is too much variability."

"The priest said something about them using it for their gods, and then Cervella said Constantinople will be the first to burn."

"Apollo's flame," Menelaus said in a whisper. "Keep this here with you. I will get the captain. It's good you brought this to me, but the goddess obviously wants you to be its guardian."

"But I don't understand it."

"Don't worry about that. We'll take it to Alexandria. There are scholars there who can help you."

He left Fausta, and she heard his heavy footsteps cross the deck above her head. She found a barrel of fresh water to quench the burning in her throat and waited. And waited some more. Men's voices startled her out of a doze she didn't know she'd fallen into, and the creaking of the ship told her it was on the way. Footsteps outside the chamber where she waited sounded wrong, so she shoved the scroll under a blanket on a bunk.

"Menelaus?" she asked.

"The Phoenician didn't make it on to the ship," the young man said. "The Varengian guard stormed the dock and captured him. But we will take you to Alexandria."

Her throat stung again, this time with tears for her friend.

IRIS CAME out of the trance, but her own throat burned with tears for little Fausta. She sensed the girl hadn't made it to Alexandria, possibly due to illness or some sort of internal damage from smoke inhalation, but she had kept her secret as to what the manuscript contained. Then the Alexandrian monks had accepted it but also hadn't known its significance, and it had gotten lost in the flotsam of time until it resurfaced at the Louvre.

And Firmin thinks I can figure out the key.

She knew she would have to reach back farther than Fausta to the mind of the author of the manuscript, but she wasn't so good at directing her talent that she could force objects to show her things, particularly not objects of low density like paper and cloth.

There must be something I can do, some key somewhere. The priest said something about one they were burning. Perhaps it's survived at the temple. But which one?

A knock on the atelier door startled her.

"Entree!"

Marie entered. A thousand questions leapt to Iris's mind, but she only asked, "How did you sleep?"

Marie's cheeks flamed, and she looked away. "Fine."

"Did you have sweet dreams of Johann?"

"Alas, the situation is not that simple. But I'm not here to talk about him. I saw Amelie Lafitte this morning. She's extremely neurotic after something happened at the student gathering referenced in Cinsault's letter."

"What happened?"

"I'm not sure, but I've sent for Davidson to investigate the church next door. That's where they met. She brought this brochure back with her."

Marie handed Iris the pamphlet, and the symbol brought her back momentarily to the evening in her father's study. "It's the neo-Pythagorean symbol."

"Yes. Can you read it?"

"I think so. It's Greek, which I'm not as strong in as in Latin. We should get Doctor Radcliffe to take a look at it—he's much better than I am."

"That's not quite what I meant." Marie gestured to Iris's hands. "What the brochure says may not be as important as what it can show us about the meeting."

"I can try, but paper doesn't hold impressions as well." She closed her eyes and focused on the brochure the impressions it gave her had the quality of candle smoke in a breeze—hard to see and even harder to sense beyond the occasional whiff. "Faint screams and rustling, that's all." She opened her eyes. "But the rustling sounds like what we heard at the marquis's chateau."

"She said something about that, and that now that the rose is open, the thorns will dance."

"The voice in the temple!" Iris had tried not to think too much about that day when Edward had saved her but lost his sense of self, but the words had been etched into her mind. "It said, 'The rose is opening.'"

"What rose?" Marie asked. "It's winter."

"It has to have something to do with the Eros Element. It can be made into a weapon, and something about the numbers in this manuscript is the key."

Footsteps on the stairs outside the atelier startled them.

"Mademoiselles?" Inspector Davidson called.

"In here," Iris said.

When he came through the door, the paleness of his face such that even his freckles had disappeared shocked Iris.

"You were right, Mademoiselle St. Jean. We found the immolated remains of what must have been a painting in its frame. You're all lucky that somehow it didn't catch the gunpowder in there. The main question is how."

Marie put a hand to her throat, and she and Iris exchanged a panicked look. They had all come too close to being blown up.

"But it may play to your advantage, Mademoiselle. You see, these were delivered to me this morning."

"What are they?" Iris asked.

He held out the photographs of Marie embracing Johann and of Johann and Frederic arguing in front of the broken window in the theatre.

"Bollocks," Iris murmured.

"I'm not sure what to pursue, a mysterious fire that could have killed all of you or the fact that someone very badly wants Maestro Bledsoe to be blamed for Frederic LeClerc's murder. Who took these photos?"

"Would you believe a spirit?" Marie asked.

MARIE MET Johann in the theatre lobby after his rehearsal but before hers, and the expression on his face told her that he had seen the same pictures she did. They passed the window repairmen, who gave them suspicious looks.

"There's nothing like blackmail for breakfast," he told her.

She tried to smile, but the tightness around her mouth that had started when she saw the photographs wouldn't let her. "That's not something to joke about. The spirit wants you out of the way. But there's something bigger going on."

She filled him in on what Amelie Lafitte had told her and

the strange burned painting in the church that didn't catch fire to any of the other very flammable things in there.

"And what of the other students?" he asked.

That at least was a relief. "Davidson is going to talk to Amelie and get their names, then try to track them down. He says not to go anywhere, though."

Johann snorted. "Right. We're trapped here, as your friend in the theatre can attest. Did you tell Davidson about him?"

Although he must have meant the words as a joke, they jolted Marie. "He's not my friend. As for Davidson, he wants to help me trap the inventor, but he's pulled too thin right now to get involved in a love triangle murder."

They reached the townhouse, and Johann pulled Marie into the receiving parlor and shut the door. He took her into his arms and bypassed the offer of her lips to kiss the top of her head.

She jerked away. "I knew it. You're disappointed in me now that you know what I've done."

"I don't consider any of that your fault, particularly as I've also acted stupidly in order to obtain my freedom."

Marie's nerves felt as though they were fringed, each end raw, and she didn't care to put on a role to deal with the situation. "So you're calling me stupid."

"Now you're determined to make me at fault. I got enough of that from my family."

"And you're trying to convince yourself that what I did doesn't matter, but your actions show how you truly feel."

"That doesn't matter to me." He ran a hand through his hair. "I need to know something, though. How do you do what you do on stage? How are you so convincing?"

Dark spots appeared at the edges of Marie's vision. "What do you mean?"

"The spirit alluded to it, and Radcliffe has observed it. When you're in a role, you change."

Bitterness came to the back of Marie's throat. This was it, the final secret. She recalled her mother's words, *Focus on Maestro Bledsoe—he is accustomed to being one thing and acting another. Ask how he manages it.*

But would he believe her? And would she then have to explain to him that he wasn't attracted to her, but the ideal woman she played?

She bolted for the door. "I have to go. I have to eat before rehearsal."

A quick glance over her shoulder told her he really was disappointed in her, but she couldn't tell him what she could do because then what if he thought that was how she'd gotten in trouble with Cobb? Or that she'd used it to ensnare him?

No, she would be better off trying to manage it on her own.

33

T héâtre Bohème, 8 December 1870

As the orchestra warmed up for the opening night performance of Light Fantastique, Johann was grateful he was familiar with the music. He'd be relying on his hands and fingers to play the notes because his mind and heart would be on stage with Marie.

She'd avoided him since Tuesday when he'd asked her his awkward question, but when he'd snuck in to watch the rehearsals, he'd noticed what Radcliffe and the spirit had alluded to. She took on the look and demeanor of the character, and when she glanced out to where the audience would be, the force of her persona hit him, club-like, in the middle of his chest.

She was his ideal, and he wanted her completely.

On one hand, he was impressed with her ability, but on the other, terror strong enough to double him over punched him in the gut at the thought of the spirit or Parnaby Cobb, whom Lucille had confirmed was in Paris, seeing her and having the same reaction.

And he knew without a doubt that she was perfect for him

even when she wasn't playing a part. He craved her kisses and wanted more, but he also admired her ability to take care of herself and her loyalty to her family. He'd never met someone as simultaneously tough and tender as she. But what he admired most of all was that she'd found the courage to stop running from what she feared the most. He understood why she had wanted to avoid the stage. Now if only she'd confide in him about what she did to return to it.

Johann couldn't see the crowd, but the murmurs and shuffling of clothing told him that it was a full house. Just after they played the overture, a hush indicated that something of significance had occurred. He glanced up to the best-positioned box to see that the empress had arrived with the emperor's cousin. The emperor himself wasn't there, and it was rumored that he was ill after his brief imprisonment by the Prussians before his spies had broken him out. The empress nodded and gestured for the actors and musicians to continue.

Marie took the stage in a fake box toward the top, and the audience applauded wildly at the reappearance of their beloved Fantastique. Once their adulation subsided, a slow clap brought all eyes to a box on the opposite side of the theatre, where Parnaby Cobb sat and didn't stop applauding until Marie acknowledged that she'd seen him.

Johann held his breath and calculated the quickest way to get to her if he needed to, but she only nodded as regally as the empress had. Johann suspected that only he saw the flash of fear in her eyes.

As the main male character descended into a madness brought on by love and opium, Johann similarly felt pulled down into the bog of his emotions. He had to watch the score, Fouré, and the stage, but he also had to ensure Cobb stayed in his box, and the return from the two intermissions was maddening waiting for him to reappear. There was an empty box that had been reserved, but it stayed unoccupied, and Johann guessed that was where the spirit watched.

And she is the idealized woman in a room full of fools and madmen.

At the end of the play, the actors made their curtain calls, and the audience showered Marie with flowers. She indicated Fouré and Johann. He was surprised to find he also received loud applause, and Fouré complimented him on his passionate performance. A few of the other musicians offered him grudging congratulations, and Inspector Davidson, who had also been in the audience, shook his hand.

"A great performance, Maestro. Makes me glad I waited to arrest you."

Johann's attention narrowed to where the inspector held his hand tightly. "Wait, what?"

"I'm sorry, but my superiors have made it clear that there have been too many strange goings-on around the theatre, and there's a lot of pressure for an arrest to show that some progress is being made."

"Can't this wait?"

"The security of Paris depends on it."

Johann tried to pull away, but the inspector's grip crushed Johann's hand.

"But I didn't kill Frederic LeClerc. I had an alibi. Two, actually."

"Your alibi is dead and disappeared. I tried but couldn't find the woman who talked to Professor Bailey."

Johann looked up to the boxes. The empress had disappeared after the final act and just before the curtain calls, and Cobb was also gone. Would he try to go backstage?

"Look, Inspector, I'll go with you willingly if you will stay with me this evening. I fear Mar—I mean Fantastique is in danger of being kidnapped."

"As long as you don't leave my sight, I will stay with her to protect her. Who do you think is going to try to kidnap her?"

"One of two madmen."

"And if I do this for you, you will help me and go willingly under arrest until I can find the real murderer?"

Johann gripped the inspector's hand in return. "So you don't believe I did it."

"No, I don't. But I need to maintain my position here to continue my work."

"At least I should be safe from the Guild in jail."

But the look on the inspector's face told Johann he might be a sitting goose, and his name would be foie gras once the Clockwork Guild could re-enter Paris or activate a sleeper agent to finish him off.

MARIE ACCEPTED the congratulations of the cast and select members of the audience her mother had deemed worthy of visiting her backstage, but she couldn't help but look around for Johann. She had managed her ability to take on the role, and while sometimes it had felt like a runaway team of horses, she had wrested control and had the best performance of her life.

Finally he appeared, and although he grinned when he saw her, the lift of his cheeks didn't match the tension around his eyes. Inspector Davidson followed behind him like a shadow.

"What's wrong?" Marie asked him.

"I came to congratulate you, and the inspector is here to protect you. Parnaby Cobb is in the audience, and we don't know what your friend downstairs is going to do."

"You didn't answer the question." She was sweating in the costume wedding gown. She thought she'd noticed the distinctive rose-colored glow of the Eros Element in the footlights, but the gas lights still heated the stage. A shadow fell across them, and she looked up to see Parnaby Cobb approaching them.

"A marvelous performance, my dear!" He kissed both her cheeks in the French fashion. "I'm so glad you've put your talent to good use during your leave of absence."

"I didn't take a leave of absence," she told him. "You fired me."

Lucille walked up to them, her mouth set into a firm line. "Monsieur Cobb."

"Madame St. Jean, you're looking well."

"What are you doing here? I told you never to set foot in my theatre again." The stage hands came from the side and back of the stage to stand around here and form a protective barrier between Cobb and Marie. Fouré stood beside Lucille.

"I'm only here to congratulate Marie and see when she wants to return to work for me."

Johann put an arm around Marie, and she leaned into him. "The answer to that is never."

"Oh, so you would prefer to consort with a murderer than with me?" He assumed his kindly uncle expression that made Marie's stomach turn because she knew that was when he was about to spring a trap.

"He hasn't killed anyone."

"Oh, really? There are photographs that are pretty damning evidence, my dear, and I know for a fact that the inspector is going to cart him off to jail as soon as the festivities are over."

Marie's mind leaped off Cobb's words. How did he know about the photographs? And Johann was to be arrested?

"By whose orders?" she asked.

"The chief of police. Paris is an unsafe enough place. There's no reason for a murderer to be walking about free, and it would be quite scandalous for a famous actress to take up with him."

"That might help my reputation," Marie said. "You don't know the French."

"I know enough of them."

The barely healed wound in Marie's heart opened again. "Fine. I get it. You have the chief of police in your pocket. I should have guessed. What do you want for Maestro Bledsoe's freedom?"

"Only for you to come back to work for me. I'm interested to find out what your friend Professor Bailey has been working on, and I have not forgotten my promise to ensure Miss McTavish's academic career. I would hate for her talents to go to waste if no school were to have her."

Marie had to remind herself to breathe. He was willing to ruin all of them to get her back.

"And what of the play?" Lucille asked. "She is the star, our Fantastique."

"I'm sure that Miss Sellers can step into the role admirably. That's why I paid for her passage here."

Iris and Edward had come backstage during the conversation. Marie was relieved to see Iris clutch Edward's arm and pulled him into the shadows before Cobb saw them. Iris mimed a puppet master pulling the strings, and Marie nodded to show she understood. Cobb had never been out of the picture. He'd only been abiding his time until they made some progress with the Eros Element.

Marie's main focus was on securing Johann's freedom. A flash of gold caught the corner of her eye, and panic exploded in her chest. A clockwork butterfly clung to the curtains to their right.

The Guild! Right, Cobb is involved with it. If Johann goes to jail, they'll have him trapped, and he won't last a week.

She swallowed the bitterness and closed her eyes, prepared to take on her most hated role, that of Marie the maid, the repentant employee.

"I will come work for you," she said.

"No!" Johann and Lucille shouted. Johann's arm turned to rock around her shoulders.

Cobb ignored them and looked her over. "You're willing to do that to buy your lover's freedom?"

"I will do as you say." Marie pulled away from Johann, who kept contact with her as long as he could and reached after her.

She'd taken two steps toward Cobb when a voice came from above them, "Parnaby Cobb, you and I have unfinished business."

The spirit, still in his metal mask and cape, rode down one of the ropes and landed with a flourish that Johann had to admire. He didn't think he'd be glad to see the spirit again, but he was happy for anything that would keep Marie out of Cobb's clutches until he could come up with some way to rescue her.

If he was smart like Edward, he could...

Edward!

Johann had seen him and Iris in the shadows, and Johann caught Edward's eye. He made a turning motion with his hand and mouthed, "Turn up the aether light!"

Sure, he didn't know whether the right frequency was up or down, but he hoped Edward would get what he meant.

Iris whispered to Edward, who nodded. They disappeared into the shadows, and Johann waited and listened. He recalled that the inspector carried a weapon, but the spirit had the same thought. The spirit grabbed Marie and held the gun to her throat. Johann kept himself from lunging after her.

"Lay your weapons down, gentlemen," the mad inventor said. "Or I shall finish Fantastique."

Davidson did as he said, as did some of the stage hands. At the spirit's direction, they threw the weapons into the now-empty orchestra pit.

"You stole my plans," the spirit said to Cobb. He still held Marie.

Cobb laughed, clearly surprised. "Oh, Paul Farrell, is that you? Why are you wearing that ridiculous mask?"

The spirit stiffened, and Johann crept behind him. He feared the madman would twitch or jump, and that would be it for Marie.

"I liberated an automaton from the tunnels, and it has allowed me to borrow its face."

"In that case, I *liberated* your designs. You didn't have the resources to implement them, and I paid you well."

"You paid me barely a pittance."

"You gambled it all away to the Clockwork Guild."

"And now I know that you orchestrated that event to keep me in your power. You don't let go of people once you have them. I want my plans back, Cobb."

Johann wondered if he and the spirit had gotten caught in a similar trap. Even if he could pay back what he owed, would he ever be free?

He would worry about that later. He watched the lights and waited for a certain tint to tell him it was time to take advantage of the other's high emotions and act.

He only hoped he'd be able to keep his own under control.

EDWARD LED Iris down the stairs to the control area for the theatre's lighting system. They'd adjusted the volume of the aether gas so that the lights still had an extra warm and flattering glow and the frequency to a benign level. His hands trembled at the thought of what he would have to do.

Patrick O'Connell stood in front of the bank of dials and levers, shutting it down.

"Stop!" Edward said.

Patrick started, and his frown deepened when he saw them. "What's happening?"

Iris filled Patrick in while Edward pulled stops and turned dials to crank the lighting system back up to full power. Thankfully it warmed up quickly.

"And Johann wants Edward to turn the aether frequency up so the mad inventor will shoot Cobb," she finished.

Her words made Edward freeze. It had been one thing when he'd taken desperate action to save Iris. While he would do anything for her, his conscience had eased with the knowledge that it was partially the Eros Element that had caused him to break through his inhibitions and boundaries to use science to destroy another human life. Now he was going to do so again, but this time with a clear head and heart.

His chest tightened, and he stepped away from the console. Iris rushed to him.

"What is it? Are you all right?"

"I can't..." He tried to breathe into shrinking lungs. "I can't do this again. I can't use it to kill again."

Iris took his face in her hands and turned it toward her so he gazed into her dark blue eyes. "Please trust me on this—"

"I trust you in everything."

Her eyes softened, and her lips turned up into a smile that he knew was only for him. "Then believe this, that Cobb must be destroyed, for if he gets hold of what you've discovered and developed, he will ruin many more lives than he already has. Firmin gave me a clue to what's possibly the next step in developing the Eros Element into a power source, and ancient peoples tried to use it as a weapon."

"And you think that's what he wants."

"In the end, yes. Not power to help, but power to harm."

The weight of the responsibility threatened to crush him. He thought about why they had pursued their quest, so the poor would have access to a power source that wasn't coal. He hated to play at being a god, to decide who would live or die, but he couldn't let what they'd worked so hard to find end up in the hands of a power-hungry madman.

"Then I'll do it."

"I'll be right here beside you," she said. "For always."

He put one arm around her, and supported by her strength, flooded the system with the aether, then closed his eyes and forced his memory back to Rome, back to the combination of tuning forks that had produced the frequency that pushed him into desperate action. He turned the appropriate dials, and the gas he could see took on a peach-rose hue.

"The rose is opening," Iris murmured. "God save us."

The tubes that held the gas glowed brighter and brighter, blinding like the airship when it had exploded. Edward wasn't sure if current experience conflated memory, but he thought he remembered it exploding in a peach-rose hue, not orange-red fire. And then there was the lone parachutist after...

"Turn it off!" Iris yelled. "It's too much."

Patrick ran to the console, and he and Edward tried to reverse it, but the Eros Element seemed to take on its own life. Edward thought he saw a rose-colored snake slither through the tubing.

"It's not shutting off," Patrick shouted. "Get out now!"

Patrick grabbed Edward and Iris and pulled them out of the room and braced himself against the door. A crackle like that of a lightning storm sounded, and then the system exploded, leaving them in darkness.

THE FOOTLIGHTS TOOK on a peach-colored hue, and Johann observed his own emotions, the building tension in his chest. He hated Cobb at that moment for manipulating of all of them, but most of all for what he'd done to Marie.

The discussion between Cobb and the inventor Farrell heated. The inventor gestured with his gun, and Johann grabbed Marie from Farrell and pulled her back toward him. The inventor continued to brandish his gun at Cobb.

Come on, come on, do it.

"What did you do?" she whispered.

"I had Edward change the frequency of the aether lighting system."

"But what if someone gets killed?"

"If we're lucky, it will be Cobb."

Farrell pointed his pistol at Cobb. "I told you not to under-estimate me!"

The entrepreneur held up his hands. "Fine, Paul, we can talk about what's bothering you. Just put the gun down."

Why isn't Cobb affected? Johann watched the tableau unfolding while backing away with Marie. Lucille and the stagehands also gave the two men a wide berth, and Johann gestured for Davidson to follow him.

A whine reached Johann's ears, and he yelled, "Not so much, Edward!"

A voice floated up from below, Patrick's—"It's not shutting off."

Johann experienced a range of emotions, from ecstasy to despair, the waves lasting only a matter of seconds. The sounds that came to him through the high pitch of the system were Farrell's laughter. Peach-rose lightning crackled from the lights. Then the theatre went dark and was silent except for the sounds of one, two, three gunshots and a body hitting the wooden stage floor.

34

héâtre Bohème, 8 December 1870

Johann threw Marie to the ground and lay on top of her. Something on her costume ripped, and cold air tickled her side.

The thought floated through her panic, Merde, *I suppose Maman was right about letting this one out.*

Had the bullets hit Cobb? Someone else?

"Are you shot?" she whispered to Johann. *Please don't be shot, please be all right.*

"No, are you?"

"No." She tried to remember who was in the theatre. "But *Maman. Maman!*" She frantically looked around, but all she could make out was lumps in the dark. Some weren't moving. The last she had seen Lucille, she could have been in the path of a bullet, especially if the shot had gone wild.

The house lights, which were on a different system, slowly illuminated. Although there was a trail of blood, Cobb and Farrell had disappeared. Everyone else stirred and checked for injuries.

Lucille rushed to Marie, and the two women embraced.

"I thought he had hurt you," Lucille said. "I would never have forgiven myself."

"Me, neither."

"I'm sorry," Lucille told her and held her hands. "For all of it. For the secrets I kept from you."

"And I'm sorry too, for running away." They embraced again.

Iris and Edward emerged.

"Is everyone all right?" Iris asked. "We heard gunshots."

"Yes," Marie said. "Although Cobb and Farrell are gone."

"So is Davidson," Johann observed. "I suspect he went after them."

"Does this mean you won't be arrested?" Marie asked. "Davidson definitely got a good demonstration of how the aether lighting affects people."

"Yes, I wonder what he was feeling," Iris said.

"So you know who Farrell was?" Marie asked Lucille. "He had talked to me once before, but he said he knew you."

Lucille looked away, and Fouré nudged her. "You need to tell her everything."

"Very well." She looked at Marie, and her eyes glazed with tears. Marie watched her, shocked. She'd never seen her mother cry.

"You don't have to do this now," she said.

"*Non.*" Lucille wiped her eyes with the handkerchief Fouré gave her. "You have a right to know, and I won't let any more time pass. Paul Farrell was an inventor and assassin I hired to take care of Cobb the first time he showed interest in you several years ago, even before you were the *ingénue* in the production that drove poor old Maurice mad. He had a grudge against Cobb, and I wanted to use that. I did not realize how truly insane he was."

"Why didn't you just warn me?"

"Because I was afraid you would let the knowledge of how

alluring you were to men run away with you like it did me. I didn't think the opposite would get you in trouble."

"I ran off with Cobb because he stole and then burned the traveling papers I'd gotten without your knowledge. And then he blackmailed me." Saying the words and seeing the hurt in her mother's eyes made Marie's stomach turn. "But wait, like it did you? What happened?"

Fouré looked down at Lucille with a grin and then gestured to Marie. "Well, you did."

Johann turned and coughed, and Marie's cheeks heated. "This may be more than I want to know," she said.

Lucille took her hands. "I do not regret what I did, for I do love your father even if we have not been able to have a traditional life together. I would not keep him from his career, and he knew he could not take me out of Paris. I was expelled by the Roma community here for becoming pregnant out of wedlock. Zokar defied our father to stay in contact with me, and I am glad you found him, but I did not want you to know of my impulsive behavior."

Marie put the heels of her hands to her head. "This is too much."

"I know it's a lot." Lucille placed her hand on Marie's cheek. "And I promise that if you have any more questions, I will answer them honestly."

"I need some time." Marie took her mother's hand and kissed it.

"Take what you need."

"Don't worry," Marie said. "I'll be in shape for the performance tomorrow night, although I'm not sure the lighting system will be."

Lucille smiled. "I will leave that up to you. Don't worry, I will not force you to take the stage again, although you're managing your talent beautifully."

"Thank you."

And for the first time, Marie felt she could drive her ability rather than it take her over.

JOHANN WALKED out of the theatre and into the cold air with Marie. She paused and looked out on the street, where a few people still milled about, but it was generally quiet.

"What are you thinking?" Johann asked.

Marie turned to him and smiled. "That I finally feel like myself."

He took her in his arms and kissed her. She molded herself to him, and she sensed he only held her, not any role or pretension. He hadn't since before Paul Farrell had jumped out of the shadows. But she had to make sure.

"Does that mean you're willing to think about being my partner in adventure?" he asked once they broke apart.

"What are you asking me, Maestro Bledsoe?"

"That once this siege is over, we finish our grand tour and go to the Ottoman Empire."

Marie looked up into his turquoise eyes. "You do realize what my talent is, right?"

He stroked her cheek. "Yes, that you can take on any role very convincingly."

"And you do remember what I was playing on the stage," she pressed. A little flicker of hope ignited in her belly, but she wouldn't fan it until she knew with certainty.

"The idealized woman. But you haven't been playing her the whole time, and my feelings for you have only grown as you learned to manage your role. Silly *fille*, I've loved you more as you've become more yourself."

Although she could have drawn from any number of heroines with a happy ending, Marie knew her joy was hers alone, as was her answer. "Then yes, I will travel with you."

Iris and Edward walked out of the theatre, and Edward put an arm around Iris.

"Did I hear someone say something about the Ottoman Empire?" he asked. "Sorry, we were just inside the door."

"Sounds good to me," Iris said. "There's something I'm missing in interpreting that manuscript Firmin gave me. I need to visit temple ruins there and see if I can find the key."

"And I do like to finish what I started," Edward added.

"Are you all right?" Johann asked.

Edward nodded, and for once his smile wasn't shadowed by anxiety or regret. "Now that I know the Eros Element was causing my mood, I'm handling things much better."

"Then let's figure out how to make this work," Johann told them. "And I know just the way. Marie St. Jean," he said and got on one knee. "We've been through life and death, airship crashes, crazy inventors with guns, and bizarre circumstances, and through it all, you've been as graceful and gracious as any man could wish. Would you be my wife?"

Marie's eyes widened, and the flicker of hope in her belly spread to become a happy glow warmer than the aether lighting. "Are you sure about this?"

"As sure as I have ever been. And I want you, all of you."

"Then yes!"

This time when they kissed, it was the fulfillment of all they'd wished and desired.

EPILOGUE

*A*irship over the French Countryside, Midnight 25 December 1870

"Are you ready, Fantastique?"

Marie turned from the window of the small pantry off the airship's ballroom and smiled.

"As ready as I'll ever be."

Iris had never looked so pretty with her white-blonde hair piled atop her head and the unusual color of her eyes particularly vivid with the satin lavender gown she wore.

"Yes, we seem to be beyond the siege lines, so we can start," Fouré said. "I won't have the Prussians upstaging your wedding with a shell."

"I'll inform the captain," Radcliffe told them and slipped out.

"You both look lovely," Fouré said, "but especially my daughter." He held out an arm, and Marie took it. Radcliffe returned, and the door opened a crack.

Amelie Lafitte peeked out. "There are so many people!"

Her loveliness had returned after Radcliffe exposed her to the Eros Element and cured her hysteria. Marie hadn't seen him look as hopeful as he did after, and she knew he would be taking off to the States soon. Although he still had work to do on his method, particularly on someone not recently traumatized, he would want to find his Claire.

But first, a double wedding and honeymoon in the Ottoman Empire so Iris could search for the key to decipher the manuscript Firmin had entrusted to her.

Amelie, the lone bridesmaid, processed toward the podium. Then Iris went out on Radcliffe's arm. Marie felt Iris's spike of excitement through the bond they shared and then the smooth calmness of the certainty that she was making the right decision marrying Edward.

The music changed to a more—what else?—dramatic entrance, and the door opened to reveal the ballroom decorated in red and green. Small aether lights twinkled in the trees along the bank of windows and seemed to talk to the midnight stars outside. Marie's gaze was drawn to Johann, now beardless and smiling and in his best tails. She wondered what Iris thought as love and lust bloomed in Marie's chest, and she smiled not-so-innocently at him. Fouré handed her off, and Johann leaned in after taking her hand.

"You look ravishing. Also like you."

"*I'm* marrying you, not Fantastique, Marguerite, Henriette, or any of the others," she murmured back.

"And I couldn't be happier."

The witnesses were Lucille and Fouré, who had finally married, as well as Radcliffe and Patrick and Zokar and Saphira. Sadly, Inspector Davidson couldn't be there. The charges against Johann had been dropped as soon as Cobb had managed to leave Paris, and Lucille had given Johann and Marie the profits from the opening performance of *Light Fantastique* as a wedding present so he could pay off the Guild when they approached him for it again.

After witnessing what had happened in the theatre and

Amelie's treatment, Davidson was convinced that the Eros Element did have the power to influence emotions and investigated accordingly. Frederic's murderer was found to be the guardsman outside the chapel who was also attracted to Marie after seeing her around the theatre, and the murder of Monsieur Cinsault was pinned on the neo-Pythagoreans who weren't keen on his exposing them to the students. The assassin acted before he had intended, thanks to Eros.

As for the third man, all they could surmise was that the neo-Pythagoreans had mistaken him for Edward.

Davidson had disappeared soon after the cases wrapped up, presumably in pursuit of Cobb and Farrell, who Lucille's sources said left together. No one was sure what to make of that, but Zokar was happy to get his automaton back even if its face had disappeared. His family and people and as much as they could bring were also on the airship headed to a new life and country.

As Marie kissed her husband, she found herself grateful to be surrounded by family and friends. It was a freedom she never thought she would have, the freedom to love and be loved for and as herself.

She knew she would take the stage again, but for tonight, she found wife to be the best role of all.

FROM THE AUTHOR

Thank you for reading Clockwork Phantom! I hope you enjoyed it – this is what happens when an editor challenges her author to write a steampunk Phantom of the Opera.

If you'd like to keep up with me and my writing, and to get a free short story, please go to http://www.ceciliadominic.com/ newsletter to join my author newsletter.

Also, if you have the chance, please leave me a review at the site where you bought the book and/or at Goodreads. Reviews are so important for us authors so we know what to do differently, but most importantly, what readers want more of. Even a single sentence like, "I liked it" is greatly appreciated and helpful for those oh-so-mysterious algorithms.

ABOUT AETHER SPIRIT

Forgetting her is impossible. Remembering him could kill her.

Left with partial amnesia after a steamcart accident, Claire McPhee tried lengthy treatment for the mental and emotional trauma. Now armed with her own training and medical degree, she helps others with combat-related neuroses hoping, she'll someday—somehow—fill in her own blanks. Particularly the elusive memory of a man she once loved.

Something about the new medical chief triggers her painful, hypnosis-induced blocks, but he keeps pushing her away before she can shove through the barriers to determine why.

Chadwick Radcliffe has faced many challenges since assuming the position of medical chief at Fort Daniels, but facing his former love—and the knowledge that her memory of him could be deadly—pains him the most. While he's had some preliminary success using the Eros Element, he's all too aware its unintended effects could harm as much as heal.

With the Union on the cusp of caving in to the Confederacy's demands, time becomes a precious commodity. Ghosts rise. The Element takes on a new, unpredictable aspect. And resurrected love could give Claire and Chadwick unexpected strength—if they have the courage to break the chains welded around them to seize it.

Aether Spirit is the third book in the Aether Psychics, a thrilling steampunk series with puzzling mysteries and elements of romance, and can be read as a standalone novel. If you like historical mysteries, sweet romance, and clever heroines, then you'll love Cecilia Dominic's Aether Psychics series.

Buy Aether Spirit to begin or continue this addictive and charming steampunk series today!

Aether Spirit is available in paperback and electronic forms from most online vendors, or you may order it from your favorite bookstore. You can give whoever's ordering it for you the following ISBN to make it easy for them to find it: 978-1-945074-41-7

AETHER SPIRIT

P*lease enjoy this preview of Aether Spirit, the next book in the Aether Psychics series...*

FORT DANIELS, *Tennessee, 22 February 1871*

Am I seeing a ghost?

Doctor Chadwick Radcliffe couldn't take his eyes off the young woman who had just pushed through Distillery Hospital's pitted wooden doors. She looked and moved so much like Claire—his Claire—down to how she shook the water out of her umbrella with three open-shut pulses. The watery light dulled her copper penny hair, but she still had the one wisp that wouldn't stay contained in her simple hairstyle, and she wore the same rectangle-rimmed spectacles that gave her blue-gray eyes and oval face an air of perpetual curiosity.

He shook his head. It was just fatigue and the fact he had been back in the Union States for a month and hadn't heard anything of Claire's whereabouts in spite of repeated letters and telegrams to his contacts in Boston. Six years had passed since the accident. What were the chances her appearance hadn't changed? He looked back at the young woman, expecting her to have transformed into someone unfamiliar, but she glanced around, her bottom lip between her teeth in her habitual thinking expression.

An accidental resemblance, then. His Claire would never have ventured so close to an active front, one of the few left in this stalemate between the Union States and Confederate States. Her family would never have allowed their precious daughter and niece so close to danger. He motioned to one of the nurses, who approached with swishing skirts.

"Yes, Doctor Radcliffe?"

"Find out who that young woman is and what she wants. She doesn't belong here, must have made a wrong turn in town and gotten lost."

The nurse's huff caught his attention. Ah, right, Nanette. The dark-haired beauty had paid extra attention to him since he arrived, but he'd ignored her. His heart was spoken for, although it would kill his beloved to claim it.

Nanette returned with an amused expression. "She says her name is Doctor Claire McPhee. She's the neuroticist sent by the University of Pennsylvania to help the soldiers recover from their mental wounds." Her mouth twisted around the word, "neuroticist".

Chad forced his hands to unclench, but not because of his hatred for neuroticists, who had been instrumental in keeping her away from him so her injured psyche could *repair itself*. It *was* her. She had arrived to find him completely unprepared.

"She asked for the chief of medicine. I told her it's you."

"I guess I am."

Dammit.

The former chief had accidentally crossed the border too close to a Fort Temperance sniper. That was how things went these days—few battles, but they picked each other off whenever they had the chance. As Chad was the only other physician there at the time—Perkins having been on a much-delayed leave—Chad had assumed the chief position. For some reason, the powers that be decided to keep him there in spite of Perkins's objections when he'd returned two weeks later.

Chad approached Claire with what he hoped was a professional air, but his heart beat a charged tattoo in his ribs. Would she recognize him? Would it injure her to do so? What did he hope would happen?

Above all, he didn't want to hurt her.

Claire studied him with her intense gaze under a slight frown, although without a flicker of recognition.

It wasn't supposed to be like this. He swallowed the lump in his throat and resisted the urge to tuck that stray strand behind her ear.

"I'm Doctor Chadwick Radcliffe, the chief of medicine. How can I help you?"

Again, nothing except an odd, measuring gaze. "I'm Doctor Claire McPhee," she finally said. Instead of holding out her hand for him to take it, she rubbed at her right temple with two fingers. She wore tan kid gloves that screamed "city girl".

"What brings you to Fort Daniels and Distillery Hospital? Were you looking for Danielsville? It's just over the ridge."

"I just came from Danielsville. Is that what you call this place—Distillery Hospital?" She grinned, and her careless amusement—the same that had attracted him to her in the first place—nearly doubled him over with grief.

Instead he straightened his spine. "Beggars can't be choosers when you're on a war front." His statement came out as a growl, but he had to get away from her before he accidentally damaged her. Or shredded his heart further.

"True." She took a deep breath, and he knew she was about to try to convince him of something. "I suppose you got my telegram? Well, not mine. The one about me. To you, the medical director."

"No. It's possible one arrived, but we've had some personnel changes."

"I see." Another breath—even under her prim jacket he could see the movements of her chest—and she launched into her spiel. "I'm here on a grant through the University of Pennsylvania to work with soldiers who show signs of nervous disease like nightmares, feeling like they're back in the situation, being easily startled, memory problems..." She rattled off a list of symptoms, and Chadwick had to remind himself to pay attention to her words, not her full lips. Plus, she described most of the young men who were there, their minds as broken as their bodies after years of tense anticipation punctuated with brief skirmishes.

"Did your superiors realize they were sending you into a war zone?" he asked and gestured around him. "It's dangerous —one well-aimed shell from just over the border, and we're toast. Plus, we don't have private consulting rooms here, just a surgery suite, and it's not someplace that will speak of comfort to a soldier."

"Oh, I recognize that, and they knew. Sometimes you don't have much to lose, you know?"

Her question, more than anything, tore his heart. What did she mean? He knew her father had died, but wasn't her mother still alive? And her evil aunt, Eliza, who adored Claire to the point of wanting to make her life perfect, at least according to Eliza's desires?

"Not really," he said, hoping she'd elaborate.

Instead, she pressed on. "The grant is to find out if we can make a difference with sympathetic conversation rather than procedures, which is the European model, and you probably know better than I how mental healing can promote physical healing."

More than you know. The elbow he'd landed on when he was thrown from the steamcart had refused to heal completely. It still ached on rainy days like this one, as did his heart.

She waved a hand in front of his face. He'd drifted again, dammit. Perhaps he had some of the symptoms she'd come here to help the soldiers with, but he'd never admit to them.

"I'm sorry, Doctor Radcliffe, but does my being here bother you? I know neuroticists still have a poor reputation in the medical world, but this work is important. This war is too close to finally being over to lose soldiers to their worst fears."

And I can't sacrifice these boys to my fears. Or the mistakes they made with her. "Fine, Doctor McPhee. I can find you a spot for your work, but every soldier you treat has to be medically cleared. By me personally. I won't let you damage them physically by digging around in their psyches."

"That's fine." Her eyebrows curved above the rims of her glasses. "Well, then, I promise I won't get in your way. If you'll have one of the nurses show me to the women's quarters so I can settle my things? I can manage my own trunk."

Nanette hovered nearby, as always. Chadwick jerked his head at Claire. "Nanette, show her around."

After the nurse took Claire out, Chadwick had to breathe slowly and evenly for a count of ten. *What have I done to deserve this? And how can I get her to agree to her own treatment?*

"Women's quarters are this way. They stick us at the end as far away from the soldiers' barracks and prisoners as possible."

Nanette didn't look at Claire as she talked. Claire trotted behind her and dragged her trunk on its little wheeled clockwork cart over as much stone-paved path as she could find. By the time they reached the squat, two-story building on the opposite end of the fort from the battle front, Claire's arms ached, one from pulling the trunk and the other from holding her umbrella aloft against the driving wind and stinging raindrops.

Claire sensed the waves of resentment coming from the dark-haired nurse who led her to the women's quarters, so she didn't ask for a tour of the fort. It seemed pretty self-explanatory, and she was good at finding her way around. Once Nanette left her to their shared room—an unfortunate happenstance that the only empty female bed was with such a reluctant roommate—Claire unpacked as quickly as she could. She hadn't brought much, having had to sneak out of her mother's house in Boston, now shared with her least favorite aunt. She'd had to keep her whereabouts a secret from most of her friends and acquaintances, who would have ratted her out to her family, especially her aunt and brother. Her family wanted to stick her in an uncomfortable marriage with a man she hardly knew.

Hell, she hardly knew herself. Her memory held huge gaps from her life from when she'd been sixteen to when she'd come aware on a neuroticist's couch in Vienna when she'd turned eighteen.

The only thing she was sure of was that the man she dreamed about—but whose face she never saw—had existed, and she wanted to find him again. She hadn't encountered him in her mother's circles in Boston, so she thought he must have gone to be a soldier of some sort. She believed in the underlying order of the universe, hence why she put herself in a position to be sent to the front. She had faith she'd find him, whoever he was, if she put herself in the right place. The grant award had seemed a long shot, but she'd gotten it, so he must be here.

Of course she couldn't start up something romantically with one of her patients, but she knew she'd recognize him when she saw him, and she'd feel all the love and affection he'd been keeping for her these six years.

Or maybe she was just a silly girl with a dream. Either way, she'd be helping people, which was all she'd ever wanted. Her neuroticist had told her to focus on that, not finding the man she missed but wasn't sure why.

She changed out of her wet clothing and into her work blouse and skirt. Hanging her clothing in the wardrobe allowed her to bring her attention to what she was doing. But thoughts swirled around in her head like the icy raindrops that had plagued her on the wagon ride from the station to the fort and after. She'd been lucky in that she'd arrived with a shipment of medical supplies, so she was able to get to the fort that day, unlucky that the freight wagon's covering was for boxes, not people.

And the unenthusiastic welcome from Doctor Chadwick Radcliffe hadn't helped. She guessed that even with his apparent expertise, he'd had to fight hard to stay in his position, or perhaps he was an interim chief. As much as the Union States may embrace the idea of emancipation, they didn't necessarily espouse the principles of equality necessary for a dark-skinned man to be accepted as a medical chief of a major fort, and she brought potential controversy with her. She wondered if he'd trained in Europe. They certainly seemed more welcoming over there, although there was still plenty of racism.

Still, she'd been more than kind and didn't think she'd given him any reason for his coldness.

Not cold, exactly, but fearful. Why was he afraid of her? He certainly hadn't been happy to see her, but nothing about what she was there to do should inspire fear, and she'd been approved by the previous director. She was there to help Radcliffe. In fact, his antipathy to her had been almost visceral, his emotions too strong to sort it out. This led to one conclusion—he, like many, had been traumatized from his time at the front. Or he was afraid she'd damage his patients. She'd have to spend more time with him to reassure him. There was no sense in getting turned away until after she'd found her hero, whoever he was.

"Oh, there she is."

Claire turned around to see Nanette and two of the other nurses waiting in the front hall of the quarters.

"Hello," she said. "Thank you, I'm settling in nicely. Is dinner this way?"

"You're not going unescorted, are you?" Nanette asked. "It would be very forward of you."

Claire pressed her lips together so her upper one wouldn't curl in disdain at the idea that a woman couldn't go to dinner by herself. This was a war zone, not a society matron's house, for goodness' sake.

"Are you waiting for someone?" she asked. "Perhaps I could tag along."

"Yes, but only three men are coming. You'd look a strange odd one out."

One of the other nurses, a blonde, tittered. "More than you already do. What kind of woman wears spectacles?"

"Well, thank you for your advice, but I'm going to head along. Perhaps I'll find my own escort on the way."

She thought she heard one of them say, "Not likely." She told herself she didn't care, that the pricking in her eyes was from the rain. How could she have made a misstep so soon?

It doesn't matter, it doesn't matter. But she knew from experience it did. Alienating the nurses at a hospital was a one-way ticket to failure.

When Claire walked out of the front door, the inviting smells of the dining hall beckoned her. Relieved that her destination was upwind so she wouldn't have to wander around completely lost, she opened her umbrella and stalked into the rain. Whatever she did, she wouldn't allow a grumpy doctor and resentful nurse to deter her from meal time.

The more emotions she soaked up, the hungrier she got, and she had missions to fulfill, both personal and professional.

"YOU SEEM PERTURBED," Patrick O'Connell said to Chad that night as they ate in the mess hall. "A waste of good food, you are. Missing the French siege diet and Ottoman spice?" He held up a beer-braised sausage on a fork, and a strand of onion dripped juice on to his arm. The Irishman licked his hairy wrist.

"And you seem to have lost any refinement you may have gained in our travels."

But Chad was relieved that Patrick's humor had returned, especially since Paris. Patrick had always been more of a doer than a traveler or thinker, and he was happiest in his workshop.

"You're grumpy tonight."

Chadwick shrugged.

"There's the difference between us, my friend. I don't let gun problems ruin my appetite." His eyebrow wiggle confirmed the double entendre. "Not that I have any."

"You're stretching with that one." Chad shook his head and pushed the greasy food around on his plate. It was fine, better than he'd expected when he arrived. The speed with which his superiors had summoned him back to the front had surprised him. But then, he'd lost track of the news in besieged Paris, and the situation in the States was becoming desperate. Public opinion was for halting the war effort and negotiating with the rebels.

In other words, against the continued sacrifice of sons who had barely been out of diapers when the war began and the guaranteed spinsterhood of a generation of daughters.

Like Claire.

No matter where his thoughts started, they returned to her unexpected arrival.

"Rough day," he said.

Patrick's face fell into serious planes. "Did you lose a patient? If so, I apologize for my insensitivity. Sometimes I do forget we're back in this hell."

"Thanks, but no apology needed. In fact, quite the opposite. I found someone."

Patrick put his fork back on his plate. "Claire?" He said her name in tones that sounded like a prayer or that he spoke of the star of a ghost story of long ago.

"The same. She just walked into Distillery Hospital, shook out her umbrella, and..."

"And?"

"And didn't recognize me." Now the food on his plate made his stomach clench—or maybe it had been the loss of hope that she would recognize him—but either way, he was done. He pushed his plate away. "No sign at all, not even the barest flicker."

"That's not surprising considering she didn't seem to see me in Vienna."

"Yes, the damn neuroticists did their job too well burying the accident so far in her memory that she doesn't remember anything about it. Or me."

Patrick scooted Chad's plate closer to him. "You're not finishing this?" It was a vaguely hopeful question.

"No, I'm not." He sighed. "Tell me about your gun problems."

Patrick lowered his voice. "Well, there's this whore... All right, nothing like that. That weapon is working just fine. I'm having trouble with *La Reine*. While the professor and I managed to corral the aether into a form we could use to light the stage at the Bohème, concentrating it to the point of aiming it as a weapon is eluding me. I haven't found the right material for the lens."

"That's unfortunate, especially since it's kept you from working on our other aim."

"Aether as a healing medium? How much more do you need? The preliminary experiments with the girl in Paris went well enough."

"Yes, but she was newly shocked and not physically injured. I dare not try it on Claire or the soldiers until I've refined the process, but I haven't had the time with us being so shorthanded."

Patrick's green eyes widened, and his brows crawled up his forehead. "There she is."

Chad looked over his shoulder and saw Claire carrying a tray from the kitchen. The rain had plastered her one stray strand to her cheek, and water speckled her glasses. She approached the nurses, who turned their backs on her and spread out so there was no room for her at their table. The medical apprentices ignored her, as did the soldiers who were well enough to eat in the mess hall.

"Hey, that ain't right," Patrick drawled in a pretty good imitation of the Confeds.

"Where did a boy from Ireland learn a horrid expression like that? You sound like one of the prisoners. Wait, what are you doing?"

But it was too late. Even if she hadn't seen them—unlikely considering Patrick's flame-orange hair and beard—the Irishman made sure she'd notice them. He stood and waved his arms.

"Hey you, girl with the glasses, come sit with us!"

Claire's face lit with relief, and Chad closed his eyes. *I've missed that smile.* When he opened them, he saw she stood by their table, her brows drawn down in hesitation. Chad gestured for her to join them.

"Thank you," she said and set her tray beside Patrick's. "Word gets around fast."

"Not fast enough." Patrick took her hand and kissed it before taking his seat again. "I had no idea our camp had been graced with such beauty."

Chad shook his head while studying Claire's reaction. Patrick was laying it on thick, but as with Chad, she demonstrated no sign of recognizing the Irishman either from life before the accident or from when Patrick had asked her for directions in Vienna.

"And brains," Chad added. "This is Doctor Claire McPhee. She's a neuroticist from the University of Pennsylvania. She's going to try to help our wounded soldiers get their heads on straight while their bodies heal."

"Oh, a neuroticist." Patrick covered his mouth. "I'll be careful what I say around you, then."

Claire rolled her eyes. "And now I've diagnosed you with a bad case of unoriginality. It's quite rude considering we haven't been introduced."

"You've wounded me." Patrick pretended she had just bayoneted him. "I'm Civilian Engineer Patrick O'Connell, tinkerer and designer of weapons."

Claire's eyes unfocused, and she pressed her right temple. "I'm sorry," she said, sounding as though she was speaking from inside a dream. "I get these headaches. I knew a tinkerer once. Or an inventor. There are lots of McPhees in Boston."

Chad rubbed his jaw to keep it from dropping. She didn't remember her own father?

"We tinkerers are a good sort," Patrick agreed with a glance at Chad. "I take it you know Doctor Radcliffe?"

"We've met." She gave Chad a wry smile. "I hope your day got better."

"Nah, he's still sulking," Patrick said. "Where did you train?"

Chad tried to kick Patrick under the table. He didn't want to force Claire into more memory than she was ready for.

"I worked with Doctor Charcot in France, then trained with the neuroticists in Vienna, and then I returned to the States to the neurology department at the University of Pennsylvania. I'm working on a grant."

"Charcot, eh?" Patrick steepled his fingers. "That's the hypnosis guy, right?"

"Yes, and the Vienna neuroticists are working on a new theory of hysteria and other mental problems, particularly judicious use of electricity, which has been shown effective for melancholia but not nervous hysteria."

"How did you get involved with them?" Chad asked to keep her talking. He had known vaguely what she'd done in Europe, but if she was going to work with his patients—and if he was going to help her—he needed to find out more. Having Patrick there was the perfect buffer. Her animated expressions and gestures dragged him into the past, when he was the focus of her attention, but seeing her gloved hands reminded him of the scars underneath.

"Well, they don't have a high opinion of us supposedly 'weaker sex,'" Claire admitted. "I was first a patient of theirs, and luckily I managed to impress them enough that they kept me on."

Patrick nodded. "And they think getting experienced soldiers back on the field by soothing their mental anguish is going to break the war's years-long stalemate and preserve the union. We'll see who makes a breakthrough first, you with your neuroticist theories or me with my weapon project."

"Deal," she said and shook his hand. "You'll have to tell me about it."

"It's top secret," Chad told her.

"But then how will I know if he won?"

"The war will be over, of course," Patrick said. "After one final battle."

"And what is the prize?"

Now Patrick looked at Chad. "We'll let the good Doctor Radcliffe decide."

Chad stood, exhausted by the day and the mental challenge of trying to dig for information without revealing too much. "If you two will excuse me, I have to round one more time before bed." He willed it not to, but his hand found the small ruby ring in his pocket.

ABOUT THE AUTHOR

USA Today Bestselling author Cecilia Dominic wrote her first story when she was two years old and has always had a much more interesting life inside her head than outside of it. She became a clinical psychologist because she's fascinated by people and their stories, but she couldn't stop writing fiction. The first draft of her dissertation, while not fiction, was still criticized by her major professor for being written in too entertaining a style. She made it through graduate school and got her PhD, started her own practice, and by day, she helps people cure their insomnia without using medication. By night, she writes fiction she hopes will keep her readers turning the pages all night. Yes, she recognizes the conflict of interest between her two careers, so she writes under a pen name. She lives in Atlanta, Georgia, with one husband and two cats, which, she's been told, is a good number of each.

You can find her at:
    Web page:
    www.ceciliadominic.com
    Facebook:
    www.facebook.com/CeciliaDominicAuthor
    Twitter:
    www.twitter.com/ceciliadominic
    Instagram:
    www.instagram.com/randomoenophile/

Newsletter:
http://www.ceciliadominic.com/booknewsletter